"You're incredibly kind," she whispered.

Her lips were half parted and only inches away. It took all his willpower to resist the temptation, her sweet vulnerability, her sadness affecting even his disreputable soul.

"May I kiss you?" she whispered.

"You probably shouldn't." He was trying to be honorable. She perhaps didn't understand what a kiss would do to him.

"I'm not an innocent."

Beau shut his eyes briefly, her few simple words permission for all he wished to do. And when he opened his eyes, he murmured, heated and low, "Let *me* kiss *you* . . . ."

And then the man known by salacious repute as Glory lived up to his name.

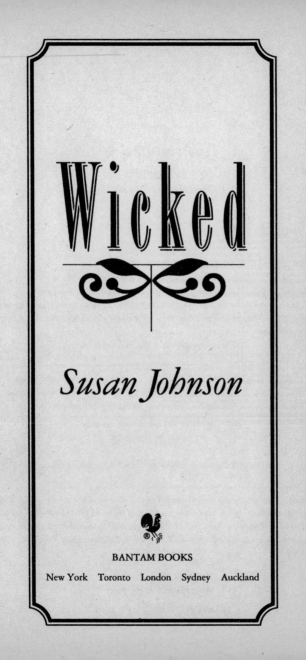

Wicked

Susan Johnson

BANTAM BOOKS

New York   Toronto   London   Sydney   Auckland

Wicked
A Bantam Book / January 1997

ISBN 0-553-57214-8

Published simultaneously in the United States and Canada

*Bantam Books are published by Bantam Books, a division of Bantam Doubleday Dell
Publishing Group, Inc. Its trademark, consisting of the words "Bantam Books" and the
portrayal of a rooster, is Registered in U.S. Patent and Trademark Office and in other
countries. Marca Registrada. Bantam Books, 1540 Broadway, New York, New York
10036.*

PRINTED IN THE UNITED STATES OF AMERICA

OPM   0   9   8   7   6   5   4   3   2   1

Wicked

1

February 1800

"Stay a while longer. It's not even morning. I'll wake the ladies. . . ."

"Can't. Have to leave." Beau St. Jules shrugged his broad shoulders into his coat and stood for a moment surveying the sleeping dancer from the corps de ballet who'd entertained him so pleasantly the last few days. Her slender, nubile body was only partially covered by the sheet, the crimson-hung bed short feet away. "Damned tempting to stay though, Albington," he murmured, his shadowed eyes half-lidded, memories of the previous night stirring his blood. Slipping a small enameled watch from his waistcoat pocket, he glanced at the painted face. "What day is it?"

"Sunday, the first."

His head came up, his dark brows mildly creased. "You sure?"

"Positive. Tomorrow I get my monthly stipend. I *never* forget that, even with cunt like this warming my bed. It's the first and soon I'll be *solvent* again." Leaning forward in his chair, the young Marquis of Albington reached across the card table for a wine bottle. "And I'll drink to that," he said with a grin, pouring a ruby stream of first-rate claret in his glass.

"Jesus," the Earl of Rochefort muttered, beginning to swiftly button up his waistcoat. "I thought it was Saturday."

"Missed an engagement, did you?"

"My sister's birthday," Beau noted with a grimace, deftly slipping the fine linen of his neckcloth into a presentable

1

knot. "The duke's going to want my head on a platter. Maman puts such store in birthdays."

The fair-haired man let out a low whistle. "I'd cut and run if I were you. You're on your way to Naples anyway. Leave early."

"I promised Nell a trip to Madame La Clerque's. Where the hell are my boots?"

"Where the feverish Miss Gambetta tossed them after stripping your clothes from you. Near the door, I'd say."

Recalling the young lady's eagerness, Beau smiled as he surveyed the shadowed environs near Albington's apartment door. "She *is* an insatiable little piece, isn't she? Tell her I'll see her when I return."

"If she's still available. Monty's after her for a more permanent arrangement. You could always set her up in Half Moon Street before you leave and guarantee her accessibility."

"Not likely," the Duke of Seth's eldest son murmured, moving toward the door to retrieve the boots he'd spied under the puddled folds of Miss Gambetta's hastily discarded azure silk gown. "I don't set up light o' loves." Nor had he any need, with the entirety of London's available females in hot pursuit.

Short moments later he was booted and reasonably attired, considering his clothes weren't crisply fresh from his valet, but then he'd had substantial practice making himself presentable after a night spent in some lady's boudoir. He *could* use the services of a barber, though, he decided, glancing at his image in a candlelit mirror. Dark stubble shadowed his jaw.

Pulling several bills from his coat pocket, he set them on the table.[1] "See that . . . ah—"

"Mariana," his friend helpfully interposed.

"Mariana gets this with my heartfelt thanks," Beau finished with a smile. "She's *damned* good."

"Good enough to make you forget your sister's birthday," Charles Albington sportively reminded him.

Beau grinned. "She actually can wrap her legs around her neck."

"Most definitely."

Amusement lit Beau St. Jules's eyes. "I guess that's worth a tongue-lashing from the duke."

"You looked as though you were enjoying yourself," Albington drolly noted. "Think of that luscious cunt when the père is flaying you alive."

"I just have to appear suitably contrite while he's chastising me for upsetting Maman. Nell don't care when she gets her new wardrobe from Madame La Clerque's."

"She old enough for all that frippery?"

"Hell no, she's only thirteen, but she wants *real* dress-up clothes." He shrugged. "So I said I'd buy her some."

"Before too many years you'll have to guard your sister from all the rakes like us."

"Not Nell. She can take care of herself. Wants to be a jockey like Maman was."

"Maybe I'll marry her myself," the Marquis of Albington cheerfully remarked. "Always wanted a prize-winning jockey."

"Then you'll have to give up all your whoring."

The marquis's eyes opened wide. This was a time of great freedom for men, married or not. Faithfulness was never a requirement.

"She's my sister, Charlie," the Earl of Rochefort softly remonstrated, his hand on the door latch. "She's different." And with that quiet warning, he left.

Later that morning, at the same time Beau was enduring a rare reprimand from his father, Serena Blythe was suffering yet another of the countless dressing-downs dispensed with righteous regularity by her employer, Mrs. Totham.

"I distinctly told you to keep your eyes down when traversing the downstairs hallways and not to speak to anyone unless asked a direct question by one of the family. Did I not?"

"Yes, ma'am," Serena quietly said, clenching her fists to

keep from striking the face of the spiteful, pompous woman seated before her.

"Yet dear Neville tells me you not only gazed at him with brazen temerity this morning but you had the nerve to compliment him on his appearance. And on the Lord's day too! I won't have it! I won't have you practicing your female wiles on my innocent young son! Do you understand, Blythe!" Her double chins jiggled in indignation.

"Yes, ma'am." It would do no good to defend herself before Neville's doting mother. Her only son could do no wrong and slimy, lying creature that he was, he'd deliberately fabricated an untruth to further assail her position in the household. She'd been fending off his unwelcome advances for a month now, ever since he'd been sent down from Cambridge in disgrace. "I can have you fired without a recommendation," he'd threatened that morning when he'd caught her coming downstairs to fetch new quills for the schoolroom and backed her up against the wall with his soft, pudgy body. "*Or* I can see that your life improves," he'd silkily added, his breath sour with the smell of last night's wine. "You're wasting your time teaching my two stupid sisters. I can set you up in style."

She'd feigned innocent dismay and slipped under his arm, not allowing herself to deal with him as she wished. She would have preferred felling him with a solid knee to the groin, but then she'd be thrown out into the street with certainty and she desperately needed her governess post. But the pressure of his advances was daily increasing, and as she stood humbly before Mrs. Totham's rebuke, she wondered how much longer she could resist Neville Totham's salacious demands.

"However the *aristocracy* might disport themselves," Neville's mother said with a virtuous sniff, "the business class has sterner morals and I won't have you corrupting Neville with your loose, scandalous ways." The particular denigration of her family was pointed and familiar. Mrs. Totham never failed to remind Serena that her father, Viscount Amberson, had gambled away his fortune and the family estate, Fallwood, before he died. "I don't want to have to remind you of your position again, Blythe. Servants are to be seen, not heard."

"Yes, ma'am," she repeated, her submission mortifying but necessary. It had been four years now since her widowed father's death, four dreadful years except for the brief ray of cheer when Julia Castelli and her father had come last fall to catalog Mr. Totham's paintings and offered her their friendship.

"In the future you are to remain in the schoolroom unless called for," Mrs. Totham curtly said. Her small eyes buried in corpulent folds of flesh narrowed to slits, raking Serena's form from head to toe with a chill basilisk gaze. "That should keep your Jezebel lure away from my darling boy. Now get back upstairs." And nodding dismissively, the wealthy foundry owner's wife reached for her cup of chocolate.

Serena shivered as she walked from the room, whether from tension or fatigue she wasn't sure. She was desperately weary of her humbled circumstances, of the constant vicious discipline, of Neville's harrowing pursuit. Unclenching her fingers at last, she felt as though she'd been wrung dry. Her eyes stung with tears as she stood in the shadowed corridor leading from the breakfast parlor to the servants' stairs, and drawing in a deep breath, she tried to stem the overwhelming urge to cry. She wouldn't allow herself to break down; tears wouldn't bring her salvation, nor would self-pity, she reminded herself for the thousandth time since entering the Tothams' employ. She'd survived four years and she'd last a short time longer. By July she'd have enough money saved to pay for her tuition at the Academy of Art in Florence. And with the money Julia had recently sent for passage, her dream of quitting the Totham household would soon be realized.

Only five months more, she reminded herself, her day of liberation etched on her liver. After these miserable years, she could tolerate mere months. The encouraging thought cheered her as she climbed the two long flights of stairs to the nursery floor.

"What took you so long?" Hannah Totham petulantly complained when Serena walked into the schoolroom. "And you haven't any quills!"

"Mama says she's lazy and worthless," her older sister Caroline sharply said, her grating voice identical to her mother's. "She never does *anything* right."

Serena's two charges were small replicas of their plain, stout mother, their mannerisms already frightening facsimiles despite their youth. At twelve and fourteen they were being groomed to enter society where their father's riches would obtain them each a husband of distinction. Vain, self-important, fully aware of their wealth, they were difficult to teach and their lack of success with French and the arts of painting and music were blamed on Serena's ineptitude.

"Why don't we take out the French pattern books and practice our list of fashion terms?" Serena suggested, knowing the girls would much prefer that to lessons in the Scriptures. In her current low spirits, she wasn't capable of suffering through a morning of sulky disinterest and apathy.

"Can we have chocolate bonbons while we work?" Caroline pressured, her antennae maliciously attuned to Serena's disheartened mood.

Serena hesitated; bonbons were strictly rationed for Mrs. Totham was trying to mold her daughters into svelte beauties—a task of daunting proportions.

"I'll tell Mama *you* ate them all if you won't let us have any," Caroline warned.

"Have all you want," Serena said with a small sigh, unequal to another struggle with the ill-natured girls. And perhaps intimidated by Caroline's threat as well. A fortnight ago when the Totham daughters had eaten all the candy and blamed it on her, their mother had withheld Serena's meals for two days. Even with the bland, frugal nursery diet, Serena didn't care to risk having her food withdrawn again. She hadn't had breakfast yet this morning.

"Caroline, you find the bonbons then," Serena said, her

voice resigned. "Hannah, take out the newest pattern book with the yellow muslin gown on the cover. And I'll tell the nursery maid we'd like chocolate and toast."

"I want heavy cream," Caroline said.

"Whipped," Hannah added. "I want two cups."

"Very well." Serena left to find the maid, who generally could be found sleeping in the sewing room next door. The girls could have asked for fried elephant and ostrich eggs at the moment and she would have agreed to order it. After her recent ordeal with Neville and Mrs. Totham, her combatant strength was depleted.

The two men seated in the Seth House study bore such a striking resemblance, the ton referred to them as the Sainted Pair. Tall, muscular, their dark hair cut fashionably short à la Titus, the lure of their stark, sensual looks exceeded only by their charm, the two men had monopolized the attention of all the beautiful women for a very long time.

When they walked into a society entertainment or a club they turned heads. Handsome as sin, flagrantly sinful, they were the bellwether for profligate vice. Their male peers were wont to grumble at the unfairness with which fate had so liberally bestowed physical advantages on the pair but the ladies were only selfishly grateful for father and son's splendid beauty and sexual largesse.

Although the Duke of Seth had given up his libertine ways after marriage to a young Scottish lass, his much-loved son, born of a youthful love affair, had succeeded not only to one of his father's numerous titles but to his vacated position as London's leading rake. And like his father before him, Beau St. Jules was more than willing to oblige all the eager ladies who wished to share his bed.

"I don't expect you to forgo a young man's pleasures," the Duke of Seth was judiciously saying, gazing at his eldest child across his cluttered desktop, his tone more resigned than punitive. "Except on these family occasions when your maman wants you home. You'll apologize and not tell her the truth."

"Of course." Beau shifted uncomfortably in his chair. He knew, despite the moderate tone, that his father's authority was not to be disregarded. "It was an unfortunate oversight."

Sinjin smiled faintly. "If I'd known Miss Gambetta held such allure, I'd have sent Davis to remind you of the time."

"You know Miss Gambetta?"

"I've seen her on the stage"—Sinjin's dark lashes lowered fractionally—"and at Farley's bachelor party last fall."

Beau sat up straighter, his gaze suddenly sharp. "Were you with her?" His father had been very young when Beau had been born and at forty-one was still the object of many a wishful female dream. Beau was well aware of ladies' interest in him.

"Do I detect jealousy?" Sinjin's blue eyes held a hint of amusement. "A word of advice. Go to Naples tomorrow; Miss Gambetta won't pine for you."

"*Were* you?" Pointed curiosity colored Beau's tone. Farley's bachelor party had kept the scandal mills grinding for weeks. Rumor had it there were three accommodating females for every man.

"You should know better," his father mildly replied. "I'm unfashionably in love with your mother. But Miss Gambetta does have extraordinary acrobatic skills," Sinjin added with a grin. "I hope you enjoyed yourself."

"Vastly." Beau rested back in his chair, his smile languid.

"In that case, the required abject apology to your mother should be an easy quid pro quo," Sinjin softly said. "Although I suggest you bathe and change first. The scent of Miss Gambetta is pungent; apparently none of your amorous play included a bathtub."

Beau's mouth lifted in a boyish grin. "Not *last* night. There wasn't time."

"I see," the duke blandly said. "I'll tell your mother you'll be down for breakfast. *You* make up a suitable story explaining your absence from your sister's birthday party." Sinjin rose and glanced at the clock, his responsibilities as a disciplinarian thankfully over. "Say an hour?"

"Yes, sir." Beau stood swiftly, grateful the interview was over. "Thank you, sir."

"By the way . . . don't take Miss Gambetta to Italy with you."

"No, sir. I hadn't planned to."

The duke's dark brows arched faintly. "I stand relieved."

"I don't like women on board my yacht for long voyages. One becomes bored."

"I see."

"You can't get away from them out in the middle of the ocean."

"A dilemma to be avoided," the duke urbanely murmured. "Davis has my supplies packed for the villa in Naples," he noted, more pertinent business interests yet to be addressed. "He'll have them transported to Dover tonight. When do you leave?"

"Tomorrow afternoon."

"The Foreign Office found you?"

"Lord Percy came around. They're interested in the foreign ambassadors' instructions at Naples. With the French marching back and forth across Italy, all is in flux at the Sicilian court. I might be able to glean some useful information."

"Don't put yourself in danger. Naples is awash with spies and thugs and mercenaries."

Beau shrugged. "I'm more interested in seeing if our estates have survived French expropriation and all the revolutionary destruction. But if I hear something relevant concerning Napoleon's plans, I'll relay it home. Lord, I *can* smell her," Beau abruptly remarked, lifting the ruffled cuff of his shirtsleeve to his nose. "It's definitely time for a bath."

After his son's departure, Sinjin stood at the window for a moment, gazing out over the sere winter garden sloping down to the Thames. Miss Gambetta had ambitions to catch herself an aristocratic husband like her cousin the new Marquess of Weyhouse. And while the Coltrans might not mind welcoming an actress into their family, he was relieved to

find that Beau's extended rendezvous with the young balle-
rina had nothing to do with love.

Beau's apology and explanation for missing his sister's
birthday was graciously accepted by his maman for she
was fully cognizant of the latest gossip concerning her
stepson. Albington's valet had discussed the ballet dancers
with his sister, who was dresser to Chelsea's mother-in-law,
the Dowager Duchess of Seth. And yesterday, over tea, the
Dowager Duchess had told Chelsea not only of Miss Gambetta's liaison with Beau but of her hopes for joining the
St. Jules family.

While Chelsea's entrance into the family had been unconventional in the extreme, she was under the impression after
listening to the details related by her mother-in-law that
Miss Gambetta seemed more intent on acquiring Beau's title
than his love. A romantic at heart, Chelsea preferred a love
match for her stepson.

"We saved you a *big* piece of cake," Nell said to Beau the
instant his apology was concluded. "Do you want it now or
after I show you the pattern books of gowns I want at
Madame La Clerque's?"

"Let Beau eat his breakfast first," her mother suggested.

"You missed out on the bestest ice cream," his youngest
sister, Sally, said. "I bet you're sorry." At five, her priorities
were decidedly different from her brother's.

"Beau doesn't care about ice cream, Sally. He just cares
about horses." Just recently ten, Jack was thoroughly enamored of horses.

Little Sally's bottom lip began to tremble. "He does *too*
like ice cream."

"I really wish I had some ice cream right now," Beau
kindly said, smiling at his young sister.

"It's all gone," Nell briskly interjected. "Aren't you
almost finished? Maman said I can have a purple dress."

Sinjin's startled gaze swiftly met his wife's across the
breakfast table.

"She's using the dresses for play, Sinjin. Don't be alarmed."

"I'm not either," Nell protested. "You'll take me out in my gowns from Madame La Clerque's won't you, Beau?"

Beau's glance quickly slid from his father to stepmother, decorum at issue, purple more apt to be worn by courtesans than young misses. "We'll find *someplace* to go," he diplomatically replied.

"Someplace *fashionable*."

"Perhaps the boys at the track will like it," Beau suggested.

"Perfect!" To Nell who was a better jockey than many of the professionals, showing off her new gown to her jockey friends would be perfection.

"Early in the morning," Sinjin murmured, his voice meant for Beau's ears alone.

Beau nodded in acknowledgment. "Would you like to come along to the dressmaker with us, Sally?" he offered.

"Beau!" Nell wailed. "It's *my* birthday present. She'll be fussy and troublesome and into everything—oh, all right," she mumbled, taking notice of her mother's stern expression, "she can come along. But she can't cry."

"I won't cry," Sally brightly avowed, her blond curls bobbing as she waggled her head. "No matter what."

"You can sit on my lap," Beau said, "and we'll both help Nell pick out some dresses."

2

A decidedly outré pose for London's most disreputable rake, Madame La Clerque decided the following morning when Beau St. Jules lounged on her pink moiré settee with his young sister straddling his knees. London's most fashionable modiste had never seen the young Earl of Rochefort in her fitting rooms without a mistress; he was one of her best customers. Normally dégagé and audacious, exuding an overt sensuality as his mistresses preened before him, he was today a gentle, agreeable brother to his sisters, teasing still but without his normal cheekiness. But whether buying for a sister or lover, he was supremely indulgent.

He purchased a dozen gowns for the young Miss Giselle, never taking issue with her selection of fabrics no matter how inappropriate, never asking the price. And when the small child on his lap became fidgety, he let her unroll a priceless swathe of China silk for her amusement and after belatedly taking note of Madame La Clerque's dismay, casually said, "Send Sally's silk along with the gowns. Perhaps my mother will find some use for it."

Heart-stopping moments aside, when Madame La Clerque thought she might lose a considerable sum to a small child's amusement, it was, all in all, an extremely profitable morning for London's premier dressmaker. And the visit offered her delicious tittle-tattle too. Most of the ladies patronizing her establishment were avidly interested in any on-dits concerning the notorious Beau St. Jules. What did he say? How did he look? Who was he with? *Really,* they would say, wide-eyed when she told them. London's most libertine rogue with his young sisters would be a delicious tidbit.

With his brotherly duties completed, Beau spent a few hours more with his parents discussing the horses he was to bring back from Naples if the animals had survived the French occupation and the royalist battles. The stables at their country villa were a halfway point for bloodstock brought out of Tunis, a resting stage before shipment home to their racing stud in Yorkshire.

"At least you shouldn't have to worry much about the French fleet," his father said.

"What French fleet," Beau said with a grin, Nelson's victory at Aboukir last year having decimated the French navy. And what was left of it was timidly commanded by Bruix, now under British blockade at Brest.

"But the privateers are always a danger," his mother reminded him.

"I should be able to outrun them."

"Is Berry sailing the *Siren*?" Seated next to his wife on a camelback sofa, Sinjin took Chelsea's hand in his and gently stroked it, understanding her legitimate fears for their son.

Beau nodded.

"Good," his father said, satisfied his son had the best captain in England. "He'll be fine with Berry, darling," he told his wife, then turned back to Beau. "And you're armed?"

"Ten cannons. We added four more last week."

"That sound ominous." Chelsea's brows drew into a mild frown. "How necessary is this trip?"

"You *could* wait," Sinjin interjected. "Naples is still a hotbed of lawlessness. If the horses survived, they can rest indefinitely at Naples."

"Now that Napoleon's slipped through the blockade and is back in France, rumor has it he may invade Italy again. I'd like to get the horses out if possible. Regardless," Beau continued, "I *want* to go. Thing is, I need some excitement."

"Beyond the corps de ballet," Sinjin blandly noted.

"And Miss Gambetta," Chelsea added with a smile.

"Is nothing inviolate from the society matrons?" Beau inquired without hint of offense. "Tell me, Maman, what is the gossip over tea? You probably know whether Monty will win his suit with the pretty Miss Gambetta. I'm sure he'd like to know."

"My information," Chelsea said, "is that Miss Gambetta is holding out for an earldom."

"Not mine, I hope."

"I'm afraid so."

Beau drew in a small startled breath; women bent on marriage were intrinsically terrorizing. "Now I'm *really* looking forward to setting sail. Not that I have anything but compliments for Miss Gambetta but, good God, I'm not in the market for a wife."

"Your papa said as much last night."

"And he's right. Jesus, maybe in ten years." Beau stood abruptly as if there were immediate need to escape Miss Gambetta's clutches. "I should check on William's packing and on my mail."

"Send us your news with the consular dispatches," his father said, his gaze amused. "Your mother worries."

"Of course, Maman." Leaning down, he kissed Chelsea gently on the cheek.

"You'll be careful now," she urged.

He smiled and nodded, his relationship with his stepmother one of deepest affection. His own mother had died shortly after his birth, and while Sinjin had taken over his fatherly duties when Beau was a baby, he had not had a mother until years later when Sinjin had married.

"And we'll expect you back in a month or so?" the duke said.

"Six weeks at the most. Even if I have to go to Palermo and mingle at court for a time, I should be back by mid-March."

When Beau arrived at his bachelor quarters in St. James a brief time later, he found Albington waiting for him, half drunk and in the company of two young actresses.

"Told them we'd see you off at Dover."

"Really," Beau softly said, handing his hat and gloves to his valet, asking William for his mail in an undertone. Turning back to his company, he took in the smiling countenances of the pretty actresses, perceived that Albington, with his feet resting on a case of rare Cognac, was once again in funds, and debated briefly whether he wanted companions on his drive to Dover. "I'm afraid I'm leaving within the hour," he neutrally said.

"We're ready right now," the marquis cheerfully replied. "Lizzie's never been fucked in a carriage before." He leered at the girl perched on the arm of his chair.

Reason enough, Beau sardonically considered. "Would you care for some Champagne?" he asked the young lady seated to one side of the couple kissing each other now with passionate disregard for their companions.

She giggled. "I've had some already. Albie ordered up your best stock."

"Then I've some catching up to do." Beau took his mail from the salver William held out to him. "I'm Rochefort," he went on, sifting through the scented billets-doux that arrived daily. His dark eyes lifted from Miss Gambetta's familiar script gracing one lilac-colored note and, pleased to be so imminently quitting London and her unwelcome designs, he said to the young lady with raven curls and a splendid bosom, "Do you like carriage rides?"

Serena locked her door against Neville's unwelcome advances Sunday night and even he wasn't brave enough to force it open, the risk of waking his sisters or parents outweighing carnal urges. He'd slunk away finally, but not before whispering ugly, graphic threats of what he'd do to Serena when he finally had her alone.

She hadn't slept after that, fearful of his return, apprehensive about maintaining her virtue against such determined attacks, more happily contemplating various ways she could dispose of his corpulent, repulsive body. It cheered her in those sleepless hours to devise and scheme, even if all her vengeful plans were only pipe dreams. She briefly wondered whether such vicious thoughts put one beyond redemption. Or did God forgive malevolent intent if it was in self-defense? She even fleetingly asked for divine guidance in her plight but no one answered her plea, nor had they anytime these last four years. So she sensibly stayed awake in the event Neville returned.

Desperately fatigued by morning, she greeted the sound of the girls stirring awake next door with a soft groan. What discourtesies and rudeness would she be subjected to today? Glancing at the calendar she'd made and posted prominently over her bed, she rallied her weary body and mind with the glorious goal of July and liberation.

The cook was in a pet because Mrs. Totham had early guests coming in the forenoon so only tea and toast were sent up for the nursery breakfast, the serving girl breathlessly explained after navigating the two flights of stairs. And Serena was fortunate to pluck a single piece of buttered toast from the plate before the Totham girls fell on the frugal breakfast like wolves on the fold. She ate hurriedly, much as a convict would in a communal cell, not sure she could defend her small breakfast from her charges.

Instructions were sent up soon after that Hannah and Caroline were to be dressed in their newest gowns and brought down to meet their mother's guests at precisely half past eleven. But on their way downstairs, Caroline's heel caught in the muslin of her hem, ripping off a foot of ruffled flounce. By the time they'd repaired to the nursery to change her frock, Serena and the girls were ten minutes late arriving in the drawing room.

The butler announced the two young girls because Mrs. Totham liked to put on airs before her friends and before Serena could pass completely through the door, she heard Mrs. Totham say in an icy tone, "Where is your new gown, Caroline?"

"Blythe is so clumsy she made me stumble on the stairs and my shoe tore the flounce."

"It's impossible to find good hired help," Mrs. Totham

acerbically said, smiling tightly at the two ladies seated across the tea table from her.

"And they have no manners," a large, thin-faced matron commiserated. "I had to sack our governess last week when she failed to meet our high standards."

Serena recognized the rector's wife, the daughter of a prosperous merchant who had traded her considerable dowry for the younger son of a baron in need of funds to maintain his rectory. And she supposed the rector's wife's high standards had to do more with deference than manners for she had neither charity nor courtesy herself.

"Take the price of the gown from her wages," the wife of the Tothams' solicitor curtly said, as if Serena weren't standing directly behind the Totham girls—as if she were invisible.

"At Madame La Clerque's prices, she wouldn't be paid for two years," Mrs. Totham pointed out with both pride and anger.

"It would serve her right," the rector's wife declared. "Isn't she the one with the viscount for a father? An ungodly, iniquitous man if I recall. A gambler and utter disgrace to the Christian community."

"You didn't know my father," Serena abruptly declared, her weariness perhaps impulse to her unguarded response.

"Apologize to Mrs. Stanton," Mrs. Totham snapped, her voice bristling with anger. "This instant."

"It was uncivil of her to revile my father without knowledge of him or his circumstances," Serena stubbornly retorted.

"You ungrateful, impudent creature. After all we've done for you! Apologize!" Maud Totham's fat cheeks were bright red with rage, her eyes virulent.

Serena stood mutinous, not even sure herself why she'd finally taken a stand, aware in the less emotional portions of her brain that she was committing a kind of suicide in her refusing. Aware as well of the breath-held censure that seemed to smother the room in an ominous silence.

The muted scrape of Mrs. Totham's chair on the plush

carpet broke the stillness, and raising her bulk from her seat with remarkable swiftness, she rushed at Serena in a rustle of silk skirts, her face and quivering chins apoplectic scarlet. "How dare you oppose me," she lashed out, her voice tight with rage, and coming within striking distance, she slapped Serena with such fury, she stumbled momentarily before catching her balance.

Struck dumb by the sudden attack, Serena stood motionless, her cheek stinging from the blow.

The girls broke into giggles, Mrs. Totham shrieked at Serena like a madwoman, and the two guests sat back with smug smiles to view the tempestuous scene.

As the crescendo of epithets, threats, and abuse broke over her, an odd, inexplicable sense of finality overcame Serena—simultaneously dreadful and uplifting. Without a word, she turned and walked away from four years of unmitigated misery.

"Don't you turn away from me!" Mrs. Totham screamed. "Come back here this minute! Do you hear?" Her shrill voice echoed in the large drawing room, acrimonious and hostile, reverberating in piercing accents from wall to ceiling to floor. "I'll have you thrown into the streets if you don't come back this instant! I'll have you thrown into gaol!"

Everyone had their breaking point, Papa always used to say about losing at cards, and she'd reached her breaking point today with the Tothams. She didn't care anymore about anything except escape—like her father when he'd taken his life after the gambling had finally ruined him completely.

She moved up the stairs, her mind remarkably cool and collected, considering she was literally out in the streets. And she began planning a hastily arranged voyage to Italy. It would have been preferable to have all her funds in hand but surely she could find work in Florence to supplement the few months' pay she was short. Governesses would be needed there too and since Mama had been Italian, she was fluent in the language. There. All settled. Neither uncertainty nor dilemma prevailed in her current resolve.

Now to pack, she purposefully decided . . . and suddenly she felt borne by a wave of stirring elation. She'd book passage here in London; the sailing schedules were as familiar to her as her name, since she'd pored over them for months. The nearest stage to Dover left from the King's Arms Inn on Knightsbridge Road; if she hurried, she'd be on the afternoon coach.

After locking the door to her room, she quickly tossed her few possessions into her two satchels. She mustn't tarry; if Mrs. Totham pressed charges against her, she'd be thrown into prison. Rushing to quit her room, within minutes she was packed, her worldly possessions minimal, only her paints and brushes of any value. She had nothing left of her life as Lady Serena Blythe after her father's creditors had stripped everything of value from their house and property, all her assets contained now in two small satchels. But she had her freedom, she noted thankfully, and picking up her valises she walked from the room.

Standing in the hallway for a brief moment, she listened for any untoward sounds from below, fearful someone might be on their way to apprehend her. But the floor was silent and moving quietly through the corridor and then down the servants' stairs, she exited the house through a little-used door to the kitchen garden.

It was a rare, sunny afternoon in February and walking briskly through the mews behind the fine houses on Russell Square, she found herself smiling as she made for the shipping line office to purchase her ticket. Even the weather was cooperating as if in propitious portent of good fortune.

By twilight she was in Dover; a deep purple sky bordered by ominous thunderclouds promised rain. Obtaining directions from the coachman, she hurried to the shipping office near the docks and caught the clerk just as he was locking up. But he assured her her luggage would be stowed away on the *Betty Lee* later that evening and at daybreak tomorrow, she'd be allowed on board.

"Is there an inn nearby?" she inquired, not sure she could

afford the added expense, but equally aware she'd need refuge from the coming storm.

"The Pelican over there." He waved in the direction of a small stuccoed building set under a craggy cliff wall. "Tell Fanny I sent you."

Encouraged by his introduction and, moments later, pleased to find Fanny not only the proprietress but warmly welcoming, Serena found the courage to ask if she could sit in the parlor for the night.

"A bit short of the bob are you?" Fanny asked, her smile understanding.

"I hadn't planned on spending a night in an inn." Serena blushed in embarrassment at having to ask for charity.

"Well now, dearie, don't you worry none. There's plenty of room in the parlor what with only four others there. But those London nabobs and their dollies could get a mite noisy." She nodded in the direction of a small group of well-dressed patrons. "You might want to stay clear of them. They've drunk up half a case of my best French Champagne and it seems likely they're only going to get louder."

Gazing into the small parlor facing the sea, Serena took note of the convivial party seated near the windows. Two handsome young nobles, their expressions amused, were sprawled in elegant languor observing two ladies' dramatic recitation.

"They just ordered up supper, too, so I'd say they're going to let them little dollies entertain them a trifle longer."

"I could just sit here in the hall," Serena suggested.

"Heavens no, child. There's not a speck of heat out here. Find yourself a spot in that corner near the fire." Fanny indicated the site with a quick lift of her chin. "If you sit nice and quiet, they won't be apt to take no notice. Rich rogues can be a danger to a young lass like you if'n you're not careful. And when Tad's done running for them fine gentry, I'll have him bring you a cup of soup and a bit of tea."

Serena's grateful thanks were casually brushed off by the landlady. And while the splendid young noblemen were engrossed in their ladies' rendition of the newest ditty disparaging the Prince of Wales, Serena slipped into the secluded corner near the fire.

Within short hours she'd be on board the ship that would take her to Florence, to her friends the Castellis, to an art school she'd always dreamed of attending ever since her mother had told her of all the renowned ateliers and collections in the city of her birth. Despite a ringing fatigue and hunger, she was comfortable and warm, protected from the rain that had just begun falling, ensconced in a cozy refuge for the night. If she believed in luck—and she did with the same gambler's spirit as her father—she'd be tempted to say her luck had finally turned.

Sometime later she ate her soup and tea while the young bloods and their ladies consumed Fanny's best cut of beef and pudding and drank Champagne and laughed . . . and kissed. There was much kissing and more than that on occasion with the young ladies sitting on the gentlemen's lap from time to time. Serena tried not to look but the noisy, amorous repartee was in too close proximity to fully ignore.

The rain had been driving in sheets against the windows for some time and between kisses and giggles and flirtatious petting, the conversation had occasionally centered on whether they would all stay the night or begin the journey back to London. The dark-haired buck didn't seem to mind if they went or stayed. And while he kissed the lady clinging to him, he did it idly, like a man with other things on his mind.

As the heat from the fire seeped through Serena's tired senses, her eyes began drifting shut and the amusements of the party from London seemed to enter her consciousness from a great distance. Until a giggling shriek jerked her awake and a swift glance was enough to know she shouldn't look again no matter the instinctive impulse. The fair-haired blade, roaring drunk and laughing, was sliding the gown from his paramour's shoulders and it appeared as though he were intent on making love to her, public venue or not.

"You might want to shut the door, Charlie, unless you're in an exhibitionist mood," Beau mildly said.

"Sha'it yourself."

"Charlie-e-e," Lizzie fretted, her remonstrance ending in a giggle as the Marquis of Albington licked a path downward between her breasts. Then she softly moaned, her eyes drifted shut, and her hands came up to hold his head to her breast, the compelling sensations of his mouth on her nipple apparently overcoming any reservations she might have had.

"It appears we're about to be entertained," Beau lazily drawled, clearing the filled glasses from the tabletop in his immediate vicinity.

"Wake up the judge!" The cry from the street outside was dimly heard, and a second later, the front door of the Pelican crashed open. A rain-soaked man burst through the portal, shouting, "Wake up the judge!" his voice like a crash of thunder in the candlelit room. "Fanny, where the hell are you?" he yelled before glancing quickly into the parlor in search of the landlady. Not catching sight of her, he spun away, racing toward the back of the inn, his voice raised in summons. "Fanny, Cap'n Darby's been killed!"

Within minutes, the Pelican was a scene of pandemonium, a score of men wet from the storm crowding into the parlor, the alarm having been raised from the docks to the inn's front door. While everyone waited for the judge to come down from his quarters above, the dead man was carried in and placed on a long trestle table near the door. Even in the dim light, the brutality of the attack was evident. The man's head and face were a bloody pulp, distorted out of all human semblance, crushed flesh and bone bleeding onto the floor in a widening crimson pool.

"It was his first mate Horton, for sure. He and Darby been at odds for years," one man brusquely said, staring down at the corpse.

"Horton were drinkin' all day at the Bird's Nest," another noted, his voice gruff.

"Heard tell he were swearing to make the cap'n pay for

them lashings he got back last year. It must ha' been him."
The man speaking nodded his head with certainty.

"Seein' how he sailed off tonight without the captain, it looks likely."

"Someone has to notify Crawford's."

"And the widow Darby."

A sudden silence filled the room.

"Fanny can tell her," someone quietly said. "They's friends."

"Can they find Horton and bring him back?"

"Not the way he knows the seas," the man with the gruff voice bluntly observed. "Been sailing since he were ten."

"He could sell the *Betty Lee* in some foreign port and live the rest of his life in style."

"He were a violent man. . . ."

The men's voices suddenly faded away in Serena's consciousness as the disastrous import of the words *Betty Lee* registered in her brain. The *Betty Lee* was *her* ship, she fearfully realized, the ship that was to take her away to Florence in the morning. It was *gone,* they said, which meant her luggage and passage money were *gone.* For a moment she couldn't breathe, so cataclysmic was the news. Everything she owned had been on that ship, including money she'd hidden in her paint box. Forcing herself to a calmness that threatened to erupt into a wail of despair, she desperately tried to deal with the devastating events.

Fighting back her tears, she reminded herself she was alive, at least, unlike Captain Darby, who was brutally murdered and still as the grave short feet away. However much ruin faced her, it was far from the stark reality of death before her eyes.

She needed options, she consciously deliberated, swallowing hard to stifle her tears. Think, she commanded her numbed mind. While she struggled to regain some modicum of reason, a cacophony of voices rose from the crowd, everyone speaking at once, when the local magistrate entered the room.

He raised his hands to quell the uproar.

As the clamor diminished, the elegant, young noble with
dark hair came to his feet, his height and patrician presence
immediately silencing the room. In a deep, temperate voice
that gave no indication of the numerous bottles of Champagne he'd consumed, he said, "Perhaps I could be of help.
Since I'm scheduled to sail soon, if you'd care to arrange an
arrest warrant—should witnesses conclude Horton did the
deed—I could see that the appropriate authorities in various
ports of call are made aware of his crime."

Everyone's eyes were trained on the tall aristocrat, splendidly dressed by London's best tailor.

He stood in placid repose as if he were familiar with
legions of gazes centered on him.

"Capital, young men," the judge exclaimed into the hush.
"Bound to say Crawford Shipping would be beholden to
you," he went on. "When do you sail and where?"

"My yacht is at the ready. I'm bound for Naples, but I'm
at your convenience, sir." Beau bowed slightly.

"Well, then, come, my boy," the judge briskly said, "and
you too, Camden. We need the particulars written down
and the witnesses interviewed."

His yacht at the ready, Serena silently mused, the black
abyss facing her shrinking by the second. Naples wasn't
Leghorn, but it was a lifetime closer than Dover, she
reflected. An option of sorts if she had the nerve. Trembling
at such a blind bargain, she considered what other possibilities were available to her with her passage money gone, her
ship set sail, and her purse so depleted she'd be destitute in a
fortnight.

She could no longer apply for a governess post in London.
Mrs. Totham would have put out the alarm with the
greatest of pleasure too, she suspected. Possibly she could
hope for employment in some outlying area of England
where London gossip rarely intruded but such an under-
taking required staying in rented quarters while she adver-
tised for a position, depleting what little money she had left.
What then, if no position materialized? And even should she

find work, there was no guarantee her new employers would be an improvement over the Tothams.

Rising suddenly, she moved around the outskirts of the assemblage filling the parlor until she came to the windows facing the dock. Pressing her face against the cool pane, she made out the dim outline of a sleek yacht tied to its moorings, its pale raking form faintly visible even in the heavy rain.

3

When he first heard the soft footfall in the passageway outside his stateroom, he glanced at the clock mounted on the ship's overhead beam.

Two o'clock.

He came fully awake.

A woman was on board his yacht.

He immediately recognized the tiptoeing gait as that of a female but then Beau St. Jules had vast experience with tiptoeing rendezvous in the middle of the night—as he had with women of every nuance and description. His amours rivaled—some said surpassed—his father's distinguished record. The Duke of Seth's eldest son wasn't called Glory by all the seductive ladies in London for the beauty of his smile alone.

That celebrated smile suddenly appeared on his starkly handsome face as he threw his legs over the side of his bed and reached for his breeches.

A female stowaway on his yacht. How serendipitous.

Entertainment, perhaps, for his voyage to Naples.

Creeping down the dimly lit passage, Serena hardly dared breathe. She'd waited until all sounds of activity had ceased on the yacht save for those of the night crew above decks. And if she hadn't been famished she wouldn't have risked leaving her hiding place in the small closet filled with female attire.

The scented fabrics reminded her poignantly of her

mother's fine gowns. Long ago . . . Before her mother's death.

Before her father's spiral into drink and gambling.

Before her own servitude as governess to the despicable Tothams.

A small sigh escaped her as she moved toward the galley she'd seen when she'd stolen aboard the yacht at Dover late last night. How far removed she was from that distant childhood—without funds, in flight from England aboard a stranger's yacht, hoping to reach Florence by the grace of God and her own wits.

Her stomach growled, the delicious scent of food from the galley drifting into her nostrils as she eased open the door and the more urgent need to eat drove away any remnants of nostalgia or self-pity.

She was adding a crusty loaf of bread to the cheese and pears she held in the scooped fold of her skirt when a voice behind her gently said, "Would you like me to wake my cook and have him make you something more substantial?"

She whirled around to find the yacht's owner lounging against the doorjamb. His smile, flashing white in the subdued light, mitigated the terror his voice had engendered although his state of undress, clothed as he was in only breeches, gave rise to another kind of fear. He was powerfully built, the light from a small oil lamp modeling his muscular body in shadow and plane, his virility intense at close range.

"Have we met before?" he softly asked, wondering if he should know the young lady, the blur of women in his life occasionally making it difficult to recall specific females.

"Not precisely," Serena replied, hesitant, not certain of his mood despite his soft voice. "I saw you in the parlor of the Pelican."

"Really." Genuinely surprised, he shifted slightly in his stance. He rarely overlooked women of such striking good looks. She had glorious golden hair, huge dark eyes, a slender, voluptuous form, and a sensuous mouth he was definitely interested in tasting. "I must have been very drunk," he added, half to himself.

"You probably were," she said, repressing an odd flutter induced by the graphic display of rippling muscle as he moved. "You didn't come aboard till almost dawn."

"Really," he said again, his voice mild. "Are we sailing mates then?"

"I'd be happy to *pay* for my passage."

His gaze raked her swiftly, pausing for a fraction of a second on the food bundled in her skirt. "But you prefer not taking conventional routes."

"My ship left without me after I'd already paid for my passage." Her eyes suddenly filled with tears.

"Please don't cry," he quickly said. "You're more than welcome aboard the *Siren*." He was uncomfortable with distraught women and she was obviously without funds if she was reduced to stealing aboard his vessel.

"I can . . . reimburse you for my passage"—she swallowed hard to stem her tears—"once we reach Italy." The tuition money she'd sent ahead to Florence should cover her fare.

"Nonsense," he murmured. "I'm sailing there anyway." He smiled briefly. "How much can you eat, after all?" Easing away from the jamb he stood upright, his height suddenly formidable to her upturned gaze. But his voice was bland when he said, "Why don't I find you some better accommodations and a real meal. Do you eat beefsteak?"

"Oh, yes." Serena salivated at the thought, her last food a frugal breakfast in London two days ago and a cup of soup at the Pelican. "Yes, definitely."

"Why don't you make yourself comfortable?" Beau suggested. "The second door on the right should do." He moved back into the passageway to allow her egress from the galley. "I'll join you directly I get my cook awake."

He didn't reappear for some time, sending a young lad with hot water and towels to his stateroom, followed shortly after by another servant with a decanter of Tokay and cookies. This would allow his beautiful passenger time to

wash and refresh herself while he gave directions for a sumptuous meal to his French chef, whom he'd cajoled out of bed
with a sweet smile and a lavish bribe.

Some sautéed scallops first, he'd requested while the
young Frenchman had sulkily rolled out of bed. "She's very
beautiful, Remy, and not quite sure she can trust me."

"Nor should she," the slender young man muttered,
standing motionless beside his bed for a moment, still half
asleep.

"But your luscious food will set her mind at ease."

"So I'm supposed to help you seduce her," the Frenchman
grumbled, his chestnut hair falling into his eyes as he bent to
pick up his trousers from a nearby chair.

"Now, Remy, since when do I need help there?" Beau
murmured, his grin roguish.

"I thought you didn't like women on your yacht?"

"You haven't seen her." Dark brows flickered sportively.
"And now I have this overwhelming impulse to make her
happy."

"Then maybe you should serve her oysters first," Remy
said with an answering grin as he stepped into his trousers.
"And save the scallops for lunch tomorrow when her passions are sated."

"She wants beefsteak too."

Remy groaned. "You English have no subtlety. Served
bloody, I suppose."

"With your mushrooms and wine sauce, *s'il vous plait*,"
Beau pleasantly added, "and I'll add another fifty guineas to
my offer."

"Make it sixty and I'll give her floating islands for dessert
as well. Women adore them."

"You're a treasure, Remy. How would I survive without
you?"

"You'd be skin and bone with all your fucking, no
mistake."

"And I'm deeply grateful." Beau's voice was amused.

"I suppose you need this all within the hour so you don't

have to wait too long to make love to this female you've found."

The young Earl of Rochefort grinned. "After all these years you read my mind, Remy darling. An hour would be perfect."

But he gave no indication of his designs when he entered his stateroom a few minutes later. "My cook is grumbling, but up," Beau said with a smile, walking over to a built-in bureau and pulling out a crisply starched shirt from the drawer. "So food should arrive shortly. Are you comfortable?" he politely queried, slipping the shirt over his head.

"Yes, thank you." Serena looked up at him from the depths of a soft upholstered chair she'd almost fallen asleep in. "The cookies were delicious . . . and the wine."

"Good." After glancing at the crumbs remaining on the plate, he gauged the amount of wine remaining in the decanter with an assessing eye.

"I'd like to thank you very much for your hospitality." The lanterns had been lit by his servants and Serena's fairness was even more delectable bathed in a golden light. And her eyes weren't dark but aquamarine, like the Mediterranean.

"My pleasure," he casually said, dropping into a chair opposite her. My *distinct* pleasure, he more covetously thought. Her lush beauty was tantalizing, more provocative perhaps after the conventional prettiness of the actresses Charlie had procured. How would she respond, he wondered, to his first kiss? "Where had you booked passage?" he asked instead, gracious and well-behaved. "Perhaps I could see that your money is returned."

"Do you think you could?" She sat forward, her eyes alight with hope.

And for the briefest moment Beau St. Jules questioned his callous pursuit of pleasure, her poverty was so obvious. But in the next flashing moment he soothed his momentary twinge of conscience by deciding that a generous monetary settlement once they reached Italy would more than compensate for his dishonorable intentions. And who knew, he considered in a more practical frame of mind, she might not be an innocent despite her enchanting delicacy. She'd stowed away, after all—not exactly the act of a proper young lady.

"I'm sure I could. How much did you lose?"

"Two hundred pounds," she said. "It was all my savings."

Good God, he thought, briefly startled. He gambled thousands on the turn of a card. "Let me reimburse you in the interim," he suggested, reaching for a wallet lying on his desk.

"Oh, no, I couldn't possibly take money from you."

He looked up from the purse he was opening, not because of her words but her tone. A small reserve had entered her voice, and her eyes, he noted, held a distinct apprehension. "Consider it a loan," he calmly replied, gazing more critically at her, trying to properly place her in the hierarchy of female stowaways—a novel category for him.

Her navy serge gown was worn but well cut, her shoes equally worn but impeccably polished; her exquisite face and radiant hair couldn't be improved on in the highest ranks of society. Was she some runaway noble wife dressed in her servant's clothes or someone's beautiful mistress fallen on hard times?

"I'm a governess," she deliberately said.

"Forgive me. Was I staring?" His smile was cordial as he counted out two hundred pounds. "Here," he said, leaning across the distance separating them, placing the bills in a neat stack on a small table beside her chair. "Pay me back when you can. I've plenty. Do you care to divulge your name?" he went on, noting her necessitous gaze, willing her to pick up the money, wanting the distrust in her voice to disappear.

"Why?" Her blue-green gaze rising to his was cool, guarded.

"No reason." He shrugged—a small lazy movement, deprecating, indulgent. "I was just making conversation. I have no intention of hurting you," he softly added.

Her expression visibly relaxed. "My name's Serena Blythe."

Definitely an actress, he thought. She couldn't be a governess with a name and face and opulent body like that. "Have you been a governess long?" he casually asked, waiting to decipher the fabrications in her reply.

"Four years. When my father, Viscount Amberson, died I was forced to make a living."

He felt his stomach tighten. A *viscount's* daughter? Did she have relatives? he instantly wondered, the kind who would exert all the conventional pressures? And then as instantly he decided any young lady so destitute must be on her own. "I'm very sorry."

She sat still for a moment, thoughts of her father always painful, and then taking a small breath, she said in a controlled tone, "Papa gambled his money away. He wasn't very good at cards after his first bottle."

"Most men aren't."

She glanced at the bills and then at him and he could almost feel that small spark of elation he suddenly saw in her eyes.

"Are *you*?" she mildly inquired.

"Best hand wins the money?" he suggested, one dark brow raised in query. "Although I warn you, I'm sober."

"It would legitimize my taking it." She smiled for the first time, a lush yet curiously girlish smile, enigmatic like her.

Twenty minutes later, when the first course of oysters arrived, she was five hundred pounds richer, the Tokay decanter was empty, an easy bantering rapport had been established, and Beau had deliberately let her win only two hands. The rest she'd won on her own. She was either very good or very lucky. But she was definitely beautiful, he cheerfully noted, comfortably sprawled across from her, his cards balanced on his chest, his gaze, over the colorful fanned rims, gratified.

As was his mood.

The chill in her voice had disappeared, the guarded

expression in her eyes replaced with animation. And when she smiled at him after a winning hand, he found it increasingly difficult to refrain from touching her.

She ate the oysters with relish.

She drank more wine when another decanter arrived and she said "thank you" so sweetly and gratefully when only the empty oyster shells remained on her plate, he almost considered giving up his plans to bed her.

But then she smiled at him and leisurely stretched and all he could think of was the soft fullness of her breasts raised high with her arms flexed above her head. Not even the plain navy serge could disguise their delectable bounty.

"Did you make your gown?" he inquired to mask his overlong gaze with politesse. "I like the lace-trimmed collar."

Leaning back against her chair, she delicately touched the white lace. "It was my mother's. I outgrew all of mine."

He swallowed before he answered, the thought of her outgrowing her girlish gowns having a profound effect on him after just having observed the voluptuous swell of her breasts.

"We could probably find you some additional dresses on board."

"Like the ones in the closet under the stairwell?"

"You were hiding there?"

She nodded. "The scent was luscious. Very French."

"I'll have my steward put together a wardrobe tomorrow," he blandly said, not about to discuss French scents or the reason they were there.

"Whose gowns are they?"

He gazed at her for a brief moment, gauging the degree of inquisition in her query, but her expression was open, innocent of challenge.

"I'm not sure," he evasively answered. "Probably my mother's or sister's." Which meant the more garish gowns would have to be culled out before offering the lady her choice. The light of loves he brought aboard for brief excursions on the Thames had a penchant for seductive finery.

"I often wished I had siblings. Do you see your family often?"

He spoke of his family then in edited phrases, of their passion for racing and their winning horses, of their stud in the north, how his younger brother and sisters were all first-class riders, offering charming anecdotal information that brought a smile to her face.

"Your life sounds idyllic. Unlike mine of late," Serena said with a fleeting grimace. "But I intend to change that."

Frantic warning bells went off in Beau's consciousness. Had she *deliberately* come on board? Were her designing relatives even now in hot pursuit? Or were they explaining the ruinous details to his father instead? "How, exactly," he softly inquired, his dark eyes wary, "do you plan on facilitating those changes?"

"Don't be alarmed." She suddenly grinned, feeling gloriously alive again after so many years. "I have no designs on you."

He laughed, his good spirits instantly restored. "Candid women have always appealed to me."

"While men with yachts are out of my league." Her smile was dazzling. "But why don't you deal us another hand," she cheerfully said, "and I'll see what I can do about mending my fortunes."

She was either completely ingenuous or the most skillful coquette. But he had more than enough money to indulge her and she amused him immensely.

He dealt the cards.

And when the beefsteaks arrived some time later, the cards were put away and they both tucked into the succulent meat with gusto.

She ate with a kind of quiet intensity, absorbed in the food and the act of eating. It made him consider his casual acceptance of all the privileges in his life with a new regard—but only briefly, because he was very young, very wealthy, too handsome for complete humility, and beset by intense carnal impulses that were profoundly immune to principle.

He'd simply offer her a liberal settlement when the *Siren* docked in Naples, he thought, discarding any further moral scruples.

He glanced at the clock.

Three-thirty.

They'd be making love in the golden light of dawn . . . or sooner perhaps, he thought with a faint smile, reaching across the small table to refill her wineglass.

"This must be heaven or very near . . . ." Serena murmured, looking up from cutting another portion of beefsteak. "I can't thank you enough."

"Remy deserves all the credit."

"You're very disarming. And kind."

"You're very beautiful, Miss Blythe. And a damned good cardplayer."

"Papa practiced with me. He was an accomplished player when he wasn't drinking."

"Have you thought of making your fortune in the gaming rooms instead of wasting your time as an underpaid governess?"

"No," she softly said, her gaze direct.

"Forgive me. I meant no rudeness. But the demimonde is not without its charm."

"I'm sure it's not for a man," she said, taking a squarely cut piece of steak off her fork with perfect white teeth. "However, I'm going to art school in Florence," she went on, beginning to chew. "And I shall make my living painting."

"Painting what?"

She chewed a moment more, savoring the flavors, then swallowed. "Portraits, of course. Where the money is. I shall be flattering in the extreme. I'm very good, you know."

"I'm sure you are." And he intended to find out how good she was in other ways as well. "Why don't I give you your first commission?" He'd stopped eating but he'd not stopped drinking and he gazed at her over the rim of his wineglass.

"I don't have my paints. They're on the *Betty Lee* with my luggage."

"We have to dock in Lisbon to alert the authorities to the

man Horton. Why not buy your paints there? How much would you charge for my portrait?"

Her gazed shifted from her plate. "Nothing for you. You've been generous in the extreme. I'd be honored to paint you"—she paused and smiled—"whoever you are."

"Beau St. Jules."

"*The* Beau St. Jules?" She put her flatware down and openly studied him. "The darling of the broadsheets . . . London's premier rake who's outsinned his father, the Saint?" A note of teasing had entered her voice, a familiar, intimate inflection occasioned by the numerous glasses of wine she'd drunk. "Should I be alarmed?"

He shook his head, amusement in his eyes. "I'm very ordinary," he modestly said, this man who fueled the scandal sheets and stood stud to all the London beauties. "You needn't be alarmed."

He wasn't ordinary, of course—not in any way. He was the gold standard, she didn't doubt, by which male beauty was judged. His perfect features and artfully cropped black hair reminded her of classic Greek sculpture; his overt masculinity, however, was much less the refined cultural ideal. He was startlingly male.

"Aren't rakes older? You're very young," she declared. And gorgeous as a young god, she decided, although the cachet of his notorious reputation probably wasn't based on his beauty alone. He was very charming.

He shrugged at her comment on his age. He'd begun his carnal amusements very young, he could have said but, circumspect, asked instead, "How old are *you*?" His smile was warm, personal. "Out in the world on your own?"

"Twenty-three." Her voice held a small defiance; a single lady of three-and-twenty was considered a spinster in any society.

"A very nice age," he pleasantly noted, his dark eyes lazily half-lidded. "Do you like floating islands?"

She looked at him blankly.

"The dessert."

"Oh, yes, of course." She smiled. "I should save room then."

By all means, he licentiously thought, nodding a smiling approval, filling their wineglasses once more. Save room for me—because I'm coming in. . . .

When the dishes were cleared away by the servants and coffee and fruit had been left, they moved to a small settee to enjoy the last course. She poured him coffee; he added his own brandy and leaning back took pleasure in watching her slice a pear and leisurely eat each succulent piece.

"Your employers didn't feed you enough, did they?"

She turned to look at him lounging against the settee arm, all languid grace and beauty. "You wouldn't understand."

His lashes lowered fractionally. "Tell me anyway."

"I don't want to," she retorted, suddenly disquieted, all the misery still too fresh. "I don't want to remember anything about those four years with the Tothams." And despite her best intentions, her eyes grew shiny with tears.

Quickly setting his cup down, he took the dessert knife from her grasp and the remains of the pear, wiped her fingers on a lavender-scented napkin, and holding her small hands in his, softly said, "It's over. You don't have to go back."

When a tear slid down her cheek, he gently drew her into his arms and held her close. "Don't cry, darling," he murmured. "By the time we get to Naples, you'll have won a fortune from me. And then the Tottles can go to hell."

She giggled into his chest.

"And I'll see that the portrait you paint of me is seen at the Royal Academy. Should I pose nude as Mars? That should draw attention."

She giggled again and pushing slightly away from him, gazed up into his smiling face. "You're incredibly kind," she whispered.

Her lips were half parted and only inches away. It took all

his willpower to resist the temptation, her sweet vulnerability, her sadness affecting even his disreputable soul.

"May I kiss you?" she whispered, her feelings in turmoil, the warmth and affection he offered inexpressibly welcome after so many years of emotional deprivation, the feel of his arms around her comforting after the recent desperation of her plight.

"You probably shouldn't." He was trying to be honorable. She perhaps didn't understand what a kiss would do to him.

"I'm not an innocent." She'd been kissed before, although against her will, by the Tothams' repulsive son, when he'd dared transgress his mother's commands. It was immensely satisfying to offer a kiss of her own accord.

Beau shut his eyes briefly, her few simple words permission for all he wished to do. And when he opened his eyes, he murmured, heated and low, "Let *me* kiss *you*. . . ."

She was lost then, a true innocent despite what she'd said, her notion of a kiss eons distant from Beau St. Jules's kisses.

He made her feel lusciously heated, melting, his mouth delicate at first, offering butterfly kisses on her lips and cheeks, on her earlobes and temples, on the warm pulse of her throat, and then his mouth drifted lower, following his fingers as he unbuttoned the top three buttons of her neckline, drew her collar open, and kissed her soft, pale skin.

She kissed him back after that and a new tremulous feeling flared deep in the pit of her stomach. Pleasure inundated her senses, her heated blood, the warming surface of her skin, and most of all, gloriously in her spirit where she felt overwhelmingly happy. "You make me feel wonderful," she whispered, too long in the wasteland to want to forgo such blissful sensations.

"You make me feel—impatient." He lifted her into his arms, moving toward his bed, his mouth covering hers again, eating her tantalizing sweetness.

"Maybe I shouldn't," she breathed moments later when he lowered her gently to the bed.

"I know," he murmured, brushing his mouth over hers. "I shouldn't undo these buttons," he whispered, unclasping another pearl button at her neckline. "Tell me I shouldn't."

"It's highly improper," she gently teased, touching his strong jaw with a trailing fingertip, smiling up at him.

"But I have this powerful carnal urge." His voice was deep, low, rich with promise.

"Should I be frightened?" Her heart was racing, her senses in tumult.

"Are you usually?" he silkily inquired, amused at how well Miss Blythe played the game.

She didn't know what to say for a moment. "No," she finally replied, trembling, eager for his touch. "I'm not."

And then the man known by salacious repute as Glory lived up to his name.

Her dress was discarded between flame-hot kisses and bewitching caresses, his hands intoxicating on her flesh, his touch incarnate sensuality, her petticoat and chemise leisurely removed, her worn slippers and much-mended stockings slipped off with tantalizing languidness. And when she lay nude before him, flushed pink with arousal, the pulsing between her thighs leaving her breathless with longing, he pulled off his shirt and placed her palms on his chest so she could feel the powerful beat of his heart. "I want you that much," he whispered, seated beside her, his large hands covering hers, his skin hot, the rhythm of his heart turbulently echoed in her own.

The rich splendor of her body incited his passions: her provocative breasts pinked from his touch, their ripe fullness his for the taking; the sensuous curve of her slender waist and hips was female sorcery; and lower, her pale silken hair was lure and magnet to his lust. Lifting her hands to his mouth, he lightly kissed her fingertips and then gently lowering her hands, he whispered, "Don't go away. . . ."

"Not likely when I'm melting inside."

"For me?" His smile was warm like his gaze.

"For you . . ." An enchantress's voice, soft, low, eager.

And when he abruptly rose to strip his breeches free she understood another compelling measure of his allure.

"You're very beautiful," she said, her gaze on his arousal. "I'll paint you for myself too."

"Like this?" He touched himself with a practiced hand, watched her eyes widen as his erection grew. "Be my guest," he softly said.

"Later," she promised, feeling fiercely independent, flushed with a precious, new freedom, a universe away from her servitude, from all her recent misery.

"*Much* later," he quietly agreed, moving over her, sliding between her thighs, guiding himself to her hot, wet cleft.

Lacing her arms around his neck, she ciung to him, glorying in his strength and power, in the unalloyed pleasure she was feeling.

He drove forward.

She screamed.

"Jesus." He exhaled explosively. "Jesus Christ . . ." He shuddered, his body convulsed by the abrupt, shocking curtailment.

"I won't cry out again," she whispered, pulling his face down to kiss, a keen hot craving overriding her transient pain, avaricious need flooding her senses. "Please."

He softly swore, unsavory practicalities pertaining to wellborn virgins suddenly in the forefront of his brain, danger signals bombarding his senses.

"Let me help," she whispered, moving her hips in a delectable enticement, reaching down to touch him.

Her fingers slid down his rigid length and he groaned, the animal sound rising from deep in his lungs.

"Don't," he said on a suffocated breath.

"But I want to."

He shut his eyes briefly against his overwhelming urges. "You can't change your mind later," he said, his voice rough with restraint.

"I know."

"You can change your mind now." He took a deep breath. "And maybe for a few seconds more," he said, his whisper hoarse, constrained, his eyes half shut against the hot-spur needs of his body.

"I don't want to change my mind." She stroked his rigid erection.

It was too much for a man known for his heedless prodigality.

Brushing her hand away, he braced his lower body, held her hips firmly between his hands, and surged forward, plunging into her with a savage, barely contained violence.

Her cry ricocheting around the teak-paneled stateroom went unnoticed as he sank hilt deep into her luscious warmth and exhaled in acute gratification, sensational feeling strumming down his nerve endings.

Seconds later her soft whimpers and the pressure of her hands clutching his back finally registered on his consciousness. And gallantly tamping his selfish desires, he exerted himself to soothe her distress, because she was his now until Naples and he had all the time in the world. . . .

Lying quiescent within her, he gently kissed away her tears, his mouth delicate on her cheeks and eyelids, his murmured words soothing, apologetic. His voice was deep, velvety, his caresses bewitching, and when her tears were gone and her hands had relaxed on his back, he promised her pleasure in seductive love words . . . conjuring up lush heated images in her mind, offering her enchantment. Until soon her senses were flame hot once again and she offered her mouth to him and smiled and said, "It doesn't hurt anymore."

"I can tell." She was sleek, wet, pulsing around him and when her hips first tentatively moved he gently glided deeper until she gasped not in pain this time but in astonished gratification.

"I'm dying," she whispered as the exquisite rapture ravaged her senses and she held him deep inside, her hands firm at the base of his spine, prolonging the blissful agony.

"Not now, but soon," Beau murmured, the words

vibrating across her mouth. "Loosen your hold for a second. There. Isn't that better?" he gently queried as he penetrated that small measure deeper.

She couldn't speak but he understood her trembling sigh and with an expertise garnered from years of pleasuring women, he slowly, gently offered Serena Blythe her first joyous glimpse of paradise.

Followed shortly by her second enchanting vision as he joined her in his own explosive orgasm.

And soon after, she experienced a third luxurious climax.

He was a man of celebrated stamina.

Much later as she lay in his arms, basking in the afterglow of a deep contentment, she said, "Do people call you Glory to your face?" Shifting slightly in the curve of his arm, she gazed up at him.

His glance drifted back from the rising sun—a brilliant saffron in the symmetry of the brass-framed porthole. "Sometimes," he carefully said, not sure he cared to discuss a subject related to his sexual prowess, not altogether sure he should have taken her virginity despite her acquiescence.

"You deserve the name," she simply said, smiling. "You're very good. How long will it take us to reach Italy?"

Her smile was flirtatious with an underscoring of naïveté so sweet, he found himself suddenly immune to misgivings and the thought of screwing the beautiful Miss Blythe from here to Naples held an irresistible appeal. "Three weeks," he said of the two-week journey. "Maybe a month if we stop at Lisbon and Minorca." He'd already decided to order the sails trimmed in the morning.

"Only a month?" she said with a luscious smile, moving against him with an enchanting gliding progress that brought her semen-damp cleft in proximity to his quickening erection.

"Longer," he murmured with a wolfish grin, "if we have to elude the privateers."

"That sounds nice. Is there any food left?"

He laughed. "Some dessert, but I'll need a kiss to get up and fetch it."

Her response was immediate, luscious, and decidedly heated.

And he gave her something she wanted more.

"*Now,*" Serena murmured a pleasurable time later, tracing a languid finger over Beau's mouth as he rested lightly over her, "I'm going to eat."

"Food?" A boyish grin flashed white against his tanned skin.

"Yes, my glory boy," she whispered, "but don't go away."

"Not likely, darling." His velvety voice licked at her senses. "But I was thinking . . ." he whispered, gently stroking the full curve of her breast. "Perhaps you'd like—"

"No," she murmured, placing a restraining hand on his muscled chest. "You have to wait."

"What if I don't want to?" He dipped his head to lightly kiss the slender bridge of her nose. "And you're so *easy* to please."

"Only now in my novice stage," she said with a seductive lift of one brow. "By the end of three weeks I'll be salaciously demanding."

"Umm," he murmured, smiling faintly, "promises, promises . . ."

"Only if I'm still alive, darling." She pushed against his weight. "I'm *starving.*"

She was serious, he realized. "I'll call Remy," he said, instantly obliging, aware of the recent privations in her past, "and you can tell him what you want."

"No, please don't. . . . There's some food left on the table." A pink flush colored her cheeks. "I mean"——her gaze drifted down his bare chest—"look at us. We're not dressed and the bed's a shambles and—"

"He's not judgmental, darling." His voice was soothing, dégagé.

Her eyes went shuttered. "And he's seen this often."

For a brief moment he considered lying, her tone suddenly moody, but then he didn't wish to deceive her about either the style of his life or her position in it. "Often enough," he quietly replied.

She gazed at him for a speculative moment, a multitude of implications in that short phrase, his answer perhaps more frank than she might have wished. "I *could* get dressed and sit in that chair over there."

"If you like," he politely said. "But Remy won't care if you're dressed or not."

"So I shouldn't be concerned with appearances."

He tried not to smile at the concept of appearances, considering their recent intimacies and the warmth of her body currently resting beneath his. "I wouldn't worry about it," he said, repressing his grin.

And then she suddenly laughed—at her absurd notion of propriety, at his gallant attempt to suppress his smile, and reaching up, she took his face in her hands and drew his mouth down to hers. "You're very sweet," she whispered.

"Not as sweet at you, lollipop."

Stretching slightly upward, she licked his lower lip, a sensuous, lingering caress.

"Anywhere . . ." he murmured, his smile cheeky, ". . . anytime."

"Because you're always ready," she purred, feeling him rise against her belly.

"I've been in training."

"While I've been waiting for you."

"Lucky me," he whispered, gently nudging her legs apart.

"Do women ever say no to you?"

His hesitation was minute. "Of course," he lied.

"Good," she asserted, looking up at him with artless

innocence. "Because if you don't feed me *right* now," she softly added, "I'll never *fuck* you again."

"Remy!" he bellowed, and rolling off her, he swiftly rose from the bed.

"You really like me," she teased, from the disordered jumble of the bedclothes, all pink-cheeked, tousled, delectable.

"Oh, yes . . . you're vastly pleasing, Miss Blythe." Gazing down on her, his dark eyes heated, his libido on full alert, he wondered for a moment whether all virgins were so tantalizing or whether Serena Blythe's naively tempting allure was unique.

The perfection of his muscled body gleamed in the golden rays of the rising sun, his broad-shouldered frame dwarfing the confines of the small stateroom, his dark beauty breathtaking in the full light of day, and Serena understood— beyond the lure of his sexual virtuosity—why Beau St. Jules never slept alone.

"Who first called you Glory?" she asked, wanting to know what woman had so aptly named him. At the sharp rise of his brows, she added, "I've overheard all the stories from the Tothams' son. He was forever trying to ape your rakish ways. 'Lady C. was seen emerging from the maze at Chatham with Glory R., her expression one of deep satisfaction,' " Serena quoted with a quirked grin. "Mrs. Totham devoured the scandal sheets too."

"Do I know them?" Beau blandly inquired, interested in deflecting her query.

"Hardly," Serena answered, entertained by the notion of Beau St. Jules seated across the tea table from the self-righteous Maud Totham. "Tell me about your name."

"Rochefort?" Reaching for his breeches, he swiftly pulled them on, an unconscious defense perhaps, female inquisitiveness invariably provoking evasion.

"If you don't want to tell me," Serena playfully chided, "just say so."

His gaze swiveled to her, his fingers arrested on the buttons at his waist. "I don't want to tell you."

"I could always sleep under the stairs again," she said in a seductive purr.

"You'd have to get out of here first."

"Are you threatening me?" A mischievous glint shone in her eyes and she wondered what it would be like to truly challenge the Earl of Rochefort. He'd killed a man in a duel last year, she knew; Neville had talked of little else for a fortnight.

Dropping into a chair, he surveyed her from under half-lowered lashes. "Just pointing out your physical limitations, lollipop," he murmured.

"Do you always bully your women?"

"I've never had to."

"Which brings us back to your nickname."

He sighed. "If I tell you will this interrogation cease?"

She smugly nodded.

Exhaling softly, he said, "A lover once referred to my height as glorious and the name caught on."

She snorted in disbelief. "Liar."

"She liked tall men."

"Certain *parts* of tall men."

An infinitesimal pause ensued before he carefully said, "Perhaps."

"*Perhaps?*" Her grin was knowing, impertinent.

"Jesus," he softly breathed. "you're persistent."

"You're not going to tell me, are you?"

"There's nothing to tell." Nothing at least that he could reveal without shocking the virginal Miss Blythe.

"I can find out."

He grinned. "Out in the middle of the ocean?"

"Later then."

Later didn't matter to him. Once they reached Italy there was no later. "Suit yourself," he mildly replied, relieved to hear Gallic curses outside in the corridor. "Ah . . . here comes Remy."

Seconds after the imprecations reached their ears, the door opened and a scowling young man still buttoning his shirt cuffs stepped into the stateroom. "I don't suppose it occurred to you that I was sleeping," he muttered, glaring at his employer.

"Don't you knock?" Beau remarked, his voice dulcet, his lounging pose unaltered by his chef's gruffness.

First surveying Serena seated in bed with the sheet clutched under her chin, Remy returned his gaze to Beau. "You sounded *excited,* milord," he impudently replied.

"Mind your manners, Remy," Beau cautioned, his tone soft as velvet. "Miss Blythe's my guest and she's hungry."

"I should have stayed in London," Remy grumbled. "Where you never eat at home."

"But then you wouldn't see the pretty signorina in Naples." Remy's penchant for a young modiste had been prominent in his decision to accompany Beau.

"Touché, milord," the young Frenchman murmured and, apparently warmed by the memory of his lover, he smiled. "So the mademoiselle is hungry," he pleasantly said, as if his previous stormy behavior hadn't transpired and, bowing with infinite grace, he courteously inquired, "What would you like to eat, Miss Blythe?"

"Nothing, that is . . . I couldn't . . . I don't wish to put you to any trouble," Serena stammered, thoroughly intimidated by Remy and even more so by the immodest circumstances of their meeting. "Beau shouldn't have wakened you."

"Good Lord, don't tell him that." Beau shifted into an upright position. "He's impossible enough already. It's not a problem to cook for us, *is* it, Remy?" he quietly inquired, a hint of steel beneath his mannered drawl.

"Not at all," the young Frenchman readily agreed, as if he'd not been churlish, as if such contretemps between himself and his employer were commonplace. "I'd be honored, milord. Perhaps I could suggest some succulent coquilles St. Jacques à la Parisienne now that morning has come," he added with a meaningful glance in his employer's direction, "or some tender veal and mushrooms. Or perhaps a sweet genoise with chocolate buttercream icing."

Even as the saliva rose in her mouth at the thought of

such delectable food, Serena hesitated. The chef's sudden volte-face was as unnerving as his ill humor.

"We'll have the coquilles St. Jacques and the genoise," Beau interposed. "I don't like veal."

"Maybe the mademoiselle likes veal," Remy delicately remarked.

"Oh, no," Serena blurted. "I mean, I do . . . but, well . . . scallops and cake would be . . . more than enough. I'm afraid even that will put you out enormously."

"Not your usual sort," Remy murmured, his comment for Beau's ears alone. "So enticingly polite."

"Thank you for your favorable endorsement," Beau sardonically replied, his voice equally subdued. "Would you like Champagne, darling?" he inquired, addressing Serena in a normal tone. "Remy tells me we have a bountiful supply."

"If you don't mind."

Remy smiled, moving a step closer to Beau before softly asking, "Does she say thank you after you fuck her too?"

"Very sweetly." Then in a voice that carried to the bed, he said, "Send the cake first while we wait for the scallops. And three bottles of Champagne."

"Yes, milord," Remy answered, his gaze sportive. "How much time will I have to rest between"—his brows rose in lecherous ascent—"meals?"

"I'd sleep when you can," Beau quietly replied. "Do we understand each other?"

"Perfectly, milord."

The cake when it arrived was magnificent. Decorated with candied violets intertwined in a latticework piping of pale yellow almond-flavored buttercream, the chocolate-iced layers stacked atop creamy praline filling that trailed down in enticing rivulets onto a luscious base of macaroons, the presentation was enough to dazzle the most jaded palate.

Lying beneath the covers, Serena held her breath, awestruck as the young serving lad carefully placed the dramatic cake on the table. Once the boy left with the remains of their previous meal, she sat up, inquiring breathlessly,

"How does Remy manage such spectacular food in a galley kitchen so far from the markets? Candied violets . . ." The delicacy had been unknown to her the last few years.

"Remy's resourceful," Beau casually replied. Beyond that blanket avowal the concept of food preparation was foreign to him. "Ask him if you like," he went on, cutting a slice of cake and easing it onto a plate. "Although I know he has a walk-in cold chest because we loaded several wagons of ice on board." Handing the plate to Serena, he took pleasure in seeing the delight on her face.

"Ice?" She looked up, her first forkful already halfway to her mouth.

"For the Champagne, I expect," he said, deftly twisting off the cork on a bottle, "and maybe these." He touched a spun sugar violet. "You don't mind having dessert first, I hope."

She shook her head, her mouth too full to speak, glimpses of paradise within touching distance as the luscious blend of flavors melted on her tongue.

Touching was very much in Beau's mind too as he poured two glasses of Champagne, although his sensations were less visionary and more graphic. She was a delicious sight lushly nude, seated in the middle of his bed, her golden hair in tumbled disarray on her shoulders, her breasts ripe and full, her slender waist and graceful hips incarnate female allure, like the pale silken hair between her legs. How exotically beautiful she was, a delicate, golden siren all scented womanhood and desire—and disarming appetites. With what pleasure she ate; what curious pleasure it gave *him* to offer her that enjoyment.

"You're not eating," she said, licking her finger after scooping up the last morsel of frosting on her plate.

"I'll wait for the scallops." Although he wasn't sure he cared to eat at all.

A tiny silence fell.

"Would you like more Champagne?" Leaning forward, he began to reach for the bottle on the floor beside his chair.

"Not just yet."

Another small hush descended.

And then he noticed her gaze on the cake.

"Would you like another piece?"

"If you don't think me piggish," she said, her tone reminding him of a young child told to mind her manners.

"Lord, no," he quickly assured her, realizing she'd been afraid to ask for more. Placing the entire cake on the bed within her reach, he said, "Eat it all."

"I feel so greedy."

"Darling, you're apologizing to the wrong person. Greed of every kind is a byword in the haut monde and that cake in contrast is the merest small indulgence. Just remember to save some room for the scallops."

She smiled. "You're very lovable."

"I was thinking the same of you, lollipop," he softly said, the husky undertone in his voice irrepressibly sensual.

"How nice," she whispered, dipping her finger in the chocolate icing and slowly bringing it to her mouth. "But Remy might come in. . . ." And sliding her fingertip into her mouth, she slowly withdrew it frostingless.

Stirred by such lascivious intent, he restlessly shifted in his lounging pose, his erection an instant response. "Why don't I lock the door," he murmured, already half rising.

"Your chef will be furious if his scallops are ruined."

"I pay Remy well enough to overlook a ruined plate of scallops," he said, moving toward the door, "or a month's ruined menus for that matter."

"Won't he pout?"

Beau half turned and smiled. "Better him than me."

"And you don't care to be deterred."

"Not in terms of sex with you."

"How flattering you are, Rochefort."

It stopped him for a moment, her utter candor when so many women preferred sugary euphemisms for lust. Turning around completely, he quizzically gazed at her. "Have you always been like this?"

"Naked in bed with a virtual stranger, you mean? Just

this once, my dear Glory, as you well know. Or do you mean something else?"

"I mean so willing to speak your mind."

"At this stage I don't have much to lose, do I? My other option is starvation on the streets of London. I prefer this," she declared, smiling. "Short of throwing me overboard, you can't chastise me overmuch for my plain speaking. And *somehow* I've gotten the impression you prefer my company to solitude on this voyage."

"Perceptive woman," he said, half to himself, surprised to find her insight true when he'd always railed against female company on lengthy cruises.

"And who knows . . . if you continue playing cards so chivalrously, by journey's end, I may be a wealthy woman as well."

"You're damned good." He grinned. "At cards too . . ." His tone abruptly altered from the overtly seductive. "And chivalry had little to do with your winning."

"I know." She fluttered her lashes at him in flirtatious parody. "I was being polite."

"A game, then, later." He felt a surge of excitement beyond the sexual, gambling one of his passions. "No holds barred."

"You could lose, Rochefort."

His grin was boyish. "I can afford it."

"While I can't."

"You've a stake at least. How much have you won from me?"

"Enough to give me independence from governess duty in Florence," she declared. "I'll never be able to thank you properly," she added, her voice suddenly hushed, a small tremor in her words. "You've saved my life."

"Lord, no," he quickly protested, unfamiliar with such warmhearted female gratitude separate from lavish gifts of jewelry. "Please . . . you'll make me feel guilty for taking advantage of you."

She shook her head, her hair shimmering tinsel bright in the morning sunshine. "I took advantage of *you*. Of your kindness and generosity, taking your money at cards, forcing Remy from his sleep twice—keeping you up all night," she finished in a playful hushed breath.

His sudden grin matched the teasing light in his eyes. "So you actually owe *me*."

"Very much, milord." Her voice was sweet, respectful, her expression that of a young maiden well schooled in politesse. Until she smiled in a slow, seductive, languorous way that had nothing to do with maidenly innocence. "Tell me what you'd like me to do," she provocatively murmured, "to repay you."

He reached behind him, and his fingers closed on the door key. The sound of the lock moving into place sent a shiver of excitement down Serena's spine.

"Why don't I show you?" he softly said.

But after rejoining her on the bed, he adjusted the pillows under his head, settled back, and mildly said, "Finish eating first if you like."

A tyro in the game of love and deeply appreciative as she'd already indicated, she thought it might seem rude to ignore him and cut herself another piece of cake. "I don't have to," she said, a degree of uncertainty in her voice, "if you'd rather do something else . . ."

"Fuck, you mean." His voice was very soft.

"Yes. I'm profoundly in your debt."

One dark brow lifted. "You're doing this out of obligation?"

"Of course not. You know better than that with amour your conspicuous speciality."

He slowly smiled. "You did seem rather more involved than mere duty would warrant."

"Odious man," she reproached, a twinkle in her gaze. "As if a woman alive could resist you."

He'd learned long ago to refrain from discussing his love life. "Are you going to eat?" he asked instead.

"I don't *have* to."

"So accommodating," he lazily drawled. "But if you're hungry, eat. I can make love to you anytime."

"Can you really?" A faint pettish note shaded her voice.

His mouth quirked faintly. "What do you want me to say?"

She made a small moue; his certainty based on the legions of women in his life could not be doubted. "Say something charming, Rochefort," she wryly said, deciding she didn't care to hear the truth. "Something sweet and romantical from your repertoire."

"I only meant we're unconstrained by time. And I don't have a repertoire . . . although," he added with a lush smile, "if I had one I'd liken you to Ovid's Corinna—your beauty's without flaw." Reaching up, he delicately touched her cheek. "Is that better?"

She ruefully wished she could be as dégagée as he. "Forgive my pettiness."

Beau shrugged. "There's nothing to forgive, lollipop."

"I don't know why I should take exception to your reputation with women anyway," Serena mused, gazing at him sprawled in nonchalant splendor beside her. "I hardly know you."

"Have I been remiss?" he gently inquired.

"Well, besides that," she replied. "And thank you very much, dear Glory, for your exceptional talent. But I mean *really* know you."

He never liked the sound of that phrase, particularly from women in bed. It always presaged their wish to insinuate themselves into his life and by definition change his comfortable existence. Restive at the familiar consequences of a woman in pursuit, he rolled up into a seated position, the flux of rippling muscle impressive. "Why don't I feed you?" he suggested.

"Why?" Perplexed, she stared at him.

"Because I want to." Beyond the need to derail her train of thought, he couldn't dismiss the tempting allure of her sumptuous body, nude, available, only inches away. And with her hot-blooded libido, he didn't doubt his ability to distract her.

"And you always do what you want."

"Almost always." His dark eyes were direct.

"Then maybe I'm not hungry right now," she retorted, taking issue with his careless authority, her servitude at the Tothams' too recent.

"Why don't we see whether you are or not?"

He spoke so softly she barely heard the words, but his languid intonation was offering not food but sex *and* the faintest of challenges.

"No." Sitting up straighter, she clasped her hands in her lap, presenting an incongruous image of nude primness.

"Just a small bite," he coaxed, as if she hadn't spoken, as if the pink blush rising on her throat indicated a far different response. Reaching out, he dipped his finger into the cake frosting and plucked a candied violet from the creamy chocolate. "Open for me," he whispered, leaning forward, his dark gaze provocative, sensual.

And heedless to all but the tantalizing promise in his eyes, a throbbing began deep inside her. His intent was palpable, his nearness overwhelming, the hard muscled strength of his shoulders and chest so close she could feel the heat from his skin. Drawn by a chrysalis desire that overlooked temperament and jealousies, she slowly reached out to touch him, the sensitive pads of her fingers delicately sliding over his powerful shoulders before her fingers splayed, her hand flattened, and her palm brushed down over his sharply defined pectorals. With the warmth of his body seeping into hers, her hand glided lower still, drawn by a hunger she couldn't resist, her fingers tracing the ridged tautness of his torso, slipping over the waistband of his breeches, her pulse accelerating as her gaze focused on the bulging prominence of his arousal.

He followed the tantalizing progress of her hand, watching, waiting, aware of her patent interest. "Touch it," he murmured.

Helpless against such manifest lust, she looked up at him for a flashing moment, her gaze hot with need.

"Touch it," he repeated, "it's for you."

And after taking a small steadying breath, her hand moved that last small distance and closed over his hard, pulsing erection.

He sucked in his breath, her touch triggering a flaring surge of excitement. His gaze flickered briefly to her small hand before lifting to hers. "Try it now, lollipop," he murmured.

Double entendre licked at her senses as he raised the sugared violet to her mouth and his enormous length grew beneath her hand, whetting her appetite.

"Open," he softly breathed.

She was wet, covetous, tantalized. And she obeyed his quiet command because she could no more resist his seductive promise of pleasure than the hundreds of women before her.

His finger invaded her mouth by leisurely degrees as if making her wait now that she'd capitulated. And when he'd penetrated sufficiently, he whispered, "Lick it off. . . ."

Trembling with expectation and need, she closed her mouth over his finger and tasted sweet violet and scented lust . . . and a luxurious, voluptuous surfeit uncommon in her world—like the nectar of the gods.

A man of finesse, he knew how to sharpen that fine edge of feeling, to intensify her quivering ecstasy. Sliding his hand up her thigh, he touched the pale silky hair of her mons, his fingers slipping downward, delicately stroking the satiny tissue of her labia. "Can you feel me?" he murmured, his question rhetorical with his fingers in two of her orifices. "Or is this better?" he asked, slipping a second finger deep into her throbbing cleft. "Or this?" he added over her low moan of pleasure, forcing a third finger inside.

Salacious feeling overwhelmed her, so violent and unrestrained she bit down hard on his finger.

Grunting at the sudden sharp pain, he jerked his fingers free. "Bloody little savage," he murmured, shoving her back-

ward with a sweeping shift of his forearm. Following her
down, he held her captive, the weight of his body lightly
braced above her, his hips cradled by her outspread thighs,
his dark eyes amused. "What are we going to do with you?"

"Fuck me," she said, relishing the blunt, decisive sounds
on her tongue, his powerful body overwhelming her senses.

"I'm bleeding." He scowled in mock anger.

"Fuck me anyway," she whispered.

"Maybe I'll exact my revenge instead." A roguish smile
played on his lips.

"I should like that immensely, milord," she breathed. "I
just know I would. . . ."

He laughed, a delicious, husky sound reminiscent of
wickedness and sin. "You're a hot little baggage, Miss
Blythe."

"You've a great deal to do with it, dear Glory." Her hips
moved in a slow, sensuous rhythm so they both felt the
pleasurable extent of his erection. "I'm enamored with my
new . . . toy."

"And you want to play again." His voice was velvet soft.

"Oh, yes . . ." she purred. "Do you think you could
arrange it?"

"I must live right to be rewarded with you, Miss Blythe."

"And you must be my reward for surviving the Tothams.
Now take these off," she insisted, working at the buttons of
his breeches, "or I'll turn tantrumish."

"A second, lollipop, before you scream," he teased, easing
away to slide the cake plate and Champagne bottle onto the
floor, then settling back between her legs. "And now, we're
at your service."

Lacing her arms around his neck, she murmured, "You're
very fast."

"For you, wild thing . . ."

"Good, because I need you, *now*." Her gaze was flame hot.

"Then I hope you can sew." Ripping off the unopened
buttons on his breeches, he freed his erection and plunged
into her. The instant he entered her, her orgasm began, her
unbridled response so precipitous and unexpected that a

second later he had to curtail his withdrawal stroke to accommodate her hot-spur urgency. Completely submerged once again, her nails biting into his back, he braced his legs and held himself hard against her womb, filling her, fulfilling her, her rapturous whimpers an adjunct to the fevered pulsing of their bodies.

She moved minutely in entreaty and he moved less delicately, understanding her, answering her, penetrating that essential, lustful distance even more.

"Oh, god," she breathed, delirium assaulting her senses, the shocking pleasure exploding in her brain, "oh, god, oh, god, oh, god . . ."

Her voice trailed away.

She was dying.

She was melting away, she was dissolving.

And a hush enveloped the sunlit room, the only sound the faint rasp of breathing.

5

Long moments later her eyes opened and then the faintest of smiles slowly curved her opulent mouth. "I couldn't wait," she softly said, her gaze heavy-lidded, surfeit in her husky contralto.

"You never have to, kitten. There aren't any rules."

"Why doesn't anyone ever tell you it's so . . . *wonderful*," she exalted.

"So you can find out for yourself," he neutrally replied, not wishing to blight such charming delight. The cynical truth related more pragmatically to the price of virginity in the marketplace than to self-realization.

"When did *you* find out?" she asked, still faintly awestruck.

"A long time ago." Feeling her honeyed warmth still pulsing around him, he wondered if she was some fairy nymph with special siren powers that could make him want her so. "It's better than anything, isn't it?" he softly added.

"Even better than Remy's genoise."

His eyes widened in mock surprise. "That good."

"Although you didn't . . . I mean . . ." The warm flush on her cheeks deepened in color.

"Don't worry, lollipop," he gently replied. "I will."

"Be sure and tell me if I'm doing anything wrong," she said with an ingenuous sincerity.

He smiled at the notion of a tutorial. "You couldn't possibly do anything wrong."

"I'm willing to learn—Oh dear—" she said on a smothered gasp. "What are you doing?"

"Can you feel this?" He drove in a fraction deeper.

And she trembled under his hands. "Oh, yes," she whispered, the sensation so exquisite she didn't wonder why he was in such high demand. "Please . . . do it—again."

How sweetly artless her request, he thought, like a child requesting a second cookie. "Like this?" Holding her hips lightly, he forced himself deeper and deeper still until she cried out softly and her breathing abruptly altered to a less tranquil rhythm. And when he shifted slightly to withdraw enough to indulge her again, her hands slid down his back to restrain him, to keep him hard within her throbbing flesh.

"Let go," he whispered, stirring against her unyielding grasp, his lower body poised to ease back.

"No." Her grip tightened.

"It gets better if you wait."

"No." A fretful, suffocated sound. "You said I didn't have to."

"Did I?" he murmured, dismissing any further contemplation of leisured foreplay. The innocent Miss Blythe must have been virginal too long for she was wildly impatient now as if making up for lost time. Clasping her tightly so they remained joined, he rolled onto his back, carrying her with him. "You set the pace, darling," he said, easing her upright, adjusting her on his hips so she was riding him. "Here." Slipping his hands under her bottom, he raised her so she slid up his erection. And when she was poised on the swollen crest, his hands glided up to her hips. "Then thusly, kitten," he murmured, exerting pressure downward, guiding her until he was sunk hilt deep inside her honeyed warmth.

She uttered a small blissful sigh.

"Ride at any breakneck speed you prefer, lollipop," he said. "I'll try to keep up."

"So I have my own personal stud," she murmured, exquisitely impaled.

"For as long as you want." A connoisseur of sensation, he

was considering keeping her beyond the journey to Naples. They were a very good fit.

"Are you always . . . this ready?"

"We try," he modestly said, this man who held most of the sexual records in the club betting books.

"How nice for me," she replied, moving upward slowly until she was hovering on the tip of his erection.

"And me." His smile was wolfish.

"Can I keep you locked away till landfall?" she murmured, inundated by joyous sensation, a new, wondrous world suddenly at her command.

When he didn't answer, she gazed down at him from under languid, half-lowered lashes and slowly slid down his rigid length. "Say yes," she whispered.

He smiled faintly. "I don't take orders—even from pretty governesses."

Rotating her hips in a sensuous, intoxicating revolution that gave new meaning to the word friction, she said, sultry and low, "You give the orders, then."

His smile broadened. "An imaginative solution."

"A selfish one, darling. But the orders better be to my liking."

"Meaning?"

"Meaning they must be confined to carnal matters."

"Really. You won't make my bed or wash my clothes?"

"My four years of servitude ended"—she looked out the window at the bright morning light, gauging the time— "two days ago, Rochefort. And I don't know how to wash clothes."

"I don't suppose you make beds either?"

"I've learned to particularly *unmake* beds now, thanks to you, my dear Glory. And I think," she said with a grin, "we're going to need some clean sheets soon."

"What if I ordered you not to climax for ten minutes?" he teased. "Would that be carnal enough?"

"Be reasonable, Rochefort." Her pout looked delicious.

"But then I'm never reasonable," he said, effortlessly lifting her free of his erection, ignoring her squeal of protest as he placed her on the bed. "Now what are you going to do?" he added, grinning.

"Attack you."

She lunged at him and he rolled away, laughing.

"You're mine, darling," she said, still in pursuit. "It's just a matter of time."

"Ten minutes, to be precise," he lazily replied, catching her as she fell atop him. "And I'm giving the orders."

"You don't really mean it, do you?" she whispered, moving her hips seductively.

"Abstinence is good for the soul," he silkily murmured, stilling her hips.

"How would you know?"

"I read it somewhere." His gaze was shameless.

"But I don't *want* to wait." She struggled against his solid grasp.

"Perhaps there's an alternative."

Appreciation warmed her eyes. "How sensible you are, Rochefort."

"While you're a sizzling little baggage. Are you religious?" he asked, as if the two thoughts were related.

"If I were, dear Glory, meeting you would have made me deeply concerned about the fires of hell."

He smiled faintly. "Then you haven't considered becoming a nun."

"Not since Dover at least."

He laughed, and releasing his hold, eased away and rolled off the bed. Coming to his feet, he held out his hand. At her questioning gaze, he said, "I'm offering you instant gratification."

She immediately clasped his hand and rising from the bed followed him. Blowing out a candle flame as he passed his desk, he lifted the half-burned remnant from the candelabra and drew her after him to the settee. "Have you ever masturbated?" he casually asked, dropping onto the small sofa, his fingers sliding from hers.

She stared at him, not certain she'd heard him correctly.

"You must not have," he noted, her startled gaze answer

enough. Leaning over, he lightly stroked her mons with the base of the candle. "I thought you might like to learn during this ten-minute hiatus."

Serena blushed.

"Everyone masturbates," he lightly acknowledged, "at some time or other. There's nothing to blush about. Would you like to try?"

She shook her head, embarrassed.

"You might enjoy it," he quietly said, sliding the candle between her legs.

"I prefer *you*."

"But you can't have me right now." Exerting upward pressure, he forced her labia open with the pale beeswax candle.

"Then I'll wait." But she was quivering slightly, the insinuating penetration, the tangible gliding pressure of the candle on her clitoris detonating tiny sparks of carnal lust.

"No need to wait," he murmured, conscious of her heated response, the sleek progress of his makeshift dildo potent evidence of her irrepressible passions. She was slippery wet, her body receptive, eager for sex. "I saw a nun in an oratory once—doing this—putting a candle deep inside her . . . up to here," he softly added, forcing the candle delectably deeper, watching Serena's face. "Can you feel it?"

Standing before him, she closed her thighs on the intoxicating sensation, his whispered words echoing in her brain, provocative, tantalizing, as if he knew precisely what he was making her feel.

"Tell me," he murmured.

She couldn't. She was incapable of conjuring words with breathless, lust overwhelming her.

"That nun had dark curls down here," he softly said, "not golden silk like this," he added, gently stroking the damp verges framing her swelling clitoris. His touch was delicate, sensitive, her engorged flesh responding, her breathing accelerating into a light panting rhythm.

"All the altar boys used to hide behind the tapestries and watch her when she'd take advantage of the privacy in the small chapel. She had a beautiful cunt," he murmured. "Turn around, darling." He nudged Serena's hips. "So we all can see you. You're almost ready to come, aren't you? Here . . . hold the candle yourself or it's going to fall out." He knew how close she was, how primed, and he smiled faintly at her swift securing grip when he released his hold on the candle.

"There now . . . you move it . . . push it in a little farther." And leaning forward, he gently kissed her silken mons. Her whimper of pleasure as her yielding flesh absorbed several inches more of the candle sounded delicately erotic in the quiet room. "Show my friends your big breasts," he whispered, reaching up to stroke the weighty undercurve of one breast. "Turn this way so they can see," he instructed, rotating her slightly, his hands on her hips. "We've seen them before, haven't we? Last week behind the altar when you thought you were alone, you undressed, didn't you? Alastair particularly likes your huge breasts. He's never seen any so big. He'd like to touch them—like this. . . ." Beau's voice was husky, low, the fantasy he evoked scandalous, wicked. She was nude, exposed, exhibiting herself before all the covetous boys who wanted to touch her. Beau's fingertips slid over the plump, flaring roundness of her breasts, then slowly circled one nipple. "Would it be all right if Alastair sucked on this hard little tip?"

Eyes shut, Serena shook her head, her body on fire, Beau's voice kindling provocative images, stirring guilt and feverish desire.

"She's shy, Alastair," Beau murmured, squeezing her nipple so hard she half swooned from the staggering pleasure. "She doesn't know you. Maybe later . . . after she's come to orgasm a few more times. But remember, she's mine first; I'm going to fuck her first."

She felt his finger trail down her stomach. "Have you ever been fucked by an altar boy?" Beau whispered.

And she came in shameful, shocking response—a wild, turbulent, scorching orgasm so prolonged it left her gasping. Beau didn't touch her until the last dying flutter had vibrated away and then, sliding the candle free, he pulled her down on his lap and held her close while the delicious heat subsided and the throbbing between her legs slowly eased. After a time her arms slid around his neck and she offered him a languorous, sated smile.

"Were you actually an altar boy?" The bridge between fantasy and reality seemed inexact and confusing.

He shook his head. "Only by association. Some of my friends were; they initiated me into a number of youthful pleasures."

"Are you saying there really was a nun behind the altar?" Bewildered now, she questioned the extent of her naïveté.

"More than one." He spoke matter-of-factly, unself-conscious and frank.

"How convenient," she sardonically noted.

He shrugged, recognizing a female tone best left unanswered.

"Did you actually watch them?" she persisted, thinking her life very sheltered in Gloucestershire.

He'd done considerably more than watch in those youthful years. "Sex is a strong focus at that age," he casually replied.

"And it isn't now?"

"You of all people chiding me?" he lightly challenged. "You can't last ten minutes."

"I could," she said in rebuff. "I just don't care to."

"I noticed," he said, the faintest irony in his tone.

"Are you complaining?"

"*Au contraire,* lollipop. You're every man's dream. But with your libido, I'd suggest you practice with this or its equivalent," he mildly said, indicating the candle he'd set on a nearby table, "because most men won't be able to keep up."

"You set yourself apart?"

"It's just a suggestion," he blandly said, not responding to her jibe.

"Do you often serve as tutor, Rochefort?" she querulously

inquired, resentful of his suave amiability that sidestepped any pertinent queries.

"I occasionally have a charitable impulse." His gaze was impudent.

"Perhaps I'm not in need of your charity," she coolly replied, temperamentally opposed to all his former charitable impulses apropos of females.

"You're bashful," he gently mocked.

"No. I simply take issue with all the complaisant students in your past. I don't care to be added to the number. If and when I decide to, er, practice these, ah, solitary amusements, I certainly don't need any help from you."

"You sound so damned prim, it's quite arousing," he murmured.

"An unusual state for you," she dryly retorted.

"We're a perfect match then, aren't we?" he said, his gaze angelic. "And you like it, after all," he went on with a simplicity that couldn't be denied. "Come, darling, consider this an indulgence for me." And rising from the settee over her protests, he carried her to the bed, where he dropped her onto the disarray of pillows. "Shut your eyes," he quietly said.

She stared at him for a heated moment, irresolute, willful, piqued by an incomprehensible jealousy that served no earthly purpose in terms of Beau St. Jules.

"If you really were a nun, you'd always have to do what you're told," he murmured, his voice deep and low. "You'd have to learn obedience; they insist on it—and devotion. So lie back, darling, and enjoy your lesson. We'll start with something simple. Put your hand here," he murmured, drawing her fingertips to her cleft. "Shut your eyes, now . . . that's a good girl . . . touch this just lightly," he coached, his fingers over hers as he massaged her clitoris. "Press here. Does it feel good?" he softly asked, guiding her fingers so she stroked and exerted just the right amount of pressure.

It did.

He could tell.

"Try it alone now," he whispered, "and think of waiting

for me . . . of how I'll come to you tonight after evening vespers, when you're supposed to be on your knees in your cell praying. Can you feel the cool tiles and the summer air?

"I slowly take off your habit while you kneel in prayer, your cowl and veil, your apron and gown and petticoat—your skin is pale in the evening light . . . luminous. When I let down your hair, you shiver in anticipation; you forget the words to your prayers because you want to feel me inside you. You remember how I feel inside you, hard and thrusting, stretching you, and you begin to rise." His voice changed and his hand drifted slowly downward over Serena's stomach with exquisite tenderness. "But I make you finish. I make you recite every prayer in order and only then can you undress me. You always liked that, didn't you? You touched me so gently, so perfectly, I never could wait. And you'd always smile at my impatience."

An austere convent cell, a young nun tempted by worldly longings, a coltish, passionate St. John heir and forbidden pleasures. The images burned through Serena's blood—rash, reckless cravings like hers, like her constant need of him.

"You loved her, didn't you?" she said, her eyes open, direct. His tone, the faint shift in verb tense had been revealing.

Horror showed in his eyes and, drawing back as if he'd been struck, he precipitously came to his feet.

His heart was beating like a drum as he strode to his liquor table, ghastly memories flooding his mind. He hadn't realized what he was saying. He hadn't dreamed of Caitlin in years. What a fool he'd been to have spoken so unwisely, he thought, pouring himself a large brandy. The associations, the words, the fantasy—all too thinly veiled—he'd been careless, foolhardy.

Watching the brandy slowly fill the glass, he felt the lacerating pain again and the old anger, the incorrigible, perverse anger he'd never been able to resolve.

How long ago it seemed when he'd first seen Caitlin walking in the convent garden with Sister Mary Martha. But unlike Mary Martha, who'd fueled all his friends' fantasies with her private carnal urges, Sister Claire was utterly chaste.

But he'd wanted her desperately—with a young boy's heedless indiscretion. He'd sent her notes and left her flowers, bought her jeweled prayer books she couldn't keep and had frantically returned. He'd been stubborn in his pursuit, however, relentless. Although none of it would have mattered had not those irrepressible vestiges of the sensual Caitlin Garrick from Ulster still existed beneath Sister Claire's hard-won piety. And one warm summer night when he was fifteen, she'd succumbed to him.

"You're spilling," Serena quietly said.

Her voice broke his disturbing reverie and he looked at the pool of liquor spreading over the polished cabinet top. "Christ," he muttered, reaching for a shirt tossed on a nearby chair.

"I'm so sorry," Serena apologized. "I shouldn't have asked."

"It's not your fault." Quickly mopping up the spill, Beau tossed the wet shirt into the washbasin. "It's other people's fault. Would you like a drink?" His voice was emotionless.

When she shook her head, he picked up the bottle and returned to the bed. Settling back against the footboard, he distanced himself on the modest dimensions of the mattress, careful not to touch her when he stretched out his legs. And then he proceeded to drink his extremely full glass of brandy without further conversation.

The silence was rife with disquietude.

Some time later as he began refilling his glass again, Serena said, "I don't suppose you want to tell me about her."

"There's nothing to tell. She died," he said in a caustic murmur. Recorking the bottle, he tossed it aside. No religion was worth such a sacrifice, he bitterly thought. He'd loved her and she'd loved him.

But that hadn't been enough when the abbess had discovered them.

She'd hung herself that night without a word to him, without caring that he loved her with all his youthful heart.

Swearing under his breath, he lifted his glass to his mouth and drained it.

"Would you rather be alone?" Serena's gaze was replete with sympathy.

"God no." He exhaled softly. "I think you must remind me of her somehow. Your eyes, I think . . . She had blue eyes like yours that shone green in certain lights. Are you sure you don't want a drink? Some Champagne . . . or wine? I could use a drinking companion about now."

"Then I'll have some Champagne."

"Good," he said with a kind of earnest relief, leaning over to retrieve a Champagne bottle and glass set beside the bed earlier. "Jesus, I detest melancholy." He preferred the amnesiac oblivion he'd constructed eight years ago.

"Then you might want to consider the speed with which you're drinking. Papa was plagued with melancholy after a bottle of brandy."

Disagreeing with a shake of his head as he uncorked the Champagne he said, "Liquor generally cheers me." He smiled faintly. "At least until my fifth bottle."

"I don't think I'll try to keep up."

One dark brow quirked intuitively and she decided he was regaining some of his normal insouciance.

"You keep up very well, Miss Blythe," he lazily replied, offering her a glass of Champagne.

"Thank you, Lord Rochefort. My maman always said a lady should endeavor to please."

"Very astute guidance," the Earl of Rochefort benevolently murmured. He raised his glass to her and dipped his handsome head in salute. "To forgetting," he softly said.

And some lengthy time later when recall of the cheerless afflictions in their pasts had been mitigated by one bottle of Champagne and two of brandy and the door that had accidentally opened into Beau's psyche had been slammed shut once again, when their mild alcoholic bliss had evolved into a luxurious exploration of sensuality, Serena found herself seated astride Beau's hips, thoroughly impaled, shuddering from the bewitching ravishment, and she lightly touched his dark, crisp hair where it met her paler curls. "Mine," she said, looking down at him, winsome, infatuated, a young maiden awash in pleasure.

Unaccountably, he thought her charming, although two bottles of brandy may have tempered his judgment. And more unaccountable yet, he slid a finger delicately over her dewy wet cleft and softly murmured, "Mine."

He didn't mean it, he would have said had some voice of reason called him to account. But no such voice did in the midst of the winter gray Atlantic a hundred miles offshore. And Miss Serena Blythe, so recently released from a long bereavement in durance vile, couldn't be expected to experience less than heady, dizzying bliss. Beau St. Jules was, after all, renowned for his competence.

And the next time she came to climax, he met her release, pouring into her unchecked, each spasm jolting, acute, the world reduced to the minutiae of riveting sensation in the familiar, safe landscape of carnal physicality he preferred. His eyes were shut, his body sheened with sweat, a tidal wave of feeling draining from his body with each convulsive stroke.

A sudden sharp knock on the door jarred his senses.

Softly swearing, he refocused his concentration, recapturing his feverish rhythm, sliding back into his heated orgasmic nirvana.

"Open up!" It was Remy's voice.

"Fuck off," he muttered, the sound half swallowed, his body convulsed, caught in an undertow of sensation.

A vigorous brisk tattoo punctuated the rhythm of heated breathing in the small cabin.

Serena shifted minutely, unnerved by the interruption. "The food," she murmured.

Her voice, wispy with apology, registered through Beau's fevered sensibilities.

Inhaling deeply, he opened his eyes and gazed down on her. "Damn."

"I don't think he's going away," she whispered. "You weren't finished, were you?"

Grimacing, he blew out an exasperated breath. "I am now."

"I'll break the door down!" Remy shouted.

"Fucking calm down," Beau growled, rolling off Serena. "I'm coming."

Serena giggled at the unintentional pun and when he glared at her, she apologized so sweetly, he decided he wouldn't actually throw Remy overboard after all. "I'll make it up to you," she said, pink and warm and unutterably cheerful.

His heavy black brows met in a scowl. "Damn right you will."

"You needn't frown so. I really will. But I haven't had coquilles St. Jacques since . . ." A fleeting poignancy trembled in her voice. "For a very long time," she quietly finished.

He sighed. "Then I'd be an ogre to refuse you."

"Which you're not," she softly said, understanding even in the brief time she'd known him that he was more compassionate than he appeared and infinitely indulgent.

Heaving himself from the bed with another sigh, he stalked to the door, threw it open with a resounding crash, and standing stark naked and aroused on the threshold, ushered his chef in with a tightly restrained, "Don't ever do this again, Remy, or you won't see Naples."

"It's a mortal sin to let these go to waste," Remy retorted, undeterred by Beau's threat. "Are you eating on the bed?" he calmly went on as though he'd not interrupted them in flagrante delicto, as if he'd simply brought morning chocolate and brioche to the breakfast room. Motioning a serving lad forward with fresh table linen and two more chilled bottles of Champagne, Remy stood with the covered platter of scallops held aloft while the young boy—careful to avert his gaze from Serena draped in a quilt—spread the tablecloth on the bed.

"Perfect," Remy pronounced when the last wrinkle was smoothed away and he placed the silver platter on the bed with a flourish. "For your pleasure, mademoiselle," he offered, grandly whisking the cover off.

A luscious scent perfumed with the merest hint of shallots wafted upward from the plate of plump scallops swimming in a creamy velouté sauce. Tantalizing bits of mushroom peaked through the sauce; a delicate sprinkling of bread crumbs browned in melted butter embellished the whole.

"*Bon appétit,*" the chef crisply pronounced, and with a graceful bow he turned on his heel, walking past his nude employer without a glance.

"No point in locking this again," Beau dryly said, pushing the door shut behind Remy and the serving lad.

"Uh-huh," Serena replied, her mouth full of scallops and white sauce.

"Don't let me keep you," Beau sardonically murmured.

Quickly swallowing, Serena looked up and smiled. "Remy's right. It would have been a sin to have these go to waste. Taste them," she suggested, making room beside her, offering him a scallop on her fork.

"I hope we have enough food to last till Lisbon," he muttered, moving to the bed and sitting down.

"You needn't be grumpy. I said I'd make it up to you. Now taste this. There, isn't it perfect?" she said, watching him chew the morsel she'd put into his mouth. "Do you know I've never seen Lisbon? Do you suppose we could sightsee?" she asked, selecting another savory portion for herself. "I'd love that. It's supposed to be ever so much warmer than England," she added, the rhythm of her words punctuated by an occasional appreciative gustatory sigh. "After this last winter at the Tothams'," she said, chewing, "I swore I'd never be cold again. You're doing a marvelous job of keeping me warm, by the way."

His searching gaze arrested her monologue.

She swallowed. "Don't you like women who talk?"

It took him a moment to answer; the women he amused himself with were not primarily interested in conversation. "I hadn't thought about it," he finally said.

"Which means you don't. What a shame. I love to talk,

although the last four years haven't offered much opportunity, as you probably can tell. Oh, dear, there I go again. Forgive me. I'm sure I can be quiet if I try." Pantomiming, she locked her lips with a key.

This young miss was a true novelty in his life, he decided, amused at her undaunted cheer. "By all means talk," he graciously offered. "You haven't been to Lisbon before?" he asked, politely encouraging her to continue.

"You're sure now?" she said. "You don't mind? You see, I don't know exactly how to behave after . . . well, ah, after . . ."

"Sex?" he amiably supplied.

She nodded, "I haven't actually ever said that word."

"You have a natural talent then, kitten."

"And I expect you know you're excellent. Not that I have any means of comparison," she quickly noted, "but in terms of satisfaction, I couldn't be more pleased."

She was astonishing, he thought, to accept her denouement so openly and buoyantly. Although he had no means of comparison either, never having deflowered a virgin.

"I don't want to become pregnant though, because I'm going to be working hard at my studies in Florence," she went on, causing him to choke slightly in midthought. "Are you all right?" she solicitously inquired as he swallowed hard. "I suppose it's not a man's concern, but Maman died when I was young and Papa naturally didn't discuss such things with me, so I feel ill equipped to deal with the practicalities. But I thought you'd be sure to know because courtesans aren't forever pregnant or they wouldn't be able to, er, do their . . . job and I expect you know one or two with your reputation, so naturally, I mean, if anyone would know . . ." Her voice trailed off.

This too was outside his area of expertise; pregnancy was not a bachelor's concern in his privileged world. Mentally running through the possibilities available out in the middle of the Atlantic, he gamely said, "I'll see what I can find on board. Would you like something right now?"

"Oh, no," she quickly replied. "Sometime later will be

fine. Surely a few hours can't hurt. Do women become pregnant on their very first time?"

A gambling man, he calculated the percentage of risk with her innocence so newly lost and uttered what he considered a benign lie. "Never," he said. But later he'd have to have Remy find him some of the sponges that had been brought on board for the kitchen.[2]

"Oh, good," Serena cheerfully pronounced, "then, once we've finished eating, I'd like very much if you'd—that is— I mean—"

"Make love to you?"

"I didn't know if I dared use that particular phrase, love having so many other connotations, and I didn't suppose rakes actually believed in love or they wouldn't be rakes, now, would they?"

He laughed. "No need to mince your words, darling. Say anything you want."

"Anything?" Wide-eyed, she seemed fascinated by such newfound possibility, her years at the Tothams' having instilled an unnatural caution.

"Anything. I'm not easily shocked."

"I like that most about you . . . well—second—and I shouldn't say it, but then I've drunk a good deal of Champagne, which is probably why I'm talking so much, but I like *that* best." She gestured shyly at a point between his legs. "I never knew there could be such pleasure."

Her sweet confession had a predictable effect on his libido, and glancing down at his rising erection, he lightly said, "He must have heard you. Come, give us a kiss, lollipop." Moving the tray of food aside, lust warming his blood, he gently added, "And then we'll see what we can do about expanding your horizons."

And when she climbed into his lap and threw her arms around his neck, all open warmth and affection and artless delight, he found himself experiencing profoundly new degrees of pleasure himself.

6

Those blissful early hours of their voyage south set a sybaritic pattern of gratification and delight for the days to come. A connoisseur of sophisticated women, Beau found himself in the novel position of tutor to a newly liberated innocent intent on trying her wings. Skilled beyond the finesse of most men, he was perhaps the most sensually gifted of all the dissolute young bloods in London. And also extravagantly indulgent to a young lady with a passion to learn.

Remy and the crew took bets on when the young couple would first emerge from their stateroom. The estimates ranged from twenty hours to three days, with much ribald comment defining the various calculations. Remy simply said, "Not before Lisbon." He knew his master well and lengthy sexual marathons weren't without precedence. What was, however, was his benevolent accommodation to Miss Blythe. While always generous to his lady loves, Beau St. Jules was rarely accommodating beyond the needs of his own selfish interests.

And he was never benevolent.

Miss Blythe was charmingly different, Remy realized. And if he wasn't aware of Beau's orders to lie in at Lisbon, he would have considered extending his estimate to Minorca at least.

When the Earl of Rochefort and Miss Serena Blythe first came up on deck six days later, it was a blustery sunlit after-noon with the capital of Portugal rising into view like a heavenly city gleaming white and pristine on the hills bordering the Tagus River.

"What do you want to do first?" he asked as she surveyed the approaching port, wide-eyed with wonder.

"I want to see everything," she softly said, her body warm against his side, the wind blowing tendrils of blond hair across her rosy face.

"Greedy puss," he murmured, dipping his head down to brush a kiss over her cheek. "You always want everything."

"And you always give it to me," she whispered, warmed by the heated look in his eyes, beginning to feel the familiar melting warmth pervade her senses. And then a man stepped into her line of vision. "The crew," she nervously noted, her gaze shifting to the men busying themselves on the deck where they stood.

"I can kiss you if I wish," Beau casually said, immune to mannered limits. "Although I'm sure they'd like to too."

"While I have a distinct partiality for you, Rochefort." But she shifted her position, as if a few more inches between them eliminated censure.

"Damn well you better," he softly said, pulling her back. "I'm not in the mood to share."

She wasn't likely to win a tug-of-war nor was propriety of much consequence at this late stage, she decided. "This is silly, isn't it?"

He nodded, his grin boyishly sweet. "I'll let you know when appearances matter."

"Does that happen in your life?" she ironically queried.

"Not often," he said. "But consider, darling, this is backwater Lisbon. You're safe from scandal here."

And, she thought with resolve, entirely free from the Tothams. Which put society's strictures in a decidedly more trivial perspective.

"It's not a concern at all, kitten," Beau said, assured of his ability to protect her.

"How clever you are," she genially said.

He gazed at her for a moment, her sudden mood shift disconcerting. "Are you all right?"

"I'm very much all right," she pleasantly said. "I'm blissfully free, financially stable, thanks to you, and about to embark on a new and independent life. And it's not as though I've always lived in a thoroughly conventional manner anyway. Papa rather did as he pleased." Her smile was open and warm. "Now then, what are we going to see first in Lisbon?"

They took a short detour to the harbormaster's office first because Serena was eager to recover her luggage in the event the *Betty Lee* was in port.

Since the British had a large trading and political presence in Lisbon, the warrant for Horton's arrest was treated with considerable respect. The *Betty Lee* had docked early yesterday, they discovered. In fact, it was being unloaded now.

"Why don't you wait here?" Beau suggested, shifting slightly in his chair to gaze at Serena, who sat behind several stacked cartons in the small, cluttered office. "Or if you like, I'll have you escorted back to the *Siren*."

"You don't know what my luggage looks like. I'll come along."

"No," he said, scowling faintly. "Just describe it for me."

"They're plain brown leather portmanteaus, two of them, and they're featureless. I'll come along," she firmly replied.

"It's too dangerous." His voice had suddenly turned cool. He wasn't in the habit of arguing with ladies.

"Perhaps Miss Blythe could wait in the carriage when we board the ship, my lord," the elderly official politely interposed. The set expressions on the lord's and lady's faces presaged a lengthy disagreement. "It would be safer, my lady, with a felon on board. We'll require an escort to bring in this Horton fellow to the authorities," he added. "I'll need fifteen minutes to assemble the guard. Would that be satisfactory?"

He was a diplomat, with the art of compromise well honed in his years of authority at a port dominated by English traders.

She would have appeared childish to refuse. "Yes, of course," Serena said.

"We'll need a man left at the carriage as well," Beau declared.

"Certainly. Could I have coffee brought for you in the interim, or perhaps ginja?"

"No," Serena abruptly said, chafing at what she considered Beau's ill-advised autocracy.

"Yes, please," Beau replied, his tone cordial.

But when the door closed behind the harbormaster, Beau came to his feet and fixed a cool gaze on her. "This Horton fellow has killed a man—and very brutally." His voice was brusque. "I don't know why you insist on coming along. Be sensible, stay here."

"It's broad daylight, Rochefort," Serena impatiently retorted, her annoyance no less than his. "The docks are abuzz with people. *You* be sensible. And surely now that I'm relegated to the carriage with a guard," she went on, a touch of acid in her tone, "I should be subject to a minimum of danger."

He shifted on his feet, his temper held tightly in check. "I'm surprised you kept your position for four years, Miss Blythe," he crisply said. "You're very outspoken."

"It appears you're only familiar with women saying yes to you, milord. However, you have no authority over my life. As for my position at the Tothams', I wasn't halfway to Florence at the time, nor so full in the pockets." Her smile was oversweet. "For both of which I thank you."

A muscle twitched along his clenched jaw. "You could thank me with some obedience."

Her brows rose. "Is that what you want in a woman? I'm surprised. I rather thought you liked more spirit."

"Jesus, Serena," he murmured, exhaling in a long, low sigh. "We're getting way the hell off tangent here. The man's a brute. Let's not argue about this."

"I should simply acquiesce, you mean." Her voice was equally soft. "Even if I disagree."

"It's only a precaution."

"Then maybe it's not necessary."

"This is senseless." Each word was staccato blunt. "I don't know why I'm even discussing this with you."

"If it bothers you to have a woman not utterly docile to your will, I could book passage on some other vessel now that we're in port," she rashly said.

"Really," he murmured.

Clasping her hands in her lap, she straightened her shoulders and looked up at him with an uncompromising gaze. "You doubt it?"

"Yes."

"You certainly are plain, Rochefort," she coolly said. "Am I your prisoner until Naples?"

"At *least* until Naples," he drawled.

"I think not," she snapped, thin-skinned and touchy, not inclined to take orders from anyone now that her independence was restored. "This very polite harbormaster will no doubt grant me asylum from your unwelcome designs."

He stood very still, his dark eyes half-shuttered. "I doubt it, but you could try."

"How ominous that sounds. What exactly would you do to keep me?" she sardonically inquired. "Tie me to your bed?"

"That won't be necessary." He smiled faintly. "My uncle heads the embassy here."

"I see." Her voice was scarcely above a whisper. She knew the British embassy was one of preeminent power in an economy dominated by British trade. "In that case," she went on, forcing herself to speak in a normal tone, "maybe I should tell him you kidnapped me."

"I think Remy might dispute that. He was witness to your, ah, willing involvement," Beau silkily murmured.

"Damn you!" she hotly exclaimed, glaring at him. "Maybe I'm no longer willing."

"Give me a minute," he softly said, "and I'm sure I can change your mind."

She drew in a deep breath, his words, the small underlying heat in his voice, triggering delectable memory. And her voice when she spoke trembled slightly. "Would you keep me against my will?"

"Never." Shameless impudence shone in his eyes.

"Bloody go to hell," she breathed, rankled by such brazen assurance.

"Give it up, darling. You don't really want the notoriety anyway, do you?"

He was right, of course. Any publicity would be disastrous to her reputation. "You needn't feel smug, Rochefort," she fiercely declared. "I intend to pay you back for this coercion."

"I never doubted you would," he serenely replied. "Just remember to stay in the carriage."

When the coffee arrived a few moments later, he politely offered her some, for a second cup had been thoughtfully included on the tray.

"I'd rather break bread with the devil," she snapped.

"I'll make it up to you," he soothed, well schooled in dealing with irate females. "We'll go shopping afterward."

"Does that calm all your doxies' temper tantrums?"

Always, he wished to say, but gracious in his victory, he said instead, "I'll beg your pardon in any way you please once this is over."

"And the cost is incidental," she sarcastically murmured, "because your family owns half of England."

"I'm sorry," he quietly said, not about to argue the merits of his wealth. "I don't suppose you'd like some ginja?" he offered, pouring himself a liberal draft of the Portuguese liqueur made from Morello cherries. And when she didn't answer, he casually lifted his glass to her in salute before drinking it down. He didn't speak to her again but waited silently at the window overlooking the harbor, sipping his coffee, seemingly oblivious to her presence.

She maintained a studied indifference that took its toll on her willpower, for the fragrant aroma of steaming coffee filled the room. She was dying to pour herself a cup and take a cake from the tray. The fruity cakes, heavy with citron and cherries, were steaming too in the coolish temperature of the harbormaster's office, the sugar glaze melting down their fluted sides giving off little tendrils of heat. Beau hadn't even glanced at them, damn his black soul, while the delicious scent and sight of them were torturing her.

By the time the carriage and guard arrived she was in a decidedly pettish mood, feeling ill used and starved. Even the harbormaster noticed and gallantly directed his conversation to Beau during the drive to the eastern reaches of the port where the *Betty Lee* was berthed. The men were engaged in a discussion of river currents as they stepped from the carriage and took leave of her with a minimum of words. But as the harbormaster gave last orders to his men who had arrived in a second conveyance, Beau paused at the carriage door. "Now don't move," he gently reminded her, "and once this is over, you can take out your temper on me with my blessing."

"You may regret such generosity, Rochefort," she irritably said.

A small smile curved his fine mouth; her raw, restless nerve was reminiscent of her untrammeled sexuality. "I'll take my chances," he softly replied.

She watched him stride away, his long, dark redingote stamping him with a sinister air, the silhouette of his tall form limned against the pale water like a darkly forbidding apparition from some stygian gloom. His black hair was spiked by the wind into a wild disheveled nimbus; the caped folds of his black coat, caught up by errant gusts, billowed out like fiendish wings.

He suddenly looked a stranger moving down the quay; dangerous, menacing, phantomlike, towering above the phalanx of guardsmen. An unnerving shiver fluttered down her spine. How well did she know him beyond the narrow confines of their heated passions? Could she truly assert herself against such ominous power?

But a second later she shook away her apprehensions. She wasn't a fainthearted, timid young girl; she was capable of taking care of herself—the way she always had, not only in the years following her father's death, but long before as well.

Which brought to mind her immediate circumstances and her guard. Sliding the window up, she leaned out to check the position of the soldier left to protect her. Turning at the sound of the window rising, he broke off his conversation with the driver and when she smiled at him, he smiled back and wished her good-day. The Portuguese phrase was one of the few familiar to her.

Resting back against the seat a moment later, she drummed her fingers against the worn leather, hoping she wouldn't have to be shut away too long in the carriage. She detested waiting, as she disliked being ordered to play the missah lady, protected and coddled like some simpleton. She knew how to shoot as well as any man and if the old harbormaster hadn't been so gracious, she wouldn't have felt the need to acquiesce so readily. On the other hand, perhaps salvaging her luggage was worth a politic show of submission.

She restlessly flicked a dust mote from her skirt, leaned over to brush a smudge from the toe of her shoe, impatiently restraightened the hem of her pelisse as she sat upright again.

Twenty seconds had passed.

Fidgety, she wondered what would happen if she stepped from the carriage and looked around. Beau was well away by now. How would he know? She briefly debated, not sure how hindered she was by her coerced agreement or Beau's orders to stay inside the carriage. Perhaps he only meant she was to stay out of danger, she conveniently rationalized. How could it hurt if she strolled around the immediate vicinity?

Pursing her lips, she gazed out the window, contemplating the possible consequences—when a gunshot exploded.

She had the door open before the second shot resounded and at the third shot she was halfway to the ground, only to be faced with the young guardsman ordering her back inside in a rush of Portuguese. Slamming the door shut once again, he stationed himself directly in front, barring her exit. Which meant she could only peer out the window to try to catch a glimpse of the disturbance. Leaning way back, she could see down the extremity of the quay. A tall, burly man was racing for the shore well ahead of his pursuers.

She suspected he was Horton; who else would flee from the *Betty Lee*? Her guard, panicking at the continued sound of gunfire, was trying to load his rifle. "Not like that," she murmured, her fingers twitching as she helplessly watched him fumble with the cartridge. Careful, don't jam the barrel, she silently commanded. "Oh, god . . ." she groaned, his clumsy operation of the ramrod excruciating to observe.

Quickly glancing out the window, she took note of Horton's progress. Beau, who was within her range of vision now, led the chase, his long stride closing the distance between himself and the sprinting man. Bullets whined around Horton as the guards shot at him. But he had an enormous advantage in distance and once he reached the street bordering the quay, he could lose himself in any of the labyrinthine alleyways winding up the hillside.

Tense and agitated with her confinement, she longed for one of her fine Manton pistols that had been auctioned off with their household goods. There had to be horse pistols somewhere in the carriages, she decided; everyone carried them. Shifting onto her knees, she quickly lifted the seat, searching the storage area beneath. "Eureka," she softly exclaimed, catching sight of an old relic of a weapon resting on a coil of rope. Pulling out the dusty pistol, she ripped away the small cartridge pouch attached to the handle and found three paper-wrapped cartridges inside. Hopefully one would be enough, she thought, swiftly loading the pistol. Horton had almost reached the end of the quay.

Her guard, well away from the carriage, had positioned himself in the middle of the empty street, the townspeople having scattered for shelter at the first gunshots. His musket was raised, braced against his shoulder, sighted in on his target. But he was shaking with nerves, apparently not blooded yet in combat. Slipping from the carriage unnoticed, Serena brought up her weapon and carefully aimed it at the man running directly toward them.

He was only twenty yards distant, his muscular legs pumping like pistons, his face set with grim determination, his speed accelerating as he caught sight of the musket pointed at him. Horton swerved just as the guardsman fired and the shot went wide. While the soldier struggled to reload, Horton bore down on him, charging headlong, the drumming of his boots on the cobblestones like thundering hoofbeats signaling the apocalypse. Steadying her pistol hand at the wrist she brought her sights up. Horton's face was fully visible now—terrifyingly close—a villainous face, heavily bearded, scarred, his eyes deep-sunk and malevolent.

She squeezed the trigger.

A feeble puff of smoke erupted from the powder pan. Swearing at the old damp powder that had misfired, she threw the heavy pistol with all her strength, hitting Horton full across his bushy black brows. But he kept coming, ignoring a blow that would have dropped an ordinary man and before Serena could gather air into her lungs to scream, he smashed headlong into the soldier, knocking him over. As the guard lay stunned on the ground, Horton savagely kicked him in the head before turning with quicksilver speed to grab Serena's arm. With a rough jerk he pulled her close, positioning her before him like a shield, his knife to her throat.

"Don't move or I'll kill her," he snarled at the carriage driver, not realizing the man had all he could do to hold the horses from bolting with the smell of blood in the air. "And now, dearie," he panted, his rancid breath repulsive in Serena's nostrils, "you're going to get me out o' here." Drawing much-needed air into his lungs, he squinted into the sun, gauging the speed of his pursuers.

Serena scarcely dared breathe for fear the knife would slice into her throat. His arm was like a vise across her waist, his knife hand hard against her chin, the blade hovering dangerously close. She recalled the bludgeoned corpse of the captain at Dover lying dead white on the table. The soldier at her feet oozed blood from his mouth and nose as his spirit slowly left his body, another victim of this man's brutality and, paralyzed with fear, she was utterly nonplussed for the first time in her life. It seemed a nightmare too horrible to contemplate. And then she heard a familiar voice calmly say, "Let her go."

Her gaze focused first on the sweet blessed sound of salvation and then a protracted moment later Beau appeared in her field of vision, standing directly before her, his tall, broad-shouldered frame motionless against the backdrop of agitated guardsmen.

"Look," he quietly said, slowly bringing his hands up, palms open to show Horton. "I don't have a weapon. I'll have the soldiers back off." He nodded slightly to the guards who retreated. "No one will hinder your escape," he went on, carefully lowering his hands. "Leave the lady. You're free to go."

"She goes with me, mate," Horton growled.

"No, she stays. You have my word no one will follow you. The driver will come down. Take the carriage."

"Your word?" Horton sneered. "That don't mean nothin' to me."

"Then take me instead. And release her."

Horton's laugh was ugly. "I like this little bit o' fluff more'n you, mate. She feels right nice."

Serena went pale.

"I'll buy her from you," Beau quickly said. "You'll need money."

"How much?" Horton said, his flinty eyes suddenly regarding Beau with acute interest.

"A thousand pounds. Enough to purchase a great deal of female company."

"You don't have it." It was an enormous sum to a man of Horton's ilk.

"I do," Beau replied, sliding his hand into his coat pocket and pulling out a roll of bills. "Here."

Was it possible he'd free her? Serena thought, a tiny fragment of hope insinuating itself into the overriding terror engulfing her. Could it all be over so easily with a simple exchange of money? And she'd be safe again? Her breath seemed in abeyance, the world momentarily arrested on its axis.

"Toss it over."

"Release the lady first."

Horton looked at the money, indecision evident in his expression, greed prompting him to want both Serena and the money, although he was uncertain how to accomplish the feat. "Tell the driver to climb down," he said.

Beau curled his index finger on the hand holding the bills, the small gesture directed at the driver. "Now let the lady go." His eyes flickered upward briefly, watching the driver tie the reins securely in place.

Horton stared at the money for a moment more and then shook his head. "Sorry, mate."

She was as good as dead, Serena grimly thought, her heart pounding so hard she could hear it thumping against her rib cage. And she felt him begin to pull her backward toward the carriage. In an eerie, pale blur of images her life flashed before her eyes during the slow retreat, Horton's knife blade lightly flicking her tender skin, each step moving her closer to her inevitable death. How long did it take one to bleed to death? she wondered.

Beau watched Serena being drawn away, his gaze locked on Horton's knife hand, silently counting the steps as they moved. Two, three . . . Jesus, she almost stumbled. He could feel perspiration trickle down his spine—four, careful—five . . . six . . . Horton had to reach up soon to begin making the ascent into the driver's seat; he had to adjust his hold if he wanted to carry Serena with him.

Just . . . like . . . *that*.

A shot rang out, a bullet whined through the air, and Horton's right eye and the top of his head disappeared in a bloody explosion of tissue and bone.

Serena's high, piercing scream reverberated up the narrow street running down to the docks as Horton's brains sprayed her in a gruesome drizzle. For a moment of ghastly horror, she watched an eyeball ooze down her arm and then a shrill, lurid cry echoed in her ears as if from a great distance—the sound drifting farther and farther away to the other side of the vertiginous darkness engulfing her.

Beau leaped forward to catch her as she crumpled in a faint. Lifting her into his arms, he briskly ordered the driver, "To the York Hotel." Stepping over Horton without a glance, he carried Serena to the carriage, the powder-burned bullet hole in his coat pocket visible when his redingote swung open. "Notify the British authorities," he quietly said to the harbormaster, who came up at a run. But he didn't wait for an answer, the carriage step already dipping under his weight.

He wiped what blood he could from Serena's face and hair on the ride to the hotel, discarding his soiled handkerchief after a time, resorting to his coat skirts to absorb the remainder of the bloody residue. Once the detritus was cleaned away, she was so deathly pale he quickly felt for her pulse. Its strong, steady rhythm reassured him. He'd heard tales of people dying from fright and certainly she'd been subject to the most appalling trial. But through it all, she'd been unflinchingly brave, not uttering a whimper despite her awful fear.

The doorman at the York Hotel immediately called for help when Beau descended from the carriage with Serena still unconscious in his arms and by the time he'd walked through the swiftly opened double doors, several more staff were offering their assistance.

"I need rooms immediately. The lady's been in an accident. Have a doctor summoned."

"Yes, sir, of course, Lord Rochefort, we'll have you escorted to your suite at once." No one questioned the relationship of the lady to the young lord. Beau St. Jules was well known at the York; the ambassador's nephew was a frequent visitor.

"Rochefort!" a voice cried out, the hubbub having drawn the attention of several guests in the lobby.

And before Beau could escape, Lord Edward Dufferin

appeared, pushing his way through the hovering staff.
Puffing slightly from having moved his portly frame with
unusual speed, he rested his curious gaze on Serena. "Been in
a bit of a scrap, St. Jules?" he queried, taking in the blood-
stains on Serena's gown. The white lace on her collar was
exceedingly soiled. "Could I be of help?"

"Nothing serious, Duff," Beau replied, inwardly groaning
at his bad luck at being sighted by a gentleman who was an
old friend of his uncle. He hadn't planned on visiting
Damien. "The lady fainted and cut herself in the fall."

"Is she English?"

It was a pointed question; he wished to know her name.

"A distant cousin, Lord Dufferin," Beau evaded.

At which unfortunate time, Serena came drowsily awake
and, looking up into Beau's face, whispered, "Darling . . ."

Eddy Dufferin's eyes widened and he cast a speculative
glance at Beau. "A cousin, you say," he murmured, his smile
one of knowing male conspiracy.

"If you'll excuse us," Beau quickly said, not about to
reveal any pertinent details likely to get back to his uncle
and family. And without waiting for a reply, he swiftly
walked away, carrying Serena across the lobby into the
colonnaded atrium onto which the rooms opened.

7

"Who was that?" Serena murmured, her eyes still heavy-lidded, her voice wispy and low.

"Nobody," Beau blandly disclaimed. "How are you feeling?"

"Alive . . . thanks to you," she replied.

"Your color's better. You were very courageous."

"If my pistol hadn't misfired, I might have slowed him down."

Beau chuckled. "You mean I'm not going to be able to say, 'I told you so.'"

"I'd be an ungrateful wretch if I didn't allow you *that*"—a small smile appeared—"although if I'd had a decent weapon . . ."

"You'd be very dangerous." His grin flashed white against his tanned skin. "Remind me to keep my pistols out of your reach."

"I'd never harm you, darling. I owe you twice now for saving my life."

"My pleasure, mademoiselle," he gallantly replied, coming to a stop before a large doorway at the far side of the atrium. "I think this is our room." He waited for the hotelier and staff to catch up, their hurried footsteps audible behind them.

"You've been here before," she said with the faintest of arched brows.

"Once or twice."

"You don't stay with your uncle?"

"Not always." Not when his wife was in residence, he refrained from adding.

"Your rooms are ready, milord," the small, immaculately dressed manager said as he reached them, moving to open the doors with a flourish. The hotel always reserved the two east suites for its most welcome guests. "The doctor's been summoned. Hot water is on its way and if milord would suggest some food items that would appeal to the lady, the chef will begin preparing them."

"Anything at all, Ramos. The lady has a cosmopolitan palate," Beau replied, a boyish grin directed at Serena.

"I can't help it if I hadn't eaten for four years," she whispered.

"A circumstance I'm doing my damnedest to remedy," Beau murmured, his gaze affectionate. "Do you need anything else besides food before this throng of people departs?"

The rooms were awash with staff opening the curtains, turning down the bed, plumping pillows, seeing that the water pitchers were filled, placing vases of fresh flowers strategically about the sitting room and bedchamber, arranging fruit bowls and sweets so they were visually alluring.

"My lord, you must be important," Serena gently teased, her gaze taking in the great number of servants. "I can see I'm going to have to be vastly more pleasing to a man of such consequence."

"No complaints, darling, on that account," he murmured. "That will be all," he said to the hotelier hovering nearby. "The lady requires some rest." He glanced down at Serena with an inquiring gaze. "And some bathwater?"

She nodded.

"Immediately," Beau declared.

"Yes, my lord, of course," the trim little man crisply replied and, clapping his hands, he waved everyone from the rooms.

"We're going to have to throw this gown away," Beau remarked, his gaze flickering over her ruined dress as he moved through the sitting room into the bedchamber.

"My luggage!" Serena exclaimed, recalling her reason for accompanying Beau to the docks.

"I'll have it delivered here. But right now we need to get rid of this gown."

Neither mentioned the bloody stains, but Serena allowed him to help her off with her dress and, not averse to being coddled after her harrowing experience, didn't protest Beau's tucking her into bed.

"I'll be right back," he said, placing a small plate of cookies near her. "Wine or water?" he inquired, bringing over two decanters. He nodded his approval when she said wine, knowing the liquor would relax her. Bundling up the navy serge dress, he placed the bell pull within reach. "If you need anything, there are forty people to get it for you. Don't move and I really mean it this time."

"I have properly learned my lesson, sir," Serena said with mocking acquiescence.

"Hmmm," he restively murmured, not certain Serena Blythe's unfettered spirit would ever be suitably restrained by man or god.

So he moved with dispatch once he left the suite, handing the gown over to be discarded, giving instructions to the manager for the return of Serena's luggage, checking on the young guardsman's fate, delivering a verbal list of orders to arrange for Serena's comfort. Yet despite his speedy return, he found her not in bed but sitting on a garden bench in the small walled terrace attached to the suite.

"You must have been a handful as a child," he said, standing in the doorway. His gaze leisurely surveyed her enticing image, her voluptuous form clothed only in petticoats and chemise. "I thought you were going to stay in bed."

"The sun's too lovely to stay inside. Isn't it deliciously warm in this little snug garden? And for your information I *was* a handful. Papa used to call me his little savage."

His brows rose. "I wouldn't have guessed."

"I've always been independent."

"Another surprise," he drawled.

She wrinkled her nose at him. "You'd be bored to tears if I was truly missah, admit it."

"I admit, darling, you bring with you more than your share of excitement." He didn't often kill a man in an afternoon, deserving or not.

Tears suddenly welled in her eyes, the shock of the recent events flashing into her mind. "Oh, dear," she whispered, beginning to shake, "is the young soldier truly dead?"

"No, he's alive," Beau said, quickly moving to her side. Lifting her into his arms, he held her close and gently kissed her quivering mouth. "We can go to the hospital tomorrow and see him if you wish."

Serena expelled a great sigh of relief and her arms, wrapped tightly around his neck, eased. "How wonderful," she whispered, although she was trembling still.

"I'm putting you to bed, no arguments," he sternly said, striding toward the bed.

"Yes, sir." Her meek reply was muffled against his shoulder.

"You're not required to be perpetually brave," Beau noted, and tossing the bedcovers back, he placed her on the bed. "I'll take care of you now." He pulled the covers up, tucking the quilt under her chin.

"You're much too kind for a rake," she whispered, offering up a tentative smile.

"And what would you know about rakes?" he teased, sitting down beside her, brushing her hair from her temples with the gentlest of touches.

"Rumor has it rakes are notoriously selfish in their motives."

"I may be as well, darling," he softly said. "How do you know?"

"Touché, but right now I'm more than willing to disregard motive and bask in your charm."

"Good, because I want you to rest until the doctor comes. Don't think about anything, don't worry or fret and don't argue with me," he firmly added as he saw her begin to voice protest.

"I don't want a doctor," she insisted. "*Please,* Beau, I'm perfectly fine."

"Let him be the judge of that. Do I have to tie you to the bed?" he asked with mock severity.

She suddenly smiled. "That depends. . . ."

He gazed at her for a moment, his dark eyes assessing, his libido reflected in their depths. "After the doctor leaves, I'll consider it," he said. Bending close, he framed her face between his palms. "*If* you behave now."

"Kiss me," she whispered, wanting to feel his ardent warmth, needing to vanquish the recurring images of death from her mind. Her fingers closed on his coat lapels. "I *need* you to kiss me."

Recognizing the stark urgency fear generated, he obliged. Cradling her face in his hands, he tenderly kissed her, the pressure of his lips gossamer light. "I'm here, kitten," he murmured. "Don't be afraid."

"Make love to me," she breathed, craving him as if primal feeling were antidote to the haunting visions flooding her brain. "Please . . ."

"As soon as the doctor leaves . . . if he agrees you're not hurt."

"I'm not hurt," she insisted, wanting him to make her forget, wanting to escape into sensation. "I'm fine." Her voice was rising on an hysterical note. "I don't want to see a doctor."

He kissed her then without benevolence, a hard, heated, ruthless kiss that took her breath away and stopped the cry rising in her throat. He kissed her until her trembling ceased and then his mouth slid down the satiny curve of her throat, glided over her delicate collarbone, traced a lingering pathway down the fullness of her breast mounded above the lacy neckline of her chemise.

Her fingers were laced through his hair, her breathing heated, and she moaned softly as his fingers pushed away the delicate fabric to give him access to her nipple. "Are you feeling better now?" he murmured, his breath warm on the taut, pink crest.

"Ummmm . . ." she purred, rising slightly to press her nipple against his mouth.

"We should wait. . . ."

Her head moved on the pillow in lazy back-and-forth negation.

"Until after the doctor," he whispered, taking her nipple into his mouth.

Her sound of protest ended on a trembling sigh and he skillfully maintained that fine balance between rapacious desire and mesmerizing pleasure until the manager knocked at the door, announcing the doctor.

"Tell them to go away," Serena softly protested.

"Do you want to be tied to this bed or don't you?" he roguishly queried.

She hesitated the briefest interval and then smiled up at him. "You're going to insist on this doctor, aren't you?"

"How long can it take?" he blandly murmured.

"I'll tell him I'm in blooming health."

His smile was angelic. "Then he won't stay long."

She cast him a small fretful look. "I suppose I owe you some consideration."

"Notice how courteous I was in not mentioning that obligation," he replied, grinning. "We'll have the doctor out of here in record time." And without waiting for her reply, he rose from the bed to open the door.

If his aplomb weren't so well honed by years of casual disregard for the world's opinion, he might have indicated his surprise by other than the merest flicker in his eyes. For the man standing before him was a frequent guest at his uncle's residence.

"Good to see you again, Beau," Dr. McDougal warmly said. "Ramos tells me you're in need of my services." A large, sandy-haired Scotsman who had settled in the English colony after his marriage to a wealthy Lisbon widow a decade ago, he was one of Damien's fellow antiquarians. Both men had discriminating collections of early Greek sculpture.

Apparently the hotel manager had assumed the ambassador's nephew would prefer the ambassador's doctor, Beau belatedly realized, but short of shutting the door in Douglas McDougal's face there was nothing to do but deal with the awkward situation.

"Come in," he said. "A lady traveling with me is in need of your expert opinion. She was involved in a nasty situation this afternoon and fainted. Since she was unconscious for some time, I thought a doctor should be called."

"Absolutely correct, my boy," the elderly man replied. "Let's have a look at the lady." As the men walked toward the bedroom, McDougal asked, "Have you seen your uncle yet?"

"We just arrived," Beau evasively replied. "And after the disaster down at the docks, I've been kept busy." He went on to briefly outline the events that took place.

Serena was seated in bed, the coverlet pulled up to her throat. The booming voice of the doctor, with its easily recognizable Scots brogue, carried through to her room, causing unease. She would have preferred the anonymity of a Portuguese doctor.

But when Beau entered the room, he merely introduced her without comment as Miss Blythe and the doctor soon put her at ease with his kindly manner. He didn't ask anything personal regarding her relationship with Beau, which strangely irritated her more than if he had. Apparently she was perceived as simply another of Beau St. Jules's transient ladies.

The doctor listened to her heart, took her pulse, looked into her eyes, asked whether she had any residual dizziness or shortness of breath and after his short examination pronounced her physically recovered from her ordeal. "But it may take more time for the bad memories to fade, my dear," he gently said. "I'd suggest a mild potion of laudanum and hot milk before bedtime for a week or so. I'll have some sent around. Will you be staying long in Lisbon?" he asked, turning to Beau, who was seated at the foot of the bed.

"It depends on Miss Blythe."

"I'm really quite recovered," she quickly interjected.

"A day or two then," Beau said, rising to escort the doctor out.

"I'll tell Damien of your mishap, although he may have heard of this Horton fellow from Captain Soares by now," the doctor said as they walked through the sitting room. "You can fill him in on the details when you see him."

"I'm not sure I'll be seeing Damien," Beau carefully replied.

"Ah . . . of course. Didn't think, my boy," the doctor said, reaching the door. "Well, she's a beautiful young lady and in fine health. I'm glad I could be of service." He put out his hand. "Perhaps we'll see you at dinner another time."

"Yes, surely you will," Beau said, shaking his hand. "Thank you for coming so promptly."

He might as well have sent out calling cards, Beau grudgingly thought, shutting the door behind the doctor. Not that he was necessarily traveling incognito, but he hadn't thought a day in Lisbon would require any social visits either.

"You knew him!" Serena exclaimed as he reentered the bedroom.

"Unfortunately, yes." He grimaced. "I should have specified a Portuguese doctor. My mistake," he apologized.

"Will he tell your uncle?" She nervously plucked at the lace edging on the sheet.

He shrugged. "Perhaps. But it shouldn't matter. If I don't call on Damien he has sense enough to know I wish to be left alone."

"Because of me."

"Yes. My reputation is ruinous for yours. I'm very sorry about McDougal, although he *should* be discreet."

"You needn't be sorry. I think I was more nervous for you. *I* don't know any of these people," she said with a small smile. "Although . . ." she murmured, her smile suddenly taking on an enticing allure, "if I *am* truly ruined, perhaps I should at least take advantage of your dissolute reputation. Would you like me to tie *you* to the bed or would you prefer to do the tying?"

He stood looking down at her for a moment, his expression unreadable. "I can't decide how naive you are."

"I understand perfectly, darling——my reputation is in tatters once I've spent time with you. But consider how little consequence I had once our money and estates were gone and I was obliged to work for governess wages. And the life of an artist I've chosen will scarcely put me in the highest circles other than as a fleeting curiosity.[3] The very finest artists may be feted for a time by the haut monde, but they're not invited to marry into the family, are they? So why shouldn't I enjoy this very pleasurable time I have with you?"

She was disarmingly astute and courageous in another sense to face so bravely a very different world from that of her birth. "You're sure now?" he said, not even aware he was questioning his own selfish needs, a rare occurrence in his profligate life.

"I'm very sure, my dear Glory. Do I look equivocal?" And she lifted aside the coverlet to reveal her bounteous charms devoid of chemise and petticoats.

"When did you do that?" he asked with a grin.

"I'm extremely eager," she murmured. "You have that effect on me."

He glanced at the clock. "The chef is making you food."

Her eyebrows rose and with wide-eyed innocence she softly said, "Cancel the order."

"You're refusing food?" His brows rose in playful query.

"I ate all the cookies."

"I see," he gently said, beginning to slide his coat from his shoulders. "Do you think you'll like being tied up?"

"You're declining the experience?" Her tone was sportive.

"Maybe later," he said, throwing his coat on a nearby chair.

"Have you ever been tied up?"

"By a lady?" He looked at her, his cravat half undone, his hand stilled.

"By anyone, darling. I'm not prudish."

He laughed and resumed untying his cravat. "Only at Eton and only once——a very long time ago."

She'd watched his eyes as he'd spoken. "And you took your revenge for it, I suspect."

"Oh, yes," he softly said, tossing his neckcloth over the chair back.

"Should I be frightened?" she teased.

He chuckled. "Hardly. I like women."

She knew he did, the whole world knew he did. His entire manner bespoke his intrinsic need for women. "I wish I'd met you in Gloucestershire," she said, wondering how her life would have differed had she met him before her poverty.

"Your father probably would have shot me," he said with a lazy smile.

"He may have liked you enormously."

"As long as you do, lollipop, I'm content," he casually replied, not about to discuss anything smacking of potential fathers-in-law.

"Oh, I do, Rochefort," she said, dulcet sweet, and settling back on the pillows, she held out her arms to him. "Show me how nice you can be."

"I'm going to postpone the food. I prefer not being interrupted by an irate chef."

"Hurry back," she teased, "or I'll go on without you."

He grinned. "That's what comes of too much education."

"I wouldn't tarry," she seductively murmured, stretching luxuriously so her breasts rose in luscious ripe mounds.

He took a deep calming breath, his libido jolting to attention. "Give me two minutes and I warn you, if you don't wait, I'll paddle your bottom."

"Ummm," she purred. "How exactly will you do that?"

"Jesus," he said on a caught breath, capricious lust flooding his senses.

"Will I like it?" Serena whispered, turning over so her pink, plump bottom was tantalizingly exposed.

"To hell with the chef," he breathed, reaching for the buttons on his trousers. And short seconds later, she was lying facedown beneath him, his erection sunk deep inside her, and he was lightly paddling her bottom to the rhythm of her panting cries.

• • •

They did eat eventually. A sumptuous meal was delivered at a more convenient time along with a selection of ladies' dressing gowns.

"How thoughtful," Serena said, reaching up to kiss Beau's cheek.

"You needed something to wear until we see a dress-maker," he noted, brushing a finger over her bare shoulder.

"Or until my luggage arrives."

"That too," he politely said, although the state of Serena's blue serge gown didn't portend a wardrobe of any distinction. Reaching down, he plucked up a garment from the array tossed at the end of the bed. "Wear this peach silk."

"You like that?"

She spoke in that polite questioning female tone he'd learned to recognize long ago. "Wear what you like, darling," he said, rising from the bed.

"I like the primrose brocade."

"Perfect," he replied. "I'll pour the wine." A portion of Beau's clothing had been brought from the *Siren* and he shrugged into a Chinese silk robe, the deep scarlet vivid complement to his dark coloring. The heavy silk fell in rich folds, the exquisite fabric stark foil to his potent masculinity and for a brief second Serena wished she weren't simply passing through his life. He would be charming to wake up to every morning, she covetously thought, her senses attuned to his blatant virility. The last hours in bed had been so profoundly moving, she could still feel the delicious heat.

"Do you need anything else?" he casually asked, securing the corded belt at his waist in a knot.

You, she thought, but realistic about his permanent availability, she said instead, "No, I'll join you in a few minutes."

After Beau disappeared into the garden, she slipped on the pale yellow robe and brushed her hair with his ivory-handled brush, silently admonishing her mirror image to get a grip on her wayward emotions. She reminded herself that their encounter had a recognizable time limit. She knew it;

he knew it. And despite the extraordinary sensual pleasure, her plans would remain unchanged—Florence was her destination.

A short time later, when she walked into the small walled garden where the table had been set, her sensibilities were suitably in hand. The food was beautifully arranged on an adjacent serving table, the delicious aromas wafting into the night air: pheasant marinated in port and stuffed with truffles; turbot with tomatoes and green pepper; crusty golden prawn rissoles; olives from Elvas; melon from Ribatejo; queijo da Ilha, a Portuguese cheese; pudim Abode de Priscos, a sweet lemon dessert; jesuitas, puff pastry cakes and marzipan sweets from Algarve. Serena sampled everything, eating with her customary appetite; Beau drank more than he ate as was his custom and they smiled at each other and exchanged kisses across the small table.

Serena talked of her life at length for the first time, less inclined now to conceal her past. She knew Beau as intimately as anyone could, and genuinely happy after years of sadness, she found herself confiding in him.

"I was Papa's best friend," she explained in answer to a question Beau had asked of her childhood. "Since Papa didn't venture much into society except for his clubs after Mama died, we spent a great deal of time together. He taught me to ride and shoot so I could go along with him when he hunted. He was my instructor in gambling too; it was our entertainment in the evenings. I learned very young the difference between risk-taking and expertise."

"Which accounts for your unusual skill."

"I could win at almost any card game by the time I was ten."

"We'll have to play again," he softly said, the challenge intriguing.

"Anytime," she readily agreed. "And we needn't play for money. You've already given me more than enough."

"There's no risk unless you play for money," he quietly said. "Indulge me."

She shrugged lightly, the candle glow shimmering on the heavy brocade of her gown. "It's your money."

A smile curved his graceful mouth. "So assured, darling."

"I beat the Earl of Montrose once."

"So did I," Beau gently said. "More than once. I look forward to our match."

"And I look forward to enriching my purse," she confidently replied.

They were seated together on the garden bench after dinner, drinking ginja under the sparkling starlit sky when a knock on the door disturbed their gentle quiet.

"I warned the manager against interruptions," Beau murmured, beginning to rise from his chair at the sound of footsteps crossing the sitting room floor.

"Forgive me for appearing unannounced," Damien St. John said, coming to a halt in the garden door just as Beau stood fully upright, "but I was concerned about you." He bore no resemblance to Beau save for his height, his fair coloring setting him apart. But his smile was winning like all St. John smiles, and his calm assurance seemed a family trait.

"I should have sent a message," Beau replied, setting down his glass. "Damien, may I introduce to you Miss Blythe," he politely said as if receiving sudden guests in dishabille was commonplace. "Serena, this is my uncle, Damien St. John."

"My pleasure, Miss Blythe," the ambassador courteously responded, bowing gracefully before turning back to his nephew. "If I could have a word with you, Beau, I won't keep you long."

"Of course," Beau quickly agreed. "Excuse us," he said to Serena, his gaze bland. And he followed his uncle into the sitting room.

"I beg pardon again for intruding," his uncle repeated, speaking softly so their conversation wouldn't be heard, "but McDougal came to tell me of his visit here shortly after I'd heard of the bloody incident from Soares." He spoke rapidly, his voice low. "And when you didn't come to the embassy, my anxiety grew. I had to see for myself that you weren't hurt. Ramos tried to dissuade me, so don't take issue with his lack of compliance to your orders. I fully understood you didn't wish to be disturbed. Consider this visit familial license." He seemed to relax after confessing his alarm. "Emma said I might as well go and make a fool of myself," he said, grinning, "as pace a hole in the drawing room carpet."

"I should have contacted you when we landed. It was my fault completely. But Miss Blythe . . ." Beau shrugged slightly. "We're both fine, as you can see. So tell me," he went on in a conversational tone, "is Vivian in England again?"

"I'm relieved of course to find you whole, and yes, she's been in London for several months."

Since Vivian openly disliked all the St. Johns, she wasn't likely to call on Beau's family in London, nor was she apt to appear at any of the bachelor revels that consumed most of his social agenda. He wasn't surprised he was unaware of her presence in England. "Is she abroad more permanently than usual?" Beau inquired, alert to a new almost light-hearted elation in his uncle's voice.

"Perhaps," Damien said with ambassadorial constraint.

"Congratulations."

"A bit premature," his uncle replied, "but a guarded thank you to you, nevertheless."

"Does Papa know?"

"I haven't told anyone yet. You're much too perceptive. But enough of that," he hastily added, not prone to discuss the uncertain prospect that he and Emma might soon live openly together. "Assure me now you're in perfect health and I'll give you back to your lovely lady."

"I'm in excellent health as you can see. Serena was the one in danger, not me."

"Her name sounds very familiar. Should I know her?"

Beau hesitated, not certain Serena cared to have her identity exposed. "I doubt you would."

"Blythe . . . it's not so common a name. Was there—
Yes." His eyes lit up with recognition. "There was a Blythe
with me at Cambridge. Robbie Blythe built himself a Palla-
dian gem of a house up in Gloucestershire; I saw his archi-
tect's drawings at the Royal Society years ago. I always
coveted that house."

"You could have bought it at auction, four years ago. He
died in poverty and his property was sold off."

"She's his daughter?"

Beau nodded. "She stowed away on the *Siren* at Dover."

"Good god!" the ambassador said, shocked. "Bring her up
to the embassy," he declared. "Emma will take the girl
under her wing."

"I'll have to ask her."

His uncle stared at him, perplexed.

"I'm not sure she *wants* to be taken under anyone's wing,"
Beau explained. "Serena's on her way to Florence to study
art."

"Without money?" Damien skeptically asked.

"She has some money."

"But a woman alone . . ."

"She has friends."

"I see," Damien softly said. "And you don't wish to relinquish her company."

"To be honest, no, but, of course, feel free to ask her."

"Now?" Damien demanded. He felt duty bound to offer
protection to the daughter of an old acquaintance.

"Be my guest." Beau gestured toward the garden.

Serena was surprised to see the men return and when
Damien invited her to come to the embassy to meet his
cousin-in-law, Emma Pares, who kept house for him in his
wife's absence, her astonishment showed.

"I knew your father," Damien explained.

Serena quickly glanced up at Beau, inquisition in her
eyes.

"He recognized your name. He and your father were in
the Royal Society together."

"I'm very sorry to hear of his death. Do let us help you reestablish yourself," Damien said. "You'll like Emma."

Serena cast another flustered glance at Beau.

"I told him you were planning to study art in Florence," he quietly said, "but he wished to ask you himself."

"I'd stay in Lisbon, you mean?" Her tone was hesitant.

"Damien thought Emma could take you under her wing."

"It must be difficult for you to be on your own, Miss Blythe," Damien gently noted.

"What do you want me to do?" she asked, gazing up at Beau. Did he wish to rid himself of her?

The smallest pause ensued before he said, "I told Damien you were the one to make the decision."

"But what do you want?" Her voice was very low, her eyes huge in the candlelight.

He didn't answer immediately. When he spoke his words were scarcely above a murmur. "I was under the impression you were expected in Florence."

"Yes," she quickly agreed. It was enough. "I have friends who are waiting for me. Professor Castelli has made arrangements for me to study with his colleagues."

Damien's gaze took in the cozy scene, the obvious intimacy. Not that he'd expected any of Beau's female friends to be with him under duress. "Well, you must come to dinner at least and allow me to send along letters of introduction for you."

He watched the young lady look to Beau for guidance again and realized she was unusually innocent, a divergence from his nephew's normal amorous companions.

"Tomorrow night," Beau said.

"Emma will be delighted. Just a family party then?"

"Perfect," Beau said and stood waiting.

"Ah—Well then, until tomorrow . . ." And with a faint bow, the ambassador departed.

"I didn't know what to say to him," Serena affirmed, still uncertain whether she'd correctly interpreted Beau's response.

"Damien meant well," Beau noted, sitting beside her again and drawing her close, "but I wasn't sure you were interested in joining the English colony in Lisbon."

"Not without you I'm not." Enclosed in the warmth and security of his arms, she spoke from her heart.

He smiled at her candor. "My feelings as well, lollipop. Now where were we," he huskily murmured.

"We need a guard posted outside the door," she said, her voice lush and low. "I'm not sure I care to have any more interruptions. I have plans. . . ."

"Such as?" Despite the darkness, his eyes held a smoldering glow.

"Such as making use of this braided silk cord around your waist," she purred, touching the colorful tasseled belt.

"An intriguing thought . . ."

She smiled up at him. "I knew you'd like it."

"You'd look good in red," he murmured, his fingers working the loosely tied knot open.

"I was thinking of *you*."

His fingers stilled briefly and then shaking his head, he resumed his untying. "I don't think so."

"You said I could later."

"I said *maybe*."

"What would it take to make that less equivocal?"

"A gun to my head?" His grin flashed in the darkness.

"You'll have to tell me about Eton sometime."

"You don't want to know. Now hold out your hands." The corded belt from his robe dangled from his tanned fingers and when she didn't respond, he lightly said, "I have the advantage."

"You'll overpower me, you mean?"

"I could if I wished." He didn't move.

"Or if I wished you to."

"That too," he softly said, his rising erection evident with his robe partially opened.

"Coercion arouses you, I see."

"Sometimes."

"Perhaps it does me as well."

"You're not strong enough," he gently said.

"I could use guile."

"You could try."

"You resist so, Rochefort. I'm intrigued that you don't capitulate in even this playful diversion. Am I not allowed a turn?" And she slid her yellow robe tie from around her waist and draped it over the tip of his jutting penis, which was framed between the draped folds of his robe.

It surged larger and higher.

"See . . . he's interested in being tied," Serena whispered, brushing her fingertips over the red pulsing crest, stroking downward over the large conspicuous veins. "You really should let me," she murmured, wrapping the slippery brocade once around the thrusting length.

"I'll think about it," he said on a caught breath.

"That's a start at least." She slid a second silken loop into place, tightening it with exquisite slowness.

He groaned, a small, reluctant sound.

"Now that I have your attention," she whispered, bending to kiss the tumescent crown rearing upward, "let's see if my wonderful toy looks pretty in a yellow bow."

His eyes shut when her lips touched him and as her mouth opened and slowly slid down his length his back arched against the fierce pleasure.

Holding his rigid length in her hands, she drew it into her mouth until it rested against the back of her throat and then pulled away leisurely. The friction of her mouth and tongue lingered sumptuously—sleek, warm, sensational. He felt as though it were his first time—as if he were young and quivering, defenselessly in rut. And when she slipped two silken loops around his testicles and tugged lightly, he moaned deep in his throat.

"How showy you are, Glory," she said, tying the primrose brocade into a firm bow. "Cock up and rock hard," she breathed, fluffing the bow out, the yellow silk bright against the dark, crisp curls at the base of his stomach. "I may just want to sit and admire you tonight." She measured his glorious erection with her fingers, sliding her hands downward to cup the weight of his testicles. "I may not let you touch me at all."

Such heresy brought his eyes open. "I'll be touching you," he said, his voice a raspy, low exhalation.

"Maybe you won't," she whispered.

He could do anything he wanted to her, was his first unequivocal thought. "I hope this isn't a contest," he said.

"And if it is?"

"You'd lose."

"So you're *allowing* this?"

He didn't answer, his reasons too complex, inchoate, and damning. He'd resisted physical coercion—however benign this was—since Eton. He'd promised himself that long ago.

"Why?" she asked.

"Jesus, Serena, how the hell should I know. You like it, I like it—it's foreplay to my fucking you," he brusquely declared. "And it's over." Jerking the bow apart, he pulled the tie off and tossed it aside.

"You have to be in charge, is that it?" She gazed at him with stormy eyes.

"Something like that."

"Do women always do your bidding?"

"I don't give orders, believe me," he gruffly said, his experience rather that of fending off females, "and I don't feel like fighting over this. Do you want a drink?" And sweeping her up into his arms, he strode through the garden into the bedroom and deposited her on the bed.

"You drink more than you should," Serena told him, sliding into a seated position against the headboard.

"And you sound like a wife I don't need."

"You've drunk steadily since Dover."

"So?" He selected a bottle of old brandy from the array on the table. "I'm not working now."

"You work?"

"Of course," he declared, turning with a rim-full glass of brandy in his hand. "You can't fuck all the time," he said with a tight smile.

"Ah, yes—your primary avocation."

"Hardly," he scathingly retorted.

"The scandal sheets disagree," she contested, watching him walk toward her—all lithe strength and grace—resentfully aware of his reputation as stud to the female aristocracy.

"They make it up."

"I don't imagine they have to fabricate much. You're an unbearable show-off," she coolly noted, her gaze on his arousal. "Always erect, aren't you?"

"Only with you," he silkily replied, coming to a halt beside the bed.

"Right," she waspishly said. "Like a virgin . . . unpracticed and naive."

"While some people apparently don't need any practice at all," he murmured, lifting his glass to her in salute. "Are you finished looking?"

"Is there a time limit?"

"There's always a time limit. But in your case I'm not concerned—you're more impatient than I."

"Is there something wrong with that?"

"Oh no," he replied, his smile smug. "That's definitely an asset."

"Like your hard cock."

"Exactly," he sardonically agreed. "Would you like to try it?"

"No, I've decided to begin a celibate life tonight. You're much too annoying."

He looked at his drink for a moment and then at her. "What if I say I'm sorry?"

"Too late."

"What if I say I'm very, very sorry," he quietly said, sitting down beside her.

"I shan't be moved."

"Not even if I offer to make amends?"

"How? With that?" She gazed blightingly at his erection.

It usually worked, he thought, but said instead, "I'll let you have your way."

"You'd do that?"

He nodded.

"For me?"

"For you."

"That's very sweet."

He smiled. "I know."

"I can do anything?"

"Anything," he unequivocally said.

"And you'll acquiesce?"

He took a small breath. "Yes."

Taking note of his faint hesitation, she realized she'd witnessed a minor watershed. "Thank you," she softly said. "And you really do drink too much," she added with a mischievous grin.

"And I really need to make love to you," he murmured, ignoring her playful gibe, tossing his drink down his throat and dropping the glass on the carpet. Reaching out, he drew her close.

"Is this open to discussion?" she queried.

"No. Do you mind?" He needn't have asked; he could see the answering heat in her eyes as he shrugged out of his robe.

"Damn you," she whispered, beginning to tremble as he moved over her.

"Damn me later," he softly said, lowering himself between her spreading thighs.

"I won't want to later."

"So don't think about it." He guided himself to her pulsing core, sliding inside that first finite distance.

"I should *resist*." Her final syllable ended in a dulcet gasp.

"Too late," he whispered, resting hilt deep inside her, the words echoing in his brain as his hands slid over her slender waist, then lower, his fingers splaying over her hips, securing her firmly beneath him. "Much too late," he breathed so quietly the words were lost in his throat. And shutting his eyes, he drove into her.

8

Over breakfast the next morning, Beau said, "Ramos tells me your luggage has arrived, but you'll have to identify it."

"Finally and with perfect timing," Serena exclaimed, sightseeing high on her list of priorities. Immediately setting her fork aside, she rose from the table. "Where is it? I'll look right now."

But the scene that greeted her when she opened the suite door onto the atrium briefly confounded her. Instead of two pieces of luggage, two dozen or more bags, portmanteaux, and pouches in every color and description were spread across the terra-cotta tiles.

"Ramos wasn't taking any chances, apparently," Beau dryly noted over her shoulder. "I'm sure I told him brown leather." He'd also made it clear the lady was to have her luggage without fail, which no doubt accounted for this vast array.

"I hope the other passengers weren't discommoded."

"We'll have the rest returned," he assured her. "Do you see yours?"

"There and there." She pointed out the familiar pieces and stepping through the doorway set out to retrieve them.

"Allow me," he said, following her.

She glanced over her shoulder when he touched her arm. "I can carry them." And had already transported them across a great portion of London, in fact.

"You don't have to; I'm here."

His hand was warm through the fine silk of her dressing

gown, his nearness a trigger to her pleasure senses. "You're going to spoil me," she whispered, wondering if every woman he touched immediately experienced lust as she did.

"How could I not?" he gallantly said, brushing a kiss down her straight nose.

But she was less easy to convince when it came to his request that they seek out a dressmaker. Her gowns, as expected, were not only démodé but shabby and he wished to remedy her lack of wardrobe.

"You know what a modiste will think if I walk in with you," Serena objected, shaking out another gown from her luggage.

"I'll introduce you as my cousin. She won't say a word."

"But she'll think it nonetheless. And I'll have to with-stand that cool-eyed censure."

"Obviously you haven't been to a stylish dressmaker lately. They care only for the price they receive. Believe me, she'll treat you with the respect you deserve."

Serena shook her head. "I doubt it. Regardless, I'll be too uncomfortable in the public role of paramour. This brown wool isn't terribly worn." She held it up for his inspection.

"But then no one wears that style waistline anymore. Would you be more comfortable going with Emma?"

"Lord no." Her brows drew together in consternation. "She's a complete stranger."

"We're agreed then. I'll have the carriage fetched around."

"We're not agreed!" She stood at the foot of the bed glaring at him.

"Why don't I order you another of those lemon desserts?" he persuasively murmured.

"Do I look like a child?"

"Not by the furthest stretch of the imagination, darling," he lazily drawled, eyeing her curvaceous form evident beneath her ivory silk robe. "How about a more enticing bribe then," he tranquilly observed, intent on having his way. "Jewelry . . . pearls perhaps or sapphires to match your eyes. Or would you prefer artwork? Portuguese mosaics are quite nice. I know the dealer my uncle patronizes near the embassy. Do you like antique sculpture?"

"Beau!" she wailed, not sure she could withstand such determined attack.

"I don't care to see you at dinner tonight in that hideous brown thing." He was lounging on the bed, his voice as temperate as his languid pose. "Let me buy you something for that occasion at least," he mildly offered.

"So I don't embarrass you."

"No, darling, anyone will tell you I'm impossible to embarrass. Just for the pleasure it will afford me."

"Then you must do something for me," she insisted.

"Anything."

"You say that so lightly."

He was surprised himself; he was notorious for never making promises to a lady. "You must have a way about you, kitten," he said, smiling faintly at recall of the previous night.

"I wish to pay for the gown myself."

"Done," he blandly said, taking note of the singular noun with satisfaction.

"So accommodating, Rochefort? Should I be concerned?"

"Not in the least. I've simply learned that when you're happy, I am as well."

"Like last night."

"Like that," he said with a wicked grin.

The dressmaker turned out to be English, which caused Serena additional anxiety and she wondered for a brief moment during their introduction whether she was capable of launching herself as an independent artist in a man's world after all. But she silently admonished herself against such faint heart and further bolstered her equivocating spirit by reminding herself that this was simply another rite of passage in her new journey to independence.

The dressmaker knew Beau, of course. What a surprise. She seemed to know him *very* well, which drew an even more jaundiced assessment from Serena. But on second look Mrs. Moore had to be too old even for Beau's catholic tastes, Serena decided. It must be his patronage the modiste so appreciated.

"Coffee with four sugars if I recall," the dressmaker was saying with extreme cordiality, "and a decanter of ginja. Would your cousin like tea?" she pleasantly asked, slightly emphasizing the word "cousin" even as she looked through Serena as though she didn't exist.

"Some cakes with the tea, too." Beau glanced at Serena's testy expression. "We'll wait in the pink room," he hastily added, taking Serena's hand and drawing her away before her tightly set mouth opened.

"You must spend a great deal of money here," Serena hissed as he bundled her into a room decorated in pink damask and gilt. "The woman is near to kissing your boots."

"Which should mitigate any concern with your reception."

"She's dying to call me your paramour."

"But she won't." He gently pushed her into a chair.

"I want this over as rapidly as possible," she said through clenched teeth.

"Then tell her the style of gown you prefer," Beau calmly suggested, seating himself in the chair beside her. "And I'll see that you have it tonight." Crossing his legs at the ankles, he settled back as though he were perfectly at home. "Have some ginja." He touched her hand, curled white-knuckled over the chair arm. "You'll relax."

"I don't want to relax," Serena heatedly retorted. "I want that woman to stop looking at me as though I were the thousandth female you've brought in here."

"Did I remember to tell the driver to wait for us?" Beau abruptly asked, standing so suddenly Serena jumped.

"Of course you did," she said, looking baffled.

"I'd better check." And he quickly strode from the room.

Left alone, Serena gazed about the sumptuous room, taking in the multitude of fashion prints gracing the walls, feeling increasingly threadbare as she surveyed each splendid ensemble. She tucked her feet under the hem of her brown wool skirt, conscious of her worn shoes in this resplendent room. Pulling her pelisse completely shut to cover her gown's antiquated styling, she suddenly felt sartorially deprived—a novel feeling when survival had been her only priority for the past few years.

Before her father died, pretty clothes were commonplace for her. She'd never felt deprived, his love and affection the essential substance of her life, their bond absolute, the creature comforts of their existence agreeable. Perhaps she did deserve a new gown; perhaps Beau understood better than she the pleasure beautiful clothes evoked. And with a small smile of discovery she decided it would give her pleasure to buy herself something elegant. Her need to pinch pennies was past now that she'd won five hundred pounds from Beau. She could *afford* a new dress. Reaching over, she picked up a stack of fashionable drawings from a table. Maybe she'd even purchase a new pelisse, she thought, running her finger over the frayed hem of her capelet . . . and a petticoat with lace too, she decided, smiling. How good it felt to be in funds again.

When Beau returned she ran to hug him. "Thank you for bringing me here," she buoyantly exclaimed, her arms laced around his waist. "What do you think of a gown in moss green or gold?" she inquired, her voice animated.

"I like either one," he replied, not questioning her sudden change of heart. In his experience, a man was better served not inquiring into a woman's reasons. "You'll look luscious in both."

"And," she gaily went on, gazing up at him with a smile, "I'm also going to buy a petticoat with lace."

"Definitely a worthwhile purchase," he genially agreed, visions of her in her new petticoat enchanting to contemplate.

"I'll need shoes too."

"Slippers are all the rage. We'll have some made to match."

She hugged him more tightly. "I'm *enormously* happy."

"I can tell," he softly said.

"And I wish to apologize for my tantrumish behavior."

"No need. I didn't notice," he chivalrously lied.

"And I shall be civil to Mrs. Moore even if *she* isn't."

"I'm sure she will be. You may have misinterpreted her attitude."

"Perhaps," Serena thoughtfully murmured, "but she did say 'cousin' with a decided snideness."

"If she dares say so again, I'll demand an apology. How would that be?" Beau gently asked, smiling down at her.

"Please, no, don't make a scene. I'd be even more embarrassed."

"I won't make a scene," he said with assurance. "My word on it. Now show me what you've found in those fashion prints."

And when Mrs. Moore came into the room a short time later, she was so gracious, Serena wondered whether she'd imagined the insults. Personally serving them from a tea tray carried in by a serving girl, the dressmaker kept up a charming chatter apropos of the sights in Lisbon after discovering Serena was interested in viewing the town.

"You must in all certainty see the old quarter. The very best of the medieval architecture remains there. It's the only surviving portion of the city after the earthquake of seventeen fifty-five. Do you like cathedrals?" she asked, her expression lively.

"I certainly do."

"Then you'll marvel at the Se Patriarchal, won't she, Lord Rochefort? It's the most lovely Romanesque design."

"I'm sure she will," Beau blandly said, content with the outcome of his talk with Mrs. Moore. When he'd gone out, ostensibly to check on the driver, he'd coolly pointed out to the dressmaker that if she dared offend Miss Blythe, he would see that no one in the English colony ever bought another garment from her. He'd further mentioned that she was under no circumstances to use the word "cousin" in Miss Blythe's presence. "She's a very good friend of mine, Mrs.

Moore," he'd pleasantly said. "You understand I don't wish her unhappy."

So Serena was treated like royalty, fawned over with quite the same sycophantic delight Mrs. Moore showed her most exalted customers.

Beau watched carefully as Serena went through the stacks of fashion drawings, taking note of the various gowns she liked, agreeing with her when she finally settled on a round gown in gold silk gauze with an overgown of silk muslin.

"Although it's so impractical," she said with a sigh. "Maybe I shouldn't."

"You can wear it to any evening occasion," Beau noted. "It's practical in the extreme. Although you might like a cashmere shawl for cool evenings. Could you show us some, Mrs. Moore?"

"Oh, no," Serena objected. "They're much too expensive."

"Let me buy you one."

"No," she flatly said.

"Just try one on. Should one of your investments do well, Miss Blythe," he pleasantly said, referring obliquely to her competence at cards, "you'd know what you like."

"I can't afford a cashmere shawl regardless how successful my business ventures, Lord Rochefort," she plainly said, intent on holding him to their bargain. "I'll have a pelisse made instead. They're so much more practical."

"One shouldn't be practical for evening parties. Ask Mrs. Moore," Beau suggested, undeterred by her refusal.

After being warned by Lord Rochefort that he didn't wish Miss Blythe to be unhappy, yet aware that *he* wished his paramour to have a cashmere shawl, the dressmaker cautiously said, "In general, a certain degree of luxury is, ah, common to evening wear, although if Miss Blythe would prefer a pelisse, perhaps we could have one made in velvet or swansdown-trimmed wool."

"Now there's a possibility," Beau cordially declared. "Why not see some of those fabrics as well as the shawls."

"Beau, no. I'd rather not." Her voice was cool.

"Consider, my dear, you won't always be on a limited

budget," he replied. "In any event," he went on, taking note
of the sudden tick in her jaw, "tell Mrs. Moore what sort of
petticoat you have in mind."

"Now *that* I need," Serena agreed, turning away from
Beau to address the dressmaker, who was thoroughly con-
fused by this time. Was the lady paying for her own purchases? With Lord Rochefort as wealthy as Croesus. Had she
misunderstood the word "friend" when Rochefort had pronounced it with such delicacy?

"Do you have any petticoats trimmed in broderie
anglaise?" Serena asked.

"Certainly, Miss Blythe," she answered, sure of her inven-
tory at least in this treacherous field of problematical rela-
tionships. "I'll have some brought in."

"And we'll need slippers made to match the gown," Beau
interposed. "Would you like colored leather or silk?" he
asked his companion.

"Leather. They'll last longer."

"Very good, miss," Mrs. Moore said, wondering why a
paramour of Rochefort's was concerning herself with such
practicalities. "When I have the petticoats brought in, we'll
take your measurements for the gown and a pattern of your
foot as well."

When the dressmaker returned, two seamstresses carrying armsful of petticoats accompanied her and after Serena
decided on a filmy muslin trimmed in elegant broderie
anglaise, Mrs. Moore delicately said, "It would be best to
measure you without your wool gown on, Miss Blythe. If
you don't mind."

"No, of course not."

"Would Lord Rochefort, er . . . that is—would you
prefer—"

"I'd prefer some more ginja if you don't mind," Beau said,
his voice temperate.

"Yes, certainly, my feelings exactly . . . I could see that
you were quite ready for more," Mrs. Moore strategically
replied. Lord Rochefort's cool-eyed look caused her extreme
discomfort; indeed, the difficulty in reading the nuances of

this "friendship" had brought an unladylike sweat to her brow. Casting a steely-eyed look of her own at one of her assistants, she said in sugary tones, "Another decanter of ginja for Lord Rochefort, Madelina."

"Really, Rochefort, you can wait," Serena chided. "Don't make the poor girl run off for more when we're almost finished."

"Never mind, Mrs. Moore," Beau graciously replied, submitting to Serena's wishes without cavil.

Silently praying she survive this unusual encounter with Lord Rochefort and his newest companion, the dressmaker signaled her seamstresses to help Miss Blythe out of her gown. How unusual it was to see Rochefort so out of character—accommodating, conciliatory, without insolence or audacity. She gave Miss Blythe high marks for an audacity of her own. Apparently her cool dissent appealed to this man who'd dressed more than his share of beautiful Lisbon women.

And ostensibly she was paying for her purchases herself.

Surely a first for the ambassador's nephew.

But the lady was less composed under the watchful eye of Lord Rochefort when she stood half undressed before him, her bare feet peeking from under the hem of her plain linen petticoat, her fine skin blush pink, her gaze avoiding his.

Taking in the well-made but worn garments, Mrs. Moore decided Miss Blythe's appeal had much to do with her fallen circumstances. Unlike the playthings Rochefort normally amused himself with, this young lady was no flitting amorous butterfly. She was oddly genuine, a word the dressmaker found curious even as it struck her consciousness—as if the other ladies he knew were female marionettes. And less conspicuous at first glance but hovering beneath Miss Blythe's cool resolve was a tremulous sexual need. How tantalizing that must be for Lord Rochefort. Women had been throwing themselves at him for years, and now to encounter this small, intrinsic resistance from the lady . . .

"Turn around," he softly said, his deep voice so hushed

the vibration hummed in the small room. "So we can see your hair."

Serena hesitated a small interval, which Mrs. Moore anticipated now that she better understood their attraction. Serena's gaze met Beau's briefly. He smiled. Then her eyes took on a carnal warmth and she slowly swung around.

"We'll need a hairdresser for tonight," Beau remarked.

"Maybe I'll have my hair cropped à la Titus," Serena murmured, lifting her hands up to balance the heavy coils of her pale hair atop her head, gazing at Beau over her shoulder.

"Absolutely not."

"It's *my* hair," she smoothly returned. "Think how easy it would be to wash."

"We'll find someone to wash it for you if that's a problem." His voice was suddenly blunt, devoid of pleasantry.

"Now who would that be?" she softly queried, responding to his audacious authority and to more—to the irrepressible passion warming her body.

"How cheeky you are, Miss Blythe." He spoke as though they were alone in the room, with the sensual undertones flagrant.

"No more than you, my lord. If I wish to cut my hair I shall."

His gaze held hers for a long moment and then it flicked to Mrs. Moore. "I'm sure you can get measurements from Miss Blythe's dress and shoes. Take them and get out."

"There's no need. Stay," Serena asserted, rescinding his order.

"Take them," Beau said, his tone so soft it was no more than a whisper.

But Mrs. Moore understood the voice of command when she heard it, and whisking up the two items, she shooed her assistants out and followed them, firmly shutting the door.

"Now then," Beau murmured, "we can discuss this in private."

"Couldn't this have waited, you damned autocrat?" She gazed at him with hot-eyed insolence.

"Don't be impossible." His voice was mild, his lounging pose unaltered.

"You can't keep me from cutting my hair." It gave her pleasure to say it.

"You don't even want to cut your hair."

"Maybe I do."

"And maybe I want to fuck you where you're standing."

"You can't."

His brows arose. "I can fuck you anywhere I want."

"Not if I don't want to."

"But you always do. Like now," he whispered, his gaze on her nipples, which were rising against the sheer linen of her chemise. "Tell me you don't want to feel me inside you."

His words insinuated themselves into her senses like small heated explosions, trembling up her spine and down her arms and deep inside her as though they were gently probing fingers. "I don't," she whispered, clenching her fists against the flaring sensations.

"That's what you said last night too," he murmured, his eyes half-lidded, impudent.

"But this isn't our bedroom." She had no intention of making love in so public a place, no matter the heated stirrings of her body. "So stay where you are," she added when it looked as though he might rise.

"I'm not going anywhere," he calmly said, recrossing his legs. "Why don't you come here."

"No. Good god, Rochefort, have some discretion."

"Like you," he impertinently said, "the lady who left England in a stranger's yacht."

"You weren't a *complete* stranger."

"At least not for long." His voice was amused.

"And now that I know you so *well*," she sardonically noted, "I'm keeping my distance. Someone could walk in, all of them could return. You smile. You'd like that, I suppose—but I'm not so decadent yet. I'll wait here safely out of your reach until they bring my dress back."

"I'm afraid Mrs. Moore won't return until she's called for."

"So she's familiar with your amusements," Serena oppressively murmured. "Like an accommodating brothel keeper. I wondered at all the divans in here. How many ladies have you entertained in this silken room? Ten . . . a dozen . . . more?" The pitch of her voice rose as the room suddenly became haunted with beautiful, willing females. "First you dress them and then you *undress* them. Mrs. Moore must prosper when you're in town."

"They'll hear you outside." Beau hadn't moved but the minute flare of his nostrils gave indication of his irritation.

"Will they think you're losing your touch?"

"They'll think I've found a tantrumish little bitch to fuck," he softly said.

"Then they'll be wrong on both counts."

His brows rose marginally. "I'm not so sure," he murmured, noting the flush on her pale skin, the agitated rise and fall of her plump breasts half revealed above the neckline of her chemise.

She took a deep breath and, meeting his half-lidded gaze, said, "*I'm* sure."

"You can be persuaded, though. . . ." he repudiated, beginning to rise.

"Damn you, sit down," she warned, moving backward, a tremor not solely of anger vibrating in her voice.

"I'd rather stand," he said, coming to his feet.

"If you move another step, I'll cut off my hair," she precipitously threatened, scooping up a pair of scissors from a nearby worktable, holding them poised over her ruffled curls.

Dropping back in his chair, Beau half smiled. "You remind me of my little sister in a pet."

"You must provoke her as well."

"You'll be sorry if you cut your hair."

"Maybe I won't; maybe I'll enjoy looking fashionably shorn." Pulling her hair back, she twisted it into a queue at the nape of her neck and glanced at her reflection in one of the numerous mirrors.

"I don't like short hair on women."

"More reason then," she said, swinging back to him.

"Don't be childish."

"Don't be feudal."

He wasn't, of course; he was being infinitely polite. Sighing, he wondered what it was about her that tantalized him despite her tedious desire for independence.

"Tell me about your Lisbon lady friends."

Her audacity startled him. "Why would I do that?"

"I'm curious."

"A gentleman doesn't discuss the ladies he knows."

"A *gentleman* doesn't fuck all the ladies he knows."

"Don't be tiresome, darling." His voice held a new edge.

"I shouldn't ask?"

"No." He disliked being pressed.

"And if I do?"

"You're wasting your time and mine," he brusquely said, grasping the chair arms. "I'll call for Mrs. Moore."

"*I'll* summon her back," Serena quickly interposed. "Don't move," she ordered, overwrought at his damnable availability, resentful of his curt dismissal. "You stay there like a good little boy and do what you're told for once in your life."

Beau went utterly still.

"There. See how easy that was," she drawled and with a satisfied smirk she turned and began walking toward the door.

He was on top of her before she'd moved two strides, the scissors pulled from her grasp and tossed aside, the weight of his body propelling her backward until she came to rest with a soft thud against the silk-covered wall.

"Now we'll see how easy *this* can be," he whispered, his face only inches from hers, his forearms flat on the wall, framing her head as he leaned into her. "But you already know how well we fit." His smile was flinty, his body pressing into hers unyielding.

"Don't you dare."

His gaze drifting over her face was impersonal. "It's not that difficult," he said, pushing her petticoat aside with a swift, impatient gesture, baring her to the waist. "Since you're so passionate—as *always*," he murmured. "Are you panting for *me*, darling, or just any cock?" he insolently queried, brushing a lazy fingertip over her parted lips.

Jerking her head aside, she breathlessly said, "I'm not panting," contradicting the scandalous quickening of her body. "And if you try this, I'll scream."

"Scream away." He was already unbuttoning his breeches, his voice so detached and indifferent she realized no one would come.

"This is too rash, Beau, even for you," she exclaimed, struggling against his solid weight. "They'll hear; everyone'll know."

"They already know. They knew from the moment we walked through the door," he qualified. "Come, darling, open up and let me in," he murmured, inserting his knee between her tightly clasped thighs, forcing them apart.

And as he moved between her spread legs, she could feel him hard against her belly, his rigid length triggering a thousand memories of pleasure. Like quicksilver, an answering heat flared inside her treacherous body addicted to his touch. "You can't, Beau," she softly protested, attempting to deny her volatile passions, trying to ignore his erection hard and warm on her flesh.

Heedless to her remonstrance, he slid her chemise down her shoulders, freeing her breasts, his fingers gentle on her skin, familiar.

"Your nipples are hard, darling," he murmured, stroking the swollen pink tips with deliberate delicacy, glancing up at her with a fleeting look. "Does that mean you want me?" he gently added, capturing the taut crests between his thumbs and forefingers, squeezing gently, forcing a small, perfidious moan from her lips.

Her body was eager and aroused even if she didn't care to admit it, he thought, smiling faintly. "This won't take long. . . ." he whispered.

"Please, not here," she pleaded, trying to pull away, but

his fingers only tightened on her nipples, spiking pleasure downward into the pulsing core of her body.

"Yes, *here,*" he whispered, feeling her tremble. "Now," he lushly promised, releasing her breasts, grasping her firmly around her waist with one hand, his other sliding between her legs, his fingers slipping inside her.

She cried out, reeling with desire as he touched her to the quick.

She was shamelessly wet, sleek and lubricated and so ready for sex he felt his erection swell powerfully in response. "You need someone to make love to you," he whispered, his fingers stroking, knowing just how to touch her, what she liked, where, how deep. "And I can help you," he softly said, his expertise masterful, his timing impeccable, her body opening for him, wanting what he wanted.

Skillful, adroit, he devoted himself to her pleasure, stroking, massaging, his long fingers buried deep in her incited flesh, teasing her, tempting her . . . leaving her breathless with need, nearly orgasmic.

And then he abruptly withdrew his fingers.

As she shuddered at the sudden deprivation, he held his hand lightly before her face. The fragrance of desire was unmistakable. "There's no point in waiting, is there?" he impudently murmured, trailing his damp fingers over her mouth.

Their eyes met—hers restive, his intractable beneath his insolent pose.

Fretful, in turmoil, she swore at him.

"I'm not sure that's physically possible," he said with a grin, "but I know what is." And placing his large hands around her waist, he lifted her slightly for better access, bent his legs, shifted his weight upward, and without further pre-liminaries entered her.

Her sigh was sanction. He knew the sound.

"You always need this, don't you," he softly said, feeling her sleek warmth yield, her breath a light panting rhythm in his ear. "Tell me how you like to feel my cock filling you," he murmured, thrusting upward until he was sunk deep inside her. "Like this . . ."

She moaned, shamed by her flagrant response, the pleasure spreading outward from the deepest recesses of her body, instant, inflammatory, all-consuming.

"If you want me to stop," he said, his voice a husky rasp, "just tell me. If you don't want to climax," he went on in a velvety hush, withdrawing slowly as he spoke, "I'll understand. . . ."

She wished him in hell, but half feverish with desire she could no more have him stop than she could cease breathing.

"What do you want to do?" he whispered, poised at the extremity of his withdrawal stroke, wickedly perceptive and waiting.

A small panic suffused her senses; her body throbbed, frantic for release. "Please, Beau," she entreated and then mortified, she dropped her gaze.

"Please?" He feigned incomprehension, wanting more.

Her lashes fluttered up for only the briefest moment. "Stay inside me." Her voice was so soft he had to bend low to hear her.

Lifting her chin lightly with a fingertip, he forced her to look at him. "How far inside?"

Her eyes held his for a shuddering moment. "To infinity," she whispered.

A wild rapacious jolt surged through his body at the possibility of such uncurbed possession. His fingers curled around her chin, his mouth came down on hers in a harsh, tempestuous urgency—for only a brief moment. Then his head lifted, his hand dropped away, and flexing his thighs, he arched his back, driving upward, wanting to reach the farthest, absolute extremity. And when he'd attained that inexorable limit, still rampant and unrestrained, he forced himself deeper still.

"Christ," he murmured, lust raging in his blood, his brain about to explode. "Sweet Christ . . ." She was excruciatingly tight as he held himself for a raw moment against the very mouth of her womb, her smooth, silken flesh according the most paradoxically caustic shock to his senses.

Almost light-headed from the rarefied sensation, he finally remembered to breathe again, at which point a shaky kind of reality intruded and he slowly withdrew, the shuddering friction exquisite. Slipping his hands gently under her bottom, he found himself acutely aware of her skin on his palms, of her scent and warmth and pure sensuality, as if his perceptions were refined, honed to a rarer pitch. He reentered her then in a luxuriously slow ascent, taking his time—for himself, for her, for them—intent on regaining that intangible feverish rush.

Trembling against the silk-covered wall, Serena was dizzy with need, waiting for what he was waiting for, almost faint from the fierce, savage pleasure. Her arms were locked around his neck, her body clinging to his with abandon, her inadvertent whimpers a small sobbing rhythm of expectation and gratitude.

"You can't scream when you come," Beau breathed, his voice caressing. "They're all listening."

Scandalized, Serena opened her eyes.

"Mrs. Moore keeps score," he salaciously whispered, "of wantonness and ravishment. . . . You have to be very quiet."

Even as she went tense under his hands, he felt her engorged flesh flutter around him, the illicit, the forbidden exciting her. "My little bitch in heat," he gently murmured, the pressure of his hands on her bottom increasing. "I'll keep you safe," he whispered, bending to nibble on the ripe fullness of her bottom lip, "because I'm going to fill you now with sperm until you can't hold anymore . . . until it runs down your thighs and legs—and puddles at your feet—and then if you're very good, I'll let you come again. How would that be?" he softly queried, his erection coming to rest inside her with gratifying sublimity, his hands hard on her bottom.

"Blissful," she gasped, waves of pleasure already beginning to swell inside her.

"Do you think you can take this all?" he softly asked, penetrating more forcefully, raising her up on her toes.

She nodded, no longer able to articulate the simplest response with the flood tide about to burst.

"My ravenous little glutton," he murmured, brushing a kiss over her mouth. "Next time we'll take off your petticoat too so you'll be nude in front of all these mirrors," he whispered, "and I'll make you watch when my prick disappears inside you so you'll feel it and see it and—"

Her orgasmic cry broke in a high, breathless, lingering cry that rippled across the pink and gilt room and echoed down the corridor outside and brought a knowing smile to Mrs. Moore's face. A heartbeat later, Beau met Serena's climax, pulsing into her sweet, welcoming body, filling her as he'd promised, inundating her with white-hot rivulets of sperm that spilled over and ran down her parted thighs.

It was a long, pure, exaggerated interval of sexual ecstasy, their bodies suspended weightless in the universe, their senses indulged, then voluptuously overindulged, as if they were drenched in dissipation before falling at last into a trembling satiety.

And when it was over and disengaged and they were panting in each other's arms, Beau summoned enough breath to murmur, "I'm not finished with you yet."

"Lock the door," Serena ordered on a wispy exhalation.

"You can't cut your hair," he decreed, ignoring her command.

"I won't if you don't want me to," she murmured, her sultry glance flagrantly flirtatious.

"You *are* a little bitch," he said, grinning.

"And you have to be put in your place occasionally."

"Any special place?" he playfully inquired.

"I was thinking about the divan." Her voice was a purring vibration.

"Which divan?" His gaze was roguish.

He was much too beautiful and much too assured, she thought, but she was ultimately more hedonistically selfish than aggrieved. "All of them, my dear Glory, if you think you can keep up."

Slipping out of his jacket, he began untying his

neckcloth. "I think I can manage," modestly replied the man who was called Glory for a particularly brilliant performance one night with the entire corps de ballet.

He didn't lock the door as it turned out because Serena forgot about it in the libidinous act of helping him undress; but they weren't disturbed as he expected. They dallied on all the divans per the lady's request and the young Earl of Rochefort's inclination and also on a chair commodious enough to accommodate their licentious play, as well as on the rose-patterned carpet when they slipped off a pink satin sofa in the course of their amorous romp. It was the most pleasant style of shopping conceivable, both agreed on more than one occasion that morning. And some lengthy time later when desire was quenched at last and Beau had redressed Serena in her petticoat and chemise, retying bows and buttoning buttons while blissfully exchanging numerous kisses and smiles, he set his own clothes to rights and left the room in search of Mrs. Moore.

Finding the dressmaker in her office, he offered no explanation of the time spent in her dressing room, nor did she inquire. He only asked whether they had all the measurements they needed.

"Yes, we're quite finished, my lord," Mrs. Moore circumspectly replied, careful not to glance at the clock, cautious also to say as little as possible with the young earl in such an unpredictable mood.

After an assistant was sent off with Serena's clothing, Beau acquainted the dressmaker with his wishes concerning his companion's wardrobe, his voice serenely composed—as though he weren't mildly disheveled and attired in wrinkled clothing. "We need the gold gown tonight as well as the petticoat and slippers. Have Miss Blythe billed for only that single frock. The rest is to be charged to me. I'd also like to have the other patterns she admired made for her; I'll leave the fabric selection to your judgment. We'll need some cashmere shawls, lingerie, dressing gowns, slippers, boots, the usual assortment," he casually added. "And unfortunately we require them in three days."

Beau calmly waited while the modiste sucked in her breath, the shock turning her pale. Once she'd sufficiently recovered, he said, "I understand under the circumstances your charges will reflect the necessary haste. And I thank you in advance." He smiled warmly. "Miss Blythe is very happy," he added, turning to go.

As was the proprietor of the small dress shop, who was rewarded once again by Lord Rochefort's incomparable largesse. But even as she returned his smile and murmured all the necessary phrases of leave-taking, a feeling of panic assailed her. She had to bring in a dozen more seamstresses—no, twenty. Immediately.

A short time later Serena and Beau emerged from the dressing room arm in arm, the lady's cheeks rosy from her exertions, her smile one of deep content. And oblivious to the whispers following their progress through the several rooms of Mrs. Moore's establishment, the young English lord and his lady seemed heedless of all but each other.

They didn't notice the couple approaching them as they emerged from the shop, nor did they immediately respond to the greeting directed at them, totally absorbed were they in their mutual postcoital bliss.

"Don't say you don't recognize me, Rochefort," the young colonel exclaimed, offering a quick knowing smile to his wife.

The tone more than his name jogged Beau's fixed attention, and looking up, he saw Tom Maxwell whom he'd known since his youth in Yorkshire. Good lord, he thought. Was his entire roster of acquaintances in residence in Lisbon?

"I told Janie it was you. What brings you to Lisbon, St. Jules?"

"A short detour on my way to Naples," Beau replied, not certain how to introduce Serena. Cousin was out of the question; he'd known both Tom and Jane too long—they knew all his cousins, although luckily neither was a stickler for etiquette. Some stiff-rumped matron would have cut Serena cold. "May I introduce you to Serena Blythe," he said, realizing there was nothing to do but brazen it out. "Miss Blythe, Tom and Jane Maxwell. They're neighbors of mine in Yorkshire."

"Are you staying with Damien?" Jane asked. "We had dinner with him last week. How happy he and Emma seemed."

"He appears in good spirits," Beau evasively replied.

"Are you new in Lisbon, Miss Blythe?" Jane inquired, thinking her very beautiful even in her dowdy gown, curious to know more about the woman Beau was being careful to protect. He hadn't wanted to introduce her.

"This is my first visit," Serena replied.

Serena's upper-class accent offered a clue to her antecedents at least, although she could be an actress, Jane mused. But not dressed so plainly, she immediately decided. What an odd style of woman to be seen with Beau. Gorgeous, of course—that was a given with his ladies—but not sophisticated, nor modish, nor preening on his arm as was generally the case. "Come have coffee with us at the Antiga," she invited, piqued with curiosity.

She saw Serena's fingers close tightly on Beau's arm.

"Do say yes," Tom interposed, oblivious to Serena's discomfort. "We haven't seen you since Felicia's wedding. And army duty is dull here, as you know, even with Napoleon's machinations to keep us alert. Fill us in on the gossip from London."

"I'm afraid we have an appointment," Beau said.

"Later perhaps," Jane suggested.

"That's possible," Beau politely replied. "I'll send a note 'round if our schedule permits."

"Did you hear him say 'our schedule'?" Jane breathlessly intoned as she and her husband watched Beau's carriage disappear down the street. "He's never included a woman in his personal life before. Women are only transient diversions for him. What was her name again? And did you see her gown?

It was at least five years old, although the fabric had once been very fine," she bubbled on. "I must talk to Emma about her. She's definitely something out of the ordinary for Beau, so innocent . . . in an intoxicating kind of way," she more slowly added, as if contemplating the exact degree of Serena's allure. "Weren't you struck by her artless purity?"

"Good god, Janie, we saw her for only a few minutes. She looked damned pretty but regardless the young lady's uncommon charm, knowing Beau," he declared in a realistic male appraisal, "she'll be gone within a fortnight."

"*I* think he seemed terribly smitten. Did you see him *look* at her? And he has to marry *sometime*."

Her husband looked at her incredulously. "If he was smitten, which I seriously doubt, it was in one sense only, believe me. I wouldn't look for a wedding invitation from Beau anytime soon."

"I'm not so sure. You didn't plan on marrying me either—at first."

He smiled. "I had to grab you before Darcy Montague turned your head."

"So why can't Beau have those same feelings?"

"Because, my darling wife, he can't distinguish one woman from another—there are too many to narrow down the field to a single female. The man has them standing in line."

"You could be wrong," she repudiated, curling her lip in a pretty pout.

"And Napoleon could have a heart of gold, but let's not bet the estate on either one."

"You men have no romance in your soul."

"Including Beau St. Jules," her husband pointedly said.

But whatever he was feeling right now was a very close approximation, for with Serena seated on his lap in the gently swaying carriage, her arms flung around his neck and her sweet laughter bringing a smile to his face, he was thinking of canceling their dinner tonight so he wouldn't have to share her company with anyone.

"Do you want to go to Damien's?" he murmured, stroking her back gently, the feel of her in his arms a jubilant kind of pleasure beyond any former experience.

"I'll do whatever you want to do," she breathed, nibbling on his earlobe.

"Which doesn't at the moment include Damien," he teasingly whispered.

"Fine. Everything is *vastly* fine, darling Glory, including the entire state of the world," she grandly extolled.

He grinned. "You're easy to please."

Her lashes came up and her languorous eyes gazed into his. "Keep it in mind."

"I won't forget, believe me. I think that last climax is permanently etched on my brain."

"Am I unforgettable?" she flirtatiously purred.

"Oh, yes."

A prescient sentiment, had he known it.

9

It gave him pleasure to show Lisbon's sights to Serena. They saw the Alfama, the old quarter shaped by the length of its history—the neighborhood a maze of sloping alleys, steep stairways, and small squares, the labyrinth of houses broken occasionally by the facade of a huge palace.

Se Patriarchal, Lisbon's oldest church, stood on the southern hillside of the quarter, its origins dating back to the twelfth century. Sturdy, fortresslike, massive in size, its Romanesque form lightened with Gothic and Baroque additions.

The Palace Square, one of the loveliest squares in Europe, offered an unrestricted view of the Tagus, as did the ruins of St. George's Castle on the heights. Begun as an Iron Age settlement, occupied by Romans, Goths, Arabs, the castle was converted into a royal palace in 1300. And standing at the entrance to the former palace, the whole of the inner city lay at their feet.

When they'd seen enough picturesque churches, palaces, and quaint winding streets, Beau took Serena to the elegant shopping street, Rua Garrett, in the Chiado. At several of the antique dealers his uncle patronized he watched her piquant interest in all the beautiful items on display. He cajoled her into trying on an opulent pearl necklace one of the dealers had on display, but she refused to let him buy it for her. Originally from medieval Saxony, the necklace had been brought to Portugal in a bridal trousseau centuries ago.

"It's too expensive," Serena murmured when Beau urged

her to accept it as a gift. And he graciously acquiesced. But she allowed him to buy her a small inexpensive amber brooch with a wildflower suspended in the fossilized stone because she couldn't bring herself completely to give up having a memento from him of their time together.

When they returned to the hotel at twilight, the boxes from the dressmaker had already arrived and Serena's eyes shone as she pulled the silk gown from its wrapping of silver tissue. "Ohhhh . . ." she exclaimed, her eyes shiny with tears, the sight of the beautiful dress bringing back evocative memories. Her mother had worn a golden dress in the portrait painted of her shortly after her marriage, her pale beauty glowing from the canvas. How many times had Serena stood before that portrait, talking to her mother as if she were still alive; how many times had she found her father seated before the picture after her mother's death, his face wet with tears.

She swallowed hard, suppressing her sorrowful emotions.

"You don't like it," Beau said, looking up from the glass of Cognac he was pouring, taking note of her tear-bright eyes.

"No. I *do* like it."

He frowned faintly. "You're crying."

"Because it's so beautiful," Serena softly said.

"You're sure? We could find you something else," he suggested, wondering if Mrs. Moore could put together another ensemble on instant notice.

"No, really," Serena replied, carefully placing the sumptuous gown on the bed. "I like it immensely."

Beau quietly exhaled, the daunting task of obtaining a new gown averted. "We don't have to stay long at Damien's if you'd rather not," he said, taking note of her pensive expression.

"I don't mind," she replied, looking at him across the bed, a tentative smile fluttering over her mouth. "And I really appreciate the beautiful clothes."

"Don't thank me," he amiably said, holding the glass

between his hands to warm the liquor. "You're paying for
them yourself."

"For your coercion in getting me to Mrs. Moore's." Her
smile was warm and familiar again. "And for your amorous
entertainment at the dressmaker's," she sweetly added.

"Entertaining you is one of life's great pleasures, lollipop,"
he said, his voice velvet soft.

"So you don't mind me tagging along to Italy."

"Try to get away."

"I suppose you say that to all the women."

Her words triggered a disconcerting moment of introspection because he never had, his possessive impulses
toward women nonexistent. And at the risk of denying his
well-developed sense of indifference, he said, "No, never,"
because he felt a rare pleasure in her company. But he
drained his Cognac in one swallow afterward, as if such rene-
gade emotions required fortification.

Not realizing the full import of his admission, Serena
lightly said, "Perhaps you might change your mind if I
become too sexually demanding."

His dark brows lifted, a mild derision in his gaze.

She laughed. "Have I touched your rakish pride?"

"I have a reputation to uphold," he drawled, cheeky and
unabashed, his expression amused. "I'm pained you should
question my zeal."

And she saw him suddenly en mode: a handsome,
teasing, profligate young nobleman playing at love. "It's just
a game, isn't it?" she quietly said.

He didn't look away, although she thought he might.
"Sometimes," he said.

She held his gaze. "And is it now?"

She'd never been aware of such quiet. The intensity
seemed to exert physical pressure on her eyeballs and
eardrums, force the air from her lungs.

His expression was shuttered as he carefully placed the
glass on the liquor cabinet. "It's different," he murmured,
his voice suddenly cool.

She never should have asked such a question, she realized.

Any woman of reason would have devoutly avoided such tactlessness. "Forgive me," she apologized. "How very gauche of me."

Her apology raised a half-smile. "I don't mind your asking if you don't mind my not answering."

Falling back on the bed with a great theatrical sigh she tipped her head back to gaze at him with an impish grin. "I've *so* much to learn about amorous repartee."

Moving around the bed, he stood beside her dangling feet, her worn brown gown oddly enhancing her glowing beauty. "Don't bother," he quietly said, her bright spirit captivating, refreshing.

"With what?" she asked, bewildered by her seriousness.

"Learning fashionable repartee . . . like all—" he paused, mentally eliminating a number of unsuitable phrases.

"The others?" Serena murmured.

"I was going to say like all the femmes fatales," he discreetly finished. "I like you the way you are."

His words conferred on her a glowing happiness, the sensation so blissful, she wondered at the power of so simple a phrase. And even while she cautioned herself to beware of charming rogues, she longed for his affection. "Do we have to stay at the embassy long?" she asked, abrupt and breathless, nervous she'd overstepped her prerogatives again.

But his eyes sparkled with amusement and his smile curved upward slowly as if in anticipation. "Do you have something in mind?"

Crossing her arms beneath her head, she gazed up at him with bland innocence. "I thought I'd test your zeal."

"I warn you," he said with a lazy smile, thinking how delicious and flaunting her breasts were with her arms raised high, "I'm regarded as the most zealous of the London rakes."

"So I should be entertained by the very best then."

"Modesty forbids me," he said, grinning.

She stuck her tongue out in playful rebuke.

His dark lashes lowered marginally. "Let's just say I haven't had any complaints."

• • •

Their dressing turned out to be leisurely, for bathing took on an entirely new dimension in foreplay and a lengthy interval passed before they were attired in their evening finery. A hairdresser had been sent for, an artistic young man who styled Serena's hair into a fashionable Grecian coiffeur while Beau lounged in a nearby chair, drinking.

He found himself in extreme good humor—the day, the evening to date, the entire last week one of unique pleasure. How often had he waited like this for a lady to dress but always in the past with restless discontent, annoyed with the tedious process of a woman's toilette. He was enjoying the quiet languor tonight, with Serena's image in the mirror occasionally smiling at him, touching him with a novel feeling of intimacy.

"Do you like this hairstyle?" she asked, putting a hand out to stay the hairdresser for a moment. "Tell me if you don't."

"It's perfect," he answered, wanting to dismiss the man, discard Serena's new gown, tumble her hair down, and make love to her for a decade at least.

"You're sure?" She spoke the way women did when they wanted to be told they were beautiful.

"You could launch a thousand ships tonight, darling," he said, lifting his glass in salute.

"Is it fine enough for the embassy?"

Setting his glass aside, he murmured, "Perhaps one thing more." Slipping his hand into his coat pocket, he rose from the chair.

"I knew the embroidered ribbon was wrong," Serena fretted, gazing into the mirror. "Should I try the gold cord instead?"

"The ribbon's exquisite. Thank you, Barcelos." The dismissive undertone in his voice was clear. And as the hairdresser bowed his way from the room, Beau drew the Saxony pearls from his pocket. "You need this to make your ensemble fine enough for the embassy," he said, slipping the necklace over her head, placing the pearls around her neck.

"You're supposed to do what I tell you," Serena scolded, looking up at his image in the mirror before her. But there was pleasure in her voice and in her eyes; the strand of creamy pearls and diamond pendant was splendid.

"I might when you start doing what *you're* told," he softly retorted, clasping the diamond latch. "Tell me you like it."

"Of course I do," she said with a wistful sigh. "It's absolutely exquisite, but—"

He stopped her protest with a gentle finger on her mouth. "No buts . . . it's the merest bauble."

"For you maybe. For anyone else it's a ransom in pearls."

But he convinced her to wear it that night, half promising to return it in the morning, and when they arrived at the embassy and Serena was introduced to Emma, the necklace immediately caught her eye.

"How lovely," Emma said, "and it's perfect with your gown. In the Van Dyck portrait of Marie-Louise de Tassis in Damien's study she wears a necklace very like that one."

"A Van Dyck?" Serena breathlessly repeated. "His eye for detail is unparalleled."

"Would you like to see it?" At Serena's instant assent, Emma waved the men toward the liquor cabinet and took Serena by the hand.

She was chatty and cordial as they made their way through an enfilade of rooms to Damien's study, talking of the various embassy functions that took place in the rooms they traversed, mentioning Beau's last visit in regard to a dinner given for the Portuguese royal family, discussing the St. Johns as though Serena were part of the family.

"Damien was worried to death after hearing from Captain Soares," she added. "I hope you've forgiven him for barging in on you."

"Of course, and Beau's so casual about . . . everything," Serena said with only the merest hesitation, for Emma was making her feel very much at home. "I'm sure he didn't notice in the least."

"The St. Johns do have a penchant for ignoring the

world," Emma pleasantly noted. "I grant you, my own disregard for convention isn't so well refined."

"Nor mine," Serena said, blushing.

"We should perhaps take a page from their primer." Emma graciously put Serena at her ease, her own unconventional position with Damien well known.

"I'm attempting to . . . that is . . . once I reach Florence I intend to make my way as an artist."

"So Damien told me and I knew you'd enjoy the Van Dyck even if your necklace hadn't been such a remarkable twin. The other artwork here is lovely of course, but more contemporary. Although I must show you my favorite Gainsborough. His Ann Ford is delectable."

"A Gainsborough too?" Serena softly exclaimed. "I adore his style. My teacher in Gloucestershire once worked with him."

"You'll appreciate his technique then."

And while Serena studied the two paintings in Damien's study, Emma studied the young lady Beau had brought to dinner. Since he'd never brought a lady to dinner before, she contemplated the beautiful Miss Blythe with a fine regard. Neither did he travel with ladies, she understood, so this pretty woman must hold enormous appeal.

Before Serena was finished viewing the paintings, the men came into the room carrying their drinks. "Beau is finding me dull company," his uncle teased. "He expressed an interest in Van Dyck."

"Do come and see it, Beau," Serena said, excitement in her voice. "His way with skin tones and hair and, well, everything is wondrous."

The image of Beau standing before the small portrait, closely examining Van Dyck's brushwork caused his uncle a decided start of surprise. While Beau understood art, he participated casually, to see and be seen at the exhibits, to be au courant in his dilettante world. "Is this deep interest in painting recent?" Damien murmured to his cousin-in-law.

"Very recent, I suspect," Emma softly replied. "Miss Blythe appears to be a remarkable young woman."

"Without a doubt. He didn't care to stay in the drawing room once she was gone."

"I see," Emma quietly said. "Then we should announce dinner soon. He won't care to visit long."

"Or at all unless he can talk of her. She apparently tried to kill this Horton fellow herself and has been making her own living under despicable conditions for the last four years. He's quite taken with her."

"She doesn't cling."

"No. And he had to cajole her into wearing the necklace he bought for her."

"She doesn't take gifts?" Emma's brows rose. "An extraordinary woman in Beau's world."

"Frankly uncommon," Damien murmured. "I'll have to send word to Sinjin of his son's newest attachment."

Dinner was hurried for, as Emma anticipated, Beau was restless, his gaze almost exclusively for his companion, his conversation reduced to minimum answers on subjects other than the merits and attributes of Serena Blythe. It was a revelation for his uncle to see such a transformation in his normally nonchalant nephew.

He ate swiftly or not at all depending on the courses offered. His companion in contrast thoroughly enjoyed all the various dishes from the shellfish bisque to the leite crème dessert. The company talked briefly of the incident at the *Betty Lee* but taking note of Serena's paleness at the mention of Horton, Beau abruptly changed the subject to one less fraught with emotion.

He mentioned they'd run into Tom and Jane Maxwell, which brought the conversation to a number of other neighbors of theirs in Yorkshire. And before long Serena's color returned. Shortly after, they retired to Damien's antiquities cabinet, where they had tea and brandy and Serena and Damien perused the various sculptures and artifacts.

"Another brandy?" Emma inquired as Beau swallowed the remains in his glass, his impatience barely restrained, his gaze following the leisurely pace of Serena and his uncle through the old patined marbles on display.

"Yes, thank you." He turned back to her, half distracted still, his easy smile a reflexive courtesy.

"I'm afraid Serena and Damien have forgotten we're here at the moment," Emma said with kindly tact, refilling his bumper. "I've seen it so often when lovers of the antique find a kindred spirit."

Settling back in his chair, Beau visibly relaxed, recognizing the evening might be extended. "I'm pleased Serena is so well entertained."

"Even though you'd rather be somewhere else?" Emma teased.

He looked up with a start, wondering if she could read his thoughts, realizing a half second later that her remark was meant in the most general sense. "As long as the brandy holds out," Beau said with a grin, "they're more than welcome to continue talking of dead civilizations. She's enjoying herself."

"She's most unusual in her education. I heard her tell Damien she spoke Greek and Latin."

"She shoots like a man as well and alarms me with her skill at cards," he said with a lazy smile. "She's a fascinating woman." He spoke the last statement in a very low voice, half to himself, and he was watching her again, unaware of Emma.

"Papa's collection had one of the rare copies of Ptolemy's *Geography* from the Basel edition," Serena was saying to Damien as they stood in the book alcove, her fingers gently gliding over the tooled leather cover of a well-preserved edition of *Geographike Syntaxis*. "He had the entire oeuvre of Palladio as well. But he preferred treatises on Greek architecture," she went on, looking up at her host, her smile amiable, like a friend of long standing. "When Lord Elgin bought the library, it comforted me to know Papa's library had found such a good home."

"His collection never actually went on the market, did it?" Damien said. "I didn't hear of it."

"Papa had made previous arrangements with Lord Elgin, for which I'm very grateful. Otherwise his collection might have been completely dispersed."

"Did you know Elgin's recently been named minister to Constantinople? I must speak of your father's collection to him when he stops at Lisbon on his way to the Turkish court. Tell me what else your father particularly cherished."

Serena spoke at some length then of the various gems in her father's library while Beau drank his way through half a bottle of brandy. Emma found the intimate mise en scene before her eyes more intriguing than the best Sheridan play of the season. Beau had the look of a fond lover, his barely restrained partiality for the beautiful Miss Blythe a decided reversal of his normal insouciant disregard. Emma had seen him holding up enough columns at numerous balls, bored, indifferent, ignoring all the flirtatious female glances, to know that Sinjin's eldest son had found a woman beyond the ordinary.

He stood finally and said, "It's getting late," in the merest undertone, but Serena heard him immediately and graciously excused herself from Damien, came across the room, took his hand, and softly apologized, the last phrases unintelligible except to her lover.

His smile could have warmed the sun or cheered the lost souls in purgatory, and turning, he bowed to Emma and his uncle. "Thank you for your hospitality," he said. "An evening with family is always pleasant."

"Yes, thank you indeed," Serena sweetly added, her small hand dwarfed in Beau's grip. "I enjoyed myself enormously."

"Come again, if you stay in Lisbon," Emma said. "Damien is most happy talking of his antiquities."

"We're leaving soon," Beau quickly replied.

Serena looked up at him, her thoughts on her paints.

"After we find some paints for Serena," he added, squeezing her hand.

"Can you read my mind?" she whispered.

"I'm learning," he murmured, smiling. "Can you read mine?"

She flushed cherry red and he softly laughed. "Excuse us," he apologized, turning to his uncle and Emma. "A private jest."

"He's in love with that girl," Emma said with conviction, the moment the carriage rolled away from the embassy door. "Like an ardent young boy; I never thought I'd see the day."

"You're too romantical, darling," Damien calmly replied, more familiar with Beau's lifestyle. He'd also seen Sinjin's single-minded pursuit of beautiful women often enough in the past to understand the difference between sexual attraction and love. "I agree Miss Blythe has charmed him, but he's very much like his father."

"My point exactly."

"Sinjin wasn't this young when he fell in love."

"Many are married much younger."

"Perhaps you're right," he politely acceded, not inclined to argue such an unlikely possibility as Beau's marriage. "I'd enjoy it if they came to dinner again before they sailed. Miss Blythe's fluent in the ancient languages and she knew more than I of the excavations at Pompeii. That in itself," he added, smiling down at Emma, "makes her a decided blue-stocking—not Beau's usual style."

"Nor is his usual style impoverished females making their own way in the world. *You* didn't see him watch her all the while she was conversing with you. She piques his interest like none of the polished society belles."

"Perhaps he's at loose ends, between affairs. Her company might be amenable on his long voyage."

"Really, Damien," Emma reproved with a snort of incredulity. "He's *always* at loose ends, between affairs. The boy doesn't know the meaning of permanence in a relationship. As for company on his long voyage, could you see him accommodating the Duchess of Willbrook or Baroness Grothier on a lengthy sea journey? He'd heave either one of them overboard before the week's end."

"I'm sorry to say, Helene wouldn't last *that* long on my yacht. Nor Cecilia. Both women are too empty-headed."

"But they both have bosoms of celebrated grandeur and very passionate natures, I'm told," Emma gently noted. "This one's different, you must admit."

"She has additional qualities beyond his usual requirements, you mean."

"Obviously. Miss Blythe has a mind, darling. And that's why he's so intrigued. It's a novelty for him."

"I'm not so sure he's looking for intellectual qualities in a woman."

"That may be, but he may find he likes it nonetheless."

The statement conjured up visions of Damien's beautiful Dresden doll wife in both their minds. "I hope you're right, darling," Damien softly said, the emptiness of his own marriage nothing he'd wish on his nephew. "Perhaps it wouldn't hurt to mention Miss Blythe to Sinjin. He and the boy are close."

"It can't hurt, surely," Emma quietly said.

10

"Damien gave you something to deliver?" Serena asked, her gaze on the two packets of letters tossed on the carriage seat opposite them.

"I'm to convey the Foreign Office's assessment of the Second Coalition to the British consuls at Minorca and Palermo." Austrian selfishness had British Prime Minister Pitt trying to decide whether he should abandon the Hapsburgs and carry on the war with only Russia as an ally. Although Czar Paul was so angry with Austria he was threatening to withdraw his troops completely. "We'll reach both ports before Damien's normal message transports."

"Do you have to worry about . . . well . . . someone seeing them?" Serena was wondering whether such important ministerial information should be so casually handled.

"Everything of import is coded." Beau shrugged lightly. "I've delivered things before. It's nothing." He didn't say the *Siren* had sailed between England and the French coast twenty-eight times in the last few years in the service of the government. "Now I need a kiss for all my patience while you and Damien were so absorbed in his collection," he said, intent on changing the subject, gratified to have Serena to himself again.

"You should have joined us," she said, half rising from the seat to kiss him.

Leaning forward, he met her kiss and then settled back again with a smile, his lounging pose one of ease, his feet resting on the opposite seat, the planes of his face cast in high relief by the shadowy interior of the carriage. "Emma was filling me in on the newest on-dits in Lisbon while you and Damien were going through his manuscripts." It was a habit of long standing when he visited; Emma thought him interested in the doings of society and he'd never been ungallant enough to tell her otherwise.

"And what did you learn?"

"Nothing of the least importance. The haut monde is by and large excessively uninteresting."

"And yet you number as one of its most active participants."

"In one area only, darling," he said, his teeth flashing white in a grin. "I rarely dine and never dance."

"Never?"

"Occasionally with Maman if she insists I attend some tedious drum with the family."

"The flirtatious ladies must grieve," she observed.

"I haven't noticed." Nor would he, surrounded as he was at social occasions by a circle of fawning females. "Do *you* like to dance?"

"Oh yes."

He rather thought she might.

"Although I've danced only at country parties. Papa lost his money before I properly came out."

She was in so many ways unlike all the women he knew, he mused. Disarmingly open, unconcerned with the superfluities of beauty, remarkably unfazed by her lack of wealth, wondrously innocent of all the female pretense and flattery. She was a refreshing intrusion into his life.

"Would you like to go to a party before we leave?" he asked, the notion of watching Serena dance suddenly catching his fancy.

"What kind of a party?" she carefully inquired, not sure she cared to enter the demimonde, certain that in her position as Beau's lover, she wouldn't be welcomed in proper society.

"Something at the embassy. There's always dancing during the evening, and Damien entertains often."

"I can't attend an embassy function," she demurred.

His dark brows rose. "Why not?"

"How exactly would you introduce me?" she sardonically queried. "As your cousin?"

"You *could* have gone to the dressmaker with Emma," he reminded her.

"I didn't know her."

"Well, you do now and she likes you," he matter-of-factly declared. "I'll have her introduce you as some family connection." His smile appeared. "You might even be able to talk me into dancing with you."

An extravagant offer—the very sweetest of bribes to a woman falling deeply in love.

"Would this be a precedent-setting occasion?" she murmured.

He stared at her for a moment, then smiled. "Definitely." And mildly expensive too.

"You think no one will see you in Lisbon," she teased. "Is that it?"

"You found me out," he lightly retorted, although with ten thousand British troops in Portugal, he knew better. Any of his officer friends attending the embassy ball would be sure to take note of the momentous occasion. His wager in Brook's betting book was of long standing; he'd forfeit five thousand pounds if he danced with a woman before his twenty-fifth birthday. "Now, you have a gown to wear," he went on, "you have an escort *and* a dance partner. You're not apt to meet anyone from your past. How can you refuse?"

She should anyway, Serena thought. The possibility of passing herself off as Emma's relative was not without risks. But the temptation was great—a bona fide ball with distinguished company and all the panoply and glamour she'd only dreamed of before. "I might embarrass you . . . or myself," she added, her voice indecisive.

"Are you planning on taking your clothes off?"

"Would that embarrass you?"

"Hardly." He smiled faintly. "You forget my usual amusements."

"You're incorrigible."

"So I've been told," he murmured. "But say you'll go anyway."

She hesitated, her faraway dream no longer a distant fantasy. "Are you sure?" The caution in her tone was overlaid with a piquant excitement.

"I'll tell Damien tomorrow."

"I shouldn't," she murmured, irresolute still.

"Don't say you're losing your nerve, darling. I wouldn't expect it from a lady who stows away in a lashing storm."

"I was desperate."

"Lucky me," he softly said.

And before they'd arrived back at the hotel, Beau had convinced Serena to jettison her misgivings and let him protect her from any censure. That he was assuming the unique role of gallant as he soothed her qualms never occurred to him.

But then he rarely indulged in introspection and *never* questioned his desires.

Those desires took on a new focus the moment he had Serena alone in their suite—although he was careful to gently remove her gown, heedful of its consequence to her, taking the unprecedented precaution of placing the filmy silk garment gently over a chair before returning to more enticing endeavors.

As promised he was zealous in the extreme during the heated hours of the night—passionate, solicitous, by degrees tantalizing and demanding, tender, playful, sweetly generous—until at last, with the sun bright behind the drawn curtains, Serena gasped, laughing, "Enough . . . enough . . . you're undoubtedly . . . the very best . . . dearest . . . Glory."

Resting on his elbows, his heated body balanced over hers, his dark hair falling in damp ringlets over his forehead, he smiled down at her. "I'm glad you approve."

"Approve's too tame a word," she breathlessly murmured, her arms wrapped around his neck. "Paradise comes to mind or something with choirs of angels and a thousand glittering trumpets."

"Or this bed with your warm body close to mine," he gently murmured.

"Better yet," she whispered, but she was afraid suddenly, such unrelenting happiness too blissful, her time with him ephemeral.

"I think I'll take you dancing this evening," he softly said.

"Take me anywhere at all," she purred.

"Have you seen the Spice Islands?" His voice was teasing.

"Only twice," she nonsensically replied, "but take me there again. I miss the sunsets."

And he wanted suddenly to take her there—not only in jest but in truth, the pleasure of Serena alone on a tropical island warming his heart. "We'll have to start more mundanely with a dance at the embassy—which reminds me . . ." And kissing her lightly, he swung away from her, slipped from the bed, and reached for his breeches.

"What are you doing? Stay with me."

"I'll be right back." Pulling his breeches over his lean hips, he swiftly buttoned them. "What do you want for breakfast?"

"Anything, everything . . ." She was famished from the hours of making love but she was more drowsy, filled with lassitude, and the energy needed to feed herself was too much to contemplate at the moment. "Whatever you want will be fine," she murmured, already half asleep.

Before Beau finished dressing she'd dozed off.

Gently covering her, he locked the door behind him so she wouldn't be disturbed and departed on his errands. First, he woke the proprietor of a small store whose address had been given him by the hotel manager, pounding on the front door until a bewildered man poked his head out of the window above. When the owner came down from his living quarters and opened the door, he was carrying the remains of his breakfast. Waving him on with his morning meal, Beau eased his way through the cramped aisles of the tiny shop, gathering up containers of paint in every shade and hue, picking up several handfuls of brushes as well, the hodge-podge of other paraphernalia foreign to him. By the time Beau's purchases were piled on the counter, the bearded old man had finished eating and helped select canvas, sizing, linseed oil, shellacs, and stretchers. "Send the packages to the York Hotel," Beau instructed when he was satisfied he'd assembled everything Serena would need, "but deliver the charges to the British embassy. And thank you, you've been most helpful."

His driver brought him next to Mrs. Moore's establishment, his arrival following on the heels of the modiste herself, who was just opening her door to her seamstresses. After apologizing for his early arrival, Beau explained his urgent need for a ballgown. And if she would give him an idea of the color, he went on with an amiable smile, assuming his wishes would be complied with, he'd find some jewelry to complement the dress. Although diamonds were always suitable, he added, half aloud, suddenly recalling a display he'd seen yesterday.

He and Mrs. Moore soon agreed on an embroidered silk gauze in a blush rose. "So perfect with mademoiselle's coloring," Mrs. Moore cooed.

"Slippers and all the rest too," he reminded her, poised to take his leave, his hand on the door latch. "And a bonus for your seamstresses if the clothing is delivered by five."

"Most certainly, milord," the modiste replied, her smile in place, already contemplating the extravagant sum she'd charge.

Stop three. The jeweler didn't take long. Beau settled on diamonds.

And then to the embassy, where he needed to explain Serena's insecurities to his uncle and Emma.

He found them at breakfast in their sun-filled garden room.

Damien refrained from saying, You're up early, and instead exchanged bland comments with his nephew on the state of the weather while Beau filled his plate from the food arranged on the buffet. They briefly discussed the condition

of the street under repair outside the embassy as Beau
settled himself and waited for the footman to finish serving
his coffee.

"That will be all," Damien said, dismissing the servants,
his nephew's extraordinary appearance at eight o'clock likely
to be a private matter.

Cutting through a thick slab of ham, Beau looked up and
said, "Do you have any event planned at the embassy
tonight?"

The ambassador cast a glance at Emma, who returned an
amused, knowing smile before Damien turned back to his
nephew. "An assortment of consul-generals are coming to
dinner," his uncle said, "along with a handful of local government officials and a few regimental officers—and their
wives too, of course. Are you interested in joining us?"

Swallowing a bite of ham, Beau nodded. "Serena's never
been to a ball, so I promised her one. Yours, as a matter of
fact." Concentrating on his food again, he speared a piece of
kipper. "I hope you have some good musicians."

His uncle concealed his surprise with effort. "Emma, who
are we having play tonight?"

"Your favorites, dear," she replied, anticipating the
evening ahead with a new and piquant interest. "The group
with the virtuoso violinist. The violinist's a young girl and
quite accomplished," Emma explained to Beau. "Somewhat
of a child prodigy at ten."

"How nice," Beau casually replied, stirring sugar into his
coffee, immune to the merits of child prodigies. "But I need
dancing music," he declared. "Is that possible?"

"Of course; their repertoire is extensive. Give us a list of
requests if you wish."

"I'll leave that up to you, dearest Em," Beau murmured,
his smile one of gratification. Turning his gaze on his uncle,
he added, "By the way, I'm about to lose that Brook's wager
tonight. I expect Monty will find good use for an extra five
thousand in his pursuit of Miss Gambetta."

"Really." Astonished, Damien was at a loss for words,

Beau's wager having been persistently put to the test by enterprising females in the past—without success.

Shrugging, Beau added another spoonful of sugar to his cup. "Serena was fearful of appearing in proper society so I offered to dance with her. Ease her discomfort," he casually noted.

"How kind of you," Emma murmured, looking forward to teasing Damien unmercifully.

"I was thinking . . . could she be some family connection of yours, Em?" Beau mused, lifting his coffee cup to his mouth. "She's apprehensive and nervous and all in a dither about being cut if she appears as my, er, well . . . friend." His brows rose and fell in self-deprecation over the rim of his cup.

"I'm not altogether certain we aren't actually distantly related," Emma said, reassuring him of her cooperation. "My steppapa's aunt married a Blythe years and years ago."

"There," Beau exclaimed with satisfaction. "I knew you'd agree." Leaning back in his chair, he set down his cup, his smile beatific. "We'll come 'round early for drinks. Before all the boring, gold-braided diplomats appear."

And he talked then about the diamonds he'd just purchased for Serena, asking Emma's advice on the best approach to take in offering them to her. "She's reluctant to accept expensive gifts. There's a change," he added with a grin.

"Apparently she's not interested in your money," Damien ironically noted.

"Apparently not," Beau ruefully admitted. "I'm playing with a new, perplexing set of rules. Tell me what to do, Em."

"If it would help, you could tell her I'll be wearing my diamonds. Although she doesn't have to wear jewelry," Emma said. "She's quite lovely without it."

"But I *want* her to," Beau said with an unabashed grin.

"In that case," his uncle interjected, "we'll expect to see Serena's new diamonds tonight."

• • •

Damien wrote to Sinjin shortly after Beau left, informing him of his son's newest attachment. I thought you might be interested to know, he wrote, that Beau intends to dance tonight. He described Serena in a few deft phrases: her beauty; her background; her unusual education; her charming manner—and then briefly outlined the unhappy events of her recent years. As you may understand, he went on, she's quite out of the ordinary and has captured Beau's interest enough that he's willing to overlook his conspicuous wager with Monty. Damien lapsed into rather strong wording to express his surprise and shock at Beau's infatuation—if that indeed was all it was, he unnecessarily commented, his letter by definition expressing his doubt. While he'd been skeptical the previous evening, he explained to his brother, the morning's events seriously altered his previous assessment. The boy would be *dancing* tonight, he wrote, underlining the word to emphasize his amazement.

The young couple was traveling on to Italy soon, he finished, and then he didn't know what more to say. Was this all cause for alarm or celebration or in the end irrelevant? he wondered and, scribbling a few more words à propos his uncertainty about even sending such a curious letter, he wished his brother and his family well.

He signed it Damien and Emma for the first time.

The paint supplies had been delivered to the hotel by the time Beau returned to their suite and Serena was already stretching a small canvas. Still in her sleeping gown, kneeling on the floor of the sitting room, she was systematically easing the canvas tightly over the wooden frame.

"I *adore* you," she said, casting a radiant smile at him as he entered. "How did you *think* of these? And the colors! They're the very best ones! How much did they cost, because I want to pay you for them. And you're sitting for me today, aren't you?" she gaily went on. "Out in the garden, I think, where the light is good."

Leaning against the door, he smiled at her elation. "I'm at your disposal, darling."

"Perfect. Come here and hold this side while I tack it."

She was totally absorbed in her endeavor, the light from the windows outlining her slender form through the sheer white fabric of her nightgown, her golden hair pushed behind her ears to keep her unruly curls out of the way, her bottom lip lightly clamped under her upper teeth in her concentration.

The vision of her voluptuous body so delectably displayed brought to mind other activities than tacking canvas, Beau reflected as he moved toward her, his body responding automatically to her sensuality.

"Why don't you pose nude for me?" Serena said, looking up at him from under her lashes as he approached.

"My thoughts exactly. Although painting wasn't in my equation."

"I'm serious."

"You wouldn't get any painting done if I was nude."

She stopped in her activity, the flat pinchers arrested in her hand. "Are you saying I can't resist you?"

"No, I'm saying I can't resist you."

Her smile was both heated and sweet. "Am I that adorable?"

"Sexy, I'd say."

"And you can't resist me."

"Would you like it in writing?"

"Hmmm . . . that sounds official. Could I use it someday to blackmail your wife?" she facetiously queried.

"I don't intend to have a wife."

He didn't, she suddenly realized, her romantical dreams evaporating on the spot. "You might want a wife *some* day."

"Yes, I suppose I might," he said, aware of the abrupt change in her demeanor. "But not today, is that all right?" he gently asked.

Her expression changed as if the curtain had gone up on a new act. "My apologies. How rude of me, dear Glory, to importune you like all the other women. You must be quite weary of it." And she went back to tightening the canvas.

"Let me help you," he said, dropping onto the floor beside her. "You tell me what to hold."

She was sweet and amiable as they worked the canvas together, careful not to move into subject areas of a personal nature. Beau told her of his visit to the embassy that morning, telling her that Emma was pleased to call her a relative.

"In truth," he said, "some stepfather's aunt married a Blythe, and she's certain there's a connection."

"How curious. Are you sure?"

"Ask Emma tonight. She'll explain it all." He was careful not to mention the new ballgown or the diamonds, hoping a more opportune occasion would arise later.

In her present disquieted frame of mind Serena decided against painting Beau in the nude, opting instead for a safer composition of the colorful terrace garden. Lying in the sun, Beau drank while she painted, half dozing at times, entertaining her when he was awake with stories of the ton. She made a sketch of him stretched out on the chaise while he slept, working swiftly in broad strokes on a scrap of canvas, and then tucked it away in a bureau drawer. She could roll it up in her luggage when it dried—a souvenir of their days in Lisbon, her own visual memory of a glorious time.

They were both on their best behavior that day, careful of their words, courteous, gracious, Serena telling herself it would never do to weave unlikely fantasies concerning Beau St. Jules and love, Beau attempting to repair the damage he'd done by speaking so forthrightly of wives. But the strain of such cautious restraint cracked when the ballgown was delivered at four.

"What's this?" Serena coolly inquired as the numerous silver boxes were deposited in the sitting room.

Beau was standing in the doorway of the garden, his tall form outlined by the setting sun. "You needed a ballgown for tonight."

"I can't afford one. Take these back," she instructed the manager who was overseeing the delivery.

"That won't be necessary, Ramos," Beau calmly said,

walking into the room. "We'll manage now. Thank you."
He guided the manager to the door.

"Look at the dress at least," he told Serena after shutting
the door.

"I *can't* afford another gown, especially a ballgown."

"You didn't mind my buying the paints."

"I needed them," she flatly said. "And they're not a fraction of the price of a ballgown. I can pay for those."

"Good god, Serena. Who the hell cares who pays for
what?"

"I care," she sharply said. "I'm not your mistress or your
latest cyprian or any of the other terms used to describe a
kept woman."

"Lover?" he softly said.

"That's different. And I consent to that gladly." Her voice
suddenly went hushed. "The subtle distinctions probably
don't matter to a man like you but they do to me." She
turned away from him and stared out the window, her emotions in tumult. She wanted him without reservation and
had to fight to maintain some hold on reality, wishing she
didn't have to think about the price of a gown or the price of
her reputation or the price of trying to hold a man like Beau
St. Jules.

She heard him come up behind her, the scent of him
sweet in her nostrils, his presence filling her senses, and she
wondered once he left her how long it would take to forget
the shivering lust his nearness precipitated.

He stood very still behind her for a moment and then gently
touched the tips of her fingers. "Could we compromise?"

Yes, she wished to say, yes, I'll do anything, but she knew
she couldn't and still regard herself separate from the
women she professed not to be. "I don't know," she quietly
said, her gaze unseeing on the half-shadowed garden.

"I don't want you unhappy," he murmured, tugging
gently on her hand to turn her back to him. "Let's talk about
this."

"So you can have your way?"

"So we can meet somewhere in between. I don't think of

you as anything other than a woman I adore. When I buy you things, it gives me pleasure, that's all; it's not meant to belittle you or your circumstances."

"I wish I weren't so poor. Maybe if I weren't it wouldn't bother me if you bought me the Italian papacy."

He smiled, just a little smile. "Since Napoleon carted away most of the papal treasures, I probably could afford to buy it for you now."

"I don't want the vestments," she said lightly. "Only the Apollo Belvedere."

"Too late," he said with feigned regret. "The Apollo's in Paris. Would you settle for a ballgown?"

Serena gently sighed.

"It's just a present," he said. "People give presents to those they love all the time."

He noticed immediately as did she.

The word "love" shimmered between them for the briefest moment.

And then as impulsively he overlooked its implications.

"Take the dress," he said. "Please, I picked it out for you at seven-thirty this morning."

"Mrs. Moore must have been surprised."

"Grateful, I'd say, that I hadn't wakened her any earlier."

"What if I don't?"

"I'll understand," he said, trying to comprehend the incomprehensible.

"Should I just give up completely and let you have your way?"

"It would solve several more, er, imminent problems."

"Such as?"

"The diamonds I bought you."

"Beau!"

"They're perfect with the dress and Emma's wearing diamonds and all the diplomats will be awash with jeweled decorations."

"I won't. No. Absolutely not."

"Should we compromise on that then? Keep the dress, don't take the diamonds."

"Are you manipulating me? Are the diamonds a ploy to make me take the dress?"

"No, I really bought them."

"I don't believe you."

"Don't move."

And he returned a few moments later with three red leather cases. "There," he said.

Serena couldn't resist looking even though she knew she could never accept them. Placing the cases on a nearby table she opened them one by one to find a dazzling necklace set with hundreds of glittering diamonds, a bracelet that shone like the sun, and pendant earrings that must have belonged at one time to a queen, they were so richly adorned.

"You're too extravagant."

"And you're too principled."

"I'll take the dress," she quietly said.

"And I'll return the diamonds."

They sealed their bargain with a kiss.

A kiss that turned after a time into something quite different because they hadn't made love all day in the beleaguered atmosphere of politesse they'd maintained and they urgently longed for each other.

11

When Serena and Beau arrived at the embassy, breathless and laughing and apologizing for almost being late, their affection for each other was so obvious, Damien took Beau aside before the others arrived and cautioned him to more prudence in the presence of their guests.

"No one will believe you just met Serena when you came to dine if you act like an impassioned lover," his uncle cautioned. "I'll expect a little more discretion. Is it possible from you?"

"I'll be the most proper of dining guests," Beau promised, "as long as Emma seats me next to Serena."

"Done. Remember, it's Serena's reputation that will suffer if you misbehave, not yours. Are we understood?"

"You have my word."

"She's quite lovely tonight, by the way. But I don't see the diamonds," Damien drolly noted.

"It was a negotiated settlement," Beau replied, his mouth quirked in a grin. "And mutually satisfying."

But Beau found it stranger than he expected to pose as a proper gentleman, for all the male guests were thoroughly enamored with Emma's young relative. They crowded around Serena at the interval before dinner was announced, they gazed at her with and without subtlety during dinner, and once the dancing began, she was besieged with partners.

He acquitted himself well through it all, playing the role of dinner partner with a well-behaved urbanity that had his uncle amazed and Serena charmed. He was gracious and affable, taking part in the conversation with apparent interest, generally overlooking the lecherous glances and conversational overtures directed at his lover before, during, and after dinner.

Serena was enjoying herself, which was the point of this evening, he reminded himself, and he'd given his word to Damien.

But he glanced at the clock often.

He happened to be talking to Tom and Jane Maxwell when the musicians entered the room and he paused momentarily in midsentence at the virtual rush of men toward Serena.

"You have rivals tonight," Tom noted. "Miss Blythe has taken the fancy of all the eligible males in attendance."

"And a good share of the ineligible ones as well," Beau dryly observed.

"Emma tells me you've promised to dance with Serena," Jane slyly said, drawing her own conclusions about Miss Blythe and Beau despite Emma's unimpeachable explanation of a relationship.

"She's only been to country parties and expressed some apprehension in so rarefied an assembly." Beau's tone at the end held more than a note of sarcasm. "So I offered to dance with her."

"She seems to be waiting for you," Jane declared.

"Can't put it off, Beau, if you promised." Tom, aware of his friend's reluctance, was amused.

"Didn't say I'd dance the *first* dance with her," Beau muttered.

"Perhaps she didn't realize that," Jane pointed out. "She's looking this way. And here comes Emma with a determined look in her eyes."

"Serena's putting off all the men clamoring to dance with her," Emma bluntly said. "I'd say it's time, dear Beau."

He took a deep breath as if dancing with Serena were

capitulating to some unknown force and then with a bow toward the ladies he moved across the polished floor.

The circle of men surrounding Serena took note of her gaze and parted on Beau's approach like doors on smoothly oiled hinges. The attraction between the two young people was immediately evident to all but the most obtuse and a hushed silence descended on the group.

Stopping a short distance away from his expectant lover, Beau stood motionless for so lengthy a time, several observers said afterward, they wondered if he'd come up to the mark.

With lust and denial simultaneously pervading his soul, he didn't realize it could be so difficult to say the words, the sensation of stepping off a ledge into a bottomless black chasm overwhelming him. But he was an honorable man for all his libertine faults and he gracefully bowed at last and murmured very low, "Would you do me the honor of dancing with me, Miss Blythe?"

Gazes swiveled from the Duke of Seth's disreputable son to the blushing young lady and breath's held, everyone waited for her reply.

She smiled faintly at first and then gloriously, tantalizing the crowd of men admiring her, each in turn wishing her smile were directed at them. "I thought you'd never ask, Lord Rochefort," she softly said. "Did the music not suit you?"

"It's been so long, Miss Blythe," he lazily replied, "it seems I've learned to ignore the sound of violins."

"But not me, I hope." Her voice was luscious and low as if she were alone with him in the roomful of guests.

He knew better than most how to overlook convention and when he spoke, lust smoldered in every syllable. "I could never forget you, my lady . . . rest assured."

Even had Lord Rochefort's wager not been so well known, the couple would have drawn every glance as they danced, their looks so fine. His dark strength overwhelmed her pale, golden beauty, but with a distinct tenderness unfamiliar to those who knew him. Serena looked very young in his arms—slender and small in the shimmering rose gown, her cheeks flushed, her gaze lifted to his. And yet being held so close by a man who was a byword for vice lent a tantalizing erotic undertone to her innocence.

The heady perfume of sin and scandal always followed in Lord Rochefort's wake.

No woman he set his sights on had ever refused him.

"He must have just discovered Miss Blythe when we first met them in the street," Jane murmured to her husband, her gaze on the dance floor. "He obviously has a hand in dressing her now—her gown's exquisite. Do you still think Beau views this woman like all the rest?" she archly queried, the quintessential image of carnal desire before their eyes.

"I stand corrected, darling," her husband acceded, fully aware like everyone in the room of Beau's libidinous interest. "One doesn't see St. Jules on the dance floor every day."

"Nor so possessive. Did you see him almost rise from his seat at dinner when the Swedish consul made too personal a remark to Serena?"

"Everyone did. That collective gasp heard 'round the table wasn't in regard to the turbot sauce."

"I must find out who she is," Jane insisted with the fervent curiosity of a matchmaking female. "She's certainly poor, we know that."

"Which matters not at all to Beau. He's remarkably republican, regardless the adverse connotation to the word since Napoleon."

"I wonder if she's truly related to Emma," Jane mused, her mind teetering with possibilities. "Do let's invite them to lunch.

"You've quite shocked everyone, darling," Serena lightly said. "No one else dares join us." They were quite alone on the dance floor.

"They're too busy drooling over you," Beau dryly remarked. "Which reminds me, I forbid you to talk to the Swedish consul."

"He's much too fat," Serena airily noted, a teasing glow in her eyes. "Not at all my style."

"No one better be your style—except me," he muttered, the tedious hours of forced good conduct taking their toll.

"How sweet . . . you're jealous."

"I'm not jealous." He said it offhand, the concept mildly incredulous.

"Well, proprietary then." Understanding the bounds of her own spirited independence, she was enjoying his need of her.

He gazed at her quizzically. "Impossible."

"Should I dance with the Swedish consul?" she inquired, her tone dulcet.

His brows came together in a scowl. "Not unless you care to see Swedish blood shed tonight."

"Must my partners be vetted by you?"

"It's a thought," he moodily noted, wondering how it was possible he cared so much with whom she danced.

"*You* could dance with me all evening," she playfully murmured.

"No, I could *not*," he softly said, a sigh of resignation flaring his nostrils. "Choose whatever partners you wish, lollipop."

"You're sure?"

"Faced with the prospect of dancing the rest of the evening, definitely yes." His gaze flickered briefly to the musicians. "How long is this dance going to last?"

"How gracious you are, milord."

His dark eyes held her amused gaze for a moment. "You're enjoying this, aren't you?" he grumbled.

"But you dance so beautifully, dear Glory," Serena cooed, like a flirtatious society belle. "Why don't you enjoy it more?"

"Because if I'm holding a woman in my arms, milady," Beau negligently drawled, "I'd rather be fucking her."

"I'm shocked, Lord Rochefort," she said, affecting the scandalized horror expected of a lady.

"I didn't realize I could still shock people," he said, smiling, "least of all you."

"And now I'm forcing you to waste your time," she teased.

"I don't mind making an exception occasionally."

"Because I'm so adorable." Malapert and cheeky, she gazed up at him.

"Definitely because of that," he softly said.

Having done his gentlemanly duty, immediately after his obligatory dance, Beau bowed to Serena, said very low and heated, "I expect you to behave," and before she could reply, he walked away to the card room. And while gambling with a preponderance of elderly diplomats didn't hold enormous appeal, it was a good deal better than dancing. He sat in on several hands, drank considerably to ease the tedium, and frequently rose from the table to stroll to the ballroom door and survey his lover's current dance partner.

He found himself counting the passing minutes on the clock or computing the exact number of crystals in the chandelier. The decorations on the consuls' coats at his table numbered a shocking eighty-five, he idly noted at precisely 11:17 and yet he played consistently well as always, gambling being a reflex action in his brain. But time crept by so slowly he found himself wondering if the elegant timepiece on the mantel was in need of repair, and more importantly how long a party for consul-generals lasted.

Some moments later, when Lord Dufferin sat in on their game, his conversation and manner that of a man well into his cups, Beau questioned whether he was still capable of counting cards properly. And when he winked periodically in his direction, Beau first thought the elderly lord had an uncontrollable tic in his eye. So he politely ignored what he considered an infirmity of old age or too much drink and concentrated on his cards, winning so much that attention was drawn to their table. The crowd was extensive, he noticed, looking up after winning another ten thousand. Dufferin was sweating now for he'd lost heavily, but in the next two hands Dufferin recouped a sizable sum and the spectators murmured amongst themselves at his luck.

"There now, that's more like it," Lord Dufferin bluffly exclaimed, beaming, mopping his brow with his handkerchief, gathering his markers with his free hand. "Needed Lady Luck back on my side and damned if she didn't appear. Although"—he winked at Beau so decisively the gesture couldn't be mistaken this time—"I wouldn't mind if that *cousin* Miss Blythe was at my side either, my boy. Something havey-cavey there about cousins, eh, Rochefort," he added with a chuckle. "But then we all must have our amusements, mustn't we."

A score of indrawn breaths resonated in the sudden hush that descended around the table.

"I beg your pardon," Beau coolly said, his gaze chill.

"The lady at the York Hotel, old boy," Lord Dufferin retorted, blundering on. "I saw you with Miss Blythe not two days ago."

Beau gently set his cards down, his hands resting lightly over them, his temper shielded behind his shuttered gaze. "You must be mistaken."

"Couldn't mistake that golden hair or . . . that face with those . . ." Dufferin's voice came to a faltering stop as he realized the room had suddenly gone still. Glancing around, he quickly took note of the shocked, rapt audience crowding near, their expressions expectant like those of spectators at a public hanging.

"I met Miss Blythe for the first time tonight." Beau's voice was entirely without expression, his posture overwhelmingly one of menace.

"I see. . . ," Lord Dufferin whispered on the merest breath, terror numbing his mind.

"So you couldn't possibly have seen her with me before," Beau softly murmured, pronouncing each word with a measured delicacy.

"Yes, yes, indeed, Lord Rochefort, as you say," Dufferin agreed in a rush. "The error is completely mine . . . completely, and I most humbly beg your pardon," he added, his voice quavering, for Rochefort's reputation for dueling was notorious.

"And that of Miss Blythe."

"Yes, of course, Miss Blythe's pardon too, of course," he quickly concurred, sweat beading on his forehead. "Yes, indeed, yes . . . certainly hers above all." He swallowed hard. "I daresay I've had too much to drink tonight. If you'll excuse me now . . . that is—if you find my apology to your satisfaction sir . . ."

For a short, silent interval Beau's gaze drilled into the trembling man and then he nodded.

Lurching clumsily to his feet, Lord Dufferin pushed away from the table and, stumbling in his haste to escape, he half fell, only to be shored up by the press of the crowd. Righting himself, he shoved his way through the spectators and fled the room.

"The entertainment is over," Beau casually remarked, his dark gaze sweeping round the gathered guests. "Someone should take Lord Dufferin's winnings to him," he tranquilly added, rising from his chair, picking up his own markers and a bottle of brandy. The crowd melted away before him as he strolled toward the ballroom, the buzz of comment erupting in a wave behind him.

If the scandal hadn't preceded him, he knew gossiping soon would apprise everyone of the events in the card room. Which necessitated telling Serena. Weaving his way through the dancers, he cut in on Serena and her partner— accosted him, the young officer later said. But it all depended on how one interpreted a lazy brush on the shoulder with a brandy bottle.

"You could be more polite, darling," Serena pleasantly murmured as he swung her out onto the floor. "I think you frightened young Lieutenant Mallory."

"Let's leave," Beau bluntly declared, never having been so long a model of restraint, his civility badly strained.

"We can't leave together."

"And particularly now, I suppose," he replied with a sigh, understanding she'd have to be told soon, with the curious already beginning to stare. "I just frightened the liver out of Dufferin in the card room." At her questioning glance, he added, "The dolt made an oblique reference to seeing us at the York Hotel."

"How oblique?" Serena slowly inquired, suddenly aware of the avid interest of numerous guests.

"Not oblique enough, damn his stupidity," Beau replied, grimacing faintly. "But he apologized up and down and sideways after I pointed out his error."

Despite his casual assessment, she could read between the lines. "You threatened him."

"No, actually I didn't. I just told him he must have been mistaken."

"That's all?" Her relief was obvious.

"Something along those lines," he noncommittally said. "It's over. No one was hurt. But lord, Serena," he exasperatedly complained, "the tedium is unsupportable. Pray this party breaks up soon because I'm about to carry you off and damn the consequences."

"Why don't you go? I understand; I'll come when I can."

"And leave you fair game to all these lecherous men? Not likely." This from a man who had previously considered sharing women a pleasant diversion.

"You *could* dance with me until the band disperses," she suggested, her expression diverted.

He groaned.

"Or you could keep Damien and his cronies company over there." She indicated the group of men deep in discussion in the alcove near the door. "And when it's possible, we'll make our escape."

"You're going to have to pay, you know—for this dull foray into respectability. I'll expect due compensation," he sardonically murmured.

"And I'll give it to you gladly," Serena indulgently replied. "I'm having enormous fun."

He was startled enough to stop dancing for a moment, the possibility of such sincere enjoyment in this most commonplace evening beyond his comprehension. "Really," he said.

"Go," she retorted, smiling at his bewilderment. "You couldn't possibly understand."

And he chose Damien's circle as the lesser of two evils, spending the remainder of the evening half listening to talk of war. He added a comment occasionally, his awareness of events au courant with his informal role as courier for the Foreign Office. The debate over Napoleon's sincere interest for peace was hotly contested. Some blamed Austria's intransigence, others Napoleon's ambitions. Pitt came under attack on several points as well.

Mention of the recent controversy in the card room never came up, although everyone in the room had heard of Lord Dufferin's remarks. No one was foolhardy enough to touch on the subject in Beau's presence.

So disaster was averted.

And Miss Blythe's first dance in society was a huge success.

12

When they returned to the hotel, Beau found himself wishing they could leave Lisbon immediately so he could have Serena to himself again without all his numerous acquaintances interfering, gossiping, asking questions he didn't care to answer. But Serena's wardrobe wouldn't be ready for another day yet, so he consoled himself with sending a note to Mr. Berry, instructing him to have the *Siren* ready to cast off at dawn one day hence.

In order to avoid meeting any more overly curious acquaintances, the following morning he offered to take Serena to the lush upland country north of Lisbon where the nobles had their summer homes. For centuries Sintra had been their retreat from the unpleasant heat of the city and the picturesque landscape was the stuff of paradise.[4] Arriving at lunchtime, they chose a cozy inn beside a stream for their midday meal. The fire was warm inside, the view of the rushing water and dark greenery, the rugged terrain of peaks and valleys outside their window like a lush, evocative painting.

They ate leisurely, enjoying the solitude of the off season and the ministrations of the proprietress bustling about, bringing them all manner of delicacies from her kitchen. And later in the afternoon they toured the Seteais Palace, the most elegant of princely abodes, its staterooms so sumptuous it seemed incomprehensible that the structure was regarded as a rustic summer retreat. They admired the Quinta de Monserrate, a Moorish castle built eight hundred years earlier during the Muslim occupation, and several other of an infinite variety of summer retreats incredible for their beauty.

On the drive back to the city that evening, they watched the sun set behind the shadowed peaks, the display magnificent, and they were both touched by the delicate, shifting colors tinting the sky as if they'd not seen such a sight before. And perhaps they never had in precisely that way, with the rose-colored lenses of love adding radiance to the world.

They stayed in that evening, although Beau politely inquired whether Serena would prefer going out, resigned to a last evening in society if she wished. Jane Maxwell's note had been waiting for them at the hotel with an open invitation to visit them.

"I like being with you best," Serena had said.

And her simple statement filled him with contentment, a rare feeling occurring more frequently of late. He was glad to be away from England, he told himself, from all the ennui of the fashionable world, where nothing changed but the women in his bed. Freedom from those cloying amusements no doubt figured strongly in his content, he reflected.

Serena was less prone to rationalize away her feelings.

She knew she was in love.

When the awaited message from Captain Berry arrived— the supplies for Miss Blythe are aboard, he'd cryptically written to his employer—Beau called in the hotel staff to pack their belongings. Serena oversaw the removal of her painting supplies while Beau attended to the gratuities for the staff, and after sending off brief notes to Damien and the Maxwells they were prepared to go.

The weather cooperated in the Atlantic, where winter gales could be hazardous, and they passed through the Strait of Gibraltar two days later without sighting any craft. But the crew had been on alert since their departure from Lisbon. The Spanish fleet at Cádiz and Cartagena, although preferring to sit out the war in safety, occasionally made forays along the coast, while the French navy base at Toulon, engaged in supplying the blockaded garrison at Malta, had all manner of craft in the Mediterranean. Either would see the *Siren* as a lucrative prize.

Their new course to Minorca put them well within French and Spanish waters, a fact Beau chose not to mention to Serena because they might well arrive in Minorca without problem. The position of enemy vessels was always a gamble and until the fourth morning through the Strait of Gibraltar, they sailed unmolested.

The sun had just begun to lighten the sky, the blackness turning to gray, the ships newly sighted on the horizon only hazy shapes to the *Siren*'s lookout. But soon the stars overhead were invisible and the lookout's accustomed eye could pierce the dimness. Watching the ships' outlines emerge as the silver of dawn started showing the faintest hint of pink, he strained his eyes, trying to make out the shape of the topsails and staysails, knowing the French carried wider upper sails and triangular staysails. Waiting, he peered intently at the three vessels ten miles dead ahead. With Britain dominating the Mediterranean, it would be rare for the Royal Navy to proceed so lightly protected, he thought, observing what appeared to be a single ship of the line with two escorts making her way north. Impatiently he fidgeted on his lookout perch until the specks creeping toward them resolved into a low, fine-bowed French frigate and two fast corvettes.

"Enemy sails in sight!" he screamed.

Waking with a start, Beau leaped from bed. Grabbing his breeches and weapons he'd placed nearby for such an eventuality, he shoved his legs into his breeches, jerked them up, buttoned them hastily, and buckled on his sword belt with a few rough tugs. Striding to the door, he brusquely said, "Stay in the cabin." He was no more than a shadowed form in the half-light, his voice a stranger's voice, detached, distracted. "There's no time to watch you," he added as if in afterthought, as if the courtesy of an explanation had just occurred to him. And pulling the door open, he was gone.

"Clear for action!" Serena heard him shout, his cry echoing down the passageway, his footsteps racing toward the hatchway, and a flutter of fear quivered through her, all the lurid stories of Barbary pirates and bloody naval battles filling her mind as the drumbeat to quarters rolled through the craft. The harsh grating of the gun ports opening gave indication of the fight to come, the rumbling of the cannon being run out both comforting and harrowing. The creaking of sails as every centimeter of canvas was spread for their run resonated in Serena's ears, generating a clutch of fear in her stomach. And whoever the enemy, there was no question this time of involving herself. In a pitched battle at sea, she was helpless, her presence on deck a liability. Moving from the bed to Beau's large armchair, which was bolted to the floor near his desk, she picked up his jacket he'd tossed on the seat last night, and settling into the deep leather chair, covered herself with his coat. His scent enveloped her, calming for a second the tumult in her brain and then, like so many in extremity, she thought about praying for the first time in years.

Standing on the deck, Beau gazed at the ships ahead. "What's their flag?" he shouted to the lookout clinging to his perch on the foremast.

"French, sir, the *Généreux* and escorts! She's altering course and leaving us to the cruisers, sir!"

The *Généreux* had survived Aboukir, Beau knew. She must have been blown off course en route to the French port at Toulon. He took note of the corvettes wearing 'round to face about and challenge them.

The *Siren*'s carronades were in place—the new lighter guns designed for close-range fighting—the decks were wetted and sanded against fire, the hoses rigged to the pumps should they take a hit below the waterline, and all fires extinguished.[5] In short, the *Siren* was readied by her well-drilled crew in a matter of minutes.

Each corvette carried eighteen or twenty guns, perhaps as many as forty, against their ten. Not exactly an even fight,

Beau reflected. But if they turned and ran, they had a great distance back to Gibraltar through hostile waters with two fast ships on their heels. Minorca was only short hours away. "Make the *Siren* fly, Mr. Berry," Beau ordered, training his glass for a moment on the corvettes bearing down on them. "We're going through them and make a run for Minorca. Mr. Slade," he called down to the seaman in charge of the gunnery, "see that the matches in your tubs are alight." With all the spray breaking aboard, the flintlock trigger mechanism couldn't be relied on until the guns grew hot, and the old-fashioned method of ignition might have to be used. Beau stared again at the vessels advancing toward them. "Mr. Berry, I want the best quartermaster at the wheel. There's not going to be much of a gap between the corvettes. I need a steady hand."

"We'll be passing mighty close," Berry cautiously noted, always dependable but aware of the tight maneuvering necessary.

"Unless they panic and veer off. We'll see," Beau murmured, standing utterly still, the strong wind whipping his hair into disheveled curls, his face without emotion. The possibility they would collide bow to bow was a calculated risk.

But if they went through them, they had a chance.

He was dressed simply, like his men, stripped for action down to breeches; some had bandannas tied around their heads to keep the sweat from their eyes, while the gunners had their ears covered against the noise of the cannon. Cutlasses, swords, pistols were at their waists and they all knew the drill should boarding be required.

Crowding on all sails, the *Siren* surged forward, slicing through the seas, making straight for the French ships, the rigging snapping in the wind, the crew poised for action.

"Stand by, Mr. Slade," Beau called down. "Fire your chase guns at eighteen hundred yards. Let's see if we can slow them down." Then from the corner of his mouth to the man at the wheel, he said, "Hold her on course."

The *Siren* was only a year old, adapted from Ozanne's

designs for the French *Diligente*, regarded as the fastest vessel ever built. Or the second fastest now, those familiar with the *Siren* asserted. And in the next few minutes, if the *Siren* could elude the corvettes' guns, she could outrun the French ships.

"They've opened fire, sir," Berry said, standing beside Beau. "Larboard bow."[6]

Beau looked just in time to see a puff of smoke blown to shreds by the wind. The sound of the shot didn't reach them. It was bad policy to open fire at long range, he thought, his anxiety over the enemy's skill lessening. Better to wait until there was possibility of doing maximum harm.

"Steady, Mr. Slade," Beau shouted. "Hold your fire."

Another puff of smoke from the corvette on the starboard bow and this time they heard the sound of the shot as it passed overhead between the yards.

Beau took a last glance up at the weathervane and at the shivering topsails. "Now, Mr. Slade," he rasped, "let's show them what English gunners can do."

Beau's gunnery crews were superb, their regular training assuring them a high degree of accuracy, and both bow guns went off simultaneously in a rolling crash that shook the ship to her keel. The billow of smoke that enveloped the deck momentarily was blown away almost instantly by the strong wind so they could see both shots crashing into the corvettes.

"Right on target, sir," Berry said, sniffing the bitter powder smoke eddying around them.

"Good shooting, Mr. Slade," Beau called out. "Use the long guns until we meet and then hold your fire on the carronades until I give the order—and dismantling shot in every other carronade."

Staring narrow-eyed at the French corvettes coming down remorselessly on them, shot pouring from their guns, foam rushing by their bows, Beau made rapid calculations, judging wind and sea, time and distance, comparing their speeds, visualizing the minimum clearance they'd need to slide through the narrow gap, hoping the French aim didn't improve for a few minutes more. They were firing wild.

"Go at them," he said, steadying his quartermaster, the distance closing between them. If the French ships let them through, they weren't apt to fire at the *Siren* and risk hitting each other. And his gunners would have one chance for a broadside. The corvettes' other option was a high-speed collision. So a bluff was a bluff was a bluff. Beau felt his pulse racing, his glass to his eye, sweeping the corvettes' gun ports, thinking the steady whine of cannonball overhead either clumsy shooting or an attempt to dismantle their sail.

With a hundred yards separating the vessels, the *Siren*'s long guns struck home, battering the corvettes. The din of firing was prodigious.

Seventy yards to close.

And not enough room to run between them.

"Steady," Beau sharply ordered the man at the wheel as the *Siren*'s deck was swept from end to end with shot for the first time. And it seemed for a minute as though the heavens were falling around him. He felt the deck leap as the shots struck home, heard screams from his men, felt splinters and debris shriek by him, and then he was struck and flung down into the blood on the deck, some of the mizzen rigging falling down and entangling him. Struggling to free himself, he got to his feet, dizzy and shaken. But he saw the quartermaster still at the wheel and knew the *Siren* was on course. "Afterguard," he roared, his voice sounding raspy in his ears. "Axes here, cut away that rigging!"

And as a rush of men came pounding up with axes and cutlasses, others were dragging wounded men along the deck and down the hatchways to the cockpit below.

He steadied himself against the rail, waiting for the dizziness to pass, wiping away the blood dripping down his cheek.

Thirty yards and still on collision course. There wasn't much time. He forced his mind to concentrate. "Hold your fire," he yelled, his voice hoarse from the smoke.

Twenty yards separated them—seconds at this speed.

Would the French risk a head-on collision?

And then the corvettes swerved violently to port and starboard and the *Siren* shot between them, passing within a dozen feet of each. Bow slipped by bow, foremast passed foremast, and then foremast passed mainmast. Beau was looking aft and as soon as he saw the aftermast gun bore on target, he shouted, "Fire!"

Mr. Slade's gunnery crews opened broadside, the *Siren* lifting to the recoil of the guns. The carronades raked the corvettes' decks from stem to stern, the sound of discharge ear-splitting. Then even before the wind had time to blow away the smoke the guns were reloaded, run out, and fired again. Once more, the *Siren*'s guns pounded the French vessels, the carronades so hot that the dripping sponges thrust down their bores sizzled and steamed at the touch of the hot metal.

Beau counted three broadsides—an unbelievable loading time—before the *Siren* broke free of the gauntlet. The smoke banked thick about the ship so it was impossible to see individuals, only the long orange flashes of the guns.

Of the corvettes all that was visible was their tall topmasts jutting above the high cloud of smoke.

"Look at that, sir!" Berry said, his form rising out of the greasy trailing wreaths of gunpowder. "They're wrecked!"

Beau tried to look through the eddying mist and then a breeze rolled away the smoke, revealing the scene behind them.

The two French vessels were in ruins, their sails hanging in tatters, mizzen, foremast, mizzen topsail, and all the crossjack yards shot away.

A loud cheer went up from the men, a screaming, jubilant cry of victory as the gap between the *Siren* and the enemy swiftly widened. Through his glass Beau could see the corvettes' decks black with men struggling with the wreck of the masts. Pursuit was impossible now. He exhaled the breath he hadn't realized he was holding and snapped the glass shut.

"That was fine shooting, sir," Mr. Berry said, his grin

shining through the haze of gunpowder still shrouding the deck.

"We blew them to hell," Beau happily agreed, smiling broadly. "Give the men my compliments, Mr. Berry."

"The frogs haven't learned to shoot any better since last time at Noirmoutier, sir," the captain said. "We took only light damage."

Beau's gaze swept the *Siren*'s masts and rigging; only one topsail and the mizzen were damaged. "After the wounded are attended to, see to those sails, Mr. Berry. I've Miss Blythe to calm and then I'll be back to help."

"Ladies don't run into this excitement every day, I warrant," the captain said, still beaming at their triumph. "You leave the rest to me."

"Tell the crew there's shore leave for everyone in Minorca and an extra month's wages to spend on the ladies," Beau said.

"Very good, sir. You're wounded yourself, sir," Berry briskly added, restraining himself from suggesting that a doctor's care might be in order.

"I'll see to it later," Beau replied and, turning away, he made for the hatchway, the haze of powder still thick belowdecks. He called out to Serena as he reached the cabin to allay her fear, to give her some warning of who was approaching her door. But she gasped nonetheless when he stepped over the threshold, shocked at the sight of him.

His body was streaked with gunpowder and splashed with blood from flying splinters and from the cuts he'd sustained when the rigging had fallen. A long gash over his right eye was still bleeding, a rivulet of blood coursing down his cheek.

"It's nothing serious," he said, his tone temperate, hoping to alleviate her alarm. And then he saw how pale she was and swiftly moving toward her he anxiously asked, "Are you hurt?" He looked for shot damage that could have harmed her as he crossed the cabin, broken glass crunching beneath his feet.

She shook her head, not capable of speaking, her ears still

ringing from the cannons, the taste of gunpowder bitter in her mouth, the sight of Beau covered in blood contradicting his bland statement of good health.

"I'd hold you but I'd ruin your clothes," he said, leaning over her huddled, frightened figure. "We're free of the French," he gently added. "All's well and we're making for Minorca. Are you *sure* you're not hurt?" he tenderly repeated. "Let me have the doctor check you."

Swallowing hard, she forced herself to speak because she didn't want him to think her so timorous and cowardly. "I'm not hurt," she whispered, trembling despite every effort to appear brave.

"Could you stay alone for just a short time more?" he quietly asked, squatting down so their eyes were on level, touching her hand lightly with his bloodstained fingers, torn between her distress and his men's injuries. "I have to help with the wounded."

She tried not to shudder at the thought of wounded, at the sight of his bloody hands and the stain on her skin where he'd touched her. "Yes," she said on a suffocated breath, nodding in additional affirmation, still too shaken by the stark reality of battle stations to converse in a normal tone.

"A half hour, no more, and I'll be back," Beau promised, standing upright, brushing away a drop of blood that had fallen into his eye. "I wouldn't go on deck yet," he softly warned.

"I won't," she whispered.

"A half hour then."

And he was gone. But it wasn't a half hour. Mr. Berry came down an hour later to bring Beau's regrets. "Lord Rochefort's had a few more things to see to," the captain said. "Could he have some food sent down?"

It was another hour yet before Beau returned because two of his men had been badly hurt and he stayed with them while the surgeon ministered to their wounds.

When Beau finally walked back into the cabin, all residue of the battle had been cleaned away. He'd showered quickly

under the seawater pump, dressed in fresh clothes, had the
doctor stitch the cut over his eye. He'd sent his steward
down to see that the glass was swept from the cabin floor so
when he arrived the only evidence of their fight at sea were
the canvas patches on the windows.

"We should be in Minorca in a few hours," he said,
entering the room. "Did they bring breakfast down for
you?" he asked, shutting the door, thinking her color was
much better.

"Yes, thank you." Serena set her book down, although
her attempt at reading to pass the time hadn't been too successful, her concentration still distracted by the tumult of
recent events. "How are the wounded men?" she inquired. "I
was wondering if you needed help, but I . . ." Her voice
trailed off. The ragged gash over Beau's eye, pulled together
with a half dozen stitches, was visible as he moved into the
cabin.

"We didn't need any help . . . the men are fine." He sank
into the soft cushioned chair near her. "Only two were seriously hurt," he said, his fatigue evident in his sprawled form,
"and McGuane tells me they're both going to recover. I was
hoping," he went on with a soft sigh, "we'd avoid the French
so you wouldn't have to experience this ordeal."

"I knew there was a risk when I decided to sail to Italy."
Serena smiled ruefully. "Or at least in theory I did. I hadn't
actually considered the reality of battle. I apologize for my
lack of courage."

"No one expects you to join in," Beau replied. "And now
that you're blooded," he murmured, "the shock should
lessen."

"You anticipate more?" She tried to speak casually but
her pulse accelerated violently.

"We should be safer now. The run to Palermo from
Minorca is short."

"How often does this happen?"

"It depends," he vaguely said.

"On?"

"On where you are, darling. Boney is slipping through the blockade every day."

"Perhaps I should polish my prayers," she said, only half in jest.

He grinned. "No need, the *Siren*'s fast. And I'll take care of you."

She experienced not only comfort but joy at his words, although she warned herself not to instill too much meaning into a casual phrase. So she responded with what she hoped was equal casualness. "I like your confidence."

"I have my share of luck," he simply declared—and vast experience, his crew would attest. "I was thinking," he went on, wishing to talk of less fearful issues, "we might take advantage of our stay in Minorca and spend some time at a small beach villa I know. How does that sound?"

"On the heels of my first battle experience, like heaven on earth. I'll even wash your clothes and make your meals," Serena facetiously said, "to express my lively sense of gratitude."

"I was thinking of some other ways you could spend your time," he murmured.

"Like painting your portrait?"

"Not exactly," he said, hushed and low.

"You don't want me to cook or wash for you—nor paint. Unfortunately I don't sing well or recite poetry with any expertise. Surely," she playfully noted, "there's not a pianoforte on a remote beach. . . ."

"Very funny," he drawled. "As if I want any of that from a woman."

"You mean every mother telling her daughter to develop those graces to attract a proper husband is wrong?"

"I can speak only for myself and my friends but I'd say the gulf between the genders is wide on that account. But we still have an hour or so to discuss this before we reach harbor," he mockingly went on, reaching for a bottle of brandy from his cabinet. "Entertain me with your vision."

"My vision has nothing to do with attracting eligible husbands, for which you're grateful, I know," she said lightly. "I intend to paint, my goals are simple, but you should eat first," she added with concern, thinking it unhealthy to begin the day with brandy.

"Are you cooking?" A teasing light shone from his eyes as he pulled the cork from the bottle and lifted it to his mouth.

"I can't now on board ship, but I *could* bring you the remains of my breakfast. Does Remy fire the guns too?" she suddenly asked, wondering how the temperamental young chef responded to sea fights.

"We can't afford to lose him. He stays below in the galley."

"I see," she whispered, her expression abruptly altered.

Sorry he'd spoken so carelessly, he said, "Could I have some of that bread and sliced beef? Does your gratitude extend to serving me?" His smile was warm and intimate.

She struggled to respond, not as familiar with accepting the bloody consequences of naval engagements, her mind still disquieted by recall of the battle.

"You promised to serve me some food," he gently prompted.

"Yes, of course." With effort she refocused her thoughts and her gaze met his. "What would you like?"

"Anything at all as long as you keep me company."

She looked at him across the well-lit cabin, the hushed sound of his voice flooding her mind with memory—of other times and other places, of this small cabin the first time she met him. And she felt a warm glow inundate her senses, an inexplicable joy. He took pleasure in her as she did in him and that happiness could erase by magic all that disturbed her. "You must sit for me like that at Minorca," she softly said, wanting to capture on canvas the essence of his dark beauty, his intense virility, the grace of his smile, the lithe power of his strong, young body—the love she felt for him.

"I warn you, I intend to drink away a good part of my days while ashore."

"I won't complain," she pleasantly returned. "A resting model will be perfect." And she understood then how he dealt with the aftermath of combat.

13

Several hours later, after the *Siren*'s crew were all settled on shore, after the British commander at Port Mahon had personally been given Damien's dispatches, after orders for the refitting of the *Siren* had been left with a company from the fort, Beau drove Serena in a little gig up the shore road to a secluded hamlet overlooking the sea. A small picturesque villa stood on a hillside above the Mediterranean, its stuccoed exterior a muted ocher framed by the bluest of skies, numerous flower-decked terraces and porticoed alcoves offering a delicate fantasy to the eye, the whole like a miniature palace built for play. From the coast road, the drive curved gently up the hill between lemon trees and blooming mimosa, the scent of flowers and sea so pungent, Serena drew in a deep breath and thought herself in paradise.

After dismounting in a paved courtyard centered around a moss-covered fountain, Beau took down their valises and ushered Serena into a blue-tiled foyer. "There are no servants to intrude, no official duties requiring our time, only peace and quiet and you and me, and hopefully a well-stocked kitchen," he added with a sunny smile. "I'm starved."

He hadn't eaten since the previous evening save for the scant remnants of Serena's breakfast, and primed as he was by a rather steady consumption of brandy, food was high on his list of basic needs.

"Whose house is this?" Serena asked, entranced by the gem of a villa. The two small parlors on either side of the

ntrance hall were beautifully furnished with a woman's
ouch, the stairway leading to the second floor embellished
vith carved handrails of climbing roses and frolicking putti,
he portrait of a lady on the landing, gowned in the Conti-
iental fashion of two decades ago, decidedly English in
ppearance.

"Gillian was a friend of my father's. She died young and
eft her house to him—Maman says because he was her
avorite lover. Papa recalls instead she had no family she
ared for."

"How romantic," Serena softly declared, the atmosphere
ne of enchantment. "How did she die?"

"The locals prefer the story of a broken heart; Papa tells
ne she was of a melancholy disposition."

"She sounds like a heroine from the *commedia dell'arte*."

He looked at her quizzically, pragmatic like his father. "I
hink she was originally from Sussex."

"Perhaps when you're less hungry," she humorously
noted, "you'll appreciate the *ambiance d'amour*." And while
he didn't know the Duke of Seth personally, she'd heard
nough stories of the Saint in the course of her employment
t the Tothams' to regard this villa in a decidedly roman-
ic way.

Within a short time Beau had assembled a meal from the
arder. Pouring wine, he waved Serena to a seat at a rustic
xitchen table where they proceeded to eat cold ham,
hicken, olives, and bread. Their simple collation absolved
erena from cooking and himself from having to eat any tyro
ood experiments.

"Should I try to make some warm food as well?" she
nquired, feeling as though she should offer to make some-
hing more substantial. "Perhaps I could find a recipe book."

He raised one brow in mock horror and motioned toward
iis glass. "Just pour some more wine, darling. That will be
quite sufficient. . . . You're not eating—what's wrong?"

"I'm in the mood for cake."

"There are two kinds in the pantry," he offered, slicing himself some more ham.

"Why didn't you tell me?"

He looked up, startled. "Mostly because I can't read your mind and also because you were too busy exclaiming over the *darling* painted tiles around the windows and I forgot. There's an assortment of other sweets too," he added. The last statement was finished to the back of Serena's head; she was halfway to the pantry. "Bring another bottle of wine," Beau called, "as long as you're up."

The muffled exclamations of pleasure emanating from the adjacent room brought a smile to his face and he reminded himself not to overlook mentioning sweets in future. And when Serena emerged from the cool pantry built into the hillside, she had a bottle of wine under her arm and two cake plates balanced in her hands. "These are absolutely wonderful," she said, beaming.

"I can tell," he indulgently replied, always charmed by her delight in simple pleasures. Such gratification from his society paramours would have required at least a costly piece of jewelry or two. "Here, let me help you," he offered, rising from the rush-seated chair, and taking the cake plates from her, he deposited them on the table.

"I think that's a caramel rum sauce on that one," Serena said, gesturing at a low oval-shaped cake and setting the bottle down. "Look at these darling little cherries made from marzipan," she pointed out, plucking a bright candy fruit from the top of the second cake.

With a startling clarity that would have mystified his jaded friends, he wished to arrest that moment in time, the charm and warmth of Serena's beauty enchanting. She wore one of her simple old-fashioned gowns, which suited Gillian's country home, her tousled hair gleamed gold under the sunlight pouring into the kitchen, and she gazed at him with such buoyant happiness, holding the cherry out to him, he reflected on the possibility of staying in Minorca indefinitely.

"Try it," she coaxed, leaning across the table, offering him the marzipan cherry.

"I'd rather have you."

"But you already do," she said without coyness, slipping the sweet into her mouth instead.

He suddenly couldn't wait, his hunger for food incidental to a more potent need. "I need you *now*," he softly said, abruptly rising, reaching across the table, sliding his hands under her arms, and lifting her to her feet, the need to possess her flaring through his senses. Moving around the corner of the small table, he swung her into his arms and strode out of the kitchen as though he had only minutes left in the world.

"Dear Glory, I thought you'd never ask," Serena whispered, her face lifted to his, her unquenchable need for him beyond reason or sense—a weakness, a craving, an irresistible desire.

As he took the stairs two at a time, lust burning through his brain, her words jarred. "I'm sorry," he murmured, passing down the corridor to the bedroom fronting the sea. "Forgive my selfishness; I'll make it up to you."

"It's nice to have you back again," she purred, understanding the intense concentration required to deal with the enemy, his crew, the aftermath . . .

"Oh, yes," he murmured, his libido in ramming speed as he pushed the bedroom door open. "I'm here."

Possessed, impatient, he didn't even undress her the first time, instead pushing her skirts aside and mounting her in seconds, his initial climax only marginally delayed for hers. Wild, rapacious, he was insatiable at the outset, taking her twice swiftly before he discarded his clothes and hers, as if only insensate release would purge the recent violence from his mind. And while her reasons differed, she needed him too, and hot-blooded, she rose to meet him, wanting him deep inside her, wanting his touch, his closeness, the blissful ecstasy, not knowing any more than he why desire fed on desire and each reeling orgasm only pitched their fever higher.

Very late that evening, their heated passions at last abated, they lay in each other's arms, the moon drenching the room in silver light. "You do . . . something to me. . . . I don't know what it is. . . ." His smile appeared. "But it's damned fine."

"Yes, isn't it," she murmured, lightly tracing a finger down his muscled torso, reflecting on the infinite degrees of pleasure she now knew existed in the world. On the love infusing her body and mind.

Brushing a kiss across her forehead, he gently asked, "Are you sleepy?"

She shook her head, still warmed by an inner glow of contentment, feeling as though she might never sleep. Wanting to hold her present feelings intact, as one wished to make a fragile soap bubble last.

"Do you care to swim?"

She hadn't swum for four years, not since her father died. Twisting around to lie across his chest, she smiled up at him. "I'd love to. Although I was wondering . . . could we—I mean . . . is it possible—in the water?"

His smile was wicked. "And highly probable."

"Well then?" she murmured, her gaze provocative.

"You prefer not delaying your next climax?"

"I adore new experiences," she purred.

They slept very late the next morning because swimming was exhausting in altogether new and delightful ways and it had been nearly dawn when they'd returned to the villa. After a leisurely midday meal of fruit and rolls and coffee that Beau had made because Serena hadn't actually ever boiled water before, Serena set up her canvas and paints on a terrace overlooking the sea. Beau obliged her by posing nude on a weathered bench, his tanned body shaded by a tumble of climbing jasmine, his brandy bottle conveniently within reach.

Sketching in the rough composition first in a pale yellow wash, she blocked in the sky and sea in light blues and greens, brushed in some semblance of the flower-decked wall and bench, and then concentrated on the beauty of the man before her.

She worked without speaking for almost an hour, carefully defining the graceful line in his sprawling pose, the broad width of his shoulders and his rawboned strength, the indolent tilt of his head, the sun glistening off his dark, silken curls. His hands were strong, slender, with the capacity for offering exquisite pleasure; she painted his hands with care. And when she started rendering his face, the modulation of shadow and plane, the purity of bone structure, the fine straight nose and sensuous mouth, she worked feverishly, intent on capturing his image before the light changed. She took enormous pains with the eyes, layering her brush strokes, adding color on color, wanting to show the depth and character, the sparkling amusement, the quixotic temperament that charmed and lured. And at the last she added the stitches over his right eye, lightly, a mere dash of color, a remembrance for her of the sea battle.

Beau emptied half a bottle while she worked, politely asking on occasion how much longer, stirring restlessly from time to time, shifting his pose, but obliging with relative good grace for a man of energy.

"The face is almost done," Serena offered when last he inquired, consoling him. "I'm starting your body now. It won't take as long."

"Are we doing erotica?" he asked, his smile insinuating.

"Not if I want to show this anywhere."

"You're showing it . . . as a portrait?"

"An anonymous one, darling. Unless you wish to be on display to the world."

"I haven't done that for a while."

"Growing up are we?" she teased.

"Marginally," he lightly replied. "Are you finished yet?"

She laughed. "Stay still for another fifteen minutes and then I can go on without you."

"That sounds familiar."

"Hush," she said. "I'm too busy for that."

Pouring himself another drink, he lay back with a sigh.

But a few minutes later, he abruptly stood. "Sorry, I need a break." And strolling over he stood behind her surveying the painting while she continued to work, defining the shadows on the muscled legs, adding a burnt ocher to the darkest shading, highlighting an area with a sweeping line of cadmium yellow. "You're as good as Gainsborough," he said after a few minutes of contemplation. "Better than Reynolds or Romney. I see a lucrative future for you."

"Thank you. You've a good eye. Reynolds is as dull as the dead marbles he copies."

"I do have a good eye, don't I," he murmured, moving closer.

She felt his presence behind her, felt the light, skimming kiss on the back of her neck. "And this pretty young artist on my terrace is as good as it gets," he murmured.

"Let me finish the body before the light changes," she urged. "I can work on the background later."

"No problem." And he strolled away to gaze at the sea.

But he was back very shortly like a restless child, standing behind her, his body brushing hers so she felt his arousal. "The light will be the same tomorrow." He lifted the paintbrush from her fingers. "Let me show you the view from the west terrace where the shade is more pleasant." And setting her brush aside, he took her by the hand and led her down a short range of stairs into a bougainvillea-shaded portico with a chaise.

"You have no patience," she softly chided, moving away to look at the view.

"About some things," he murmured, watching her pad barefoot across the worn marble.

"About sex," she said, turning back to him.

He smiled. "That's one of them."

"You've been indulged too long."

"Are you going to pout if I take you away from your work?"

"No," she replied, inhaling the perfumed air. "I'd always rather be with you."

She had no subterfuge; he found it charming. "I could hurry."

"As long as my pleasure isn't stinted."

He tipped his head and gazed at her with teasing scrutiny. "You expect satisfaction every time?"

"Every time," she declared, swinging her arms like a happy child. "Or I'll have to find a new dance partner."

"They'd have to get by my dueling pistols."

"I should look for men who are excellent marksmen then."

"You're much too saucy; I'm not sure I like that in a woman."

"The only thing you like in a woman, darling, is accessibility."

"An endearing quality. Did I mention nudity? You're overdressed."

She laughed and pulled off the loose shift she wore and opened her arms to him.

He gazed at her for a moment, struck by her cheerful abandon, wondering how she'd survived as a drudge in the Tothams' household for so long. Glad she'd been set free for him.

And when he reached out and pulled her into his arms and held her close, he thought for a moment he heard Gillian welcoming him to her home.

"Let's stay here forever," Serena whispered, her chin on his chest, her eyes summer-sky blue and adoring.

"If the war stopped we could."

"Let's stay a *long* time anyway."

"Yes," he said, though he knew his orders for Palermo were pressing. "Tell me what you'd like to do."

"Make love to you and paint. Paradise on earth."

"Leave out the painting for my paradise."

"You're single-minded."

"With you I am." And he kissed her then as he'd never kissed a woman, with genuine affection, with delight separate from passion. It was strangely appealing; he was surprised.

"Have you ever thought about having children?" she asked in the sweet afterglow of that tender kiss.

He gelt a jolt of terror run down his spine. "Maybe . . . a very long time from now," he said.

"Did I alarm you?" She'd heard the sudden reserve in his voice.

"No, but let me find the sponges. I'm not planning on becoming a father today."

She was lying on the chaise when he returned, her body pale in the scented shade. "Sorry to have panicked you."

"It's not panic."

"Fear?"

"That's it," he said with a small smile. "I'd be a terrible father and a worse husband."

"Is that a warning?" Merriment shone in her eyes.

"Could we change this conversation? It's having an unfriendly effect on my libido."

"Like a new form of contraception?"

"Damn right." And sitting down beside her, he lay back in a restless sprawl. Placing the packet of sponges on her stomach, he said, "I don't think I can do it."

"Then I'll have to put you at ease or tempt you or both," she lightly challenged, lifting the small muslin bag, opening the drawstring top. Taking out one of the pieces of sponge she'd cut into a convenient shape to fit inside her, she held it up for him to see. "Why don't you watch this," she suggested, "to reassure yourself. Now pay attention, darling," she genially declared. "I'm taking this impregnable sponge," she went on with a smile, "and placing it here." Her fingers slipped inside her vagina and pressed the sponge upward. "Would you like to check it to see if it's in all the way?" she softly asked.

He looked at her for a moment, his gaze drifting down her body. He shook his head. "I need a drink."

"Courage?"

"Delay."

"I have the impression none of your ladies have asked you about having children?"

"No."

He was deathly quiet, almost grave. She was startled at the change in him. "Why don't I get your brandy for you?" she said, rising from the chaise. "And stop worrying. I don't want a child any more than you do." Her smile was pleasant, comforting. "My question was one of curiosity—no more."

"Good," he said, but he didn't smile back.

But he did later when she walked down the stairs into his line of vision, his mouth curving into a wide, captivated smile that erased his faint frown. "This is your idea of temptation?"

"Liquor, nudity, and sweets. How can you go wrong?" She struck a languid pose short feet away, the brandy bottle half raised to him in salute, his glass in her other hand, and brilliant against her pale skin glistened two marzipan cherries molded over her nipples—delicious ornaments for her plump, ripe breasts.

"The question now is what should I do first," he playfully intoned.

"Your eunuch mood has passed?"

"That bright red is very attractive," he politely declared, his wicked grin saying something very different.

"I thought you might like the cherries. Did I say they're soaked in brandy?"

"A woman of intelligence," he murmured.

"He approves too," she softly said.

His gaze flicked down to his rising erection. "Marzipan is one of his favorites."

"You have to have one drink first before you can touch me."

"Do I now," he lazily drawled.

"If you want the full experience, Lord Rochefort, I'd recommend it."

"I've heard that phrase a great number of times in the brothels of the world." His voice held a new wariness. "What is this going to cost me?"

"Nothing you can't afford. Just the use of him," she gently said, gesturing with the empty glass at his fully erect penis. "One drink. How can it hurt when you've emptied most of this bottle already?" Pouring a glassful, she held it out to him.

He hesitated a flashing moment, vigilant after too many women wanting things from him he didn't care to give.

"I'm harmless," Serena said.

"Yes and no," he murmured, taking the glass from her. She would have been far more harmless had he wished to discard her after two days in his normal pattern.

"Now drink it."

"Is it poisoned?"

"With love," she purred, smiling.

"What kind of love?"

"Sex love."

His grin flashed, familiar, warm. "To your health, mademoiselle," he silkily drawled, and lifted the glass to his mouth.

"Am I allowed to touch you now?" she teased.

"Be my guest," he said with a wave of his hand, his mood abruptly altered. And when she straddled his hips and smiled at him a moment later from very close range, he delicately touched her marzipaned nipple and said, "Dessert."

Reclining on the chaise, he drank his brandy leisurely, savoring the sight and scent of her, reaching up to touch her lightly, his fingers brushing the flaring swell of her breast, sliding upward to the warm hollow behind her ear, slipping down her jaw and across her mouth. "You could bring a eunuch to orgasm," he whispered, stroking the delectable fullness of her bottom lip.

"I thought I might have to."

"A temporary fit of terror."

"Since abated."

"Oh yes," he huskily breathed.

She could feel his erection on her back, the warm, velvety skin rubbing against her in a leisurely rhythm. And when she leaned forward to take his empty glass, his penis slid sensuously between her buttocks. "Now for dessert," she murmured, setting the glass aside, lifting her breast slightly so the bright red cherry grazed his mouth. "Take your time. . . ." she murmured, a torrid undertone in her words.

He did. He sucked away the sweet confection with deliberation and finesse and then licked off all the syrupy residue left on her nipples, shifting back and forth between her thrusting breasts, scrupulously democratic in his ministrations, fair and equitable and so exquisitely tactile, she suddenly climaxed in a fierce, panting tremor.

"You're so easy," he teased, sliding his tongue across the underside of her breast before falling back against the soft cushions. "And safe."

Her eyes were shut, the air felt like silk on her heated skin, her body strummed and throbbed like the hum of bees on a hot summer day. And she wondered with both languor and a ripple of alarm whether she'd ever have enough of him. Then his words registered in her brain. "Safe?" she queried, opening her eyes.

"You can't possibly get pregnant doing that."

"You're fixated."

"Damned if I'm not," he grudgingly murmured, talk of babies and romance like a nail in his brain.

A small flare of annoyance disrupted Serena's blissful reverie. "I'm *not* intent on marrying you."

"I've heard that before."

"I don't care what you've heard before," she said, glaring at him. "So are we not making love again? Is that what you're saying?"

"Jesus, Serena, relax."

"I find it offensive to be compared to all the grasping women in your past. And I don't care to be penalized for their sins."

"Penalized?" The word trembled between them. "Is there some quota here?"

"No, I suppose not, but . . ."

"Lord," he said, grinning, "I've fallen into nirvana. You want to fuck *more?*"

"I don't know about more, but . . . well . . . you can't

expect me to get a taste of this delicious pastime and then just stop."

"Convince me." Amusement shone in his eyes.

"Meaning?"

"I don't know if I care to make love again," he said.

"Are you serious?"

He arched his eyebrows and shrugged.

"Beau—" she began heatedly.

"You probably could change my mind." His drawl was honeyed and blissfully wicked.

"Oh." A tiny small sound of revelation. Then she smiled and arched her back and stretched leisurely. "Let me think of something," she murmured. "Something safe," she delicately noted.

"As long as you're happy, you mean." He smiled faintly.

"Isn't that the point?" Her gaze was as innocent as virtue. "Now if you'll just move down a little," she said, with a demure little pat on the chaise cushion, "I'll continue my pursuit of happiness."

And when Beau slid lower on the chaise, Serena rose up on her knees and said, "Look up."

He chuckled when he lifted his gaze to her lush genitals poised above his face. "Are those for me?" he cordially inquired.

"There are only two."

"I see that, and very pretty too." Two marzipan cherries were lodged in her pink pouty labia. "If you want me to taste them, you'll have to come closer," he whispered.

She did and he did and it grew very hot in the shade of the portico as he licked and ate at her and tasted the sweetness of Serena Blythe and marzipan candy. Her orgasm trembled down her braced thighs that time and up to her brain in a slow, sensuous burn and he held her up so she wouldn't crumple on top of him and said, "You're welcome," when she thanked him.

She licked his belly later at the place where she'd been seated and the marzipan had liquified and then moved down his body, following the feathery trail of dark hair that ran through his navel and down his lower stomach to curl luxuriantly at the base of his rigid penis.

He stopped breathing for a second when her mouth touched the glistening tip and deciding in a split second that he'd been celibate far too long—at least five hours—he pulled her up, rolled her under him, and damning the consequences, proceeded to live up to the unspecified but expected quota.

He slid into her so easily, he felt as though he'd found his long-lost home and she said, "Thank you" again in a whisper that further roused him, her innocent gratitude, her open need for him intoxicating, her hunger for sex, for him, like an aphrodisiac.

She was at his mercy, craving what he could give her but he wasn't so sure his appetite for her was any less dependent. He'd already decided to stay at the villa as long as the dispatches would allow. And in his current heedless disregard for even the stark fear of fatherhood as his body plunged and thrust into her, he considered alternatives for delivering the messages to Palermo.

But then she whispered, "I need your cock inside me all the time," and such protracted erotic possibility erased all but feverish sensation from his mind.

14

At the same time Serena was painting Beau, a footman was depositing mail on the large partner's desk in the office at Seth House. The door closed quietly behind him and the Duke and Duchess of Seth smiled at each other over their papers. Outside a light rain fell, the windows were streaked and dappled with water, lamps illuminated the desktop where Sinjin and Chelsea were going over bloodstock reports. Tomorrow's sale at Tattersalls' held some racers of promise.

"A letter from Damien," Sinjin said, lifting out a folded sheet from the stack of correspondence. "And here's one for you from Jane Maxwell," he added, handing it across the green leather desktop. "Do you want to see the invitations now?" At her refusal, he set several missives aside and continued sorting through the mail. "Why is Edward Dufferin writing to us?"

"Some hunting party I suppose," Chelsea murmured, slipping a small silver knife under the waxed seal on Jane's letter. "Did you know Vivian's in London again?"

Sinjin looked up, Damien's letter open in his hand. "Again?" His gaze was speculative for a moment before he shrugged away his curiosity. "As long as I don't have to see her, I don't care where she is. All the better for Damien, I'd say." His attention returned to his brother's letter. "A damned shame he won't divorce her," he murmured. "Beau stopped in Lisbon, Damien says. Did you know he was planning on that?"

"He didn't mention it. Jane's in Lisbon too," Chelsea noted, reading the first few lines of her note. "I thought she and Tom were still at Hammond Hill."

"He was reassigned to embassy duty in Lisbon last month," Sinjin said, his gaze racing down Damien's startling message. "Listen to this, darling. Apparently Beau's taken a fancy to a young lady and intends to dance with her tonight . . . or six—no, seven nights ago now," he added, checking the date on the letter. "Damien seems alarmed or concerned, I can't tell which; he goes on to say this girl is traveling to Italy with Beau."

Chelsea stopped reading, her brows raised in surprise, the relinquishment of her son's long-standing dance wager of less consequence than the fact that he had a woman on board the *Siren*. "Doesn't he abhor women on long sea journeys?"

"So I recall him saying," Sinjin ironically noted. "Damien describes this paragon of womanhood in glowing terms and Beau must agree if he's welcomed her aboard for the entire trip."

"Who is she?"

"A Miss Serena Blythe from Gloucestershire. She's impoverished, Damien relates, although since charming Beau, I suspect she's improved her finances."

"So cynical, dear. Are you saying she's a fortune hunter?"

"That would be my first guess."

"And your second?"

A faint smile graced his handsome face. "A cyprian with an imagination."

"So you don't think a well-bred girl could fascinate our son."

"I think he has an aversion to girls of good family. Partly it's his age. Young women bent on marriage are to be avoided when you're twenty-two."

"That would be *most* difficult aboard the *Siren*."

"Yes, wouldn't it?" Sinjin quietly said. "A very resourceful ploy by Miss Blythe."

"Like mine when I met you."

"Your proposal did have a certain, ah, shock value," Sinjin replied, the recollection bringing a smile to his face.[7]

"Perhaps it takes something inspirational to catch the attention of the Sainted Pair," she murmured, her eyes twinkling. "One has to give Miss Blythe credit for audacity."

"A powerful allure to our wild young son, I expect. Although by the time he returns, Miss Blythe will no doubt be forgotten."

"You didn't forget *me*."

"But then, darling, there's only one like you in all the world," he murmured, his voice affectionate.

"You resisted me for months."

"Until you convinced me with a dose of cantharides." He smiled at the memory of how she'd slipped the aphrodisiac in his cognac that night at Seth House.

"Resourcefulness isn't exclusively a Gloucestershire trait, darling."

"For which I consider myself the luckiest of men. A shame Damien couldn't have been so fortunate. But then," the Duke murmured, recalling his brother's attitude, "he was always too kind to women."

"Unlike you."

The Duke shrugged in a kind of apology or acknowledgment, realistic about his past and the women in it. "I was looking for different things."

"We know what you were looking for, darling, as did all of England. Do you think Damien was ever in love with Vivian?"

Sinjin gazed out the window for a moment as if trying to remember. "We weren't very close when Damien married," he finally said. "I'm not sure."

"I don't suppose there was any doubt Vivian was intent on capturing Damien's fortune."

"She didn't marry for love," Sinjin retorted, his dislike of his sister-in-law evident in his acerbic tone. "Hopefully, Damien will divorce her someday. He *did* add Emma's name to his letter in closing this time. But perhaps he's—"

"Did he *really*? Show me!"

"—only being courteous," Sinjin finished, handing the sheet to his wife.

She cast him a disbelieving look. "Damien isn't known for his spontaneity. My heavens," she exclaimed, glancing at the signature and smiling broadly. "I think you might warn the family barristers to begin lining up support in Parliament."[8]

"Let me see that again. Hmmm." His gaze scrutinized the brief signature as though willing it to speak. "If you're right, it's about time," he said, setting the letter down. "With his boys grown, away from home, why not allow himself some happiness. And I like Emma; she's good to him."

"*Everyone* would be pleased if he married Emma. He'd have to resign from his ambassadorship, though—a divorce isn't likely to be accepted abroad."

"Perhaps Vivian could die in an accident," Sinjin murmured.

Chelsea's eyes widened momentarily before casting an admonishing look at her husband. "Don't tease, Sinjin."

"Who's teasing?" he negligently drawled.

"Much as a number of people might agree with you," she admitted, "it wouldn't be proper."

His eyelids lowered marginally. "And I've always been concerned with propriety."

"Sinjin!"

"I shan't, I won't, I promise," he instantly appeased, grinning. "She's safe from me as long as she stays out of my reach. Beyond that I can't guarantee anything. Is that fair?" he playfully inquired.

Although they'd been married for years, he found he loved his wife more deeply now than he'd thought possible in his youth. And he'd not offend her more benevolent nature even if he felt Vivian's cruelty deserved retribution. "I suppose Damien's old enough to handle his wife himself."

"He probably feels he is, darling, even if you wish otherwise."

"You needn't look at me like that," he said, "with all that worry and concern. I'll behave." But he intended to see their barristers first thing tomorrow. It never hurt to have all the arrangements in place should Damien finally rid himself of his malevolent wife.

"My goodness, Jane's seen Beau too," Chelsea remarked, perusing Jane Maxwell's flowing script. "She's more discreet than Damien in her reaction; she only mentions meeting Beau and Miss Blythe outside a dressmaker's."

"Ah . . . the Gloucestershire miss will be much better dressed now. And I imagine she has a bit of new jewelry too." Sinjin was well acquainted with beautiful young ladies proficient in adding to their fortunes. His tick at modistes' and jewelers' in his youth was always a point of heated discussion with his bankers.

"Tom and Jane were also at the embassy the night Beau danced," Chelsea said. "And Miss Blythe was wearing a dazzling gown—Jane describes it as rose colored."

"Did she mention its cost?" Sinjin sardonically queried.

His wife looked up in mild remonstrance. "Jane is only politely letting us know our son is more smitten than usual."

Miss Blythe must be very good in bed, Sinjin thought; smitten wasn't a man's word.

"But no one saw them after that, Jane goes on, and now the *Siren* has sailed."

Sensible of the extraordinary inducements necessary for his son to give up a wager, Sinjin reflected the lady must have wanted to dance very much—and knew how to be convincing. Perhaps he should direct the barristers to check into Miss Blythe as well. "I *do* hope," he said, a small concern in his voice when he thought of the length of time this woman and Beau would be together until Naples, "we won't soon become grandparents." A child would be a powerful bargaining chip.

"Do you think Beau's serious about this woman?" Chelsea regarded her husband with interest.

"I think the woman may be serious about him, which worries me more. I'll write to Damien and have him send additional details."

"Perhaps Beau's found someone he loves."

"I don't begrudge him love no matter who the lady. But

I'd not like him taken advantage of by some scheming female."

"He's too much like you, dear—dare I say, ruthless about women. I doubt there's a female capable of scheming her way into his heart," she pointed out, hoping Miss Blythe's affections weren't involved, for her son's affairs were always brief. "But on the subject of scheming women," she softly said, "I have a small confession."

"Don't tell me you've already invited Vivian over."

"No."

"Thank god."

"It's something . . . more personal."

"You've overspent your allowance." He smiled. "I don't care, you know that. I'll tell Berkley to give you more."

"It's not about money."

"You bought that Arab filly we disagreed on."

"I should have but I didn't and now Kendall has her. But it's something else. Do you remember the night at Oakham when we decided to stay at that inn instead of riding back to our hunting box?"

"I remember. Fondly." His eyes warmed with memory.

"How strongly do you feel about not having more children?"

"What are you saying?" He pushed aside the papers before him on the desktop as though he needed clear space between them to understand the implications of her question.

"Tell me." She watched him intently.

"I don't want you risking your life. Some women can have children like steps each year, others can't. *You* can't." She'd lost their first child and Chelsea's last pregnancy had been difficult too.

Her heart was beating much too fast and when she spoke, her voice was lacking in volume. "I didn't use a Greek sponge that night at Oakham."

"You lied to me?" His cool tone matched his gaze.

"Everything was too heated. I wasn't rational at the time. . . . I'm sorry."

He inhaled slowly, his eyes drilling into her. "You're pregnant?"

She nodded, unable to respond to the terrible accusation in his eyes. And then she said very, very softly, "I want you to be happy about this."

"No," he growled. Drawing in a steadying breath, he shifted in his chair, restlessly raking his fingers through his glossy black hair. A baby! Dread inundated his senses. Agitated, he abruptly stood, paced two steps, stopped, swung around. "Jesus, Chelsea," he incredulously said, "Jesus!" Gazing down at her, his mind in foment, he could think only of her peril. "I would have found some other way to please you that night. Why didn't you tell me?"

"I won't ride this time," she promised in a rush, "or do any of the training work with the horses. If I hadn't ridden in those races so late, maybe I wouldn't have had problems when Sally was born."

"You don't know that. Maybe the riding had nothing to do with it," he said, frowning. "Do you think I want to lose you?" Shaken, touched to the core, he softly asked, "Are you sure? Could you be mistaken?"

"I'm sure." She spoke in very low, distressed tones. "But Sally's five now, Sinjin. I'd like another child."

He turned and walked away, standing motionless before the window, his tall form tense, unyielding as he looked down on the rain-swept square. The bare branches of the trees were dark and wet outlined against the gray sky, their spring buds still tightly curled against the cold. The melancholy day suited the melancholy news. "It shouldn't have been your decision alone," he said, bracing his hands against the cool glass, wondering how he'd live if he lost her.

"I didn't deliberately plan it. We wouldn't have stayed if the weather had been better. I'm sorry, I was thoughtless. . . . I'm sorry," she whispered. Why couldn't he be pleased the way she was?

"A September birthing," he murmured to the square outside. He remembered the night at the inn; it had snowed.

"Do you want the child?" He spoke too low to be heard, and turning around, he repeated his question, his tone raised just enough to reach her.

"Don't ask me that with such a cold look in your eyes." That he could take all the pleasure from her joy sent her voice and temper flaring. "I don't care what you think," she heatedly said. "I'm happy about the baby."

"I want midwives hired. I want them here tomorrow," he curtly said as if she hadn't spoken. "And you're not allowed to ride."

"Don't you dare give me orders." Rising from her chair, she glared at him, resentment burning in her eyes. "When you're ready to deal with this rationally, come and talk to me." And she turned to walk from the room.

Furious, he plunged after her, caught her by the arm, and spun her around before she'd moved half a dozen feet from the desk, his eyes bright with anger. "How the hell do I deal with this rationally!" he harshly exhorted. "You might be dead in September! Tell me how I set that aside and smile and tell you I'm happy," he said, flint hard, sullen.

"You're hurting me," she bristled, twin spots of color rising to her cheeks.

His hand dropped away, a muscle twitched across his cheekbones. "Don't walk out."

And they stood inches apart, the tension between them vibrating in the hushed room.

"Nothing frightens me but this," he said quietly. He ached with powerlessness—this man of wealth and power. "I want to at least minimize the risks."

"And I want you to be happy for us," Chelsea whispered, the child inside her *their* child.

He exhaled and looked up at the ceiling, at an earlier Duke of Seth allegorically portrayed in his chariot triumphant, riding to heaven. An unhappy vision in his current state of mind. His gaze swiftly jerked away, returning to his wife, whom he loved more than life itself. "I can't be happy right now," he murmured, wishing he could take back that night at Oakham.

"Could you try?" she gently asked, touching his strong hand. Their love was rare in the world of privilege where marriages were arranged for reasons of fortune and political power.

His fingers abruptly closed over hers, his grip so tight, she involuntarily squeaked in dismay but he loosened his hold only marginally. "If I try to deal with this, will you listen to the midwives?"

"How many midwives?" she asked, smiling faintly.

"As many as I can find." His smile was still sad.

"I'll try," she answered as he had.

"If something should happen to you—"

"Hush, you'll frighten the baby."

He found himself visualizing the child for the first time when she spoke of it with such certainty, but then she'd had weeks already to get used to the idea. "Sally will be jealous."

"She likes you best. You'll have to spend more time with her."

"Nell will be appalled, of course. How can you do this to me? she'll say." His mouth quirked faintly at the thought. "And Jack—"

"Will ignore it all." Each time he spoke of the baby she felt an overwhelming love for him. "Jack's indifference is at least preferable to resentment," she said, "and we could hire a new Italian dance master for Nell. Every young girl forgets all else with a pretty young man about."

"Just so long as *you* don't look at him."

"I'm sure a matron with four children would be outside his notice."

"You're still not allowed to look," he brusquely said. At thirty-one his wife was one of the most beautiful woman in London. And he'd bedded enough married ladies in the past to know that the designation matron didn't restrict amorous adventures.

"Yes, dear," she sweetly murmured. "Do you think then

this fifth child might put to rest some of those pursuing females constantly trying to gain your attention?"

"What females?" His gaze was studiously blank.

"The ones who *still* send you billets-doux."

"Pims has standing orders to toss them."

He knew. How could he not? At forty-one, he still drew every eye with his grace and beauty. "I'm reassured."

"As well you should be with a faithful husband."

"A rarity, I know. Thank you."

"You must be careful now and take no chances." His fingers tightened against the fear flooding his mind. "Promise me."

"I promise."

"No riding."

"No riding."

"And carriage rides only on well-maintained roads."

"Yes, dear."

"I'll have the stud moved down to Enfield."

"Really, that's not necessary."

"Humor me," he firmly said. "And you shouldn't be walking. I'll carry you."

She laughed at his worried expression. "Please, darling, I'm feeling quite well, but after the baby's born, you may carry her or him all you wish."

"I'd rather carry you."

"I know," she whispered, stroking his hand, which held her close. "Would you like to carry me to our bedroom now? I have this craving for kisses."

"Just kisses," he warned, her new fragility unnerving.

"Of course, just kisses," she lied. "I feel so tired suddenly . . . and you're so strong," she purred, "and we haven't made love since last night."

"I shouldn't have."

"But you did and see—I'm fine."

She kissed him as he carried her down the corridor and the maids giggled and blushed when they passed but the Duke of Seth didn't hear them, immune to the sight of servants in a house staffed by eighty. And Chelsea didn't care, her warming senses already heated with desire.

Lord Dufferin's irate letter lay unopened on the desk.

But then the Duke and Duchess of Seth already knew their eldest son was reckless and hot-tempered.

15

As the *Siren* leisurely sailed to Naples that month, Bonaparte was at Malmaison and the Tuileries, with Duroc, Lauriston, and Bourrienne, preparing for his march on Italy. The Reserve Army was being built up at Dijon with units drawn from all over France. Chambarlhac de Laubespin, forty-six years old and a former officer of the king, set out from Paris at the head of the First Division. Watrin's troops came from Nantes, joined by Loison's men from Rennes and the Chabran division. From the West Indies came Boudet, a native of Bordeaux, to take over the command of battalions formed from both experienced troops and raw recruits at the depot. Artillery and stores were being assembled at Lyons.

General Dupont was made chief of staff to Berthier, and Macdonald, senior lieutenant-general. Generals Victor, Duhesme, and Lannes were appointed lieutenant-generals. The First Consul's aide-de-camp, Marmont, was in charge of the artillery and Marescot, the inspector-general of Napoleon's army, commanded the engineers.

Murat's arrival at the Dijon headquarters was an occasion for universal rejoicing. He was a courageous and brilliant young man, happily married to Caroline, the First Consul's sister. To assist him, he had General d'Harville and 2,300 horsemen commanded by Champeaux and Kellermann, the son of the victor of Valmy.

To Dijon came a crowd of actors and musicians, the circus rider Franconi and his troupe, and Garnerin the aeronaut with his balloon. The troops quartered in the region had a very good time and there were dances in the châteaus, all the young officers full of gaiety and high spirits. Within a few short weeks Napoleon's high-stakes gamble would be in place and 60,000 troops would be poised to invade Italy.

And when all was in readiness, Napoleon would leave Paris to command the Reserve Army in person.

16

Palermo was cool and overcast when the *Siren* arrived the first week in March. Accommodations were difficult to find with the royal court displaced from Naples by the French.[9]

"There's no need to stay long," Beau had promised Serena when she'd expressed discomfort with any proximity to court life. "I'll give Damien's dispatches to the British envoy, Sir Hamilton, and even if he insists on offering his hospitality, I'll politely refuse. We should be able to sail again within a day."

"Good," she'd replied, although her feelings were torn between wanting to leave and sadness at the diminishing time left them. Once they sailed from Palermo, Florence's port at Leghorn was only two days away.

And then the man she loved would leave her.

But Beau hadn't reckoned with Lady Hamilton's interest in beautiful young men and before he'd been able to extricate himself from the British minister's home, he'd promised to bring his sailing companion and their luggage to the Hamiltons' palazzo.

"You simply can't miss our celebration dinner for Admiral Nelson, Lord Rochefort," Lady Hamilton had cried, her propensity for drama marked in her words. "He's the savior of England!"

He was, too, as anyone with the slightest interest in the war could attest. Had Nelson not defeated the French at Aboukir in the summer of '98, Napoleon would have continued unchecked on his march of conquest.

England had appeared almost on the verge of revolution that summer, so widespread had been discontent, and Boney's sound defeat and humiliation at Aboukir had been a glorious achievement. At Weymouth, where the king first received the news, he'd read Admiral Nelson's letter aloud four times to different noblemen, his excitement and relief plain. After five unsuccessful years of war with France, Britain had desperately needed that victory.

"I can't stay with the Hamiltons," Serena protested when Beau returned with their invitation.

"There's no protocol to speak of here, darling. Consider, Emma Hamilton, a blacksmith's daughter, is confidante to the queen. Quarterings on your family crest aren't a requirement at the court of the Sicilies. And if you happen to hunt, you're guaranteed the king's favor—that's almost all he does."

"However lax convention is, my position as your lover will hardly make me presentable."

He hadn't thought her that naive. "Believe me, no one will comment," he simply said. Society in Sicily was more licentious than most, although there wasn't a court in England or on the continent that didn't have mistresses prominent in society.

"Nevertheless, I'll be uncomfortable."

"You weren't at the embassy in Lisbon. A 'cousin' is no different here."

"I don't have anything to wear," she said with that female finality meant to cut short further argument.

"You have your ballgown from Lisbon, or if that doesn't suit, we'll find you something," he blandly declared, knowing her entire wardrobe from Mrs. Moore was still secreted on board the *Siren*. There had been little need for fashionable clothes or clothes at all on their voyage from Lisbon.

She shook her head. "You go to the Hamiltons'. I'll stay here."

"You can't. The men have shore leave and Remy's gone

off to Naples already. It's not safe for you to be left alone on the waterfront."

"Have you thought of everything?"

His smile was beautiful. "I've a carriage waiting outside."

Emma Hamilton had been one of the great beauties of her time, painted by the celebrated artists Romney and Lawrence on numerous occasions, her portraits displayed to admiring crowds at the Royal Society exhibits. And while she'd lost that first bloom of youth for which she'd been rightly esteemed and at thirty-eight was passing into matronly plumpness, she still had the most beautiful eyes and expressive face on seven continents.

Her manners and birth were too rustic for those in English society who viewed blue blood as the only essential to a person's worth, while her marriage to the elderly Sir Hamilton after years as his mistress was treated by many with scorn.[10] But Serena found herself liking their effusive hostess from the first.

"Come in, come in, you darling young people," Emma exclaimed on their arrival, running out to meet their carriage in the courtyard. And on being introduced to Serena, she turned to Beau and said with a sweet smile, "She's quite as lovely as your mother, Lord Rochefort. And I remember when all of London was abuzz with talk of the Scottish lass who'd captured your father's heart."

Her gaze swiveled back to Serena. "Did you enjoy Minorca?" she asked. "Lord Rochefort tells me you spent some time there."

"It was quite lovely," Serena replied, blushing at recall of their passionate interlude.

"How divine," the British envoy's wife said. "She blushes. Where did you find this charming young lady, Lord Rochefort?"

"She's a distant cousin, Lady Hamilton. From Gloucestershire. And I've promised Miss Blythe not to embarrass her with the connection."

"Then I shan't bring it up again and we'll pretend Miss

Blythe is visiting us entirely on her own. Which I wouldn't mind in the least," she said, turning to Serena. "Lord Rochefort tells me you're a painter of note."

"No ... hardly, I mean—perhaps someday, Lady Hamilton. Lord Rochefort's too kind."

"Yes, I imagine he is," she gently said, "and why shouldn't he be to a wonderful young woman like you? You may go on, Lord Rochefort, and fill Sir William in on all the dreadful talk of war." She waved Beau away with a graceful gesture. "And Miss Blythe and I will have a cozy chat about our toilettes for tonight."

Beau cast Serena a questioning glance.

"Perhaps Lady Hamilton can tell me if my ballgown will suffice," Serena said.

"Of course I will. Now leave us be, Lord Rochefort. She'll be quite safe with me. Miss Blythe will be in the Pompeii suite when you and William have finished talking."

He hesitated still.

Serena smiled. "I'm sure you and Sir Hamilton have much to discuss," she politely said. "I'm fine."

His bow was the epitome of grace. "Until later then."

Lady Hamilton escorted Serena to the Pompeii suite, and gesturing to a small table near the windows set for tea, invited her to sit down. Two maids were busy unpacking the luggage being brought into the room while the ladies drank their tea, the superb view from the window absorbing their interest and conversation.

"You needn't be nervous about dinner tonight," Emma declared when their discussion turned to Lady Hamilton's favorite subject, her lover, Admiral Nelson. "Horatio is the most gallant of men and the company will be light-hearted and gay. The queen has promised to come; you'll find her charming like her sister, Marie Antoinette, poor soul. But my dear Horatio *saved* the royal family *here,* bringing the court away from Naples during the most dire night of peril. The whole and sole confidence of their majesties reposes in dear Lord Nelson," she theatrically declared, "despite what that horrid admiralty says. My," she said, interrupting her customary lecture on the short-sighted judgment of the admiralty that was insisting Nelson leave Palermo, her gaze suddenly struck by the vast number of gowns spread about the room. "Your wardrobe is lovely, Miss Blythe."

With her back to the maids, Serena hadn't seen the display, and shifting in her chair at Emma's comment, she choked on her tea. Immediately jumping up from her chair, Lady Hamilton bustled over and began slapping Serena on the back, calling for water from the maids in an imperative voice. A few seconds later, Serena had drunk some water, recovered her breath, and was able to smile weakly and apologize.

"No need to apologize, my dear," Emma pronounced, shooing away the maids as she sank back into her chair. "No need at all. But you must tell me your dressmaker's name. Such lovely, *darling* gowns. They must be French. *However* did you get them in these times of upheaval?"

"No ... that is ... I'm sure they're not French," Serena stammered, taking in the extraordinary number of gowns piled on the bed and various pieces of furniture and she realized then why Beau had engaged a wagon for their luggage. "It would seem ... I mean—I believe a modiste in Lisbon can be credited with their creation."

"You believe?" The small drama enacted before her eyes piqued Lady Hamilton's interest; the young lady had obviously never seen her wardrobe before.

"I mean ... it was so rushed when we were in Lisbon, I don't specifically recall each gown."

"Lord Rochefort might remember," Lady Hamilton sweetly said, watching her.

"His memory for ladies' wear is quite acute," Serena replied, her temper rising, not only at consideration of his expertise in the area of female clothing, but at his arrogant presumption that he could disregard her wishes. "I'm sure he would recall all the details," she tightly said.

"Wealthy young men have a particular charm, don't you

think?" Lady Hamilton lightly said, her own experience with wealthy young men vast and varied.

"On occasion they overstep their bounds," Serena coolly replied, although her smile was gracious.

"But then they're all such children, aren't they, my dear—men, you know. I say allow them their little whims. And I must admit, dear, your charming wardrobe will quite take everyone's breath away. Do let's pick out a gown for tonight," Emma gaily said, rising from her chair. "I scarce know where to begin with such a delicious array," she added, standing for a moment in contemplation. "What color do you particularly like?"

Lady Hamilton it seemed liked a muted lavender velvet with pearls embroidered on the sleeves, the low neckline framed by a Vandyke collar of priceless cream lace. "This is the one you must wear," she declared after surveying each gown. "The queen will *love* it," she exclaimed, stroking the soft velvet. "And you must wear pearls at your throat. Horatio will adore it as well," she said. "There, it's all settled," she pronounced, with the same confidence that had brought her from her humble birth to her present position as confidante to a queen. "I'll send up my hairdresser once he's finished with me. Oh, won't it be fun! The men will cluster around you like bees."

After her hostess left, Serena allowed her fury release, pacing and fretting, her resentment building with each gown she passed in her stalking perambulations about the room, her relegation to St. Jules's harlot, with all its attendant privileges and favors, stinging her self-respect.

A dozen—no, more—twenty gowns, she counted and then, God in heaven, she realized, opening the armoire doors, there were more. *Thirty* gowns! The armoire was stuffed, the lingerie she hadn't noticed at first carefully folded in the drawers, along with silk stockings and sleeping gowns and beautiful corsets. He'd like those, of course, she fumed, her temper at tinder point. And she thought for a moment about tearing them all to shreds before cooler reason prevailed or perhaps the waste of such beauty stopped her. But she despised what he'd done—what he'd done to her.

"How dare you!" she cried when Beau finally entered the room.

"You saw the gowns," he calmly said, surveying the colorful collection scattered about the room.

"Is that all you can say—you saw the gowns?"

"Did you find the diamonds?"

"Oh!" she squealed, turning a violent shade of pink.

"I had them brought up from the yacht; in the event a brigand came aboard the *Siren* tonight, Sicily being what it is," he nonchalantly added, loosening his cravat.

"Damn you! Don't think you can calmly ignore me!" Her hands were clenched at her sides, her spine rigid.

"When you get rich on your painting commissions, you can pay me back," he said, shrugging out of his coat as though he were immune to her fury. "It's not that much with the Portuguese exchange rate," he dismissively went on, "and with the queen in attendance tonight, I thought you might like a choice of gowns."

"You *thought*." She was quivering with rage. "Did you ever think what I might like?"

"I know what you like," he softly said, tossing his coat on the bed atop a gauzy green confection. "And after Minorca," he lazily murmured, his smile sinful, "I've added a few more subtleties to the list."

"Everything isn't about sex," she hissed.

It's about money and power too, he cynically thought. "I know, darling," he murmured, his voice placating, soothing, his graceful hands unwrapping his cravat from around his neck. "And I'm sorry if I offended you."

"Sorry?" Her voice was scarcely a whisper. She was without words, her rage trembling down her nerve endings, his casualness outrageous.

"I'm very, *very* sorry," he gently said, standing a short distance away, relaxed, the strength of his powerful tanned neck and chest visible at the open neck of his shirt, his expression bland or expectant or perhaps amused.

"I'm not your tart."

"I know, of course not." He took a step toward her.

"What are you doing?"

"Nothing." Moving forward another step, he watched her retreat. "Did you like your tea with Lady Hamilton?"

"No . . . yes . . . it was . . . tea, for god's sake. Don't think you're going to touch me," she snapped, easing around a small table behind her.

"I don't want to fight over some stupid dresses," he quietly said, following her, his polished boots soundless on the fine carpet.

"Let's fight about the diamonds then."

"What diamonds?"

"The ones you were supposed to return."

"I'm not sure. Maybe I did," he lied; she obviously hadn't found them.

"Stop!" She held her hands up, palms out.

And he stopped, diverted momentarily by her sharp fiat. And then he softly said, "Don't want to," and lunged for her, lifting her off her feet in a great sweeping hug, twirling her around, smiling down at her. "Cut up the dresses into little pieces for all I care, but don't be angry, lollipop," he playfully murmured. "I apologize for everything—everything," he cheerfully added. And he kissed her and laughed a second later at her surprise and then he kissed her again—a sportive, baiting kiss at first, full of jest and amorous challenge but before long it changed into a heated, devouring kiss, a sighing, breathless, lingering kiss. And when at last he set her down, she found her agitation had indelibly changed.

"I don't want to fight," he murmured, his mouth brushing hers, his hands gently massaging her back.

"And I don't want to be treated like your newest whore." Her voice quivered with more than anger now.

"Never," he whispered, touching the corner of her mouth with a butterfly kiss.

"You embarrassed me."

"I'm sorry." His mouth drifted leisurely over the curve of her upper lip.

"Beau, listen to me." She struggled in his embrace.

"I'm listening. You don't want the dresses, so throw them out. Hmm . . . you taste good," he murmured, restraining her easily, fitting her body more snugly against his.

He felt delicious as always and tempting . . . so damnably tempting, it took a moment to regain her train of thought. "Lady Hamilton already picked one out for me to wear tonight."

"Keep that one then and toss the others." His lower body stirred against hers, his erection rampant.

"You'll say anything, won't you, when you're in rut?"

"Not anything." There was amusement in his voice. "Have you seen the mirror over the bed?"

"There's no mirror."

Releasing her marginally, he held her at arm's length. "There's a mirror under the shirring of the canopy," he softly said.

"How do you know?" A flash of pique shone in her eyes.

"Sir William told me."

"That's quick, Rochefort."

"It's the truth; I haven't stayed here before."

"Am I supposed to be diverted now by the possibilities of a mirror?"

"Why are we fighting? This is so trivial, lollipop. If the gowns are a problem, we'll get rid of them."

"It's not just about the gowns," Serena said with a small sigh, wondering if she was expecting too much from a man who viewed women as objects of pleasure and her new wardrobe as insignificant.

"I know." The jest was gone from his voice.

"Really?"

He nodded. "I misjudged your—"

"Reaction?"

"No, your sense of respect. And while we may not agree on the definition"—he'd lived too long in the Ton to be overly concerned with reputations of any kind—"I understand your feelings."

"You're insightful after all."

"Just not obtuse, darling."

"No, definitely not that," she softly replied. This man understood refinement of sensation better than most.

He heard the hint of clemency in her voice, the auspicious tempering of her resentment, and having learned long ago how to take advantage of a lady's compliance, he kissed her with that fine nuance between tenderness and temptation that was his special gift.

"I'm still going to make you pay," she whispered when his mouth finally lifted from hers, desire alive inside her.

"Anything," he breathed. "I'm at your command."

"I shall flirt unmercifully tonight."

"Then I shall too." Mocking eyes met hers.

"You're not allowed. You must watch me as your penance."

"Cut out my heart instead," he said with whimsy. "How can I watch you tease other men when I adore you so."

"Do you really?" Artless and flattered, she forgot that a man of his notoriety adored women indiscriminately but never for long.

"I do . . . desperately," he whispered, pulling her closer. "So you must stay by my side tonight and not look at other men and make me happy."

"Then you must do as much for me."

"I don't like men—that way." His dark eyes were teasing until she punched him in the stomach and a delectable heat replaced the amusement. "And in terms of women," he softly said, "I prefer you above all."

She had no experience combating such fluent charm, nor had any woman, experienced or no with Beau St. Jules's potent beauty so near. "You won't look at other women?"

"Never." His mouth warmed her temple and then her cheek and as it gently covered her mouth, he whispered, "I promise."

A moment later, he tossed a half dozen gowns on the

floor without regard for their delicacy or cost and lifting Serena, placed her gently on the bed. Lowering himself over her, he pushed her skirts up, settled with the ease of much practice between her thighs, his breeches already unbuttoned and guiding his hard length to her dewy wet cleft, he murmured, "Welcome to Sicily."

His hard length slid into her with excruciating slowness so she felt her body opening to him with a degree of ecstasy she marveled at, and she wondered if he knew something about Sicily she didn't. His body was warm through the fine lawn of his shirt, heated her flesh, her bare thighs rubbed against his nankeen breeches, the soft leather of his boots brushed her calves. The powerful rhythm of his lower body, driving, plunging, eradicated all but shuddering sensation. The panting shock, the pervasive need, the acute, staggering pleasure—all were beyond the ability of her consciousness to comprehend. Always . . . always with him she felt it.

And she wasn't alone in her rare, attenuated pleasure; Beau St. Jules wasn't so sure she hadn't spoiled him for other women. A heretic thought he quickly discarded for more immediate sensations. He pressed deeper and she cried out in pleasure. He pressed deeper still and she came as she always did, swiftly, with little panting moans that stirred his libido, that excited him and brought him harder, that propelled his own hurtling, shuddering climax.

He brought her to orgasm twice more in quick succession, a kind of dazed surfeit melting her limbs at the last and then he made love to her with measured languor, sustaining each soul-stirring sensation for prolonged moments, curbing her impetuous haste, making her wait until he knew she couldn't wait any longer. And when she'd climaxed in a wild exaltation, he only paused briefly before beginning again.

"No, no . . ." she whispered. "No." And half stupefied, she gazed at him and saw herself in the mirror above, her eyes languid, sated.

"Yes," he murmured, sliding back into her. "Just a little more . . ."

Perhaps it mattered that there would be men tonight

wanting her, perhaps he wished to leave his mark on her because of that or perhaps he only wanted to keep her in his arms and under him, impaled on his virility because the degree of satisfaction and bliss was so intoxicating.

And later when she was replete beyond measure, he sat with her in his arms in a chair near the window while she slowly returned to the cooler reality of twilight in Palermo. The overcast sky turned somber gray and then darker still as evening fell and he talked quietly to her as one would to a sleepy child, telling her stories of the officials and royals, nobles and odd characters in Sicilian society. Making the court seem strangely real and unreal at the same time the way picture books bring an unknown land to life within a narrow confine. He explained the well-known ménage in Sir Hamilton's household. Lady Hamilton and Admiral Nelson, lovers and in love, enjoyed the friendship and favor of her husband. Sir Hamilton, British Envoy Extraordinary and Minister Plenipotentiary at the court of Naples for twenty years, at sixty-nine and in ill health, understood both the beauty and corruption of the world and recognized the uselessness of jealousy.

Queen Marie Caroline, "the only man in Naples," as Bonaparte had described her, had been longing for revenge against the French ever since her sister, Marie Antoinette, had been guillotined. She'd already asked her son-in-law, the Austrian emperor, to send her a good general who could put some energy into what passed for the Neapolitan army. It was she, in fact, who virtually ruled the kingdom since her husband avoided royal duties. He was passionately devoted to the slaughter of animals and fornication, which left little time for the business of ruling. "The queen's intelligent, devious, devout, and proud of her white skin and white hands. You might want to compliment her on them," Beau said, "but avoid any discussion of the French," he warned.

What he didn't warn her against was the overwhelming number of women who seemed to know him personally.

When they entered the reception room at the Palazzo Reale that evening, Beau was immediately surrounded by a rapt audience of fawning females inquiring into his plans. How long would he be staying in Palermo? In Naples? Since the *lazzaroni,* the mob, had taken control, the city was dangerous. Would he dance later or play cards? Did he remember where they'd met? Could he be persuaded to sit by them at dinner?

Holding Serena firmly by the hand, he fielded the flirtatious demands and questions as graciously as he could. Her anger became a palpable energy at his side after the Countless Niollo shamelessly reminded him of their rendezvous at Capri last year. Ignoring Francesca's insolence, Beau said, No, he wouldn't be staying long in Palermo, nor in Naples either and he was promised to Miss Blythe for the evening. It was her first evening in Palermo. A regretful sigh drifted through the throng along with less benign reactions to the beautiful, superbly dressed Englishwoman at his side—icy glares; heated, angry looks; snide, impertinent comments having to do with boudoirs and expertise.

He extricated them from his former lovers in short order but Serena's silence warned him that a profound degree of delicacy was going to be required to restore the agreeable companionship they'd enjoyed before coming to the palace.

"I told you I didn't wish to come to court," Serena hissed, trying to free her hand from his, smiling artificially at Emma, who was waving at them from across the room.

"If Admiral Nelson wasn't being honored tonight we might have refused," he said. "Here they come. We should be able to leave in three or four hours. Admiral, how nice to see you again. And Emma, you look ravishing in blue." Her dress was decorated with nautical themes in honor of her lover's achievements; the bandeau around her forehead was emblazoned with Nelson and Victory. "May I introduce Miss Blythe to you, Admiral? Miss Blythe, Admiral Nelson, England's greatest hero."

Nelson was a small man, not remarkable in person although he was dressed in full regalia tonight, all his honors and medals adorning his uniform. The empty sleeve of his right arm, amputated after the battle of Santa Cruz, was pinned to his chest with the Star of the Order of Bath. A curate's son who'd made his way up the perilous ladder of promotion by boldness and bravery, he had a quietness about him that belied his exalted position. "It's an honor to meet you, Admiral," Serena said, bowing with grace.

"Isn't she just adorable, Horatio?" Emma said, her hand resting on her lover's arm. "I told you she had the sweetest smile."

Serena blushed at such fulsome praise.

"And she blushes too. Isn't that wonderful."

"Like an English rose," Nelson said with an adoring smile for his mistress, then turned back to Serena. "I'm afraid you'll find Sicily quite different from home."

"But a stalwart ally to England," Lady Hamilton interposed. "Thanks to Horatio's presence."

"Nothing can console the queen but my promise not to leave them." The Admiral's weather-beaten skin creased into a faint smile. At forty, he looked much older, the loss of upper teeth cautioning against smiling broadly, the sight in one eye irreparably damaged from shrapnel, his other eye partially filmed over, his hair completely white. "Spring is the very best time here," he went on. "I hope you enjoy your visit."

"Thank you, your grace." Beau addressed him with the courtesy accorded his new title, Duke of Brontë, which had been recently given to him by King Ferdinand.

"Lady Hamilton is making our stay exceedingly pleasant," Serena added.

While Emma beamed, the admiral turned away to listen to an equerry and moments later he and Lady Hamilton took their leave to wait on the queen.

"He doesn't look like a hero. He's so small and soft-spoken," Serena said, her pique with Beau forgotten in the company of so great a man. Nelson's name and victories had been feted in England for years, beginning with his victory over the Spanish Fleet at Cape St. Vincent, followed soon after by Aboukir. The Lord Mayor had given a banquet in his honor at the Guildhall, the king had received him and invested him with the Order of Bath, a knighthood had been bestowed on him and then a barony, the East India Company had rewarded him with ten thousand pounds, schoolchildren were given holidays on news of his victories, church bells rang, bonfires were lit, special prayers said and songs composed.[11]

"His personal touch as a leader sets him above other commanders," Beau said. "His men will fight for him against any odds. But he likes his acclaim as well. Watch Emma show him off tonight. It pleases him."

And the dinner was a glorious fete for the admiral with speeches and songs and sonnets proclaiming his victories. The queen presented him with a diamond-hilted sword for his rescue of the court from Naples. To the accompaniment of the court orchestra Emma performed "See the Conquering Hero Comes." Several local officers presented their thanks to the admiral in flattering speeches. Fireworks completed the festivities.

After dinner Serena was presented to the queen. At forty-eight, having borne eighteen children, eight of whom had survived, Marie Caroline was not a prepossessing woman and at best the Hapsburgs were no more than attractive, but she was gracious to Serena, and more than gracious to Beau, taking him aside for a few minutes of personal conversation.

"Another conquest?" Serena asked when Emma and the queen strolled away to mingle with their other guests.

"I've known her for years," Beau blandly replied. "With our stables outside Naples, the Neapolitan court is fairly familiar to me."

"A familiar of the queen," she said. "Does that require any special duties?"

"She likes young men," he casually noted. "You'll see several about her tonight—but not me."

"So very kind of you, Lord Rochefort to be so restrained. But tell me, is there a woman here you *haven't* bedded?"

He wasn't likely to answer that question, at least not honestly, and his smile was sweetly boyish. "I've reformed since meeting you, darling."

"That's not precisely an answer."

"The music is beginning. Would you like to dance?"

"I thought you didn't like to dance."

"I do with you."

"All the females making eyes at you are hopeful as well. I'd say you're going to be much in demand on the dance floor."

"*You* dance with me instead."

How could he so casually dismiss all the women, how could he ignore her jealousy? The result of long practice, she suspected, which only nettled her more. "I particularly dislike the Countess Niollo," she moodily said, the stylish vixen currently in her line of vision.

"You have to overlook Francesca. She's known for her boldness."

"*You* apparently didn't overlook her."

"I didn't know you last year. Oh, hell," he muttered. The lady in question was now bearing down on them in a flutter of sheer white muslin that only minimally concealed her voluptuous form.

"Darling," she cooed, her mouth lush, crimson, her smile intimate, her greeting disregarding Serena and the entire ballroom of guests. "You know how I love to dance, my scrumptious Glory. Come . . ." And she held her hand out to him.

"I've promised the dance to Miss Blythe," Beau said, declining with a courteous smile.

"Why don't I claim the young lady's hand instead," General Mack interposed. The handsome Austrian noble sent by the Hapsburg court to command the Neapolitan army, arrived a half step behind the Countess Niollo.

"How perfect, Karl," the countess purred, touching the general's arm with an affectionate little squeeze that couldn't be mistaken for casual friendship. "Dear Glory and I haven't seen each other for far too long. I'm sure this little miss would much prefer dancing with a general."

"She wouldn't." Beau's voice was flat, curt. He knew

Baron Karl Mack von Leiberich; the man was a rake and a scoundrel who spent more time with women than his troops.

"I'd love to dance," Serena announced looking up at the general and smiling prettily.

"If you'll excuse us, Rochefort," the army commander said, his voice laced with derision. "I'll show the lady how we"—he hesitated an insinuating small second—"waltz in Palermo."

Beau's mouth was set in a thin straight line, his temper barely leashed. And he held Serena's gaze for one flashing moment before she fluttered her folded fan at him and walked away.

"She seems to have a mind of her own, darling," the countess purred. "A large measure of her appeal, I'm sure. Would you like to beat me tonight, dear Glory, and release all that frustration?"

"It's a thought, Francesca," Beau muttered, his gaze on the couple whirling away. Their blond heads were far too close, their smiles too intimate. His rage grew so intense, he flexed his fingers to ease his tension.

"Dance with me," the countess whispered. "Or better yet, come away with me. I was lustful from the moment I saw you tonight; you know what you do to me—those days in Capri . . ." She sighed, swaying closer so he could feel the swell of her breasts against his arm.

He should go, he thought, and a month ago he would have without hesitation. One woman hardly differed from another then, his libido indiscriminating, sexual release the ultimate goal, pleasure a by-product of the amorous game.

Why *didn't* he go?

His gaze swiftly passed from Serena to the countess and back again, as if the comparison or the lack of it would answer his question. But nothing fell so conveniently into place and yet, he knew, gut-deep, that he couldn't leave Serena in that rakehell's arms.

"You're jealous," Francesca murmured, surprised.

He turned back to her. "Don't be ridiculous."

"She's very fresh." No fool, the countess.

"She's no younger than you."

"Ah—and yet . . ." murmured the lady he'd made love to for a fortnight in Capri last year, her understanding keen. She glanced at the dance floor. "Karl will eat her alive."

Beau smiled for the first time. "I don't think so."

"So she keeps you under control," Francesca softly mused. "A formidable woman beneath that pale blondness and pastel velvet."

"She keeps me interested."

"Harder yet, darling, for a man of your amusements. Where did you find her?"

"She's a distant connection," he smoothly replied.

"Very distant, I suspect. How polite you are, Rochefort, when you're never polite."

"She needs protection," he said, his gaze flicking back to the dancers. "She's not familiar with this world."

"All the better for her. Have you told her how dull it all is and only glorious men like you mitigate the boredom?"

He looked at her quizzically. "You should marry again, Francesca."

"Are you proposing?"

His eyelids lowered gently and his gaze, half shuttered, was forbearing. "You know better than that. I like my freedom."

"And I mine. Thank god the count died before I killed him. He was the most annoying man. And if I were you, my sweet, I wouldn't leave that young miss out there too long with Karl. His suave golden charm has turned many a young lady's head."

"Perhaps you could take him off my hands tonight."

She tipped her head flirtatiously. "As a personal favor?"

"As a personal favor."

"I'll expect a suitable reward once she's, er, gone wherever the women in your life eventually go. Your word on it?"

"My word on it."

"Well then," she said, making a trifling adjustment to the extremely low neckline of her gown, any more forcible movement likely to release her bounteous breasts from their moorings, "let's see if Karl notices my new gown."

"What gown?" Beau sardonically murmured.

"Precisely. How pleasant that these naked Grecian styles are in fashion while I'm still young enough to take advantage of them. And just to make it interesting—a small wager? Will these breasts overcome that sweet innocence?"

"It's only a question of time, darling," Beau drawled, knowing General Mack's tastes. "I'll put a monkey on thirty seconds."[12]

"I'll have him netted in twenty and then you owe me a night of special entertainment."

He hesitated, understanding her interpretation of the word "special."

"Not necessarily this visit, darling, any time," she offered, her talent for understanding men her greatest accomplishment.

"Done."

And when Beau escorted the Countess Niollo out onto the dance floor, they hadn't waltzed for more than a few bars before intercepting the general and Serena and bringing them to a halt.

"Karl, darling," the countess exclaimed in breathy accents, "you simply must dance with me. Don't you remember we danced to this song in Vienna last summer." Inhaling with a captivating buoyancy as if recalling the great fun they'd had, brought her splendid breasts in imminent danger of spilling out of her bodice, their ripe weight straining against the sheer, flimsy muslin of her gown.

The general was mesmerized; he had the look of a trencherman offered a bounteous banquet.

"Don't you just adore Vienna in the summer?" Francesca murmured. "All that sultry heat and whipped cream on all the iced drinks . . ."

"I particularly like the whipped cream," Beau acknowledged when it appeared the general was unable to speak.

"Karl and I went up into the mountains one day, didn't we, Karl," the countess reminded him, sliding her fingertip over the gold braid on his tunic collar. "It was so cool and refreshing. We swam. Do you remember, darling?" she went on, knowing he'd not forgotten their wanton play. The countess took the general's hand. "If you don't mind, Lord Rochefort, I'd dearly like to have Karl to myself."

"She's practically undressed," Serena said, watching the couple dance away. "And you put her up to this I suppose."

"They're old friends," Beau noncommittally replied.

"I could tell. All those allusions to heat and whipped cream weren't very subtle."

"Karl isn't a very subtle person, unfortunately. But he dances well, as does everyone at the Hapsburg court. Did you enjoy yourself?"

"You needn't be so smug about your little scheme. I was considering exposing my bosom and making poor Karl choose."

"First I wouldn't have allowed it and second," Beau said, grinning, his gaze straying to her luscious breasts mounded above her fashionable lace-trimmed décolletage, "decisions always overwhelm General Mack, as anyone familiar with his command of the Neapolitan army will tell you."

She smiled. "So I must content myself with you."

"I'll see what I can do to keep you amused." His gaze quickly surveyed the reception room, her tempting breasts bringing to mind more interesting uses of his time than playing the gentleman at court. "Do you want to stay or go?"

"Will anyone notice if we leave?"

"Not if we stroll out onto the terrace first."

Discreetly making their escape, they walked hand in hand back to the Palazzo Palagonia through the Reale gardens, a sliver of moon lighting their way.

"Forgive me if I spoiled your evening," he mockingly drawled, swinging her hand, "but you wouldn't have liked Karl anyway. His sexual repertoire's without finesse."

She glanced up at his profile and saw his smile flash in the semidarkness. "So you saved me from a dull evening of uneventful intercourse."

"More or less."

"But then I never intended to bed him anyway," Serena sweetly said.

"Really." His voice was mild.

"You must be thinking of the other women you know."

"Really," he repeated, a hint of astonishment flavoring the word.

"The general was very pretty but too empty-headed, darling. And he kept calling me Miss Blight. You've quite spoiled me, Rochefort," she playfully murmured, "for other men."

"Really," he said once more, this time so softly she didn't hear. And for a man who considered sexual congress as a benign form of social intercourse, strangely, her words warmed his heart.

The *Siren* left port very early the next morning in the event Serena might change her mind about the general. But if asked, Beau would have said it was necessary to lift anchor that early in order to catch the tide.

17

On March 5, the same day the *Siren* sailed for Leghorn, Bonaparte at last disclosed his plans to his generals. General Massena, the commander-in-chief of the Army of Italy, received the following directive:

> I am collecting a Reserve Army at Dijon, which I shall command in person. In eight or ten days I shall send you one of my ADC's with the plan of operations for the coming campaign, when you will see that your role will be important and within the means at your disposal. During March and April, if I were in your place, I should have four-fifths of my force, say 40,000, in Genoa. Then I should have no fear of the enemy capturing Genoa. The months of May and June are another matter, but by that time we shall have started our campaign and the instructions which I send you in ten days will serve as a guide.... Finally, I repeat, I feel you are in a strong position. Make the most of it. In the positions we hold, we cannot be beaten if we really want to win. Remember our great days! Fall on the enemy with all your force as soon as he makes a move.

The French invasion plan of Italy was en train.

18

On their voyage to Leghorn, Serena felt as though time were precious. She found herself gazing at Beau with a more discerning regard, wanting to remember exactly how he looked as he stood or walked or lay, how he smiled, how his strong hands gripped the wheel of the *Siren* with the same grace as when they moved over her body, how he gazed at her with affection, with passion. She needed the memories to sustain her in the wilderness of her coming solitude.

She'd touch him at odd times to comfort herself and he'd glance at her and smile and her heart would ache with sadness. Too soon . . . too soon—he'd be gone from her life.

And when the busy port finally came into sight on the second day, she was overwhelmed with despair.

Could she speak politely at the end when he took his leave? Could she be civil and dispassionate as expected, as required of a discarded lover? Could she behave with obliging good grace?

The sight of Leghorn occasioned unusual emotions in Beau as well, his feelings curiously discontent, restless, without clear motive or explanation, novel sensations for a man who always bid farewell to his lovers with relief. He'd really miss Serena, he reflected, mildly surprised—and not just her lush, wanton body. In minutes he'd be leaving her, a not altogether satisfying thought until sudden inspiration struck him—motives of personal gratification suggesting a reexamination of his options. "Would you like me to ride with you to Florence?" he asked, wondering even as he spoke if he might still be drunk from last night, his conduct so out of character.

"Oh, yes," Serena answered, her gloomy world suddenly taking on a golden glow. "I'd like that very much."

"Good," Beau succinctly said, gratified—no, exhilarated, a sensation he didn't question beyond its carnal implications, his mind already contemplating the nearest inn with a large bed.

The sixty-mile journey to Florence took several days, the country inns so much more tempting than the carriage and dusty road, making love so much more tantalizing than saying good-bye. Neither was quite reconciled to ending their agreeable liaison.

But eventually, even at their laggard, sybaritic pace, they arrived in Florence and on reaching the Castellis' address discovered that Serena's hosts were away in Rome for two months. The neighbor was sympathetic but without the means of ingress to their apartment. She was very sorry . . . perhaps the landlord could be persuaded to allow Serena entrance, but he too was in Pisa at the moment visiting his daughter.

"They weren't expecting me until July," Serena said with a sigh, gazing up at the shuttered windows, her thoughts sober as she contemplated the next months alone in a strange city. But even more lamentable than loneliness, without the Castellis' she was denied access to the ateliers and workshops where she wished to study.

"We'll have to find you lodgings," Beau briskly said. "Which side of the Arno would you prefer?"

"At least I can afford lodgings," Serena declared, smiling faintly, Beau's energetic reaction bolstering her despondent mood. "Thanks to you."

"No—thanks to your skill. And I'd suggest the north side—you'll be closer to everything." Taking her hand, he gave it a squeeze of encouragement. "I'll tell the driver to wait for us at the Piazza della Signoria while we look for an apartment." The hired carriage, piled high with luggage, almost completely blocked the narrow street. "And I was thinking maybe I'd stay a few days more until you're settled."

"Would you?" Serena breathlessly replied and then realizing how gauche her response to a man overfamiliar with clinging women, she more circumspectly added, "Although I'm afraid I'd be taking terrible advantage of you."

"Let's not consider who's taking advantage of whom or I might be forced to recognize I have a conscience," he said, smiling. "As for my staying, I'd enjoy it." Glancing down the cobbled street, he surveyed the buildings crowding out the sun. "Now tell me what you think you can afford?" he added, careful after their argument over the dresses to be more heedful of her finances.

Three hours later, after climbing countless stairs and navigating their way through residential blocks and narrow byways, they stood in the salon of a sunny apartment facing the Arno, a stupendous view of the goldsmiths' bridge to their left, the afternoon sun glinting off the gently flowing river below, the green hills on the horizon framing the picturesque scene perfectly as if arranged for their delight.

"I can't believe this apartment is so reasonable," Serena happily said, twirling away from the windows to survey her new home. "After all the other much smaller ones we looked at."

"I think the landlady liked you—or liked having an English lady in her building." Beau stood behind her, pleased that she was pleased, the money he'd given to the landlady overcoming her disinclination to rent the apartment for only two months. "Why don't I pay you for the entire year," he'd said as Serena was investigating the small kitchen in the back. "Would that be helpful?"

It was.

And when Serena emerged from the back hallway, she'd been greeted by the landlady's beaming countenance and a rapid flow of directions to the nearby markets, churches, and shops. Because Serena's Italian was flawless and the landlady

was much pleased with the donna inglese who spoke with a
Florentine accent, their discussion eventually included a
lengthy interrogation concerning Serena's mother's family.

"She certainly seems to know everyone north of Rome,"
Beau remarked once the landlady departed. "You at least
won't lack for someone to talk to," he added with a grin.

"She might even be able to help me find out a bit about
my mother's family. Papa knew so little."

"A fault of men," he said and in that vein dismissed any
further interest in family antecedents. "I'm off to bring the
carriage and luggage back. Why don't you decide where you
want your easel? And think about rearranging the bedroom;
I'm going to see if the landlady has another bed."

"You don't like the bed?"

"If I was a foot shorter I might like it."

"Are you staying then?" Her mood was buoyant.

"At least for a few days and I don't care to suffer."

She didn't suppose the Duke of Seth's glorious son had
suffered much in his life. And she also understood more
practically that the small bed wouldn't suit him. "Ask the
landlady where we can eat too."

"If you get hungry have some of that bread and cheese we
bought at Badia. And I'll bring back something for dinner.
Ciao, darling," he said, blowing her a kiss.

Serena wandered through the rooms, pleased with the
arrangement and size of the apartment. The salon was large,
with a diminutive balcony overlooking the river; a small
parlor suitable for an office or sitting room opened off the
salon; the bedroom was more than adequate for her needs;
the kitchen had a little porch, the scent of lilies rising from
the garden below. She could paint in the salon; the light was
wonderful. This was her first real home since Fallwood and
alone in a strange land, she was more happy than she
thought possible. Or not quite alone, she mused, which no
doubt accounted for her good spirits.

As for the future, she wouldn't allow herself to think of
Beau's leaving.

• • •

He came back two hours later, running up the stairs, shouting he was home, making her heart sing with happiness.

He'd said "home."

And even knowing better, she relished the intimate word.

Several porters followed him upstairs, bringing sections of a bed he'd found, the luggage, flowers, and vases.

"This bed isn't from the landlady—it's new. I can't afford it," she softly said, wishing there was some way on earth to keep him.

"Fight with me later," he murmured, his dark eyes sparkling, "when the bed is set up. I'll let you win."

"If I win, will you take it back?"

"If you win, I'll let you buy it from me."

"With what, pray tell?"

"I thought we could barter . . . something," he said, wicked and lecherous and charming still.

"Do I have a choice?"

He pretended to consider for a second and then grinned. "Actually, no. And before you get all wrathful," he gently added, noting the flush rising on her cheeks, "I brought back food for supper."

"Am I not allowed to argue?"

"Not until the bed's assembled." His voice was equable, a half-smile on his face.

"You're impossible," she said. "Like a battering ram." And then she exhaled in a breathy sigh. "You're going to avoid discussing any of this, aren't you?" It was impossible to be angry with him. He utterly disregarded her resentment, his good cheer and impertinent charm unimpaired.

"Let's talk about it after we eat," he pleasantly offered.

But he wouldn't and maybe she was a fool even to consider resisting his largesse.

While they ate and drank wine and watched the sun drift behind the low hills surrounding the city, the workmen set the bed in place.

"If you stay around long enough, I'll become spoiled again," Serena remarked, "waited on like this."

"Time enough for you to work when I leave."

The word "leave" strummed in the air between them, her sudden feeling of abandonment shocking, incomprehensible considering she'd always known his company was transitory.

"But I'll stay for a time. . . ." he murmured, sensing her discomfort, his own emotions in flux. "If you don't mind."

"I'd like you to," Serena quietly replied, because she couldn't be modishly coy or unsusceptible even if the Earl of Rochefort might prefer less feeling in his amours.

"Well then." He inhaled as if he'd run a great distance, and smiling at her, he said, "What should we do tomorrow?"

He stayed for another week and they strolled for hours each day through the streets of the Renaissance city, spending leisurely hours viewing all the art treasures of note, climbing to the top of the Duomo and campanile to see the city spread out before them, walking through the endless corridors of the Pitti Palace and the serpentine paths of the surrounding Boboli gardens, marveling at Ghiberti's sublime doors to the baptistry, standing in awe before Michelangelo's David—the eyes so lifelike the marble took on a warm humanity. The Palazzo Vecchio imbued with hundreds of years of Florence's history reminded Serena of how fleeting life was, as did the Uffizi, awash in masterpieces collected by the Medicis, men of great passions and power, room after room filled with works of art so precious, she was speechless before them.

They often rode outside the city too, taking in the Etruscan and Roman ruins at Fiesole as well as the monastery Michelangelo had designed in the hills north of town. And they ate and drank and made love in their hours of leisure as lovers have done since the beginning of time, completely engrossed in each other, preoccupied with all the variations of pleasure, basking in the lush world of sensuality.

• • •

Late one night, Serena's monthly courses began and Beau, sitting up in bed after she left his side, lit a candle and silently watched her wash the blood from her thighs and deal with the necessary procedures. She slipped on a nightgown when she was finished and lay down beside him again, her mood reserved, strained.

"Does it hurt?" He drew her into his arms.

"A little."

"Would you like a brandy?"

She murmured no and then subsided into an unnatural quiet.

"Did you think you might be pregnant?"

"I was concerned." She spoke softly but brusquely, grudging the words.

"After ... well—after so long," he obtusely said, "*I* thought you might be pregnant."

He'd noticed, she thought. And would it have mattered, she sullenly mused. "As you see"—she forced herself to smile—"you're quite safe."

"Since we weren't always ... practical," he said, euphemistically referring to their occasional intemperate lapses in contraception, "it's fortunate."

"Extremely fortunate for me," she coolly noted, wondering how many times Beau St. Jules had had to extricate himself from the responsibilities of impending fatherhood.

He heard the repudiation in her voice. "I would have taken care of you," he softly said, "if there'd been a child."

"I imagine you would. You're a very generous man."

Her tone implied volumes more. He'd heard that pitch and resonance and implication before—not over a child, for he was normally cautious, but over his numerous departures from women's boudoirs and lives.

He didn't answer. He knew how useless words were at that stage. But he held her in his arms because he wanted to and she allowed him. A curious sense of sadness filled his mind as if he'd lost something, and the feeling was impossible to ignore even for a man who ordinarily ignored emotions having to do with ladies and amour.

She should have felt relief her courses had come, Serena thought, lying in Beau's embrace, and in the rational portion of her brain she did. But in the wishful, unreal part of her mind where longing and need overlooked practicalities, she grieved for the baby she might have had. She might have had his child to love when he was gone from her life. But she wouldn't now. And her tears were real.

He felt the dampness on his chest, heard her small muffled sobs, but he wasn't certain he wished to know the reason for her tears, suspicious, overcautious after too many adventuresses in his life.

Beau's indifference hurt deeply, his silence speaking more powerfully than words. Her tears erupted in a deluge, and abruptly pulling away, Serena scrambled from the bed. Realizing almost too late that she intended to leave, Beau grabbed at her, his hand closing on her wrist just as her feet touched the floor. "What did I do?"

It was what he hadn't done, she thought, sniffling, wiping her tears away with her free hand. "You haven't done anything," she lied. "It's just my courses. . . . I cry easily when I'm . . ." Her voice trembled to a stop.

"Let me help. Should we do something . . . go somewhere?"

Biting her lip, she shook her head, feeling forsaken when she should know better, when he'd never promised her anything at all.

"You're sure?" His gaze was kindly, perplexed.

She tried to smile but her mouth quivered and he found himself filled with bewildering remorse. Rolling on his side, he drew her back down beside him and holding her close, stroked her hair, her face, the gentle curve of her back, molding her body to his, murmuring words of comfort, sweet, consoling words, his voice gentle. "Everything's going to be fine . . . don't cry," he whispered. "Don't cry . . . I'm here."

But he wouldn't be for long, she despairingly thought, which only made her cry more uncontrollably, and sobbing, she hiccuped, "I'm . . . sor . . . sor—ry . . . for . . . crying."

"Don't be," he murmured, gently brushing her hair away from her temples. He wanted to give her something; it was all he knew about making amends, and racking his brain, he wondered what he could purchase in the middle of the night. "Let me buy you something," he said, thinking a promise might suffice until morning, knowing it wouldn't but at a loss to console her.

"You . . . can't." She hiccuped, sobbing harder, distraite, heartsick, no longer caring about discretion or embarrassment or whether she was mortifying herself beyond redemption.

He could buy anything. "Tell me. It's yours."

She looked at him through a blur of tears, his beauty spectacular even veiled by a despairing mist. "I want . . . *you,*" she blurted out, the words exploding into the quiet like an artillery blast. As shocked as he at her boldness, she shoved at his chest, breaking his hold, and leaping from the bed, fled the room.

He lay very still listening to her agitated breathing in the adjacent room, his mind riveted on her words, the phrase locked in his brain as if gear wheels had jammed at her demand. As with any demand from a lady, the more cynical of his friends might say.

He blew out his breath.

And then he heaved himself out of bed and searched for his breeches. This was a conversation that would require at least a minimum of clothing.

When he walked into the salon, Serena looked up from the sofa where she sat curled up in one corner and spoke firmly. "There's no excuse; I shouldn't have said it. Feel free to leave—now if you wish."

He sat down in a chair across the room.

Safe, she thought. He's done this before.

"I don't want to go," he murmured. "But I can't stay forever either."

"Whatever you like." Her tears were gone, burned away by her humiliation.

"I like being with you." His voice was deep, rich, sincere.

But he kept his distance, she noticed, wary after too many women crying for him to stay. "I can't believe I said what I did." She pulled her knees up under her chin and gazed at him over her nightgown-clad knees.

He found the openness in her eyes enchanting as he always did. "You're more emotional now with—"

"My monthly cycle," she said, helping him out. She'd had time to bludgeon her emotions into a semblance of normalcy.

"With that." His grin was white in the moonlight.

"We'll pretend this never happened." Following his dégagé lead, she could even smile with equanimity.

"That'd be damned convenient." He slid down in his chair, relaxing, his legs sprawled out before him.

"And I've appreciated *your* convenience," she said, the sardonic lightness in her voice familiar. "All ten inches of it."

"When you're feeling better again, we're here for you," he lazily drawled. "In the meantime, let me take you shopping tomorrow."

"Buying off another woman's tears, Rochefort?" The irony was mild, her eyes amused.

"Assuaging my conscience."

"I didn't think you had one."

"I didn't think so either," he softly said.

They went shopping the next day because he convinced her it was useless to resist; she should understand that by now.

She did. He was right.

So for a few days more she'd allow him to mollify his conscience because the futility of continuing to fight against his wishes would soon be moot and her principles and ethics had lost their fine edge last night, inundated in the flood tide of her tears. It was very clear too, after their cordial, nonchalant conversation in the middle of the night, that once he left, he wouldn't be coming back.

He bought her a dozen pair of slippers in a dozen different colors and two lush carpets from Baghdad and the

sofas and chairs and mirrors and tables he hadn't dared buy
the day he brought home the bed. Then he also purchased
the tapestry she admired of the *Primavera*—a very close
approximation, he thought, Botticelli's lithe blond maiden
like Serena Blythe from Gloucestershire. And over her
protests, because even her disregarded principles took notice
of the exorbitant price, Beau bought her a necklace of gold
and pearls and a robin's-egg ruby. "Think of me when you
wear it," he said.

She would think of him every minute of the day with or
without the necklace, she knew. He could have saved his
money.

He stayed almost two weeks more in her lavishly furnished apartment and then one afternoon, he turned from
the window where he'd been contemplating the view of the
river for some time and said, "There may be messages for me
at Palermo, which I have to bring back to England."

"I understand."

"I'd like to stay longer."

"I know."

"If Sir Hamilton has no news, I could come back."

He wouldn't. "I'd like that," she said.

"Are you going to be all right until the Castellis return?"

"I'm going to start painting. Then I'll have some work to
show when I enter an atelier." She wouldn't cry; if she didn't
think of him leaving, she could keep her feelings in check.

"You have plenty of paints?"

He'd bought out two stores for her. "Thank you, yes."

"What are we going to do tonight?" He tried to speak
casually, but he found it difficult.

"I thought I'd fuck you to death."

He laughed and felt better. "A woman after my own
heart."

If you had one, my dear Glory, she thought, understanding beneath her derision why a man like Beau St. Jules
had never acquired one. "We're a good match then, because
I like your cock."

He covered the short distance between them in three

swift strides, and grabbing her shoulders, half lifted her from her chair, bending down to kiss her, his mouth harsh, his fingers biting into her flesh. A second later he pulled her completely to her feet, spilling the prints in her lap to the floor and jerking her hard against his body, forced her mouth open with his, drove his tongue deep into her throat, anger and frustration eating at his brain. He couldn't bear to think of her saying that to another man. She was his.

Or at least tonight she was, cooler reason reminded him, and suppressing his rankled territorial emotions, he lifted her into his arms and walked into the bedroom.

They stayed up all night, neither wanting to waste a moment of their last hours together. They made love with tenderness, with exquisite slowness, and at the last when dawn was breaking, they burned flame hot, stung by the searing finality, by the inexorable end of their affair.

He said he didn't want breakfast when she asked.

He was packing swiftly, tossing his clothes into his portmanteau, and his gaze when it lifted to hers was startlingly blank. "If I reach Leghorn by dinnertime I can catch the evening tide." His voice too was without emotion.

"Would you like me to make you a lunch?"

He smiled then—a flash of the man she knew. "If you could, I'd say yes." She'd not yet mastered the most rudimentary cooking. "But thank you for asking."

"I *could* help you pack."

"I'm almost finished. Have you seen my watch?"

"It's in the parlor; I'll get it."

When she returned to the bedroom, his portmanteau was strapped shut and he was slipping on his bottle green coat.

He took the watch from her, threaded the chain through his waistcoat buttonhole, and slid the timepiece into his pocket. "Thank you for everything," he said, standing a foot away but his voice already distant.

"You're very welcome. But you've been infinitely more generous than I. I'm in your debt." She spoke in an even, level tone, as capable as he of politesse.

"Certainly not." His tone was clipped, curt. Then his eyes held hers for a moment. "I wish you well," he softly added, and reaching for her hand, he pulled her close. "Kiss me," he murmured, "although I hate good-bye kisses."

"No more than I," she whispered, lifting her mouth to his, willing herself not to cry.

And for that warm, tender moment as their lips met, the world was filled again with wonder.

She was the only women he'd ever left with regret, he thought, the scent of her sweet, redolent of lush passion—and yet he had no intention of tying himself to one woman, however tantalizing.

His mouth lifted away.

"I'll probably see you next as the toast of the Royal Society. You paint like an angel."

"I'll send you an invitation to my first exhibition." She hoped she sounded as casual as he. But she wanted him to leave before she humiliated herself by begging him to stay. "Pleasant voyage," she said.

He looked at her for a moment more, his expression masked, and then he turned away to pick up his valise.

Straightening, he smiled, dipped his head in a faint bow, and a second later he was gone.

"Look in the top dresser drawer," he called back before shutting the apartment door. And she heard his footsteps racing down the stairs.

She ran to the window and watched him enter the carriage, waited until it disappeared from sight. Walking back into the bedroom, she pulled open the dresser drawer. The red leather boxes were nestled among her silk stockings and a note lay atop the largest.

Every lady needs diamonds, he'd written in a loose, open scrawl. And he'd signed it, "Fondly, Beau."

She opened the elegant cases one by one, the dazzling collection of diamonds enough to buy her years of security—the necklace, earrings, bracelet ablaze with hundreds of enormous diamonds. Beau St. Jules couldn't give his heart, but in all else he was the most generous of men.

• • •

She cried all morning, then slept for two days, escaping from her pain and unhappiness in the cocoon of the bed Beau had bought for her and when, finally, toward evening two days later, she decided to reenter the world, she began to paint. She worked as though her life depended on it and perhaps it did in those first days; she hardly took time to eat or sleep. She painted with fury and passion, with fervor and rage; she painted tall, handsome, dark-haired men in every conceivable pose and genre and mood. She cried at times as she splashed paint across the canvas, impatient with the unfairness of life. And then on other days she felt such overwhelming love from her joyful memories, she smiled while she worked and hummed light-hearted tunes.

But it was the very worst at night and often she painted through those melancholy hours when she wanted desperately to be held in his arms. And on those nights when she was defenseless against the pain of her loss, she hoped against hope this time she might be carrying his child. But her cycle came again the following month, the stark crimson blood mocking her dreams, and she couldn't even paint for a week afterward so deep was her despondency.

He'd forgotten her by now, she knew.

While Serena was painting her way through her melancholy, Beau was drinking himself numb in a futile attempt to suppress the heated images flooding his mind, of pale blond hair and blue-green eyes, of passion and desire. He'd called for a bottle of brandy when he boarded the *Siren* and hadn't stopped drinking since, sitting on deck their first night out, not speaking to anyone, brushing away Remy's offers of food.

He washed and shaved the next morning and put on fresh clothing but he was changed inside, consumed. No one knew how to respond to their employer's new subtle acidity. His voice was different when he spoke, his observations cynical, a rueful disillusion investing each word.

He was drunk as a lord when they reached Palermo and

when he returned from his visit to Lord Hamilton and the court a day later, Countess Niollo was on his arm. Francesca's estate, Baccate, bordered on St. John land; she'd invited herself along ostensibly to check on her properties. "Fine," Beau had said when she'd approached him, his gaze gently sardonic. "I'll save you from the republicans and you can save me from boredom."

Both properties were distant enough from Naples to have escaped the destruction of the city's defense and when they reached Beau's villa, Di Cavalli, the bucolic green countryside lay untouched by armies and revolution.

"There's no need for you to go on to Baccate immediately, is there?" Beau said as he helped Francesca dismount in the courtyard of his villa.

"Would you like me to stay?" she flirtatiously asked.

"I'd like to fuck you, Francesca, for a week or so," he drawled. "Are you interested?"

"A charming proposal, Rochefort," she pettishly retorted.

"Do you or don't you?"

"I'm not sure, you graceless man."

He was looking for oblivion, not romance, and he'd never led Francesca down anything remotely resembling a garden path. "Suit yourself. I need a drink."

"You have to pay attention to me," she said, "not just your brandy." A direct, self-indulgent woman, she always knew what she wanted.

"Don't worry, darling, you'll have all the attention you want." In his current black mood, the thought of fucking himself to death held real merit. "I hope you can keep up."

"That sounds intriguing. . . ." Her gaze took on a heated glow.

"I intend to intrigue the hell out of you, darling," he said, his voice low-pitched, bland.

He did.

She was.

And neither noticed that a week had gone by.

He drank from the moment he woke in the morning, a liquor bottle always conveniently within reach on his bedside table. But he maintained a preoccupied kind of sobriety despite his intemperance as if his acid thoughts burned away the alcohol, as if his all-consuming need for Serena allayed the brandy's potency. And Francesca de Bruni, Countess Niollo, enjoyed the passionate rewards of Beau's rage and discontent.

He found a servant girl to warm his bed when the countess left for a time to see to her estates and when she returned to find a pretty housemaid in his arms, being a woman of sophisticated tastes, she joined them.

Beau no longer knew what day it was; he didn't care; he didn't care to care. He just wanted to forget the pale blond beauty who persisted in his thoughts, who haunted him.

And after a month, he found he didn't care about anything much at all.

19

In the early days of the dissipated ménage à trois at the St. John estate, far to the north, the Austrian offensive opened and made rapid progress against the French on all sectors. On the eastern flank General Ott captured Recco and the dominant Monte Becco, forcing the French right wing back to Nervi, five miles east of Genoa. In the center Hohenzollern stormed the important Bocchetta Pass on the main road northward from Genoa to Tortona, while Melas's main drive secured the Cadibona Pass and broke through to the coast at Vado, thus separating the groups of Soult and Suchet. After three days of stiff fighting Melas had gained all his first objectives and had driven the French from their forward line on the crest of the Ligurian Apennines, though at the cost of serious casualties. Massena had put up a stubborn resistance against heavy odds; the Austrians outnumbered him five to one.

While the residents at Di Cavalli passed April in self-gratifying pleasures, in the environs of Genoa, Austrian pressure continued and the French were gradually driven back through Voltri and Sestri, harassed all the time by the fire of the British sloops who blockaded the coast. By April 20 the French left flank was withdrawn to the mouth of the river Polcevera, only three miles west of Genoa; on the right flank they had withdrawn to the river Sturla, while in the center they were holding the fortified enceinte and the detached forts to the north and east of it. General Massena in Genoa was now entirely cut off from his base at Nice and from Suchet's corps.

On April 24, Admiral Keith from his flagship, HMS *Minotaur*, sent a parlementaire to Massena, summoning him to surrender in view of the hopelessness of his position; otherwise, the admiral said, he would have to bombard Genoa. Massena promptly replied: "Genoa will be defended to the last extremity," and immediately opened fire on the British ships from the Lanterna battery. On the same day Massena sent off Major Franceschi, one of Soult's ADC's, to run the blockade and carry a dispatch to Bonaparte, giving an account of the operations to date and saying that, by still further reducing the troops' rations, he could hold out "for another ten or twelve days, perhaps fifteen."

Captain Berry arrived at Di Cavalli near the end of the month with letters and news. He found Beau and his small harem outside, the women lounging on chaises in the garden and sipping on champagne, their indolent gazes on Beau, who was working with one of the barb horses that had been brought out of Tunis. A profusion of blooms colored the greenery in the garden, the scent of roses heavy in the air.

"Could I offer you a drink?" Beau casually inquired when Berry reached the riding ring, sliding from the saddle, handing the reins to a stable boy. He offered the captain a small flask from his vest pocket.

"Thank you, sir, don't mind if I do. The ride from the coast was a mite warm and dusty."

"Even hotter here inland; drink it all. There's more over there," Beau added, gesturing toward the ladies. A sheen of perspiration burnished his skin. He wore only riding boots and buckskins, a vest with the requisite pocket for his flask unbuttoned in the heat. His tanned arms and shoulders, his powerful chest were gilded with sweat, the contrast of male strength and the delicate embroidery on his linen vest striking.

The captain emptied the flask, and handing it back with a smile, said, "If you're otherwise engaged, sir . . ." He glanced at the women seated in the partial shade of a flowering apple tree, their lacy boudoir robes revealing, their voluptuous sensuality blatant. "I'll wait in your office."

"I've been otherwise engaged," Beau sardonically murmured, "for weeks now. They won't miss me overmuch if I take you inside. Have you met the Countess Niollo?"

"Once briefly, sir—on Capri."

"Ah . . . yes, well, come and make your bow and then we'll retire to the coolness of my office." With a courteous small dip of his head, he waved Berry before him.

It was only a short distance to the garden and when Beau introduced the women, he treated them with equal deference, regardless one was a countess and the other his housemaid. The countess nodded minutely in the captain's direction, her notions of consequence requiring no more than the merest acknowledgment to a man of his rank. Thebia, the pretty maid, jumped up and bobbed a curtsy for the captain, her smile open, warm.

He'd have to see that she was well rewarded when he left, Beau thought, her engaging charm bringing a smile to his face. "If you'll excuse us, ladies," he urbanely said, as if the two women in dishabille were at a drawing room for the queen and not just recently risen from his bed. "The captain has some messages for me."

"Don't be gone long," Francesca said, cherishing an inflated sense of her prerogatives after a month with Beau.

"Will this require much time, Berry?" Beau drawled. "The countess is impatient."

"I'm not certain, sir." Although he felt his news was significant enough to interrupt Beau's hermitage regardless, he had orders not to disturb him.

"Duty calls, Francesca," Beau casually declared, understanding Berry wouldn't have come without good reason. "Perhaps one of the grooms could entertain you in my absence. I mean riding of course. Do try that pretty barb."

Thebia giggled behind her hand.

The countess glared at Beau for a moment and then said, "I found him wanting, darling, don't you recall?"

Scandal never affected Francesca; her beauty insulated her from censure as did her dead husband's generous marriage settlement. "In that case I must endeavor to make haste," he smoothly replied.

Captain Troubridge, one of Nelson's subordinates, had taken the islands of Ischia and Capri, Berry told him, perched on the edge of his chair in Beau's office, his voice clipped and rushed as he detailed the campaign. The British were once again in control of the harbor of Naples.

"Pitt won't commit land troops," Beau said, seated across his desk from him. "How do they expect to drive the French from Naples?"

"Ruffo's on the march with his Army of the Holy Faith."

"Ah . . . Ferdinand's bloody hand of God. The pillaging must have reached a fine pitch by now."

Berry acknowledged the assessment with a grimace. "And Massena's done, they say at Genoa."

"And Bonaparte?"

"No one knows."

Beau gazed at his captain, his eyes sharply direct. "Perhaps someone should find out."

"My thinking, sir."

"Am I obliged to give up my amusements then?" He leaned back for a moment, a faint smile on his face, a crackling excitement obliterating his monthlong ennui.

"I took the liberty of having the servants pack you a bag, sir."

"The countess will never forgive me," Beau cheerfully said.

"I'm thinking she will, sir, seeing as how you left her in Capri last year and she seems to have, er, forgiven you."

"Did I really?"

"She was screaming something awful, sir. I distinctly recall our departure."

"I must have sent her something."

"Two diamond necklaces, sir."

"Ah. I don't suppose you brought any along with you?"

"The jewelry case is in your room."

Beau grinned; Berry's organizational skill was impeccable. "I imagine our itinerary is planned as well."

"Palermo first, sir, and then—"

"Genoa."

"Yes, sir."

"I should be sober by Palermo."

"You'll find Lock in charge, sir," Berry calmly remarked, knowing Beau was competent sober or not. "Sir Hamilton has been formally recalled."

"All the twittering biddies finally got to the king then."

"There are those who take scandal seriously, milord."

"Luckily no one of interest to me."

"Just so, sir."

Beau and Captain Berry left Di Cavalli within the hour, the countess less prone to sustain a temperamental fit when offered free rein in a jewelry case. She was greedy, as Beau expected, and she sniffed in outrage when Beau selected two items of jewelry and gave them to Thebia. He'd left orders for his steward to pay the young woman a handsome sum as well once Francesca was gone, in the event Thebia's sojourn in his bed had irreparably damaged her reputation. The steward had rather thought not, mentioning that the young maid's casual disregard for propriety wasn't a recent manifestation—two of the footmen were special favorites of hers.

That bit of information had absolved Beau's sense of chivalry from any serious penance and he rode off in high good spirits.

The past month had mitigated the worst of his desire for Serena and he could almost convince himself that with time he'd forget her completely. He had no wish to seriously consider marriage and he couldn't offer her less in a permanent relationship. Or could he? a wicked voice suggested; even a viscount's daughter might be persuaded to the status of mistress. But, he decided in the next pulse beat, he didn't know if he could actually relinquish his bachelor ways, and recalling her temper he knew Serena wouldn't agree to any amorous license for him.

And it was all moot anyway because even the merest intimation of permanence unnerved him.

"Why did you never marry?" he asked Berry, mulling over his disparate thoughts.

Berry turned slightly in the saddle, wondering at Beau's inference.

"Just a general question," Beau dissimulated.

"Never found a woman I loved that much," Berry said.

"My thinking too," Beau murmured.

On reaching Palermo, Beau went to call on Charles Lock, the British consul-general deputizing until the new envoy replacing Hamilton arrived. The Hamiltons and Nelson were off on a pleasure cruise to Malta and Syracuse before beginning the long journey back to England, the embassy butler said when Beau inquired. All talk was of Cardinal Ruffo's success on his advance toward Naples, the major domo volunteered on their passage to the first floor offices.

There were indications the French were withdrawing from Naples, the deputy-consul explained when the courtesies and greetings had been discharged.

"On orders, no doubt," Beau said, seating himself in a comfortable chair.

"With Genoa under siege and in desperate straits, Massena needs reinforcements, I expect." Charles Lock nervously tapped his watch fob. "But there's been utter silence from Napoleon. Our usual sources seem to have dried up."

"Certainly Bonaparte's campaign should begin soon, especially with Massena and his troops bottled up."

"Moreau struck at Kray in Prussia just last week."

"Do you think Bonaparte's considering a German campaign then? Will he leave Massena turning in the wind?"

The consul shrugged. "No one knows—certainly not the prime minister's damned council . . . nor do they know how to run a war."

"And you can't trust the Austrians. Thugut has his own territorial agenda."

Lock heaved a sigh. "Since the beginning."

"I was thinking of going up to Genoa and talk to some ADC's I know on the Austrian staff. Berry and I might ride north from there and see what we can discover."

"Everyone would be grateful, Rochefort," Charles Lock said, a worried frown creasing his forehead. "We're completely in the dark. With Lord Hamilton gone and Sir John Acton on his honeymoon, most of our sources are uncertain of their new loyalties."

"Did Sir John actually *marry* his thirteen-year-old niece?" Beau's eyebrows rose marginally.

"A fait accompli, sordid as it is."

"How costly was the papal dispensation?"

"Affordable apparently. The young thing tried to run away, dressed herself like a boy in breeches and bolted. But they caught her and now the *happy couple*," Lock sarcastically noted, "is aboard the *Foudroyant* with Nelson et al."[13]

"Sir John's damned old."

"Sixty-four."

Beau grimaced. "Can't see myself doing that to a child."

"The Actons are keeping the inheritance in the family."

"Seems to me a barrister or some political maneuvering in parliament would have accomplished as much."

"But then we're neither of us sixty-four," Lock gently said. "More brandy?"

"No." Beau held his hand up to check the consul's movement. "I'm on the cure. Berry tells me I'm going to need everything working in prime condition for our jaunt north."

"If anyone can do it, Rochefort, you can," the consul-general said with a benign smile. "And not wishing to put any undue burden on you, but we're all counting on you."

Smiling, Beau rose from his chair. "On that oppressive note," he lazily said, "I'll bid you good day. We'll send our reports back to the blockading squadron to relay to you. At that point, I wish the prime minister good fortune convincing the Austrians to work with him."

"We should have our own army in the Mediterranean. I couldn't have agreed more with Commander-in-Chief Stuart. The campaign in Holland was a disaster, as anyone with half a brain could have told them."

"I'll see what I can find to convince Pitt to send land troops to Italy."

"And I'll relay your information in the strongest possible language."

In the meantime in Paris that same night, May 6, at four in the morning, Bonaparte, accompanied by his secretary Bourrienne, rapidly descended the great staircase of the Tuileries leading from his rooms to the inner courtyard and stepped into a black berlin drawn by a team of post horses. The gates opened and the carriage dashed off at a gallop. He would not be long away—it was just a routine inspection, everyone was told.

They traveled at breakneck speed. Two days before, Duroc had left to prepare the relays; the postmasters were at their stations with their best horses harnessed and waiting; the unharnessing and reharnessing were carried out without changing postilions. The secretary inquired as to the name of the village and they galloped off again.

They reached Avallon at 7:30 in the evening—150 miles in fifteen hours—ten miles per hour, including relays. On May 7 Napoleon reached Dijon and very late on the eighth he was in Geneva, where Berthier was working at full pressure so the movement of the Reserve Army could begin on the tenth in accordance with the First Consul's plan. There was a three-day delay while waiting for the artillery to complete its preliminary marches, during which time Napoleon inspected the troops and made speeches designed to delude Austrian agents concerning the destination of the Reserve Army.

And then the ascent of the Alps at the Great St. Bernard Pass began.

At that time of year the pass was a huge mass of ice; a rough mule track, covered in snow for ten months of the

year, gave access to the pass, which linked the Swiss valley of
the Rhône with the Lombardy plains. Fifty-three thousand
men, 5,000 horses, 60 cannon, and 300 wagons, were to
move into the Aosta valley, at the threshold of Piedmont, by
covering twenty-five miles of sterile valleys, defiles, rocks,
and snows, in a season when the cold and the wind were still
terrible and avalanches were of daily occurrence. In preparation for this journey each soldier had been issued nine days'
rations and forty cartridges. From Martigny, the road, wide
enough to allow the passage of a small carriage, climbed
alongside the wild, seething Drance, running close to
precipices without parapets, crossing frail, ramshackle
bridges, and finally reaching Bourg St. Pierre. The road
didn't go beyond this point. It gave place to a mere path
by which one could reach St. Rémy, the first village on
the Italian slope.

The higher the army went, the rougher and narrower the
road became. At Bourg St. Pierre mechanics dismantled the
guns; gun carriages and wheels were numbered; the provi-
sions were packed into small boxes and loaded on mules, the
gun barrels were lashed on to hollowed-out tree trunks and
sledges. Watrin's and Loison's men hauled them along, 100
men harnessed to each gun, ten men apiece for the mount-
ings carried on stretchers. When they came to the snow line,
the ice cut through their shoes and they had to change them
every three to four miles.

It took two days to move the artillery from St.-Pierre to
the Hospice of St. Bernard at the top of the pass. After ten
hours' march through regions of wild desolation, hurricanes
and snow, wreckage and wooden crosses, the soldiers came
to the monastery buildings where the monks had set up
tables laden with food arranged for by Bonaparte, who'd
sent money and wine ahead. On May 16, the harsh, bare
plateau presented a picturesque sight with all the paraphernalia of war hauled up to 8,120 feet and the soldiers dining
on boiled salt beef, mutton stew, dry vegetables, goat's
cheese, Gruyère, and an old white Aosta wine.

Then the Reserve Army began the downward journey, even more difficult than the ascent.

On May 14, Beau was at General Ott's forward head-quarters at Rivarolo di Sopra. He was renewing his acquaintances with the Austrian staff officers he'd met at Vienna last fall during negotiations for a Second Coalition against France. No one expected Massena to hold out much longer. The Austrians had cut the Due Fratelli aqueduct, which supplied waterpower for the flour mills in the city the end of April. Admiral Keith's ships stood in every night and bombarded Genoa at close range.

In desperation, Massena had attempted a breakout on May 11, but his troops were too physically exhausted to fight, and with Massena himself covering their retreat, they'd been forced back into the besieged city.

The Austrians had no word of Napoleon, but they were of the opinion the French would move to defend Provence against a threat of invasion, once Genoa fell . . . which surely it would. In the meantime, the Austrians were distracted by the siege.

Leaving Rivarolo the following day, Beau and Berry rode north to reconnoiter around Alessandria with plans to move on to Pavia and Milan next. If no rumors of French troops were heard and no indication of their presence could be found in the environs of the Alpine passes into France, perhaps Germany would be the site of Napoleon's summer campaign after all.

On the sixteenth, Napoleon's Reserve Army's advance guard descending the pass reached Aosta and captured it; the following day Lannes routed 1,500 more Austrians at Chatillon. But he ran into trouble on the nineteenth when he reached the Fort of Bard, a formidable obstacle in their path. A small fortress perched on top of a precipitous rock controlled the single road through the narrow valley.

By the twenty-first, the Austrians had been driven out of the village of Bard but the 400 soldiers in the fort garrison

with their twenty-six cannon had been able to hold off
Lannes's desperate assaults.

The fort commander had immediately sent word to General Melas in Turin of the French invasion; if the general
acted quickly, he could block the French advance.

Beau and Berry met Commander Bernkopf's messenger
from Bard riding hell-bent for Austrian headquarters with
news of the French invasion. Napoleon had done the impossible if he'd brought his entire army over the snow-covered
pass, and attaching a note of his own relaying the startling
information to Admiral Keith, Beau and his captain made
for Bard. They'd need numbers to assess the strength of
Napoleon's advance. Was this a feint through the St.
Bernard or was an entire army advancing on Genoa? Melas
would need to know.

As they approached the fort two days later, the sound of
cannons rumbled in the distance and when they came within
visual range, they could see the entire village was invested
with French troops. But estimating the strength of the
enemy after more calculation, they realized the assault
wasn't manned by an army of any magnitude.

They spent the remainder of the day scouting the surrounding countryside and late that afternoon, they discovered two footpaths that bypassed the fort farther to the west.
Sitting silently on their mounts they gazed at the stark evidence of a large force having passed through the narrow
defile.

"They're heading east," Berry said.

"He's fallen like a thunderbolt," Beau murmured,
frowning at the trampled ground over which thousands of
soldiers had passed. "How many and where are they
bound?" he quietly went on, half musing, his mind already
sifting through possibilities.

"Not to Genoa I'd bet," Berry said. "And where's his
artillery?"

"On the far side of the fort, I'd say. Those footpaths

wouldn't allow them to bring the artillery. But we need to find the army before we report back to Melas."

By evening, they were overlooking Ivrea, which had the look of a center of operations. They didn't know that Napoleon was in bed at the time, sleeping peacefully with the knowledge that the enemy was still completely baffled as to his whereabouts.

Beau and Berry slept in the hills that night, needing daylight to better survey the army's strength. At dawn the French army broke camp and continued east.

"Jesus, there's at least fourteen or fifteen divisions." With his field glass raised to his eye, Beau scanned the troops strung out for miles on the road below. "And they're marching on Milan, I'd guess. Bonaparte's going to leave Massena to perish."

"Bonaparte needs artillery to fight a war."

"And the Austrian arsenal is only ninety miles away at Milan. *Merde*," Beau swore.

They rode the forty miles to Turin in record time, stopping frequently to buy fresh mounts. But when they reached Melas's headquarters, the seventy-year old commander-in-chief dithered for two frustrating days, still not entirely convinced that an army of that size had moved into the Po valley.

Shocked at the irksome, plodding mechanisms of authority in the Austrian chain of command—it could hardly move without orders from the Aulic Council in Vienna—Beau talked to anyone who would listen, exhorting them to speed. But not until the morning of June 1, when two of Melas's commanders relayed news of French attacks, did the commander-in-chief send orders to Ott to lift the siege of Genoa immediately and march northward to join him. He finally had to act with the French approaching Milan and Turin.

At Genoa, Ott had just received word that Massena would consider terms of capitulation. He put Melas's order in his pocket and ignored it. After eight weeks, he had no intention of lifting the siege hours short of victory. He

would have Massena's capitulation. But Massena procrasti-
nated with the negotiations, allowing Napoleon the time
he'd said he needed until June 4. The final terms of surrender were signed that day.[14]

By then Napoleon had entered Milan and now stood
squarely in the line of Austrian retreat.

When Beau heard of Milan's fall a moment of panic
assailed him. Full-scale war would soon spread over all of
northern Italy. And Serena was in Florence, perhaps not in
the first line of attack, but certainly in danger.

During the days he and Berry had ridden in search of the
enemy, he'd considered the threat of invasion to Florence,
the thought a small, persistently suppressed rumination.
Perhaps the campaign could be contained in the rich valleys
of the Po, Venice and the Cisalpine regions that offered
bounty and riches to the conquerors. But when Milan fell so
quickly, all of Italy could soon be overrun.

How deeply was he concerned . . . or responsible for
Serena's safety? Was he in even the remotest sense her
keeper?

He'd done what he'd come here to do—warn Admiral
Keith and Charles Lock, he reflected, punctilious, exact in
gauging his liability. The rest was out of his hands. He was
under no obligation to save Serena Blythe.

After making his farewells to the admiral, Beau set sail
for Palermo and from there, with a brief detour to Di Cavalli
for his horses, the *Siren* would chart course for England. But
as the *Siren* cruised nearer to Leghorn, Beau grew increasingly restless. He paced the deck, silent, high-strung. Berry
noticed but kept his counsel, knowing his comments
wouldn't be appreciated.

They passed the harbor, the city only a distant prospect
on the port side, the sea lanes busy as they approached the
hub of English commerce in Italy.

Beau abruptly went below.

Stalking into his cabin, he made straight for his liquor
cabinet, his hand shaking slightly as he poured himself a
drink. In the past weeks he'd not allowed himself to dwell

on his personal feelings. He and Berry had been constantly on the move in any event and while he'd thought occasionally of Serena, any opportunities for lengthy reflection had been curtailed by more immediate problems of staying alive.

And he'd neatly reconciled his sense of obligation in the last few days; he had none.

But as Leghorn became visible, he found himself obsessing again. And no matter how he forced away the images from his mind, they returned lush and provocative, demanding. He had no explanation for their intensity; he'd thought them gone after Di Cavalli. He'd thought himself restored to his familiar habits, his casual ease, his undemanding assessment of himself and his world.

Even if on impulse he gave into his obsession, he mused, staring into his brandy, and suddenly appeared at Serena's door, what would he say?

Just thinking about it sent a chill down his spine as if he were committing himself to some unknown, unwanted, unacknowledged feeling he'd always instinctively resisted.

Emptying his glass, the liquor burning his throat, he quickly poured himself another drink. Consuming the brandy with brusque outrage, tumult boiling in his brain, he sat slouched in his chair, regarding the bed where he'd first made love to Serena. And he wanted her again, now—more with each passing moment.

Her image lured him like a Lorelei—an enchanting apparition, her seductive witchery amplified with each glass of brandy consumed. He imagined meeting her again and when she saw him standing on her threshold, he would simply say, "Be my mistress. I'll give you anything . . . and safety from the French." Or perhaps, he cynically thought, bitter and disgruntled at his hungry need, reality shredding away the veil of illusion, he could more practically say, "I can't marry you, Miss Blythe, but whatever else you want is yours. A house, an estate, a ransom in jewels, entry into the Royal Society." In the mercenary world of the ton, nothing more had ever been required of him. And if some ladies wished for his title, they'd always settled for his wealth in the end.

But not Serena, he thought with a discontented grunt.

She wasn't for sale.

An unpalatable, stinging concept.

Damn her. He opened a second bottle.

Not till he'd broached his third bottle did he rise from his chair, hie himself up to the sun and breeze above, and lazily stroll across the deck with that careful, inebriated walk of a man well into his cups. "Where are we?" he drawled, standing beside his captain, scanning the distant shore with a distracted gaze.

"Nearing Piombino, sir."

"New shipping orders, Berry," Beau said with a smile, although his eyes were flint hard. "We're back for Leghorn."

20

The Castellis had returned to Florence a month ago and Serena was now enrolled in two ateliers: the studio of a fashionable portrait painter and that of a landscape painter of note. She was intensely busy, arriving at the studios very early in the morning and, once her workday was over, often painting at home again in the evening.

She'd discovered her rent had been paid for the entire year when she went to tell the landlady she was moving at the Castellis return. So she'd stayed in her own apartment rather than impose on her friends. It was a kindness she much appreciated and her eyes had filled with tears at Beau's thoughtfulness. She might despise him for his selfishness, for not caring enough, but his generosity couldn't be faulted.

Julia and Professor Castelli had introduced her to all their friends in the course of the past month, their weekly salons filled with intellectuals, with lifelong friends, with cousins and relatives of all descriptions. And Serena had been besieged by suitors. A young lawyer had been paying assiduous court since she first met him, and Julia's cousin Sandro, a celebrated sculptor, had offered his heart should she want it, he'd said with his glorious smile. Two younger sons of a local count, splendid in their Austrian uniforms, were faithful in their attendance at the Castelli salon and in their attentions to Serena. The local prefect sent her flowers daily and a young priest was struggling with his conscience over Signorina Serena. So she wasn't without entertainments or friends and she partook of the festive amusements with good grace. But she never offered more than light flirtations to her many suitors. None had captured her heart like Beau.

She still cried over him on occasion, but there were fewer days now that she fell melancholy over her unrequited love. Each week hastened the task of forgetting or made her loss less devastating. Or perhaps she kept herself too busy to notice that Beau St. Jules was missing from her life.

Reports of Napoleon's triumphant entry into Milan reached Florence shortly after the event and the utter defeat of the Austrians at Marengo twelve days later meant France was once again in control of Italy. And those Florentine citizens with something to fear from the French began packing or hiding their valuables. The Austrian Grand Duke's household, for instance, installed in the Pitti Palace, and those local officials under the hegemony of the Austrian government left the city.

Julia explained the history of the French investiture of Florence in 1799, and after warning Serena of the possibility of mob violence that could be avoided by staying in at night, she noted that the routine of life for ordinary people was generally unchanged.

Lulled into a sense of security with no French army marching through the gates of Florence and the war far to the north, Serena was shocked by the sudden appearance of a troop of French soldiers in the Tribuna of the Uffizi one afternoon in mid-June.

She was copying Bronzino's Mannerist depiction of *Lucrezia Panciatichi* along with several other students as an exercise for her portrait class, her easel set up in the Tribuna.

The officers in the forefront were splendidly dressed hussars, their leopardskin pelisses slung over their shoulders, fur caps embellished with plaited cords and tassels set at a jaunty angle on their heads, their richly embroidered dolman jackets resplendent as a sultan's garb, their swords and sword belts chased in gold.

The small troop moved swiftly into the octagonal room, taking no notice of the students' astonished glances. The

senior officer pointed at one of the paintings on the wall and
then another, a clerk beside him writing rapidly on a small
pad while soldiers lifted the selected paintings from the wall
and carried them out.

The party paused briefly beside the *Lucrezia Panciatichi*,
admiring Bronzino's loving depiction of the elegant beauty.

"That one too," Serena heard the officer say to the clerk at
his side. And when he turned away from the painting, he
saw Serena.

He stopped, put a hand out to stay the men behind
him, then half turned his head to murmur something to his
colleagues.

All the magnificent hussars stared at her.

And then the young officer in charge walked up to
Serena, his spurs clinking delicately in the sudden quiet.
"Bonjour, mademoiselle." He bowed gracefully. "You look
very much like someone I've met before."

"You must be mistaken, sir," she politely said, answering
him in French, trying to present a calm facade, setting her
brush down so he wouldn't see her hand shaking.

"You speak French?" His statement was in the form of a
question.

"It's the language of Europe, sir," she neutrally replied,
hoping he wouldn't ask her more, desperately hoping he
would turn and leave as abruptly as he'd appeared.

"General Massena will like that you speak French. She
speaks French," he repeated, turning to his fellow officers.
"We'll take her too," he briskly said to the clerk.

"No!" Serena cried.

"No one will hurt you, mademoiselle," he gently
declared, his gaze swiveling back to her. "General Massena
likes blond women." He didn't say she looked the twin of
Countess Gonchanka, who'd given the general such pleasure
in Zurich last year. In the pillage of Europe, all beauty was
fair game. He nodded to the soldiers to seize her.

"Where are you taking me?" Serena's voice was trembling, the soldiers holding her arms guiding her toward the
door.

"To the general," the officer mildly replied.

"I have to tell my family." She tried to keep the hysteria from her voice. "Let me at least send a note."

"Of course, mademoiselle." She could have been asking for the use of his handkerchief, so bland was his tone. "Tell François here what you wish. He'll see that they receive your message."

She was taken away then, half in shock, she and her escort moving in the wake of the plundering troop that was plucking the treasures of the Uffizi from the walls as if they were produce in a market. And in the piazza below, she saw dozens of covered wagons being loaded with the artwork. Before she was lifted into a carriage, the clerk came running up and she was allowed to dictate a brief message. "I'm being taken to General Massena," she wrote to her friends. "Please help me."

The note Julia received several hours later only said, "I'm going to see General Messena." The signature wasn't Serena's.

And no amount of pleading with the local authorities to help in the search met with any aid. The advance guard of General Massena, newly appointed commander-in-chief of the Army of Italy, was beyond the authority of local government.

When Beau appeared at Serena's apartment later that week, the landlady fell into his arms with sobs for salvation. "She's gone, taken by the French. God help us, you came—I prayed, I prayed you'd come."

Beau gently moved her away, her words frightening, thinking he must have misheard her. Holding her at arm's length, beating down his alarm, he said, "Speak very slowly."

She told him what she'd heard, answering his curt, sharp questions, repeating all she knew a dozen times.

Minutes later he was pounding at the Castellis' door and Julia recognized Beau immediately as the subject of the numerous paintings in Serena's apartment. Serena had confided little to her but she'd surmised an affair had ensued during the journey from England. He was brutally handsome; she could see why Serena had fallen under his spell.

When Beau introduced himself as a friend of Serena's, the Castellis invited him in. Apologizing for his abruptness, he immediately asked for any information they might have concerning Serena's capture.

He listened to their brief explanation of the bare facts, his brow furrowed, then scrutinized the note and silently cursed himself for not coming sooner. When he discovered Serena had been in the enemy's power for four days already, his stomach constricted, knowing full well how pillaging troops took their pleasures.

Julia was speaking in a low, quiet voice, describing all the people they'd conversed with: the students who'd seen Serena taken; the workmen who'd helped load the wagons; the young boy who'd delivered the note for the clerk. And in the course of her calm narration Beau put aside futile anxiety and planned his pursuit.

When he briefly outlined his purposeful journey a short time later, Julia offered their assistance. "Let us help; we'll go with you."

"General Massena's headquarters are in Milan," Professor Castelli added. "We have friends there who could be useful."

"I appreciate your offer," Beau politely replied, "but I can travel faster alone." They'd be in the way.

"With the British at war with France, you'd be in less danger traveling with us," Julia pointed out.

"We often journey to Milan to authenticate paintings." Professor Castelli was a small man, not much taller than his daughter. "I can shoot straight and handle a sword, milord," he went on, drawing himself up to his full height. "I'd be honored to assist you."

"Thank you, but a swift passage is less difficult with fewer people. And if Serena should somehow return in my absence," Beau dissimulated, knowing she wouldn't be kindly returned, "I'd feel more comfortable if you were here. I *will* need to see a banker before I go, if you could arrange it," he went on, rapidly assessing all he'd require for his trip to Milan, hoping Massena's chief of staff was still avaricious. "Someone who could advance a large sum on letters of credit." Solignac's greed was common knowledge; some said Massena too had a penchant for ducats. Beau was depending on it.

While the Castellis weren't wealthy, they knew merchants who were, and before the day was over, Beau had enough gold in his luggage to buy a dozen women from the general. And papers from the banker that legitimized him as a representative of the banking firm Allori and Sons.

Beau rode through the night, the moon full and bright, a raiding moon they called it in Yorkshire, he grimly mused, the concept appropriate to his intentions. He planned on raiding the general of one of his coquettes—for a considerable price if possible, if not, with violence.

Whatever it took, he'd have her back, he vowed. Regardless whether she wished it or not.

He didn't question how he'd accomplish the task. He was a master of opportunity, his skills honed in his role as liaison for Pitt.

Most of his assignments were those lesser men would decline. Danger exhilarated him, his detractors said, as if he were heedless beyond the need for excitement. Those who knew him better recognized a man equal to immense tasks.

On their journey to Milan, delayed by frequent stops at wealthy monasteries and convents where Colonel Solignac, Massena's chief of staff, would obtain a "donation," Serena was treated with courtesy. She had her own room at night wherever they stopped, the colonel had his orderly personally serve her her meals, additions to her wardrobe had appeared with steaming bathwater the first morning after her abduction, and Solignac had sent a kind note by his adjunct along with several books to ease the boredom of her journey.

She felt very much like the goose being fattened for

Christmas dinner and while she was relieved she'd not been molested by any of the hussars, she understood that as Massena's prospective property she was protected.

She tried not to dwell on the outcome of their journey, refusing to give in to her fear until absolutely necessary, thinking instead of possible means to extricate herself from her dilemma. Surely in the apparently wholesale plundering of the subjugated territories, some other of Massena's subordinates might well have found a woman who would appeal to the general more than she. Perhaps that lady was already cozily installed in the general's apartments and she'd be superfluous.

A not altogether pleasant thought, she suddenly realized, with the full array of junior officers no doubt similarly in need of females. Perhaps she should count her blessings, she decided, Massena as protector no doubt superior to her other alternatives.

But any rationalization, however objective, couldn't long overcome the weight of despair crushing her spirits. Leaning her head back against the leather squabs of the carriage seat, she shut her eyes against the tears threatening to spill over. Feeling lost and stranded, a terrifying, unknown course before her, she was overwhelmed by hopelessness.

Why me? she lamented, twin paths of tears gliding down her cheeks. And utterly despondent, she wondered what further disasters awaited her.

But at a post stop north of Parma, as she waited in the carriage for the horses to be unharnessed, she saw a young woman with two children begging for alms beside the road and her own difficulties in contrast seemed trivial. Unlike the ragged, starving young family, their faces pinched with hunger and need, she was well fed, well clothed, actually pampered by the colonel—so she'd arrive unblemished, in prime form for his general.

Slipping the pearls from her neck, the ones Beau had given her in Lisbon, she called the woman over to the carriage, and placing the necklace in her hand, she wished her good use of them. "Take these, and feed your family."

The young mother burst into tears at the lavish gift, kissed Serena's hand, and thanked her, her words over-wrought with emotion, tears streaming down her face. Trying to pull her torn garments into some semblance of order, she apologized for her appearance, embarrassed by her shabbiness. "We're not beggars, signorina," the woman softly said. "Or we wouldn't be if my husband hadn't died. But the children—"

"Please, I understand," Serena interposed, feeling a philis-tine in her elegant gown and guilty for her own self-pity when this woman scarcely had clothes to cover herself or food to eat. "No apology is necessary. Please—bring your children up so I may meet them," she added, wishing to cur-tail the woman's self-conscious atonement, catching the shy glance of the little girl clutching her brother's hand.

Pulling her children forward—a thin boy and a small girl who smiled timidly at Serena—the woman urged her youngsters to give Serena thanks.

"Thank you, signorina," the young boy gravely said. "Our papa died in the war." His eyes were too large in his thin face, his arms and legs emaciated. But he stood protectively over his sister, holding her hand firmly.

"Papa dead," his little sister piped up, understanding the calamity if not the concept and Serena's eyes grew wet with tears at the children's poignant words.

"Giovanni died at the battle of Magnano last spring," the young mother said. "And"—her mouth quivered—"it's been very hard. . . ." Her voice broke for a moment. "We have no relatives and it's difficult to find work with two small chil-dren," she quietly finished.

"I know someone who can help you," Serena said, impelled to aid the unfortunate family. "Do you know how to take the post to Florence?"

At the mother's immediate nod of affirmation, Serena searched her pocket, remembering the single florin she always carried for emergencies. Taking it out, she handed it to the woman. "Take the post coach to Florence and go to Professor Castelli at the Accademia dell'Arte. Tell them I sent you; the professor will know who will buy the necklace."

The flash of hope that shone from the young mother's eyes struck Serena with such impact, it eclipsed her own problems. Before the colonel ordered the troop back on the road, Serena was able to give the young woman definitive directions to the Castellis'. "Tell them I'm well," she added at the end, "and am on my way to Milan, I think. I'll contact them again as soon as I'm able," she finished in a rush, for the carriage was pulling away.

The children waved and smiled and the woman's heartfelt thanks echoed in Serena's ears long after the troop left the post station.

Feeling revived, almost invigorated after her meeting with the unfortunate mother and children, if it were possible to experience such a positive sensation under the circumstances, Serena straightened her skirt, smoothed out the wrinkles in the elegant white georgette gown the colonel had sent to her, adjusted the yellow silk bows decorating the ruffled sleeves, as if readying herself for the fray. Her mood was almost light-hearted as she looked out the carriage window at the bright summer landscape.

She wasn't the only lady in Italy faced with the prospect of being conciliatory to the country's new conquerors, she reminded herself.[15] Nor would she be the last if Colonel Solignac and his compatriot's sense of extortion continued unchecked.

Now, how exactly did one befriend a commander-in-chief?

Apparently not with the usual ploys, she discovered when she was ushered into General Andrea Massena's quarters the following day.

He looked up from his desk when Colonel Solignac brought her in, silently surveyed her for the space of two heartbeats (hers very violent despite her intentions to appear calm), and immediately returning to the papers before him, said, "Take her to my apartment."

He was already dictating to his two secretaries before she'd left the room. A maid greeted her at the commander-in-chief's suite in the Palazzo Mombello, showed her the armoires filled with female clothing in one of the dressing rooms, told her to help herself to anything she wished. With a bobbing curtsey, she said she'd bring some refreshments for the signorina and the signorina was to consider the general's apartments her own.

From the maid's experienced tone, Serena realized she wasn't the first lady to share the general's quarters.

Massena hadn't looked like what she'd anticipated, she thought, generals in her experience being old and portly. Massena's hair was gray (the result of his starvation diet at Genoa during the siege) but he was hawk-faced and lean; he had the look of a corsair. His eyes, ice blue and wintry, had assessed her with a swift, fleeting arrogance. But then he had complete authority in all of Italy; she supposed a degree of arrogance went with the rank. He wore none of the accoutrements of his position, though; his simple blue tunic had been partially unbuttoned, his shirt beneath as plain as his uniform. He almost looked out of place in the gilded opulence of the palazzo.

After the maid returned with a tea tray, she busied herself in the room, pouring Serena's tea, unpacking the few of her belongings an orderly had brought from the carriage, placing her books atop a splendid pietre dure table near the sofa in the salon where Serena had decided to sit. As she went about her duties, she scrutinized Serena with an obvious interest, as if placing her in the hierarchy of women privy to the general's life.

"The general's very kind, signorina," the maid said, offering encouragement to the young lady who sat stiff-backed on the sofa like a schoolgirl.

"I'm pleased to hear it," Serena replied, keeping her voice neutral, not sure whether the maid was there to serve her or guard her.

"And he's devoted to his officers."

As they are to him, Serena thought, wondering how many other staff officers brought back captive women for their commanders. "How nice," she said.

"More tea?" The maid hovered at her elbow.

"No, thank you."

"Another cake?"

"Thank you, no."

"Would you like me to find you something more comfortable to wear?" the girl inquired. "The general dines late, you see. You may have to wait some time."

"No, I'm comfortable," Serena said, not yet capable of playing the courtesan with ease, her posture the antithesis of relaxation.

"Very well, signorina." The maid fluffed the last pillow on the settee across from Serena, surveyed the room quickly for any duty left undone, and seeing none, said, "Ring for me if you need anything."

Serena passed three nerve-racking hours anxiously waiting for the general to appear, rehearsing a variety of demands and pleas, courteous and not, wrathful and gracious, debating the best procedures required to expedite the process of her release.

But he didn't come and dinner passed without his appearing. Serena ate alone at a very large dining table in an enormous dining room, the vast interior gilded and mirrored and lighted with hundreds of candles. Massena's chef was of the first rank, the food superb, the service regal.

For a moment before dinner, she considered refusing the food as a form of protest against her capture, but it was impossible after surveying the delectable choices put before her. The table was covered with beautifully prepared dishes: dozens of choices in the opening course—soups, hors d'oeuvres, removes, and entrées, and before taking her first bite of veal with sorrel sauce she chastised herself briefly for being without firm principles.

After dinner she spent the evening making a pretense of reading, and at ten declined the maid's offer to assist her into bed. She preferred to sit up and read for a time, she told the maid, dismissing her for the night, intending to avoid sleep—the thought of being surprised in bed by a strange man too daunting.

She fell asleep in her chair with all the candles burning.

Like a young child afraid of the dark, the general reflected with a faint smile when he went to his chambers near midnight to fetch a document and looked in on Solignac's pretty present. A shame, he thought with a twinge of regret, that he couldn't ignore his pressing correspondence and take pleasure instead in the mademoiselle's delectable body. But he couldn't, he decided with a sigh, and returning to his office, he kept his secretaries up until three. After a short nap in his dressing room, he rose again at dawn to begin another day of demanding administrative duties.

Napoleon had called Massena to Milan shortly after Austria's defeat at Marengo and then immediately left for Paris, where the politics of fluctuating conspiracies required his presence. Massena was left with the onerous tasks of reorganizing and reequipping 70,000 troops of the consolidated Reserve and Army of Italy, none of whom had been paid in six months.

The morning activities in the adjacent dressing room woke Serena, the sound of bathing, the murmur of voices bringing her nerves on full alert once again. What should she say to the general when he first came in? What *could* she say without fear of reprisal? But the voices remained comfortably distant as Serena slowly came awake, stretching her stiff muscles. The chair, while luxuriously soft, had not offered the amenities of a bed.

As Serena nervously awaited her denouement, Franco, the general's batman, entertained his master with the latest on-dits as he dressed him for the day, and the occasional sound of the men's laughter reached Serena through the closed doors. The valet served up all the freshest rumors for Massena's edification, the general's understanding of local affairs always dependent in part on Franco's intelligence reports. Once the elderly servant had run through his repertoire of current gossip, he said with a nod at the doors to the adjoining bedchamber, "Sylvie says the mademoiselle wouldn't go to bed last night no matter how she coaxed her."

"I noticed," Massena murmured. "Send her some bauble from me today."

"The countess liked emeralds."

"She did, didn't she? Well, send this one emeralds; Solignac's young lady does have the look of Natalie, doesn't she?" Massena's memories of the Countess Gonchanka brought a smile to his austere face.

"Solignac has a good eye."

Massena laughed softly. "Now if I can just find time to enjoy my prize."

"It's not your fault the army's in a mess," the orderly grumbled, his loyalty unswerving, his understanding of army politics consummate after fifteen years of serving Massena. "They expect too much of you."

"As usual, Franco. And then the complaints begin when I lash everyone into shape."

"They're ungrateful pigs." He shook out a fresh shirt, displeasure in every snap of his wrists.

"You and I know that," Massena said with a grin, sliding his arms into the crisp shirt his batman held out for him now. "But then we must consider the politics of survival."

"Hmpf. As if Bonaparte would be First Consul without you to win his wars."

"Or I an efficient soldier without you to take care of me," the general murmured, standing still while his cravat was carefully draped into appropriate folds.

"It's an honor, sir."

"I'll try to dine with the young lady this evening." Massena shook his cuffs down. "Come and remind me at eight."

"Unless another hundred dispatches arrive this afternoon," Franco mumbled, protective of his master, concerned with the heavy schedule Massena kept after so recently suf-

fering at the siege of Genoa. He'd endured the same scant
rations as his men and his health wasn't completely restored
yet. "You should try to sleep more."

"I'll try," Massena politely agreed, his mind already distracted by the most pressing of his appointments for the day.
"Bring coffee to my office," he added, picking up his tunic
himself, waving his orderly away. "See that it's very black
and very sweet, Franco." He was already halfway to the
door. "I have to see the monseigneur first and he always
gives me a headache."

"Hang the old sinner." With republican zeal, Franco
viewed the papacy as expendable.

"There are times I'd like to when he boldly lies to me,"
Massena said with a flashing smile, shrugging into his coat.
"But then, the French Treasury needs the money he tells me
he doesn't have."

The procurement of cash for the pay of the troops was
always an exasperating problem, although it wasn't the first
time Massena had been faced with it. The French consular
government had inherited from its predecessors, the Direc-
tory and the Convention, the principle that the French
armies had to be fed, clothed, and paid at the expense of the
occupied enemy territories. Strictly speaking, though, the
provinces of Northern Italy occupied by Massena's army
were not enemy territory but neutral states, whose popula-
tions the French government wished to conciliate and attract
into the French political system as buffer states against Austria. So from the first, it was obvious that any contributions
exacted from the local governments would be bitterly
resented and would be insufficient to meet the requirements
of the French troops.

Napoleon had promised that any shortfalls would be
made up by cash payments from the French treasury. They
never would be, of course, Massena knew, and his greatest
difficulty was imposing contributions on those who, in his
opinion, could best afford to pay them.

He spent the morning with local government officials

trying to appear fair and reasonable to men who strongly objected to the sums required of them.

His afternoon was given over to tiresome and acrimonious disputes with the Austrian high command over the line of demarcation that was to be established between France and Austria per the Convention of Alessandria that had ended the campaign—an instrument still to be ratified both by the government in Paris and by the Aulic Council in Vienna. And due to the vagueness of the terms laid down in the Convention by Napoleon's representative, Berthier, and the Austrian chief of staff, Zach, the disagreements would take weeks more.

Once the Austrians had taken their leave late that afternoon, a dozen new dispatches were handed to Massena and the next time he looked up, an ADC from Napoleon was being ushered in by Solignac. Both men's faces were wreathed in smiles. The envoy from Paris had brought nine million in gold for the army paymaster. It was an occasion for celebration; Solignac had already left instructions with the chef. All further administrative duties should be curtailed for the night, he affably suggested, and at a cheer from the staff, Massena agreed with good grace.

21

Serena received orders, albeit couched in polite terms, to appear in the dining room at nine.

The emeralds had arrived from the general that afternoon, a magnificent necklace and earrings carried in by Franco, who with a graceful bow handed Serena the gold casket containing them. "Compliments of General Massena," he'd said.

And when the maid arrived to dress Serena, she conveyed a message from General Massena that he "would be pleased if the mademoiselle would wear the emerald jewelry that evening."

What a long way she'd come from her quiet upbringing in Gloucestershire, Serena thought. Wondering what other orders she'd be required to fulfill before the evening ended, she watched servants carry in copper buckets of water for her bath. Tonight she was slated to become the latest of General Massena's paramours. And she didn't know what to do.

What if she were to refuse him? What would happen to her? A small shiver fluttered down her spine. Or did one yield with good grace and pretend it didn't matter that you were reduced to the status of courtesan?

She was mute as she was bathed and dressed, feeling like a prisoner about to be led to the scaffold, her silence apparently unnoticed by the maid who ordered her lowly minions about with the authority of her exalted position. She commanded and they obeyed, bringing soap and towels and more water. The shampoo was discarded twice before the proper scent was accepted by the maid, the fragrance of jasmine apparently preferred by the general, the scent heady in the steam of the bath chamber.

The maid selected appropriate lingerie when Serena said she didn't care what she wore. The delicate silk of a chemise and the gossamer bit of corset slid over her skin with a luxurious whisper as she was laced in and beautified for the general's pleasure.

The abbreviated corset was nothing more than boning covered with lace that served to boost her breasts well above the low décolletage of the filmy bit of white mousseline de soie passing for a gown. There was no question of her purpose in such revealing attire, the undergown of flesh-colored silk blatantly suggestive, clinging to her hips and legs when she moved.

Her hair was dressed à l'antique in a fall of blond curls pinned high on her head, and the emerald necklace lay on her exposed bosom like a sensual invitation to look, to touch.

A lodestar of the first magnitude, a score of men concluded as she entered the dining room. Each one turned to stare at her standing at the door, the emeralds drawing the eye, her full, plump breasts holding their awed gazes. And each officer envied the general walking over to greet the young lady Solignac had brought from Florence.

"Good evening, mademoiselle," Massena said as he reached her, bowing slightly. "Solignac tells me your name is Miss Blythe. Welcome to Milan." He didn't introduce himself and she wasn't sure whether it was arrogance or diffidence. Unlike several of his fellow officers, arrayed in full dress uniform ablaze with gold embroidery, he wore a severe black uniform without medals or ribbons. "The emeralds are very lovely on you," he added, his voice without inflection.

"I'm not sure what to say, sir." Did one thank one's captor for his gift, regardless it was probably someone else's in the not too recent past?

He smiled and took her hand, drawing her into the room, gesturing gracefully in her direction; his hand, she noticed, was strong, tanned, devoid of jewelry. "Comrades, Miss Blythe has consented to bear us company at dinner tonight. Please welcome her."

A hearty round of applause greeted his remarks as well as a number of more exuberant cheers from the younger subalterns.

"As you can see, Miss Blythe," he softly said, smiling faintly, "your presence is much appreciated. Could I offer you some wine?"

"No thank you." She tried to keep her voice from trembling, but the struts of the fan she held in her hand were near to snapping.

"I won't take advantage of you, Miss Blythe, if you have some wine," he remarked with amusement, taking note of the strained curve of the ivory-and-lace fan. He waved a footman over. "The lady would like a glass of wine."

The footman reappeared with the filled glass, and Massena handed it to her, watching as she obeyed him and lifted it to her lips. "The evening won't seem so threatening after a glass of wine," he gently said. "I have no intention of hurting you. Now come," he went on in a less cajoling tone, "Solignac is impatient to talk with you. He's a connoisseur of art and he tells me your painting was very good. He'll talk endlessly of his collection, so when you've endured enough, simply walk away. I've already warned him you have my permission to ignore him."

She smiled, as she knew she was expected to do, and leaning over the merest distance, so his mouth was nearer her ear, he murmured, "That's better."

Perhaps the wine *did* help or the general's urbane chivalry reassured her or the officers' amiable courtesies calmed her worst fears, for after a time she found herself relaxing in the convivial company. Seated beside the general at dinner, she listened to the good-humored fellowship, the talk not of war but of families or horses, of homes they'd left behind and of who was most apt to win the bank tonight at faro. She found herself laughing too on occasion and when Massena spoke to her, she no longer weighed each word before responding. It

was very strange at first when she realized these men were
little different from those she might have dined with at a
country party in Gloucestershire. And she even forgot for a
time that she was not a guest but a captive.

They retired after dinner to a large drawing room that
had been arranged for cards, and while several officers
played faro the general invited her to sit with him at his
table, where the game of choice was loo.

He handed her some gold coins and without asking, had
the dealer allot her cards as well. Under the circumstances
she would have had to make a scene to refuse.

He knew that of course. He'd been watching the alarm
diminish in Serena's eyes throughout the evening, taking
pleasure in wooing her. He wanted her to play cards because
he'd see that she won and ladies liked to win.

And then later in the evening, he'd play a very different
game with her. One that he'd win.

She was many ducats richer before long, as he'd ordered,
although the lady had a refreshing expertise that made him
question her pose of innocence. In his experience, women
that skilled at cards were also skilled at other more pleasurable amusements. The paradox between her naïveté and that
gamester facility more likely seen in the demimonde piqued
his interest; he'd have to inquire into her background.
Although countess or maid, the pleasure they offered was
identical. Massena wasn't looking for permanence, only
orgasmic diversion.

They drank some excellent wines and laughed more often
as the evening progressed and empty bottles accumulated.
Serena had decided the general was right. The inevitable
conclusion to the evening would be more palatable with a
glass or two of wine. And she had no illusions as to the general's intent.

An orderly interrupted their game shortly after midnight,
apologizing as he handed Massena a note.

Scanning the message, the general said, "Show him up,"
and then finished dealing the cards. "A merchant from Flo-

rence wishes to discuss a donation from Fiesole," he abstractly noted, Solignac's questioning look requiring some response. "I'll ante four thousand."

"Who from Florence?" Solignac retorted, cautious of businessmen arriving at so late an hour.

"A Signore Allori. A banker, I'm pleased to say. Are you playing, Solignac?"

The chief of staff quickly perused his cards and tossed them down.

"Solignac's passing," Massena blandly remarked. "Is anyone else standing?"

"I will," Serena said. "Did you say four thousand or ten thousand?" she casually inquired.

"I like reckless play in a lady," Massena softly said. "I believe it was ten thousand, mademoiselle," he added, sliding several more markers into the center of the table. "And what will you do now?" The ice had thawed from his cool eyes; he had an insidious quiet charm. And she began to understand why his men would follow him anywhere, why rumors of his unbridled appetite for women held genuine merit.

"I think I'll relieve you of your money, mon général. Pam-flush," she pleasantly said, slowly turning over each of her cards until they were all faceup on the green baize—four diamonds and a jack of clubs.

"It's a pleasure losing to someone as beautiful as you, Miss Blythe," Massena murmured, pushing his cards aside. "What are you going to buy with all your winnings?"

Before she could answer, Massena's attention was diverted, his gaze shifting away from his companions. "I see our banker has arrived," he said, bending over to whisper something to Solignac, whose head swiveled around with a snap, his attention hard on the man walking toward them.

Taking note of the men's intense scrutiny, Serena looked up and gasped.

Turning around at the sound, Massena watched Serena's face suffuse with a rosy blush. "Do you know Mr. Allori?" he softly inquired.

"No—I'm not certain . . . I don't think so," she stammered, averting her gaze from Beau, not wishing to give him away or add to the danger of his position.

His leisurely progress across the large room drew everyone's attention, not just for the unusual time of his arrival but for his appearance. The dust of the road clung to his clothes, his hessians, chamois breeches, and dark coat a haze of pale ocher, the leather saddlebags slung over his shoulder clinking loudly as he walked, the faint jingle of his spurs counterpoint to the sudden stillness of the salon. He walked slowly, his expression composed, aware of the interest his entrance had produced. He'd seen Massena once at the Truce of Leoben, Beau recalled. Would the general remember him from the crush of people at Schloss Eggenwald that day?

The orderly preceding him announced his name as he approached Massena's table. "Mr. Allori, sir."

"What brings you to Milan, Rochefort?" the general genially asked. "And in such haste." His cool blue gaze drifted over Beau's dusty garb.

"A matter of business, general," Beau smoothly replied. The general's coup de l'oeil was remarkable. Leoben was three years ago, there were over a hundred people in the conference room, and he'd never been introduced.

"Government business?" Massena inquired, utterly calm.

"No. Private business." Beau's gaze was drawn to Serena, dressed like a courtesan at the general's side—or rather, *un*dressed like a courtesan, he thought, resentful and jaundiced. "Collecting jewelry, mademoiselle?" he murmured, a cutting edge to his voice as he noted the emeralds lying on her breasts. Only Russians created necklaces like that.

Serena drew in her breath as if she'd been slapped and then she flushed bright pink. How dare he think she was here by choice.

"Ah . . . ," the general said in abrupt understanding. Coolly surveying the other officers at the table, he dismissed them with a nod. As they rose, he motioned to Beau to sit down. "So you know Miss Blythe?" Massena casually inquired. The anger in Rochefort's eyes when he looked at her had been so obvious he needn't have asked.

"Very well." A whip-sharp murmur.

"Miss Blythe wasn't sure she remembered you when I asked."

Beau glanced at Serena briefly. "Perhaps I'll have the opportunity to refresh her memory."

"Why would I let you do that?" An indolently tossed gauntlet.

"Because I'm willing to make it worth your while," Beau softly said.

"Are we negotiating for the lady's time?"

Beau shook his head in negation, a barely discernible movement. "I've come to buy her from you."

Massena's dark brows briefly arched into half-moons, but his voice when he spoke was mild. "Have you bought women before, Rochefort? I wouldn't have thought you had the need."

"Mistresses always cost money, General. You and I both know that."

"Some more than others," the general agreed, recollecting Countess Gonchanka's extravagant tastes, unlike those of the pretty seventeen-year-old ballet walk-on who was content with bonbons and new dresses. And then there was Teo, he thought with a pang of regret, who wanted only his love. And he'd failed her.

"I knew you'd understand," Beau said, breaking into Massena's reverie. "Name your price, General, and I'll take Miss Blythe off your hands."

"I'm not for sale, Lord Rochefort," Serena snapped, leaning forward pugnaciously, furious at his effrontery. "I'm not a horse or a painting or a bit of property you covet!"

"Miss Blythe was your mistress?" Massena queried, his attention restored by Serena's revealing outburst.

She seemed oblivious to the flaunting spectacle she presented, Beau irritably thought, her pale, bounteous breasts almost spilling out of the flimsy bodice as she shifted forward to confront him. He wanted to cover her nudity with his coat, rankled that other men openly gazed at her. "I brought her here from England," he said, a muscle twitching high on his cheekbone, only an iron will keeping him seated.

"You've been in Florence? A bit of a campaign backwater for a man of your talents." Massena knew Beau St. Jules was one of Pitt's best and brightest young men.

"He *left* me in Florence," Serena acerbically said, her gaze scathing.

"Did you lose interest, Rochefort?"

"He always loses interest," Serena tartly interposed, hating him for so casually walking in, for discussing her as though she weren't there, most of all for his shocking, carnal appeal—all command and demand and authority.

"I'm not sure the lady wishes to go with you." The general's shrewd gaze drifted between the two people, assessing.

"She doesn't always know what she wants," Beau brusquely replied, his dark eyes hot with temper.

"She seems rather displeased with you, Rochefort."

"I've always been able to change her mind if I'm imaginative."

Serena blushed.

"A sexual allusion, I presume," Massena drawled. "While *I* haven't yet tasted of Miss Blythe's pleasures. I'm afraid you've come too early, Rochefort. You can't expect me to give her up without"—he shrugged delicately—"enjoying her lovely charms."

Was he serious about wanting Serena or merely raising his price? Beau wondered. Not that any subtlety, real or imagined, mattered after Beau realized Serena was yet untouched by the general. "Perhaps I could change your mind," Beau said, and reaching down for his saddlebags, he heaved them up on the table, where they landed with a resounding thud.

"This is outside governmental boundaries?" Massena queried, the obvious weight of the gold altering his notions of possession. The normal course of his day required constant bargaining and deal-making—the corrupt politics of victory more cynical than making war. He'd welcome the gold to augment the constant financial shortfall under which he operated his command. And if it was English gold, so much the better.

"This is strictly personal," Beau declared. "And there's no point in haggling. I'll pay whatever your price."

"Wait," Serena indignantly rebuked, stung by the unceremonious consignment of her body. "Just a damned minute!"

Both men looked at her for a moment, surprised at her fury. In their masculine world women were essentially disenfranchised.

"I have a proposition," she said into the silence, bartering for some mastery in the cool disposal of her body, determined to exact revenge for Beau St. Jules's presumptions. "Something more interesting than this bourgeois exchange of gold."

Massena inclined his head.

"One game of loo to decide this issue. If I win, I leave here tonight. If not, I stay with the victor." Her voice was level, the heat of her anger so intense she was without fear. And if her rage had been so powerfully provoked earlier, she might have been bold enough to consider the notion sooner.

Massena didn't hesitate a second; one of his best qualities as a strategist was his ability to make instant decisions. He reached for the deck of cards. "Loo or faro?" he inquired. "Or something else. The choice is yours, Miss Blythe."

"Loo." It was her virtuoso specialty, as sex was for Beau St. Jules.

"Is that amenable to you, Rochefort?" the general inquired, his courtesy faultless, his mood agreeable; there was a piquant excitement in a game of chance with a lady as prize. And he had two opportunities to win—his hand and Rochefort's. If St. Jules won, he'd still charge him for the pleasure of taking the lady away. He liked the odds.

"Fine," Beau said, sweeping his saddlebags from the table.

They cut for the deal and Massena had high card. He had

the advantage now of playing last, but seated to his left, Serena would lead—a slight benefit.

The cards were dealt, three each, and a ten of hearts turned up for trump. "I think five thousand ducats will do to start," Massena said, counting out his markers, "or its equivalent in florins, Rochefort, if you prefer."

And the game began.

Serena had only one trump, a king of hearts—high but not an ace. Should she lead with it and gamble no one had the ace or play more conservatively and wait to see what the others had? She had to win two out of three tricks to win the game. Now wasn't the time to play conservatively, she decided, letting her instincts drive her. She led with her king of hearts.

A risky move, Beau thought, and gave her high marks for courage. If Massena had the ace, she'd lose her lead. He placed his nine of hearts on the table.

Massena followed with a queen of hearts.

And Serena's pulse rate slowed to a more manageable level. She'd won the first trick.

"Congratulations, mademoiselle." Massena smiled faintly, recognizing she'd risked all leading with her high card. "Your luck is holding," he pleasantly added.

"Perhaps that's why they call it Lady Luck," Serena genially replied, buoyed by an irrepressible sense of good fortune.

Beau scowled. She'd gone for broke on that lead—not the work of an amateur.

"Some people don't like to lose," Serena sweetly said, glancing at Beau over her cards.

"Keep it in mind."

"I certainly will, Lord Rochefort. But you have two more chances to win, so you needn't become surly yet."

"Children, children," Massena lightly chided. "I so dislike controversy."

"My apologies, sir," Serena quickly interposed, not inclined to anger the man who might let her walk free. "I'm quite ready to begin."

And she quickly perused the two cards left in her hand. Sometimes you can smell it, her father used to say—the winds of providence. Her nostrils flared as she inhaled, and gambling that Massena didn't have any more trumps or he wouldn't have played his queen, hoping Beau wasn't lying in wait with the ace of hearts, Serena led with her ace of spades. And for a second she hoped she wasn't *tempting* providence. She desperately needed this trick. The low card left in her hand was useless.

Damn her, she played recklessly, Beau disgruntedly reflected, forced to admire her nerve—she could lose her ace with any low card of hearts. But required to follow suit, he was obliged to play his only power card—the king of spades.

Massena played a five of spades.

And Serena allowed herself a restrained smile of triumph. She'd taken the second trick.

"Thank you, gentlemen," she politely said, as if her life hadn't hung in the balance. "It's been a pleasure."

"You're a marvel to behold, Miss Blythe," Massena stated, impressed by the lady's true proficiency displayed for the first time that evening. "Where did you acquire such skill?"

"At my papa's knee, General."

"You never played like that before," Beau said, his eyes penetrating, cool.

"I was never about to be purchased before. And you know me very little, Lord Rochefort," she mocked.

"For now," he said between his teeth.

"For*ever*, milord," she countered, rising from her chair. "And now if you'll excuse me, I'm keen to begin my return journey to Florence."

"I'll send an escort with you. Solignac," Massena called, beckoning his chief of staff over.

"I appreciate it, sir." Serena was not foolish enough to refuse. A woman alone on the road was fair prey to anyone.

"The mademoiselle is leaving us, Solignac," Massena mildly said when his aide approached. "I'd like you to escort her back to Florence."

"Yes, sir." Solignac's face was expressionless; he'd hear the details in good time, he knew.

"Ready a troop," Massena ordered, "and Miss Blythe will be down directly."

"Thank you, sir," Serena said as the colonel turned and left.

"Solignac doesn't always make wise choices," Massena noted with a shrug. "But perhaps we'll meet again."

"I appreciate your kindness."

"Take the emeralds. As part of your winning hand. And the ante."

"I couldn't, sir."

"I insist." His expression changed subtly; he was once again the commander-in-chief.

"Thank you," she sensibly replied. "You're much too generous."

"Remind Solignac we're in need of him here once he gets to Florence. I know how avaricious his collecting zeal is."

"I don't think he'd heed me, sir."

Massena laughed. "The lady's a realist, eh, Rochefort?" He cast a glance at Beau, sprawled glowering in his chair.

"Supremely," Beau murmured.

"Come now, Rochefort, Miss Blythe won fairly. Give her her due."

"I intend to," he ominously returned.

"And I'll bid you gentlemen adieu," Serena airily said, waving away Beau's threat. "Pleasant journey home, Lord Rochefort, my thanks to you, General." She curtseyed, the emeralds twinkling on her shapely, quivering breasts and she was gone a moment later, only the scent of jasmine lingering in the air.

"Rochefort, you're taking this too seriously," Massena cajoled. "You didn't lose that much—a few thousand florins and there are hundreds of other women to replace Miss Blythe, lovely as she is." A rueful philosophical edge colored his voice, his premise put to the test this year without Teo. "What matters *whom* you fuck," he said, "as long as the woman's willing and available. Tell Pitt that—

he drinks too much and doesn't fuck enough. It makes him unimaginative."

"Not Bonaparte's problem," Beau sardonically replied.

"My point exactly." The general seemed to relax again, his familiar insouciant tone restored. "Tell me what you want—another fair-haired beauty? Londes will find you one to soothe your dark mood. And now that we're about to sign a peace treaty with Austria once again, I won't even confiscate your gold. Smile at least for that," Massena said, his mouth faintly quirked, past memories neatly closed away. He could take the gold if he wished; he could take it all and keep Beau prisoner too if he wanted, with England still conditionally at war with France. But the island kingdom was without allies at the moment now that the truce was signed, without a land army of any consequence, not likely to prove a difficult adversary at least for the immediate future. He could afford to be magnanimous.

Beau smiled at his gracious host, at the general who was the most capable of all the marshals of France. And then he said, "What kind of a blond woman?"

Massena roared with laughter and waved over his ADC Londes. "Lord Rochefort will be joining us this evening and he prefers a blonde. Whom do we have that would appeal to him?"

By inclination and choice Hippolyte Londes enjoyed his duties as procuring agent for the headquarter's staff. There were always ladies of every persuasion who weren't disinclined to enjoying the favors of the victors. "The Contessa Figlio, sir, is decidedly blond and very passionate."

"Could you have her brought here, in say—an hour?"

"And for you, sir?"

"Bring me a Gypsy. I'm suddenly tired and beyond wooing." And prey to the disillusion and insidious melancholy Teo's memory always evoked.

22

Londes appeared at the general's table in an hour as directed. "The ladies are waiting, sir."

Massena looked across the table at Beau. "Have you had enough of cards, Rochefort?" The men had been drinking and idly playing vingt-et-un, discussing mutual friends in the officer corps of their respective nations. Massena had served fourteen years in the Royal Army before the revolution; he had acquaintances in both England and the royalist camp, while Beau had met many officers over the past few years in the course of his missions for Pitt.

"Mustn't keep the ladies waiting," Beau pleasantly said, "although after days without rest I'm more apt to sleep in bed tonight."

"Not after you've seen Countess Figlio, Rochefort," Massena noted, coming to his feet. "Her husband was very old."

"Was?"

"He died in bed after some strenuous activities." The general's smile was eloquent.

"Surely a gratifying way to go," Beau murmured, rising from his chair.

"I can guarantee you'll be satisfied, Lord Rochefort," Londes asserted, directing them with a small bow toward the double doors leading to the hall.

"You've tried her," Beau mildly said, the faintest query in his statement.

"Hippolyte prides himself on his dedication to duty, don't you my boy?" Massena's drollery was softly put.

"I'm only concerned that the women are worthy of your interest, sir." The young fair-haired adjunct's eyes were as innocent as his tone.

"He does damned fine work, Rochefort. You won't be disappointed. Did you bring Delfine?" the general went on, the men striding side by side down the broad candlelit corridor adorned with murals of Olympian gods and goddesses.

"She was most eager, sir."

"She's a greedy little thing in more ways than one. Thank you, Hippolyte. I think I've been working too hard."

"You always do, sir. I'll tell Franco you're going to sleep late tomorrow."

"Breakfast at nine, Rochefort?" Massena said. "Or is that too early for you?"

"Nine's fine. I should start back for Leghorn tomorrow." His expression went grim for a moment at the thought of his useless journey, of his wasted thoughts for a woman who had more avaricious priorities.

"Give my regards to Madelina," Massena said, stopping at the entrance to his suite. "Hippolyte will show you to your rooms." His eyes were half-lidded from weariness but he smiled graciously. "A pleasant adventure, Rochefort."

Londes escorted Beau to a doorway a short distance away and, like a perfect host, showed him into his room and introduced him to the countess. It could have been the most respectable occasion for all the courtesies displayed; it might not have been one-thirty in the morning and sex the transaction.

"Forgive my appearance," Beau said when the door closed behind Londes. "I'll bathe first."

"I'll bathe with you. We met at Naples once, you don't remember."

His gaze came up; he'd been about to toss his saddlebags on the floor. "Where?" The thud of gold punctuated his query.

"At the Reale and later at your apartment in town."

"At my apartment?" He looked at her more closely. "I must not have been sober."

"No, but you were exceptional," she said, a husky intonation to her voice.

"I'm sorry," he replied with a rueful smile. "Demon rum and all that. My apologies." He tried to place her in the profusion of women who had passed through his life: small; cornsilk gold hair; exquisite breasts and she knew it. Her dress was revealing.

"I didn't quite believe Londes when he said you were in Milan. But it was worth coming to see for myself."

He grinned. "Well, I'm pleased to renew our acquaintance, Countess."

And when she dozed off toward morning, Beau found he couldn't sleep regardless his orgasmic oblivion, regardless they'd made love for hours and his days without sleep. Some niggling voice deep in the recesses of his brain badgered him, then eventually turned bullying.

Go after her, the small voice said. Go after her and take her back.

He found himself hastily dressing short moments later as if he were late for a mission. He left a note for Madelina—another apology and a generous sum of gold for her time. He wrote a swift note to Massena as well, thanking him for his hospitality, and within minutes was on the road to Florence.

She was five hours ahead of him.

But she was traveling in a carriage and he could outride her. Quickly calculating, he decided he could overtake Solignac and the carriage by noon.

Dead tired and consumed by spleen, he spurred his mount.

Solignac had given his troop permission to rest on the outskirts of Piacenza for no one had slept the past night and the heat of the day was enervating. While the men found soft beds in the stables, the colonel had taken rooms for him-

self and Serena at the inn, and weary with fatigue, he'd
fallen asleep immediately.

Serena found sleep elusive, no matter that she'd eaten a
hearty meal and was almost tranquilized by the creamy
tagliatelle and zabaione jam tart she'd been served. Lying on
a rustic pine bed in a second-floor chamber with the window
open to the summer afternoon, she should have been lulled
to sleep by the sound of bees in the garden below. But her
thoughts were in turmoil, a litany of logic wrangling with
intuitive needs and emotions in her brain. She was right,
though, she repeated for the hundredth time since Milan, to
have walked away from Beau St. Jules.

Of course she was right.

He was selfish beyond the bounds of normal indulgence
and gallingly arrogant to think he could buy her release
without so much as a nod in her direction. As if he hadn't
been the one to leave *her*. Did he expect her to have been
waiting precisely where he'd last left her like a china doll put
away on a shelf until he was ready to play again?

Apparently he did.

Too . . . damn . . . bad.

Let some of the other thousand women he'd bedded offer
him that compliance.

But as easily as her anger flared, so did a covetous need
for him distract her. She knew better than to give in to such
reckless feelings. He'd only hurt her again when she'd at last
made some peace with her loss.

But he'd come *back* to Florence, she thought in the next
beat of her heart, a capricious leap of hope warming her
senses. Had he come for her?

What did it matter, though, why he'd arrived in Florence
and then in Milan? she restlessly mused a second later, her
emotions vacillating fitfully. His conduct in Milan had been
outrageous and rude. And the love she wanted from him
hadn't been evidenced in a single glance or word. Suddenly
smiling at recall of their game of loo, she took pleasure in
her swift and conclusive victory, in Beau's churlish response.
It was gratifying to triumph, to win her freedom on her own

terms. A lesson to Beau St. Jules that all women weren't obedient to his will.

She'd felt invincible last night at the moment she'd suggested the game, even before the hand had been dealt, as though she'd known how the cards would fall. Her father had taught her to recognize that sensation, that small shiver of excitement and she'd almost blurted out, "I'm going to win," so intense was the feeling.

But she'd concealed her emotions; she'd learned that too from her father. And she knew Beau was left wondering whether she'd simply allowed him to win in the past, whether a woman was truly his match.

At midday late in June, the sun was sweltering hot and even if Beau hadn't been chafing and embittered, the broiling sun would have taken the edge off his good humor. Not to mention he was about to approach one of the most corrupt men in Italy and try to convince him to disobey orders and turn over a woman of possible interest to him. Beau had no illusions about Solignac's morality; like Londes, he no doubt tested the ladies gathered for Massena's pleasure.

The one positive note in his distasteful deliberations was the fact that Solignac could be bought; that was a given. But the question was, how blunt could one be in his approach? Or to what degree would diplomacy be required in convincing Solignac to relinquish his prize?

Colonel Solignac was called Massena's extortionist. Or simply his own, those loyal to Massena contended. It was a dubious distinction in a system that paid and fed its army with enforced levies from its conquered territories.

When Beau stopped to change horses at a small posting station later that morning, he learned that a French troop escorting a lady in the carriage had passed through less than an hour before. Spurred by the news, he helped saddle his fresh mount, too impatient to wait for the stable lad to finish the task. He almost had her, he thought, as he swiftly buckled the bridle in place and adjusted the bit.

The carriage first caught his eye some twenty minutes later, the vehicle pulled off the road into the shade of some trees beside an inn. How solicitous Solignac was to the mademoiselle's comfort, Beau resentfully thought, how careful that the carriage interior was kept cool for the lady. Knowing Solignac took what he wanted, Beau decided he was probably sleeping with her, and the jealous rage he'd rationalized into submission on the pounding ride south flared afresh.

Cautious with a troop of French soldiers serving as escort, he first determined their location, and discovering them asleep in the stables, proceeded to find Solignac. The colonel was upstairs, the proprietor said. He didn't wish his sleep disturbed.

Brushing the man aside, Beau took the stairs in a run and barged into the colonel's room, shoving the door open with such force it slammed into the wall with an explosive crash. Standing on the threshold, he searched the front room for Serena, his gaze sweeping the small chamber. A bed and Solignac—just Solignac.

"Where is she?" he barked, any diplomatic inclination overwhelmed by jealousy. The door's concussive impact had set a crucifix on the wall swinging wildly, and as if his harsh voice had suddenly snapped the string holding it, the statuary slid to the floor and shattered.

Solignac groggily surveyed the angry man at his door, his drowsy gaze drawn away by the brittle sound of breaking gesso to the colored bits of plaster lying in splinters on the floor. Then, as the identity of the intruder clarified, he heaved his legs over the side of the bed and sat up. "Can I help you, Rochefort?" he said, sighing heavily. "You didn't let me sleep long."

"She's not here." There wasn't room under the bed nor in it and no other door into the bedchamber.

Still not completely awake, the colonel took a moment to

synthesize the pronoun. "Massena wouldn't have wanted her here," he finally said, his voice arid.

"And you always obey?"

"Always, my dear young hothead," the general blandly said. He didn't, of course, but the woman was to have safe passage, he'd been told. And without a ready profit motive, there was no point in crossing Massena.

"Where is she?" Curt, sharp, more grim than the first time he'd asked.

Solignac's head came up and his eyes from under heavy brows searched Beau's forbidding face. "Down the hall, sleeping. Alone. You wanted to know that most of all, didn't you?" he softly added. Standing, he lazily stretched and then gazed about the room as if seeing it for the first time. A brandy bottle on the table caught his eye. "Would you like a grappa?" he inquired, not easily intimidated after fighting France's wars the last decade.

"No." Beau shut the door.

"I think I'll have one since I'm not likely to go back to sleep now," the colonel ironically said, realizing Lord Rochefort wanted privacy, recognizing the probable reason why. Solignac specialized in deal-making, for which Napoleon should thank him profusely, he often thought. Walking stocking-footed over to a small table, he poured himself a brandy, and waving Beau to a chair, sat down himself.

"You probably know why I'm here," Beau said, crossing the small room and dropping into a sturdy wooden chair painted an intense yellow.

"I have a suspicion," Solignac murmured, stroking the uneven surface of his glass, taking note of the heavy saddle-bags Beau had placed on the floor beside his chair.

"Well then . . ." A sigh of distaste or vexation punctuated the silence and the colonel didn't think he'd care to be the young lady a few moments from now. "Would you like to set a price," Beau quietly asked, "or should I make an offer?"

"You first, Rochefort. I'm curious what you'll pay for the mademoiselle."

"You don't anticipate any problem with the exchange?" Beau queried.

"None," Solignac complacently replied, smiling slightly.

"I have gold florins."

"Florins are fine."

"I have slightly less than a hundred thousand."

"That will do nicely."

"Will Massena be informed of this transaction?"

"Probably not." The colonel shrugged. "One never knows when a confession is required, but I doubt one will be. Would you like a grappa now that our business is concluded?"

"No, thank you." Quickly rising, Beau set the saddlebags on the table, his restiveness blatant.

"I recall a woman long ago who heated my blood like Miss Blythe does yours," Solignac gently said. "I envy you the feeling."

Slipping a small purse from a snapped compartment of the leather bag, Beau turned to look at the colonel, his gaze chill. "And I appreciate your understanding."

Perhaps not love after all, Solignac decided, reevaluating the young man's motives. "For one hundred thousand florins, my boy, I can be infinitely understanding," he said, smiling, the lady no longer his concern. "Her room is three doors down to the right. Take the key on the bureau. I wasn't certain she could be trusted to stay, so I locked her in."

"One more thing," Beau murmured, sliding the purse into his coat pocket. "How soon will you be leaving?"

He didn't want witnesses, Solignac thought. "As soon as the horses are saddled." One hundred thousand florins also bought a speedy exit.

"Then I'll bid you good day, colonel." Beau's bow was courteous, his smile slightly forced.

"A pleasurable afternoon, Lord Rochefort. And you'll like the food here. The proprietor's wife is an excellent cook." He didn't suppose the jealous young man would be leaving the inn any time soon now that he had the mademoiselle to himself.

Beau inclined his head in acknowledgment. "Thank you for your time, Colonel," he soberly said. Picking up the key from the bureau, he strode from the room.

23

He stood outside Serena's door for a moment, drawing in a calming breath, tamping down his temper, and then he raised his hand and knocked.

Without waiting for a response, he placed the key in the lock and let himself in.

She was standing by the bed, although the coverlet was rumpled where she'd recently lain. "You can't come in."

"Too late," he murmured, shutting the door behind him, his hair almost brushing the low timbered ceiling.

"I don't want to see you."

"Then shut your eyes, because I'm here."

She tried to remain composed when his powerful presence inspired anxiety on several levels. "You must have bargained with Solignac," she said. "He has fewer scruples than Massena."

"He has no scruples, darling." His smile was one of triumph.

"I'm not your darling," she pettishly replied, taking issue with his smile and the reasons he was here. "Those were the other thousand women in your life. You left me in Florence three months ago and I've forgotten you." She lifted her chin a fraction, challenging him.

"Have you really?" he softly asked.

"Yes, I have," she lied. "So I'd prefer you not walk back into my life. I'm sorry if you paid Solignac but he shouldn't have taken the money. He doesn't have the authority."

"I thought you were a realist, dear. He has considerable

authority at the moment, which is why I paid him. Where Massena has principles, Solignac has none. He could have killed us both, taken the money, and never missed a second of sleep."

"Well, thank you then for saving my life," she sarcastically replied. "I'm sure you had altruistic motives."

"That depends on your interpretation of altruism."

"And yours is?"

"An unselfish regard for your pleasure." She looked lush, dew fresh in her yellow sprigged muslin gown, her hair tousled from sleep, her scent perfuming the small room.

"In that case my pleasure would best be served if you left."

"I may not be *completely* unselfish," he said, his voice a velvety murmur.

"You've come a long way for nothing, Lord Rochefort," she reproved. "Your pleasure and mine are quite different."

"They never used to be."

"I've found new interests."

"Like Massena," he mildly said. "He paid you well for your time, didn't he? Those emeralds are worth a fortune," he murmured, stricture in every smooth syllable. "I'm surprised you left so precipitously. Did I scare you away?"

"I was captured. Solignac took me from the Uffizi, along with every painting that caught his eye," she levelly said, her gaze unflinching under his taunting scrutiny. "Why would I be interested in Massena?"

"You looked as though you were enjoying yourself when I walked into the card room."

A twinge of guilt caused her discomfort as she thought of her ready laughter that evening. "They were reasonably kind," she stiffly said.

"As I can be, darling," he interposed as though he'd been waiting for her cue. "So be practical. I came here to offer you carte blanche as my mistress along with a degree less disruption in your life. The Austrians are sure to break the truce before long and you'll very likely find yourself in the thick of battle if you stay here."

"You came all this way to offer me the position of mistress?" The icy chill in her voice would have stopped a lesser man. "What an honor, Lord Rochefort, although the roster must be lengthy by now. What number would I be?"

He didn't answer immediately and when he did, his voice was hushed. "I've never set up a mistress before."

"A signal honor then. My heart is palpitating wildly," she declared, her voice brittle. "What did I do to deserve such recognition from London's premier libertine? Tell me because perhaps I could market those skills to a broader audience. Was it my kissing you liked—or my instant response to your desire? Did you like that I'd stay up all night fucking you?" she sardonically murmured. "Or did my facility at cards win your approval?"

"Are you through?" he coolly inquired, his temper barely controlled, her tone galling when he thought of all the changes he'd made in his life because of her, the days and nights he'd spent drinking away her memory, the distinction of his offer—if not to her, then to him.

"What more is there to say? Do I kiss your hand now? Tell me, what's the protocol in the St. John family on momentous occasions like this?"

"Fuck off," he growled.

"Precisely what I was going to tell you," she derisively retorted.

"Sorry, that's not an option."

"What options do I have?" Haughty, imperious, she looked at him with a basilisk gaze.

"None."

"So," she said, drawing in a shallow breath, her nostrils flaring, "I'm to be your mistress, or—"

"There's no or." Decisive, final.

"I see." The words were bitten off. "For how long?"

"Are we bargaining?" he mocked, his smile vicious.

"No, it's a simple question. How long will I be your mistress? Answer me."

He couldn't of course. He didn't know and she waited as the silence lengthened and then said, "You see."

"There's nothing to see." His voice was laying-down-the-rules brisk. "I want you as my mistress preferably by choice but if not—some other way will suit me as well."

"Meaning?"

"Meaning you're mine for the duration," he simply said.

He suddenly loomed even larger in the small room—massive and powerful and don't forget wealthy, she resentfully thought, so when he spoke plainly like that people always listened. But she wasn't a dancer or a courtesan (although perhaps that would be open to debate in some quarters—but she wasn't in her heart) nor was she destitute as she'd once been, or a tradesman or servant or minor nobility who wanted something from him. "You can't always have what you want," she retorted, knowing she couldn't be forced to comply graciously.

"But I can." He always had.

"Not this time, Beau. I don't care how much you paid Solignac. You can't force me to want you."

"I can make you want me." Assured, confident, he spoke softly as though the words needed no inflection.

"That's a different kind of wanting."

His dark eyes slowly drifted down her shapely form. "I'll settle for that," he said, his half-smile insolent.

"You can't make me stay even then." She wouldn't; not ever when he smiled like that.

He didn't respond immediately, not with conflicting answers—none mild enough not to alarm—racing through his mind. "I can keep you," he said at last.

"For how long though, tell me that," she heatedly said.

"For as long as I want."

Her brows flared upward. "I'm surprised you'd trouble yourself so," she said with dripping sarcasm. "Surely there are women enough you needn't force."

Nonplussed by the simple statement, he gazed out the window where the hum of bees resonated in the summer heat. But he'd always dealt directly with his emotions and the brief uncertainty passed. "I prefer you."

"I *don't* prefer you."

He shifted on his feet, restless, enervated by her contentiousness. "Don't make this complicated."

"Just submit, you mean."

"Jesus, Serena," he wearily said, exhaustion suddenly hitting him like a wave. "I haven't slept for days. Could we talk about this later?"

"I haven't slept much at all since you left me."

"*Merde,*" he breathed, leaning back against the door, shutting his eyes in exasperation. "Fuck," he softly swore, the expletive exhaled in a disgruntled rush of air and then he opened his eyes and pushed away from the door. Walking a half dozen steps, he dropped into a chair. The silence suddenly seemed palpable, heavy and querulous, humming with dissatisfaction, and Serena felt a drifting sadness insinuate itself into her anger and scorn. She could never have him, she thought, as if a door had suddenly closed on their shared memories.

He was contemplating the toes of his dusty boots stretched out before him when he began speaking again, his slouched pose graphic with disaffection. "I'm not sure I've slept either," he murmured, his voice a husky rasp, "not since I left Florence, but then I haven't been sober much, which blurs recall. And if other women could have made me forget you, I would have, believe me." He grimaced at the comfortless memories.

"So what are we going to do?" Serena cautiously asked. He was different—his tone, his words, the insolent contempt gone.

His gaze came up and he stared at her from under his lashes. "I know what *I* want to do."

"You're persistent at least," she whispered.

"I'm mostly tired. If you keep talking long enough I'll fall asleep and no longer be of danger to you."

"You're not dangerous to me." His exhaustion suddenly showed and she realized with an elemental profundity that his search for her was driven by more than casual desire and force majeure.

"Come closer then." His voice was hushed, sleepy. "I won't ravish you. I don't have the energy."

She moved away from the bed and slowly approached him. "How long have you been on the road?"

She could see the effort it took him to concentrate. "Four or five days; I'm not sure."

"Because you love me." She said it very softly, trembling as she spoke, made bold perhaps by her success with Massena, thinking she had nothing to lose if she were viewed by Beau as mere chattel.

He shook his head and looked away. "I don't think so. . . ." And then he shifted restlessly, slowly recrossing his ankles, leaving new smudges on the hooked carpet from his boots. "I don't know . . . maybe . . ." He slid lower in his chair as if protecting himself from demons. "But I'm resisting like hell," he murmured, contemplating some distant view out the window.

Surely not an admission to bring unalloyed joy, but Serena smiled anyway, recognizing the effort it took for him to voice the words, however ambiguous.

"I don't suppose you want to get married."

His gaze flashed upward, wide-eyed, shocked. "Christ no. I'm only twenty-two."

"We should be sensible then," she said, her happiness destroyed. "You don't want to be married. I don't want to be your mistress—it's such a transient role in your life," she pointed out as though he'd not noticed. It wasn't as though compromise was possible with such disparate views, she thought, and much as she loved him, she loved herself as well. "So thank you for coming after me," she went on, her voice trembling with regret, "but I don't see a reasonable solution."

It was hard to think when he hadn't slept for so long, but he didn't want to let her go and he knew he couldn't force her to stay for long. Furthermore, she'd been constantly in his thoughts—for months—which had to mean something, he decided with blunt male practicality. "What if"—he paused, the shocking thought paralyzing his tongue for a

moment—"what if we were to marry?" he cautiously negotiated, plunging dubiously into an unknown world, the words
sounding foreign in his ears, incomprehensible. "Neville and
Harper married and it didn't change their life much," he
murmured half to himself like a convincing argument. "And
Freddie Stennis too."

"I don't want that kind of marriage," she said, knowing
she should be more hopeful and just say yes.

His lashes half shaded his eyes when he looked up at her.
"You're damned hard to please."

"It would break my heart a thousand times to see you
leave me for another woman or hear about it over tea."

"Other wives survive." He'd bedded scores of them.

"I don't want to just survive."

"Jesus," he muttered, the thought of fidelity alarming,
impossible. "I don't know how to be faithful," he said. "I
can't."

"I understand." And she did. He was too young and the
wealthy son of a wealthy duke could aspire much higher for
a marriage partner—in that far-off time when he could contemplate the act without such trepidation.

She'd known it from the beginning.

She'd known he would never be hers.

What she didn't understand however, was Beau St.
Jules's force of will—arbitrary, occasionally despotic, irrepressibly unhampered by discretion. And when he suddenly
rose from his chair like a striking deadly force, his lethargy
replaced by a graphic power, she came face-to-face with that
resolute will.

"Now then," he softly said, towering over her, forcing her
back a step, wanting what he wanted, no longer interested
in appeasement, "*you* may understand—whatever the hell
that platitude means—but your understanding doesn't solve
my problem. I came here—actually I rode across half of Italy
so I could fuck you and," he went on, forcing her back
another step, his voice dropping to a whisper, "I intend to."

He advanced and she retreated in a pulsating, smoldering
silence until her back was to the wall and when he spoke

next his mouth was only inches away. "What do you think of a mutual orgasm?" he murmured, gently placing his hands palm down on the wall, framing her head, capturing her, leaning forward so his body lightly brushed hers. "Or would you rather be just friends?" His smile was wicked, his erection swelling against her, his mouth so close she could feel the warmth of his breath.

"Would you force me?" she whispered.

"Is that what that flush on your cheeks means?" he softly breathed. "I thought it meant something else."

"Please, Beau . . ." She tried to bring up her hands and push him away, but he quickly caught them, forced them back down, pinned them against the wall.

"I think I'll make you pregnant this time," he said, dominant, intractable. "I'll keep you here in this country inn and fill you with sperm . . . day after day . . . after day." His dark eyes bored into hers, bold, shameless. "Would you like my child?"

She would, the thought a living hope in the weeks since he'd left her. But she'd found her way out at last from the grief of his departure. She'd worked very hard at making a life for herself without him and she knew better than to live on futile dreams. "Would you be faithful then?" she pointedly asked.

Startled, he pulled back slightly and gazed at her. When he finally spoke his voice was brusque. "I don't know. How the hell do I know? . . ." Goaded that infinitesimal distance too far, her query stinging nerves already raw with doubt and jealousy, he rasped, "Screw it," and his mouth came down harshly on hers, taking what he'd come to take, what had driven him for days and haunted him for weeks and months. "You're mine," he hotly whispered. "Now, tomorrow, next month . . . maybe next year."

He grabbed handfuls of her skirt and pulled it upward, forced her legs apart with his knee, and leaned into her. "We'll do it the first time standing. You used to like that," he murmured, lust twisting in his belly, his fingers nimbly

unfastening his breeches. "And after that, we'll take this"—
he swept her skirt aside—"off."

But when he entered her a weight of memory saturated
his senses and his hands gentled on her shoulders. "I missed
you," he whispered, her fragrance striking familiar chords,
the feel of her engulfing him. And he kissed her then with a
tenderness.

And wishing she didn't and not wanting to, she breathed,
"I love you."

His eyes went shut briefly, a feeling of peace, contentment overwhelming him.

She was his.

He had her back.

It didn't matter where they were; it didn't matter that
they'd come together in frustration and anger. It only mattered that they were together, joined in passion.

"You're staying with me," he said, his voice low, intense,
his lower body firmly set, plunging, withdrawing in a ravishing, penetrating rhythm.

She clung to him, wanting him as she always did, hot-
blooded desire coursing through her veins, all the thorny
difficulties dissolving.

"You're staying," he repeated, his hands sliding down her
back, cupping her bottom, securing her for his upstroke.

"I don't know," she weakly equivocated, trembling,
already near orgasmic.

"*I* know," he said, tightening his grip, plunging deeper.
"This time you're having my baby," he whispered, withdrawing marginally, driving in again, restless, forcing himself to the finite limits. "Do you hear me?"

She was shuddering, a millisecond from climax. "Yes,"
she gasped, no longer grounded in logic, irrepressible need
blurring reality. And she felt it begin, the explosive ecstasy,
the heartfelt delirium. It had been so long. . . .

He felt the same wildness, as if he couldn't wait a second
more, his need to possess her so violent he shuddered under
its spell. His fingers bit into the tender flesh of her buttocks,
his lower body took on an annihilating force. "You're mine,"

he growled, convulsing into her, his savage ejaculatory thrusts punctuation to his words. "Mine . . . mine."

"I should hate you," she panted, bliss and torpor numbing her senses, dying away in his arms. "I should . . ."

"Not now," he murmured, holding her up as she leaned weakly against him. Maybe later, he candidly thought, resting his forehead against the wall, utterly drained, drawing great gulps of air into his lungs.

When he could breathe again and a degree of consciousness returned, he took note of the bed, and lifting Serena into his arms, he carried her over to it and placed her on the rumpled covers. He stripped away her gown and chemise, her slippers, stockings while she lay drowsy and replete, his actions competent, efficient—like a man with a mission. "And now we'll start working off those hundred thousand florins," he said, trailing a proprietory fingertip down her wet cleft.

"A formidable task even for you, Glory," Serena breathed, her face flushed from passion, her body still pulsing, carnality animate, alive inside her. "Undress for me," she softly said. "I haven't seen your grand body in months."

His brows quirked briefly—he was always surprised by her calm acknowledgment of her sexuality—and then he quickly discarded his clothes, like a man who'd done it countless times before. "Well?" he said brief moments later. "Do I pass?"

Her assessing gaze slowly ranged over his tall, athletic form. "Oh, you always pass, Rochefort." She smiled the way he might in flattering a woman. "I have a taste for you."

He disliked her easy charm; it smacked of masculine privilege and accessibility when he wanted her locked away for his eyes only. "My taste for you borders on obsession," he murmured, spleen in his soft tone.

"Does it really?" she purred. "And you hate it, no doubt."

"I'll survive," he muttered.

"As you'll survive without me, you mean. Don't look so sullen, darling. I won't make you marry me. As if I could.

There. I like your smile better. I like to fuck too, Rochefort. It's not exclusively your domain."

His scowl reappeared.

"Are ladies not supposed to say that?"

"You're not." She'd never seemed like all the others.

"You can't stop me."

"I can . . . I will."

"But not for long, we both know that. See, I can be realistic too. All women don't want to be shackled to your title. You're leaner, darling." Her gaze traveled leisurely over his body, his powerful muscled form honed, attenuated, like a monk too long in the wilderness. "Have you been fucking yourself to death again?" No monk, the Earl of Rochefort.

"I've been looking for Bonaparte," he said, his voice still fractionally sullen, not sure he liked her arch and dégagée anymore than he liked her contentious. "I've been on the move."

"Perhaps you could move in my direction then. That hard cock's caught my fancy."

"Don't talk like a whore."

"You just paid a hundred thousand florins for me. For that amount do I classify as a courtesan instead? Is that more to your liking? Although *I* particularly like your cock," she silkily added, sliding up on the pillows. "I always have. So come and give me my favorite toy," she murmured, slipping her hand downward to rest between her thighs.

Voluptuously nude, pinked from her recent orgasm, she languorously spread her legs and offered him a salacious display. As she gazed up at him, her fingertips lightly stroked her clitoris. "You taught me this, remember?" she insolently reminded him. "You taught me all of this, Rochefort—this hot wanting, this uncontrollable need, this hunger for sex. . . . I should thank you." Her lashes drifted seductively lower, her gaze warmed, the glisten of moisture materializing under her fingers.

And a barbaric anger suffused his brain as he thought of her thus disposed with another man—or men . . . with Massena or Solignac, with Londes, who sampled all the ladies. She was the hottest piece he'd ever had—and tutoring had nothing to do with it. "You can thank me by screwing me," he said, low and heated, overcome with jealousy.

"Of course, darling."

"Don't call me darling," he bit out, annoyed with her flippancy.

"Yes, milord . . . forgive me. You prefer more deference from your whores? I'll keep that in mind."

"I prefer more silence from my whores," he grimly said, moving to the bed in two strides, brushing her hand aside, settling between her legs in a graceful flow of muscle and sinew. "So kindly fuck me without any added commentary."

"Yes sir," she murmured, her voice laced with mockery, her eyes blazing up at him. "Whatever you wish, my lord."

He covered her mouth with his, cutting off her sarcasm with a bruising kiss and, hot-tempered, plunged into her tantalizing body. Instantly, her legs wrapped hard around his hips and she uttered a small luscious sound of delight, annoying him, reminding him how infinitely receptive she was. "Did you sigh like that for other men too?" he asked in a low, savage tone.

"Maybe I did." Furious, she raked her nails down his back.

Grunting at the sharp, stinging pain, he jerked away. Exhaling a string of obscenities, he lifted her bodily and flipped her on her stomach. "We'd better keep your hands where I can see them," he growled. "Up on your knees," he ordered, slapping her rump the way one would a horse that had to be moved.

When she didn't respond, he slid his hands under her hips, raising her on all fours. Clamping his arm around her waist to hold her firmly in place, he moved up against her from behind, touching her vulva with the tip of his penis, nuzzling it, teasing and rubbing against the sensitive flesh until she stopped struggling and began squirming, whimpering.

"That's better," he whispered, caressing her bottom with

his warm palm in a sweeping arch from waist to heated cleft, inserting the swollen crest of his erection the merest fraction, readying her. "Would you like it rough now? Should I repay you for this blood dripping down my back?"

He pushed into her even before she could answer.

But as he moved inside her, she found herself moving too—out of shameful need, rocking back to meet each plunging stroke, craving him, an unbearable hunger intensifying with each gliding flow, the desperate, blissful sensations so compelling, so impossibly acute she felt faint from the pleasure.

She moved against him more and more urgently, insistent, demanding, and with the need to restrain her no longer an issue, his hands shifted, cupping her heavy breasts, caressing them as they swayed with the rhythm of her hips, tugging her taut nipples so she felt the bewitching frisson in her toes and down her spine and hotly in the melting center of her body.

Bending over her back, he bit her earlobe, the nape of her neck, nipping at her like a rutting animal, tasting her. "Jesus, I could fuck you mindless," he muttered, his voice husky, ragged, his hands clamped hard on her breasts, his body imposing his will on her, stretching her, making her shake, quiver with desire. He thrust into her hard, harder, his strength, his sexual demand unmistakable, seething, as if he could bludgeon her with his penis and make her submit.

"Tell me you want it," he hoarsely growled.

She was panting, frenzied, wanting him so fiercely she felt as though she were drowning. "Yes," she said on a sobbing breath.

He rammed himself further into her and she cried out, her climax jolting her like shock waves, her knees buckling as the exquisite rapture flared, flooded through her body.

Following her down, he didn't miss a stroke, agile in extremity, a curtailed orgasm unthinkable.

And dizzying moments later, momentarily sated, collapsed on her back, he said between labored breaths, "Christ, you're a good fuck."

Twisting around, she bit him.

"What the hell?" Sucking in his breath in surprise, grabbing his shoulder, he rolled off her.

She was already scrambling off the bed and standing beyond his reach a second later, barricaded behind the sturdy table, she coldly said, "I'm not here for your use."

"Yes you are," he said, his voice low, seething with fury, his palm coming up bloody. "And if you bite me again," he added, licking the blood from his hand, "I'll bite you back. Now get your ass over here."

"The first time you look away, I'll run." She spoke in a quiet, poisonous tone.

"No you won't," he said with suppressed violence, rising from the bed. "You like the fucking too much."

He was still aroused as he walked toward her, his erection waist high, hard, turgid.

Backing away, she retreated until she came up against the solid barrier of the wall.

"Come here," he said, arriving at the far side of the table, his voice chill.

She didn't move.

He gazed at her briefly before beginning to clear the table. Setting the sturdy brass candelabra on the floor, he neatly stacked the dishes from her lunch and placed them on a chair, the silence so intense that the clink of pottery was jarring. Straightening the coarse linen cloth, he carefully evened the edges as if the symmetry mattered. "Put your cunt right here," he said, tapping the tabletop with his forefinger.

"I don't perform on cue like a strumpet."

"But you always perform beautifully," he silkily said. "Better than Julia Johnstone or Amy Dubochet or any of the randy society ladies. I think I'll eat you first."

Her face colored at his reference to London's fashionable courtesans and his last words, hot, intrusive, pulsed through her body. "Stay away from me," she commanded, her gaze flicking from him to the table.

He shook his head. "I don't think so." His voice had

calmed to a dispassionate drawl. "I'm wondering if you still taste the same."

The throbbing inside her accelerated.

"Remember the terrace at Minorca?" His dark gaze drifted downward, coming to rest on her pale, silken mons. "I don't have any marzipan here but I could improvise."

Her breath caught in her throat.

He noticed. "Do you want me to carry you?" She was holding herself rigid against the wall, but he knew it wasn't from fear. "I haven't been able to see marzipan cherries since then without thinking of you," he murmured, moving around the table, advancing on her. "You were in rare form that day."

"Give me a time limit," she quickly said as he neared. "When you'll let me go."

"Why?"

"I need that."

"And I need you." He came to a stop and drew in a small breath. "I can't give you a date."

"I cried for weeks after you left."

"I won't let you cry this time," he said, as if he could stop the world in its tracks.

"Beau, please . . . just let me go."

"I can't." He took the last two steps and she could feel the heat of his body next to hers. "I wish I could," he brusquely said and abruptly bending, he slid his hand under her knees, lifted her into his arms and moved toward the table.

"I'll stay with you today and tonight," she bargained. "Then let me go."

"Sorry."

He deposited her on the rustic table and as she opened her mouth to speak, he gently touched her lips with the pad of his finger. "This isn't negotiable. If it were I wouldn't be here. Talk to me tomorrow or two days from now. Maybe I won't care then."

"So I don't have any choice at all?"

"Something like that," he murmured, running his palms up her inner thighs, spreading her legs with a gentle pressure. "Tell me how much you hate this." The heels of his hands had come to rest against the cushioned base of her pelvic bone, his splayed fingers cupping the soft flesh of her mons, his thumbs warm inside her. Gazing down at her, he said, "Tell me this is hell for you. How your cunt isn't throbbing around my fingers. How impossible it is for you to climax. How we don't fit together like perfection."

"And when you leave me—what then?" She was helpless with wanting him . . . terrified.

"No one's leaving; I've offered you carte blanche. I'll lay London at your feet." His hands were caressing her, exerting a sensuous pressure and she felt herself opening for him, her treacherous senses concerned only with the self-indulgent moment.

Aware, attuned to female arousal, he lightly hooked a chair with his foot, pulled it close, and sitting down, lifted her legs over his shoulders. "You can have anything you want," he whispered, adjusting her hips to the proper angle, opening her delicately with his fingers. "I'll give you anything," he breathed, and leaning forward, he licked a cool path up her gleaming wet labia.

The sudden rush of pleasure spiking through her senses exploded in a rapturous cry and before she could draw another breath or further debate the shame and iniquity of her passions, his tongue plunged inside her and her perfidious whimper was audible capitulation.

He was meticulous in his attentions, taking pains to please her, his tongue caressing her clitoris and vulva slowly, gently, until she ached with desire, his fingers stroking her swollen, sensitive tissue, probing the sleek passage beyond until she was writhing beneath his hands and mouth, her fingers tangled in his hair, holding him close, her moans graphic with need. She was wet with longing—her pearly fluid converging into little jeweled droplets that coated her genitals and slid over his tongue and fell from time to time onto the tablecloth in a tantalizing display of sexual yearning.

"Do you think you're ready for me?" he unnecessarily

said, rising from the chair, standing between her legs, her thighs lightly balanced on his forearms.

Eyes shut, she clutched at the table edge, her back arched, her pelvis provocatively raised to meet him. "Open your eyes," he quietly ordered. "So you can see me fuck you. Now," he added, his voice gruff.

Her lashes lifted in a slow, languorous movement. "I'm watching," she whispered. "Is that better?"

He smiled. "It is for me. Now open yourself."

She hesitated for the merest heartbeat and then her hands moved down and parted her pink, gleaming folds.

"Ask me," he gently said.

"Please, Lord Rochefort," she said, no hesitation now, her gaze direct. "I need you."

"*Only* me." He couldn't help himself. She was too sumptuous to be allowed her freedom.

"Only you in all the world," she whispered, having reached a point of selfish and selfless realization in the burning hot core of lust—where barriers no longer mattered, only raw feeling.

"I'll take care of you." His eyes were strangely grave, his voice no longer confrontational. "Although I can't offer you hearts and flowers."

"I don't need that."

"Thank you," he said about something else entirely. And then he kissed her—a fragile kiss, tender at first and then not tender at all.

She guided him into her honeyed warmth, trusting her own emotions, welcoming him with all the splendor he remembered. She had a volatile, aggressive energy that lured and baffled him, challenged him more than anyone ever had.

But in the chaos of their relationship was also a rare purity of passion—wild and tumultuous, primal—as if they were meant for each other.

Clinging to the table, she lifted to meet his plunging assault, carnal and abandoned, dipping and rising scented flesh, offering herself, surrendering. And bracing his feet on the floor, he reached above her, gripped the table for added leverage, and devoured her.

And when they climaxed in the rustic inn outside Piacenza with the scent of summer flowers in the air, they felt alive again, together, sated and content—in a special place all their own.

But their deprivation had been too painful, too desperate, and they weren't content for long. They needed the touch and taste, the smell and heat and fury, the contact and nearness, the unequivocal union. And they made love that sultry afternoon in every imaginable way, crazed and ferocious, tantalizing, languorous, taking turns at initiating and acquiescing, sensation the touchstone—the only reality—when all else was discord.

24

She stayed a week because he wouldn't let her go. He didn't let her out of his sight for a second and after a very short time in the sweetest of paradises, she no longer wished to go.

He wooed her, gallant and solicitous, amusing and tantalizing, always pleasing her whatever his mood. And she burned for him, wanton and impatient, and hungered for him and loved him with all her heart.

And a second week passed.

She wavered at times in that nirvana of the senses, torn by doubt and self-recrimination, calling herself weak and cowardly, wondering how she could debase herself so and yield so easily to his seduction. How could she allow herself to want only his touch, his kisses, his sex?

If someone had forced her to answer in those days of heated passion, she couldn't have. She only felt and craved, eager for his joyful pleasures; she only opened her arms to him . . . and her body and heart.

She loved him as much as a woman could love a man.

He showed her new and intriguing delights in the rustic bedroom tucked under the eaves and gratified her and proved to her that some things couldn't be explained with words. Or reason. And he conscientiously fulfilled his promise to make her pregnant, depositing his seed in the fertile ripeness of her body, glutting her, deluging her, lavish in his prodigality.

He was tender with her spells of moodiness, indulgent now that she'd given herself up so completely. He composed an ode to her one day, a pretty play of words that made her smile. But most of all he catered to her lustful yearnings, pleasuring her joyfully—with inspiration, artful competence, and an open heart.

He knew by the end of the first week that he'd stepped over the familiar boundaries of sensation into a new blissful elysian sphere. His feelings were perhaps inchoate but he was happier than he'd ever been in his life.

Late one afternoon, when they'd returned from fishing in the small stream behind the inn, Beau decided to ride to the vineyard that produced Serena's favorite wine and see if he could arrange for a substantial supply to be sent back to England.

His reference to London and home brought all her uncertainties flooding to the fore, contemplation of the future immeasurably depressing. She couldn't accept becoming his mistress or docile wife, both roles no more than a casual accessory to his life, and he'd never brought up the subject again anyway. Exhaustion may have been impulse to his utterances that day. He'd not spoken of marriage since.

But after he left with a smile and a wave, she ran to the window like a lovesick young girl, wanting to catch a glimpse of him while he waited for his horse in the stableyard below. She was utterly besotted. How tall he was and beautiful, like a young god, she tenderly mused watching him, his strong body toned and fit, its power evident beneath his shirt and form-fitting breeches, the muscles in his shoulders rippling under the fine linen of his shirt as he idly swung his quirt. His dark hair gleamed in the sunlight, silky curls framing his face, his profile pure of line, classic in its configuration, his head bent slightly, listening to the groom.

The man seemed to be relating a humorous story as he saddled Beau's horse because Beau laughed several times, the men's conversation engaging their interest so neither noticed the serving girl come out of the small dairy building attached to the stables. But when she called out something both men looked up; Beau shook his head no, returning his attention to the groom.

Seconds later, the young girl was at his side and throwing her arms around Beau's neck. She pulled him around so abruptly, he stumbled briefly before regaining his balance. In a flash she was kissing him, melting against him, and a second later, he broke away, but with a polite smile, and quickly moving out of her reach, sprang into the saddle. The groom sharply rebuked the girl, but she ignored him and tugged at Beau's leg. Leaning down, Beau spoke to her—a few words, a half-smile on his face before gracefully easing his horse away. And with a laughing response to a comment from the groom, he cantered out of the yard.

Serena's heart was beating in her breast as if she'd run for miles. The scenario that had taken place before her eyes left her breathless with alarm. The prophecy of things to come was frightening. He could never be faithful; he'd been quite clear on that point. And if she stayed with him, she'd be obliged to accept his licentious conduct; he expected personal freedom like all men of his class. She'd hear about his lovers in the tittle-tattle of London gossip or see them together on some public occasion like today, laughing and kissing. Just contemplating the humiliation sent a stabbing pain through her heart. She could never remain silently submissive while he indulged in amorous intrigues. She'd die of heartache.

As she stood utterly still before the open window, the warm summer air bathing her skin, a cold dread chilled her, an awful conclusion finally realized. Although she'd always known their rendezvous in the country would come to an end, her tearfulness of late was probably intuitive foreboding; that sorrowful time had finally arrived.

Turning from the window, she stared for a moment at the small room where she'd realized unprecedented happiness and plumbed the depths of sensual delights, wanting to fix it forever in her memory. Her gaze lingered on the bed for a lengthy time and then she shut her eyes and took a deep breath.

It was time to leave.

She didn't allow herself to think beyond that stark truth because she'd never leave him if she gave herself the slightest excuse to stay. And she'd be nothing more than a kept mistress and eventually a cast-off mistress—both too ignominious to contemplate. Moving swiftly now, she pulled her cloak from the armoire, counted out enough gold to see her to Florence, and leaving everything else behind, ran down the stairs and raced to the stables as if haste were required to outdistance her longing.

Hiring a groom to escort her, she was on the road in minutes, her last sight as she exited the yard that of the serving girl, with a gloating smile, standing at the gate.

An omen, she darkly thought, of her future if she had stayed. She would have been nothing more than an amorous pet to a man of licentious tastes.

That small fury kept her depression at bay for several hours, but her resentment soon gave way to sadness and by Parma she wondered if she'd made the right choice.

When Beau returned it was almost twilight and he knew immediately when he walked into the room that she'd left. He knew even before he saw the serving girl sitting in the chair by the window.

"So," he said, inhaling deeply, thinking it would help right now if he could hit something. "Can I help you?"

"She's gone."

"I see that."

"I thought you might like some company."

"I see." He pulled his coat off, reaching for a liquor bottle as he dropped his coat on the floor. But he didn't sit down or move beyond uncorking the grappa and swilling several inches of brandy in one long draft. And only then did he look around for the first time.

She hadn't taken her clothes, the ones Solignac had given to her on their journey to Milan, all neatly packed by the maid when she'd left Massena. The armoire doors were open; so she'd departed swiftly. But why hadn't she taken the gold she'd won at loo that night and the emeralds, both still on the armoire shelf, the leather money pouch and blue jewelry cases evident even in the dim light?

As if it mattered.

As if anything she did mattered.

Bloody fucking hell. He'd never gone to so much trouble for a woman.

He cursed her for coming on board the *Siren* that stormy night.

He cursed her bewitching beauty and tantalizing body, her eager desire and flaming passion.

And he cursed himself most for wanting her still.

"Would milord like a bath?" The girl had materialized at his side, her voice suggestive of more than a bath.

He hesitated for a brief moment, not sure what he wanted, and then nodded his head. "And another bottle of this too," he brusquely said. He forced himself to smile an instant later because she'd flinched at his tone. "I'm not angry with you," he explained. "It's just been a long day . . . a long month or two—or five," he gruffly murmured, the memory of a February night at sea searing his brain. May Serena Blyth burn in hell, he thought, lifting the bottle to his mouth again and then to the girl in gentle salute. She looked young, although she didn't feel young, he remembered. "A bath sounds very nice," he politely said.

Before long he found himself seated in a surprisingly commodious tub in company with the young hot-blooded signorina. He performed his function as stud with civility if not passion, but he wanted it to end before she did. And when her passions were quenched at last, he politely sent her away, called for a case of grappa, and locking his door after it was delivered, sought oblivion from his anger and frustration.

By the afternoon of the second day, he'd gone through the case of grappa and he felt like hell. A glance in the mirror shocked him into a moment of sobriety, and opening the bedroom door, he stepped out into the narrow hallway and yelled for food, bathwater, a barber, a servant to pack for him, and a groom to saddle his horse.

Dead drunk, shaky from hunger, not sure he hadn't lost his mind, he leaned weakly against the door frame, listening to footsteps racing up the stairs, and smiled.

He was off for Florence.

While Beau was making himself presentable for his journey to Florence, Serena was kneeling over a chamber pot in her apartment, vomiting. It was the second time that day, the second day in succession, and she wondered if she'd caught some stomach upset on the road.

Immediately she'd arrived at her apartment, the cooking odors from her landlady's kitchen below had nauseated her. She'd never noticed the pungent aromas before and decided she was just fatigued from two days' traveling. She'd slept like the dead till almost ten the next morning and then sent a note to the Castellis telling them of her return.

Julia had come immediately and in the course of the next hour, Serena had calmed her worst fears. She was perfectly fine, Serena assured Julia, no harm had come to her on her journey to Milan, yes, she'd seen Lord Rochefort, he was in Piacenza she thought, no, Massena wasn't a monster with three heads and cloven hoofs, although she wasn't so sure Solignac wouldn't make a pact with the devil if there was money involved, and yes, she was also very happy that she'd returned safely to Florence, and certainly, she'd be sure to come to their "at home" on Thursday evening; she wasn't in trauma at all.

But, no, please don't tell Father Danetti she was back in the city because she was planning to sleep for a day or so and didn't care to have him read prayers over her or gaze at her with soulful eyes—at least not until Thursday.

Julia had smiled then and said, "You might have to make up your mind soon and pick one of your suitors as husband. It's not fair to keep so many men in misery."

"But I'm not in the market for a husband," Serena pleasantly replied. "And I'd appreciate if it you'd disperse that information to any who will listen."

"I'm afraid they'd all find it unacceptable, dear," her friend said. "You'll have to give them the bad news yourself."

"As if I haven't tried to any number of times," Serena declared with a small sigh.

"Lord Rochefort seemed concerned with your safety,"

Julia noted, a hint of query in her tone. "I thought he might return with you."

"He's busy, I'm afraid." Serena struggled to keep her voice bland. "He's actively engaged in assignments for Pitt."

"I'm glad he found you at any rate."

"Yes, it was kind of him." A very tame word, she thought, for the pleasure and pain of knowing Beau St. Jules.

"Now, you'll recognize everyone Thursday tonight. And I'm warning all our friends not to plague you with questions about your abduction. So feel comfortable saying as much or as little as you like. They won't pry. It's so wonderful having you back safely," Julia said, leaning over to take Serena's hands in hers. "We were desperately afraid."

After more catching up on the events of the past weeks, including news of the young mother and her children who'd arrived safely in Florence and were happily settled in town, Julia left and Serena went to sleep. She slept a good part of the following days, her energy levels low, her emotions overly sensitive, her susceptibility to tears acute.

In her waking hours, she found herself contemplating her paintings of Beau, the canvases everywhere she turned, leaning against the walls, some smaller ones hung, an unfinished portrait on her easel.

She wished for the impossible one minute and told herself the next that he'd only make her unhappy. Beau wasn't in love with her or with anyone, he probably never would be— a man of his propensities was not romantically inclined.

Perhaps she should put away the paintings so she wouldn't be reminded of him at every turn, she thought one day when her feelings were more stable. She considered beginning an assignment for her landscape class. But instead of putting the canvases away, she began painting another Beau St. Jules.

She threw up only once the next day, in the morning when she woke and then again the following morning, her nausea coming over her while she was talking to her landlady.

Mrs. Calvacanti had just brought up her laundry, and when Serena bolted from the room with a stammered apology, she called after her, "I'll bring a damp cloth."

Bustling in a moment later, she helped Serena to her feet, and leading her over to the bed, covered her up and put the cool cloth on her forehead. "My boy babies always made me throw up early in the morning—never my girls. If you eat some dry bread before you get out of bed, it helps."

The matter-of-fact comments made Serena's stomach heave ominously again although there was nothing left to expel. And when her queasiness had passed, she said, dumbfounded, "A baby?"

"Now you have that nice milord marry you," her landlady ordered. "Julia told me he's in Piacenza. We'll send a letter."

"That's impossible," Serena whispered, still in shock.

"We'll have the professor write to his father, then," the landlady pronounced, her ideas of paternal responsibility exacting. "He'll see that the boy marries you."

"No, please, I don't wish to marry him." Her mind was racing, her thoughts in disarray. A baby? Was it possible?

"Marry Sandro then," Mrs. Calvacanti briskly suggested, wondering why Serena wouldn't marry such a handsome young man but open to alternatives. "The bambino needs a papa."

Good lord, a baby, Serena tremulously reflected, still trying to absorb the wonder of it, her nausea explained in a miraculous way. And if she was indeed carrying Beau's child, she had no intention of marrying Sandro or anyone else.

A fictitious husband would serve her just as well. And even that subterfuge wouldn't be required until she returned to England.

"I don't wish anyone to know just yet," Serena cautioned. "Perhaps it's not true."

The mother of ten grown children smiled knowingly. "It's true enough, signorina, but my lips are sealed," she promised. "You should marry soon though so there won't be whispers about the bambino when he's born."

"Maybe the baby's a girl," Serena offered, smiling, wondering if she'd have dark curls like her father.

"It's a boy, mark my words," Mrs. Calvacanti declared. "And I should know after seven boys. Now Father Danetti

would make a fine papa," she cheerfully said, insistent on
Serena marrying. "I'm not sure God has taken him completely yet and he's very handsome."

"It's a thought," Serena politely said, not about to discuss
marrying a priest, however kind and handsome.

"Make sure you eat well, signorina," Mrs. Calvacanti
ordered. "The baby needs plenty of food to grow strong and
healthy like his father." She'd talked to the groom who'd
escorted Serena to Florence and knew of Serena and Beau's
stay at the inn, so she had little doubt assigning paternity.
"I'm making a zuppa inglese in honor of your home-
coming. The baby will like it. Now you sleep and I'll clean
up here. You're going to need more rest."

Serena didn't argue, a benevolent lethargy seeping through
her senses. She was having Beau's child, she blissfully thought.
He wasn't gone from her life after all. And when Mrs. Calvacanti brought up the rich custard dessert later that morning,
Serena ate two servings—one for herself and one for the baby.

Beau had a multitude of tasks to accomplish when he
reached Florence, and reinvigorated after two days of sobriety,
he set to work, taking rooms at the Locanda della Rossa and
immediately calling for a tailor.

His other requirements were fulfilled, while the tailor and
a dozen assistants called in to help, sewed and fitted and set
the Earl of Rochefort to rights.

The consul-general arrived in breathless haste shortly after
the first bastings were adjusted on a pair of black trousers. A
summons from Pitt's young man required a speedy response,
not to mention the necessary respect due the Duke of Seth's
heir. Then a priest was called in and a jeweler, two jewelers
ultimately when Beau required a sapphire in addition to a diamond ring; a clerk (to write up a marriage contract) was
added to the throng as well as a florist, all of whom awaited
instructions from the young man being fitted for a new suit in
the middle of the large suite, an army of tailors with pins in
their mouths bent to the task.

Beau issued orders with polite authority, intent on speedily achieving his aims. He didn't get himself a wife every day of the week and a certain amount of work was required to accomplish his purpose, none of which he cared to wait for overlong.

As his minions labored around him, putting his plans en train, he cautioned himself to woo Serena more gallantly this time. He'd reason with her—speak of romance, say all the flattering things lovers say when proposing. Flowers should help too; women like flowers. He called the jewelers over to study the rings he'd selected again, scrutinizing the stones with an eye to Serena's tastes. Large, but not too large; she'd not appreciate a nouveau riche ostentation. He liked the sapphire best but women usually preferred diamonds—the diamond he'd been told was newly arrived from India.

He glanced at the clock, impatient to be off on his mission and mildly nervous too. Marriage was a huge step, but he couldn't have her any other way, he realized. *So . . .* He drew in a steadying breath.

An hour and a half later with the consul-general and the priest in tow, Beau set out for Serena's apartment, the carriage filled with bouquets of flowers, two small ring boxes in his pocket. The men spoke of the newly signed truce on the short ride to Serena's, none too optimistic of its holding for long, and they discussed the state of Austria's readiness to take on Napoleon again.

Mrs. Calvacanti met Beau and his entourage in the courtyard, so very pleased to see him again, she said, beaming, the young lord's carrying flowers a gratifying sign. Miss Blythe was at the Castellis "at home" that evening she told him. And she just knew Miss Blythe would be thrilled to see him.

Beau debated waiting until Serena returned but wasn't in the mood to delay what he'd come here to do and neither did he care to keep polite company with the consul-general and the priest until the entertainment at the Castellis was over.

He could send a note asking her to see him, but he wasn't sure she'd respond, regardless of what Mrs. Calvacanti implied. Serena's manner of leaving Piacenza denoted resentment, if not a more volatile anger.

Which left only a single avenue.

25

For some reason he hadn't visualized her surrounded by admirers when he walked into the Castellis' salon. He'd imagined a more poetic, sentimental moment of recognition and delight.

She didn't even notice him when he entered the room, for she was laughing uproariously at something one of the men had said and instant recall of a similar image as he'd entered Massena's headquarters at Milan burned through his brain. She'd been equally at home with the roomful of French officers that night. Taking immediate affront, his jealousy never within reasonable bounds with Serena, he had to force himself to respond civilly to Julia, who'd come over to greet him.

"Actually I arrived only this afternoon," he replied to her question. "May I introduce Mr. Winthrop, our consul-general, and Father Alegini," he politely added, his gaze drawn back to Serena across the room. "Miss Blythe survived her journey well, I see," he murmured, his tone aggrieved.

"We can't thank you enough for your intervention with Massena," Julia declared, unaware of Beau's displeasure. "Serena didn't go into much detail but I'm sure your presence in Milan was instrumental in gaining her freedom."

"I was of minor help, perhaps," he replied, bringing his gaze back with effort from the odious scene of his lover flirting with a dozen men. "Could I offer you some flowers, Miss Castelli, and beg your forgiveness for coming uninvited to your evening soiree." Serena had just thrown her head back in a peal of laughter at something a tall, blond man had said and he was no longer in the mood to woo her with flowers.

"How lovely of you," she said, taking the large bouquets he held out to her, "and you're welcome to visit anytime, Lord Rochefort. If your guests would like to make themselves comfortable, Papa has some very good sherry on the table by Plato's bust over there. I'll bring you to Serena."

"Thank you, but I'll wait till she's less busy."

Julia laughed lightly. "Then you'll wait a very long time, my lord. She's never without a circle of admirers."

"I see," he said, his smile tight. "In that case, I'll hope to find an opportune time to break into her conversation. Please, see to your other guests; I'll admire your collection of paintings while I wait." And after speaking briefly to the consul-general and priest, informing them they might be staying for a time, Beau took himself off into a quiet corner and watched Serena charm a crowd of men.

The room was large, the number of guests considerable, and the men surrounding Serena sufficient to screen Beau from her view. Julia didn't feel comfortable disregarding Lord Rochefort's wishes so she didn't approach Serena with news of his arrival. But she surreptitiously watched the young Englishman standing near the library door, one shoulder resting against the paneled wall, his arms crossed negligently across his chest. His gaze held a startling chill.

She didn't have to speculate long regarding his motives for he soon pushed away from the wall and strolled over to the gathering around Serena, all thoughts of gentle wooing effaced.

He wasn't in her line of sight until he was quite close and Serena abruptly stopped talking when she saw him. The group all turned, following her gaze, and Beau walked between two men who'd stepped aside to better view the object of Serena's attention.

He was no more than a foot away, her perfume pungent in his nostrils, when he bowed slightly. "May I have a moment of your time, Miss Blythe?" he queried, his voice expressionless. Without waiting for her answer, he pulled her forward and began drawing her away.

A hand clamped hard on Beau's shoulder, arresting his progress. "The lady may not wish to go," Sandro said, scowling.

"We're old friends," Beau silkily said, insinuation flagrant. "Tell him, Miss Blythe, how well we know each other," he softly taunted. And jerking his shoulder free, he stood poised, combative.

"I'm fine, Sandro," Serena quickly interposed, not sure Beau wouldn't be grossly crude, his body taut beside her, his clipped order resonating in her ears. "I'll be back shortly."

"And then perhaps not," Beau drawled, tightening his hold on her.

"Grow up," she lashed out, as hot-tempered as he, and turning back to the men observing her, she offered them a bland smile. "I won't be long."

Beau's lashes lowered fractionally in silent contradiction but he didn't speak, satisfied he was about to take her away.

"No one asked you to come here," Serena snapped, walking swiftly to keep up with Beau's long stride as he moved across the room. "And you're not taking me out of this gathering or I'll scream."

He abruptly stopped, scrutinized her, gauging her sincerity, then quickly surveyed the room, moving a second later toward a set of bookcases framing a large painting of a Tuscany landscape. "It didn't take you long to get back into circulation," he said, sullen and glowering, his black coat and breeches somber like his mood.

"I have no intention of living a secluded life."

"Obviously."

"You have no control over my actions, Rochefort—by your choice, if I recall. You didn't think you could settle for one woman, I believe you said. I prefer a variety of men as well."

He pinned her against the leather bindings of the books so swiftly she sucked in her breath in surprise. "I came here to marry you, dammit. Fuck the men."

"Let me capture this moment in time," she sarcastically retorted, "so I can forever remember this enchanting proposal."

"Just say yes and we can get the hell out of here," Beau churlishly muttered.

"But I don't wish to marry you," she coolly replied, "despite your gallant offer." If he wanted to marry her, it wasn't for love, judging by his tone of voice. And she didn't expect that faithfulness was a component with such an uncharitable attitude.

"Here," he said, taking the two ring boxes from his pocket. "Take these." And lifting her hand, he placed them in her palm.

"I don't want your rings."

"What do you want then, dammit?"

"What you can't give me, Beau—your love."

"I thought we went through all that already."

"We did. And therein lies the problem, darling."

He was encouraged by the endearment, no matter that it was sardonically uttered. "Well, I think I do now."

Her brows rose faintly. "You need some lessons, Rochefort, to be convincing."

His nostrils flared as he drew in a breath. "I'm not a good actor."

"I know. A shame." She wished he was; she truly did.

"All you have to do is say yes," he whispered, leaning into her, his strong body familiar and heated. "Say yes, just say it. . . ."

"I want you to love me."

He took another deep breath, the black abyss yawning. "I do."

"This is harder yet, Rochefort," she said, smiling faintly at the two breathless words he'd uttered. "You have to love *only* me."

His familiar smile flashed, his dark eyes lit with amusement. "That's easy. I've never loved anyone else before. There now, say yes. I've the consul-general here to marry us or a priest if you prefer—I didn't know if you were Catholic. The license is in my pocket. You only have to say you will."

"What of all your women? Not love this time, Rochefort, just the sexual amusements."

He exhaled, stared at her for a very long time, his face closed, his expression unreadable. Then he grimaced. "Why not?" he obtusely muttered. "They're gone. Satisfied?"

"Somehow that admission lacks a certain sincerity," she breathed.

"Christ, Serena, you drive a hard bargain."

"I don't want it to be a bargain." Her voice was soft but intense with emotion.

"It sure as hell seems like it to me," he exasperatedly muttered. "What the hell are you giving up?"

Damn him, he wasn't marrying for love; he was giving things up to marry. "Fuck you," she resentfully exclaimed.

"Now *that* I understand. Would you like to do it as a married lady?" His smile was wolfish. "I'm ready."

"You're always ready, aren't you? Tell me how long this transient impulse to marry will last. Until the next female crosses your path?"

He stood perfectly still for a moment, staring at her, frustrated by her thwarting cavil, knowing if this was a transient impulse he could have lived his life without misery anytime these past three months. "Don't move," he quietly ordered, holding her lightly by the shoulder. Shifting his stance slightly so he could address the guests, he shouted, "She's having my baby and she won't marry me!"

"How did you know?" Serena gasped.

He spun back to face her, a smile slowly unfolding across his face. "I didn't. I just said that so your friends would pressure you to marry me. You really are?" he incredulously murmured. "Just teasing, folks!" he called out over his shoulder, ignoring the shocked, horrified expressions conspicuous among the guests. "Now you *have* to marry me," he added in a whisper, his mouth inches away from hers. "You're having my baby."

"That's not reason enough to marry."

"Damn right it is."

"If you sleep around, I'll kill you," she warned, wondering if she was actually agreeing to take on the daunting task of keeping him faithful.

"Ditto," he countered. "Well, maybe not *kill* you," he amended, "but you'd be locked away on one of my remote country estates for the rest of your life."

She looked directly into his eyes. "We understand each other then."

"Perfectly." He blew out a breath. "This is going to be different."

"You may actually like it." A small giddy jolt reminded her of the blissful degrees of happiness he could evoke.

He smiled. "I do already. A wife and a baby all in the same night. Two for the price of one."

"You're not buying me, Rochefort, the way you've bought everything else you've wanted in your life," she sternly admonished.

"Don't I know it, darling. I would have had you as my mistress months ago if you'd been for sale."

"And I'm staying in Florence until I finish my studies," she peremptorily asserted, knowing she'd be overwhelmed by him if she allowed it.

"Don't I have anything to say about it?" he mildly questioned. "The French are going to be in Florence in a few weeks."

"Perhaps we could discuss it later," she said, smiling for the first time.

"When later," he murmured, basking in her smile, knowing everything was finally resolved when she smiled like that.

"Tonight," she softly said.

"After our wedding."

"After that."

"On our honeymoon, you mean."

She offered a flirtatious caveat. "I warn you, dear Glory, I can be very demanding."

"I remember," he said, smiling faintly.

"You don't mind?" she seductively murmured.

"I'm here to serve you, ma'am," he drawled. And then the easy mannered style of the rake altered. "You have my heart, lollipop," he softly added, all the insolence stripped from his voice. "You really do."

"You've had mine from the first," she whispered.

"And you don't have to worry," he gently said. "I'll never cheat on you. My word on it."

Her eyes filled with tears. "It's a lavish gift."

He shook his head in negation. "It's nothing. From now on we'll only have glad days and soft breezes and sunshine. I've put in my order," he said with a lazy smile and lifting her chin, he gently brushed her lips with his. "For us and the baby."

"I've wanted your baby from the first too."

"Not from the very first. Not on the *Siren*."

"After Minorca I did."

He smiled. "Minorca was nice."

"But *you* didn't want to be a father," she reminded him, not sure even now she could visualize the possibility.

"At least not till now."

A sudden terrible thought struck her. "Do you have children?"

He shook his head. "The ladies I know aren't interested in motherhood."

"Will they be surprised?"

He shrugged and said, "Who knows?" when he knew everyone in the Ton would be wildly astonished.

"Should we move to the country to escape your paramours?" she teased.

"I know how to say no," he casually replied, understanding that no matter how distant the country there would always be women, so he had to be certain of that. "And I needn't remind you I expect you to be equally incorruptible."

"I know how to say no as well."

"Really? When was that?" he impudently murmured.

"So I find you irresistible. Am I supposed to apologize?"

"Not for a thousand years at least," he said, grinning. And leaning over to kiss her he paused midpoint. "When did it become so quiet?" Swiveling his head, he took note of the keen scrutiny focused on them, all activity arrested as if they were performing on a stage. "Haven't they ever seen a man and woman talk before?" he murmured.

"Your remark about my pregnancy may have piqued their curiosity," Serena sardonically noted.

"Give me the rings," he briskly ordered, reaching for the boxes in her hand. Plucking the rings out, he slid them on her fingers. "Now we're *formally* engaged," he said, patting her hand with avuncular complaisance.

"Will it be a long engagement?" she asked with levity.

"Longer than I'd like—ten minutes, maybe eleven. . . . Now smile, darling, for our rapt audience." And swinging her around with him, Beau proclaimed, "Miss Blythe has had a change of heart." He held her hand with the glittering rings aloft. "She's done me the honor of accepting my marriage proposal. You're all invited to our wedding—to be celebrated forthwith."

A collective gasp masked Serena's whisper.

"If the Castellis allow us the use of their salon," Beau added, reminded of their hosts.

Beaming, Julia nodded her approval.

"Do we need a priest?" Beau inquired in an undertone.

Serena shook her head. "But we need Mrs. Calvacanti. She's been adamant I marry. She wouldn't want to miss this."

"Marry whom?" A small scowl formed between Beau's brows.

"Preferably you but she wasn't fussy. Father Danetti was one of her numerous candidates."

"*Numerous* candidates?" he repeated with heated male affront.

"Hers, not mine. *I* had no candidates."

"You'd better not have had."

"Don't take that tone, darling, or I may find I prefer a priest after all."

"You're marrying me," he curtly declared. "It's *my* child."

"Maybe," she sweetly said.

"What the hell does that mean?"

"It means I'll marry whom I please." It never hurt to set boundaries.

"Just so long as it's me." Another boundary setter.

Serena's mouth twitched into a smile. "I can see you're going to be difficult to control."

"Impossible, I think, is the word generally used," he softly murmured, his answering smile luscious as sin.

"Our life should be interesting then."

"And happy . . . *madly* happy."

"Yes," she whispered. "Always . . . with you."

"Come here," he said, pulling her close. "Where I can keep you safe from the other matrimonial candidates until the wedding, my sweet seductress . . . my joy, my delight—"

"My honeymoon fantasy," she breathed.

He paused an infinitesimal moment, her hand enclosed in his, the scent of possibility nearly palpable. "In an hour," he quietly said. "We should be married by then. Can you wait?" he graciously asked, because he knew she often couldn't.

Her eyes sparkled with merriment. "I'd like an abbreviated ceremony."

"Done," he said, competent and assured.

"And a *long* honeymoon."

"Would a lifetime do?" Whisper soft, he offered her paradise.

"I'd like that," she said, her eyes suddenly filling with tears.

When he kissed her—a boyish, deep-in-love kiss—an outburst of applause rippled over them, followed by gasps and giggles as their kiss deepened, took on risky undertones of scandal. Raised eyebrows, broad smiles, and knowing glances ensued.

But the Earl of Rochefort and his bride-to-be didn't notice.

They were conscious only of the warm magic of love.

EPILOGUE

They were married in the Castellis' parlor a short time later, the ceremony delayed only briefly, awaiting Mrs. Calvacanti's arrival and the delivery of several cases of Champagne. Most of the guests were delighted by Serena's nuptials and those men disgruntled at the news soon realized that she was enormously happy and contented themselves with that.

The honeymoon lasted a month, until the French armies approached Florence, as Beau knew they would and then he persuaded Serena to go back to England at least for the sake of the baby. She couldn't argue with such sound logic, and after packing all her paints and canvases, the young St. Jules couple left for Leghorn on the first stage of their journey home.

They were feted at Palermo and then at Minorca, where they stopped for an amorous fortnight holiday, the news that the Earl of Rochefort had been caught so precipitously a great wonder to all who knew him. The ladies wished to meet his new bride, who had managed what no one else could, and the men were fascinated to see the woman who could hold Beau's interest.

Serena was large with child when they reached London, although it was still early fall, and Chelsea immediately said, "Twins" when she saw her daughter-in-law, while Beau said with a pleased smile, "Who is this?" of the baby in his step-

336

mother's arms. He was introduced to his two-week-old baby brother by his other siblings, who now felt very grown-up with a newborn in the house. Serena immediately asked if she could hold Ian and father and son stood apart from the noisy, milling group cooing over the baby and exchanged complacent glances. Life was good.

The twins came early, as is often the case—the first week of February—and the Earl and Countess of Rochefort welcomed a tiny boy and girl into the world. The infants were very fragile but a score of midwives kept them warm with hot bricks wrapped in lamb's wool and they thrived. By spring Felicity and Seth were plump and cooing, the absolute center of their parents' life.

And the young Earl of Rochefort found he preferred his country home and his family to the gaming rooms and vice-ridden activities in his past. "Can't explain it," he'd say when his friends would rail at his tame amusements and lack of interest in their amorous play, "but I recommend it. Vastly."

NOTES

1. See page 2. When Great Britain plunged into the revolutionary wars at the beginning of 1793, her national debt amounted to £230,000,000. From that point the war was financed by means of loans to such an extent that the funded debt for Great Britain and Ireland at the time of the Peace of Amiens in 1802 had risen to the astounding sum of £507,000,000. The figure is perhaps best understood when contrasted with the funded debt of England at the outbreak of World War I. In 1914 it amounted to no more than £587,000,000.

Both in England and on the Continent during this period, there were doubts as to the durability of the British system of credit, particularly after the Bank Restriction Act of 1797, which released the Bank of England from the obligation to redeem its notes—an obligation it didn't resume for twenty-two years. Great Britain had a paper currency throughout the whole of the revolutionary and Napoleonic periods.

2. See page 74. Sponges as a form of contraception have been used since ancient times and Mediterranean sponges were always readily available. The sponge in various forms, with or without strings attached for ease of removal, functioned as a mechanical barrier to sperm.

3. See page 97. Angelica Kauffman and Mary Cosway are two examples of female artists much feted by British society in the late eighteenth and early nineteenth century. Kauffman, Swiss-born and trained in Italy, spent the years 1766–81 in London, where

she became a founding member of the Royal Academy of Art. Her neoclassic history paintings garnered high praise throughout England and Europe; she was much in demand for her portraits as well. Her client list included a glittering array of international nobles who paid her enough to make her a wealthy woman. Married when she was young to an imposter masquerading as a count, she separated from him immediately when his duplicity was revealed, but she wasn't able to remarry until he died in 1780. Her second husband was the Italian artist Antonio Zucchi.

Mary Hadfield Cosway, born in England and trained in Rome, married Richard Cosway, a painter of miniatures who had the patronage of the Prince of Wales. Her paintings, mostly poetical—Cupid and Venus, Psyche, Rinaldo and Armida—were first exhibited at the Royal Academy in 1780.

She and her husband enjoyed entrée into the finest aristocratic circles and their receptions were always crowded with the most select lords and ladies. They lived as ostentatiously as the wealthiest of aristocrats, but after the prince regent turned his portly back on Richard Cosway because of Cosway's imprudent sympathy for the French Revolution, the splendid crowds melted away.

The haut monde was always fascinated and intrigued with the newest fashionable artists but with a dilettante and fleeting interest. Artists were reguarded as distinguished craftsmen, not equals, no matter how charming their social aquaintance might be. As for those nobles who dabbled at painting, they never actually *sold* their work; it would have been déclassé.

4. See page 169. Lord Byron in *Childe Harold's Pilgrimage* had sung the praises of Sintra—that "glorious Eden." He writes to his mother in August 1809: "The village of Cintra, about fifteen miles from Lisbon, is, perhaps in every respect, the most delightful in Europe; it contains beauties of every description, natural and artificial. Palaces and gardens rising in the midst of rocks, cataracts and precipices; convents on stupendous heights—a distant view of the Sea and the Tagus. . . . It unites in itself all the wildness of the western highlands, with the verdure of France."

5. See page 172. The Carronade was a short, lightweight ship's gun developed by the Carron Ironworks in Scotland in 1778. It was a

weapon of particular attraction to the merchant marine. Because it was light, it was also relatively cheap and could be handled by a very small crew, an important consideration on merchant ships.

The gun was optimal for short-range work.

6. See page 174. Larboard is the port or left side of a ship as one looks forward.

7. See page 198. Chelsea's proposal is on page 12 of *Sinful* by Susan Johnson.

8. See page 199. Divorce in England required an act of Parliament. Disturbed by France's legalization of divorce on grounds of mutual incompatibility in 1792—after which the floodgates of divorce opened in France—conservatives in England attempted to make divorce harder to obtain.

The first concrete attempt to turn back the tide of divorce petitions to the House of Lords was the introduction by the lord chancellor in 1798 of a new set of Standing Orders, known as Lord Loughborough's Rules.

The first of the Standing Orders of 1798 demanded that an official copy of proceedings for separation in an ecclesiastical court be provided to the House with every bill of divorce. The second Standing Order was more far-reaching. It ordered that every petitioner must present himself at the bar of the House, to be cross-examined about possible collusion and prior separation.

In the hands of an energetic and intelligent lord chancellor, these Standing Orders offered a formidable weapon. Even before their passage, Lord Thurlow, lord chancellor from 1778 to 1792, had shown that it was possible, by relentlessly harassing petitioners, both to drive down the numbers applying and to increase the proportion of bills that were rejected. Whereas in the fourteen years before he took office, all 37 petitioners for divorce had been successful, during Thurlow's chancellorship the success rate fell to twenty-five out of thirty-two. (Note the small number of divorces—thirty-seven in fourteen years. Divorce wasn't an option generally considered except in extreme circumstances.)

In 1801 Lord Eldon succeeded Lord Loughborough in the office of lord chancellor; he was to hold it for over a quarter of a century, until 1827. Using to the full the new powers of investigation offered by the Standing Orders of 1798, Eldon by fierce cross-examination almost single-handedly succeeded for at least his first twenty years in office in frightening off petitioners and greatly increasing the number of bills that were abandoned, withdrawn, or rejected.

Under those conditions, it behooved a petitioner to have a strong phalanx of supporters in his camp.

9. See page 209. When King Ferdinand's Neapolitan army was routed from Rome and the French followed the retreat in hot pursuit, the royal family fled Naples. But the escape had to be kept secret or the populace—at times more resembling a mob—might try to prevent the king from leaving the city.

Prior to their departure, the royal family's possessions, including the crown jewels and the state treasury, were secretly brought down to the quay from the palace in covered wagons in the dead of night. And on the evening of December 21, 1798, under the cloak of a grand reception for the Turkish minister, the Hamiltons, and royal family along with numerous courtiers, diplomats, ambassadors, and household servants, surreptitiously slipped away from the festivities and made their way on foot to the quay, where boats took them out to Admiral Nelson's ship in the bay.

After a storm-tossed journey in which the royal family's young son died and many passengers feared for their lives in the turbulent seas, the *Vanguard* at last sailed into Palermo harbor on the twenty-sixth. The royal court would remain in Sicily until the Peace of Amiens was signed in 1802.

10. See page 211. Emma Hamilton had come a long way from her humble birth as the daughter of a blacksmith in Cheshire. Sent out to work as an under-nursemaid at twelve, by sixteen she was the past mistress of one of the Prince of Wales's most intimate cronies, Captain John Willett Payne, and the current mistress of Sir Harry Fetherstonhaugh. She had a daughter at this time, fathered by either of those men, and soon after when she was deserted by Fetherstonhaugh, she came under the protection of the Hon. Charles Greville, second son of the Earl of Warwick and nephew of Sir William Hamilton.

When Emma was twenty, Greville found a rich heiress to marry—a necessity for a penurious younger son—and wishing to dispose of his mistress, struck a deal with his uncle to have Emma come stay with him in Naples. Sir William was reluctant although he found Emma very pretty and likable. He knew she was in love with Greville.

But Greville persisted and Emma was sent to Naples ostensibly, for a brief visit. She didn't know her exile would be permanent.

As the months passed and Greville didn't appear in Naples to fetch her home, she became frantic with anxiety, writing him poignant, pleading letters asking him to come to her. Receiving no reply, Emma was forced in the end to realize Greville had no intention of coming.

Although she was fond of Sir William, she still resisted his polite advances. But after a time rumors began circulating that they were married; she began serving as hostess for him and was accepted as such by Neapolitan society. On returning to England in 1791, Sir William received the king's permission to marry Emma and they became husband and wife September 6 at St. George's, Hanover Square.

Sir William never regretted his marriage. "I have no reason to repent of a step which I took contrary to the approbation of the world," he told Lady Mansfield. "Marrying Emma was my own business. I knew what I was doing for as you know I had lived with her for five years before I married. . . . Look round your circle of prudent well assorted matches in the great world and see how few turn out so well as our seemingly imprudent one."

11. See page 223. £10,000 in today's terms is equivalent to £600,000.

12. See page 227. "Monkey" was the slang term for fifty pounds.

13. See page 253. Sir John Acton officially held a minor ministerial post in the government of Sicily, but was one of the most influential advisers to Queen Marie Caroline. Sir John had intended to remain a bachelor and to bequeath his estate in Shropshire to his younger brother Joseph. But since Joseph had served in the French army, he was disbarred from inheriting. So Sir John asked his

brother for the hand of his daughter, who was not yet fourteen.
Joseph had no objection: a papal dispensation for Sir John to marry
his young niece was forthcoming. But the girl herself was naturally
reluctant to marry an uncle sixty-four years old. She hid under the
sofa while Sir John and her father discussed her disposal and then
attempted to escape from the house in boy's clothing. Caught as
she was running across the courtyard, she was brought back and
married in the Hamiltons' house by Lord Nelson's chaplain.

14. See page 259. During the siege of Genoa, Major Franceschi
had been sent off by General Massena on April 24 with a dispatch
to Bonaparte detailing the serious condition of the garrison. On
May 27, after leaving Antibes in a rowboat, he slipped past the
British corvettes blockading Genoa and swam ashore with a letter
from Bonaparte written a fortnight previously, informing Massena
that the Reserve Army had begun to cross the St. Bernard Pass.
This was tremendous news for Massena, who knew the Austrians
would be compelled to turn round to face Bonaparte in a few days
and abandon the siege. Massena calculated that Bonaparte might
be able to break through to Genoa and raise the siege by the thir-
tieth. He was determined not to capitulate before that date—the
latest his rations would last.

April 30 was a day of some emotional excitement, as this was
the day when Bonaparte's arrival was expected to raise the siege.
But it was a false hope. That evening General Ott and Admiral
Keith, realizing that the garrison must be at its last gasp,
despatched Count St. Julien under a flag of truce to the French
outposts at the mouth of the Polcevera, repeating their previous
offer of an honorable capitulation. But Massena still temporized,
for he felt that Bonaparte must now be threatening the Austrian
rear and in a day or two would relieve Genoa. On the thirty-first a
number of his troops began deserting to the enemy lines and the
civilian population was getting out of control. Hundreds were
dying daily of typhus and starvation.

On June 1 Massena sent Colonel Andrieux to Ott's forward
headquarters to discuss terms for the exchange of prisoners.

On the morning of June 2 the three armistice delegates met and
discussed the terms of the capitulation. Matters were not eased by
the arrival of Massena's private secretary with a message saying

Massena would refuse to sign any document that contained the word "capitulation." No agreement was reached before nightfall. The conference was renewed at noon on the third and continued for eight hours. The British naval representative proved the most stubborn, for he insisted unyieldingly that all French vessels in the harbor must be handed over as prizes. That morning Massena was informed by his chief commissary that only one more day's ration of food remained in the depots.

The three principals at last met at 9:30 A.M. on June 4 to settle the final terms and sign the convention. It was finally agreed that 8,110 French soldiers (all who were capable of marching) should leave Genoa by road for the French frontier with all their arms, artillery, and baggage, while the British navy would transport the remainder of the garrison to Antibes. Admiral Keith was still obdurate about the French vessels in the harbor, insisting that naval prize law was enshrined in the British constitution and that he could not concede anything without reference to London. Massena's grim face relaxed for the first time. "My Lord," he said, "after taking all our big ships from us, you might at least leave us the little ones." Keith graciously replied, "Really, General, one can refuse you nothing."

The convention was signed at 7 P.M.

As the conference ended, the admiral seized Massena's hand and said, "General, if only England and France could get together, they would rule the world." Massena with a withering look replied, "France will be enough."

Massena's dogged resistance at Genoa contributed materially to the success of Bonaparte's Reserve Army, which was now pouring into Italy through the Alpine passes and had already occupied Milan. On June 15, the day after the battle of Marengo, when the campaign in Italy was over, the Austrian chief of staff said to Berthier as he signed the Armistice of Alessandria, "You won the battle, not in front of Alessandria, but in front of Genoa."

15. See page 270. Very few of Napoleon's officers were models of conjugal fidelity when on campaign. Many took mistresses with them. This behavior was normal practice among the military leaders of the Revolution and Consulate and Napoleon's attitude in the matter was as self-indulgent as his officers'. In commenting

on Murat's conduct during the Marengo campaign, he said, "What faults Murat committed in order to set up his headquarters in châteaux where there were women! He needed one every day, so I have always allowed my generals to take a strumpet along with them in order to avoid this trouble."

ABOUT
THE AUTHOR

SUSAN JOHNSON, award-winning author of nationally bestselling novels, lives in the country near North Branch, Minnesota. A former art historian, she considers the life of a writer the best of all possible worlds.

Researching her novels takes her to past and distant places, and bringing characters to life allows her imagination full rein, while the creative process offers occasional fascinating glimpses into complicated machinery of the mind.

But perhaps most important . . . writing stories is fun.

Dear Reader,

Last year I was plagued with a painful muscle trauma that was misdiagnosed for six months. Needless to say, my writing fell behind schedule, as did my replies to my mail. I'm in blooming health once again and I'd like to take this opportunity to express my appreciation for all the wonderful letters you've sent me. I enjoy hearing about your lives and loves, your interests, likes and dislikes, hopes and dreams. And I'm pleased to be able to share my great love of history and romance with you.

My current infatuation is with General Andre Massena, who appears as a secondary character in *Wicked*. I became so enamored with this extraordinary man as I researched *Wicked*, I knew he had to be my next hero. My husband and I are off to France and Switzerland next week to study the sites of the battles Massena won for Napoleon in 1799. My hero will be a fictionalized version of the French general—allowing me the artistic license necessary to create the story I wish. But the details will be authentic and faithful to the bold courage and captivating charm of the man Napoleon called "the darling child of victory."

I'm looking forward to introducing you to *my* general and the woman who captures his heart, in my next novel, *Taboo*.

Best wishes,

Susan Johnson

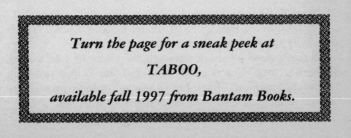

Turn the page for a sneak peek at

TABOO,

available fall 1997 from Bantam Books.

French Army Headquarters
Sargans, Switzerland
March 3, 1799

"Beauve-Simone brought in Korsakov's wife."

General Duras looked up from the maps spread over his desktop, his dark gaze piercing. "Korsakov's *wife*?"

"In all her glory," his aide-de-camp said, grinning. "She's in your parlor. Beauve-Simone couldn't think of another room in camp suitable for a Russian countess wrapped in sables."

"How the hell did she turn up fifty miles behind enemy lines?"

"Her Cossacks apparently took a wrong turn at Bregenz. Her carriage is elaborate—a bed, food, two maids . . . very self-sufficient. They had no need to stop anywhere, so weren't aware of their error. Beauve-Simone's troop intercepted them at the bridgehead north of town."

Duras leaned back in his chair and sighed. "Her timing could have been better. We're attacking along the whole front in three days. Jesus, I can't send her back *now*."

"Maybe Korsakov's corps will be in retreat by next week."

"And?"

"I thought—I mean . . . " Colonel Bonnay's voice trailed off under the general's sharp scrutiny.

"I could send her back through the chaos of a retreating Russian army?" Duras coolly inquired, his brows raised in cynical speculation. "Even her Cossacks couldn't protect her in that anarchy. How many does she have with her?"

"Four."

"Four fucking men between her and the rabble. Perfect," Andre Duras disgustedly muttered.

"Could the Countess Gonchanka look after her?"

Duras's dark brows jerked upward, tart reproach in his glance. "I don't think so," he sardonically replied. "Natalie isn't known for her kindness to women. In fact," he went on, quickly glancing at the clock on the wall, "you'll have to divert Natalie posthaste. She's planning on having dinner with me very shortly."

"She doesn't listen to mere colonels."

"Relay a note from me." The general reached for paper and pen. "I'll postpone dinner tonight . . . and don't mention Korsakov's wife is here."

"She may have heard already. News like that travels swiftly."

"Which means the Austrian spies will soon have the information. *Merde*," General Duras swore, swiftly scrawling his regrets to his current mistress. "I don't need this added problem right now. All the men and supplies have to be in place by the morning of the fifth," he declared, waving the sheet of paper briskly for a moment to dry the ink before folding it and handing it to Bonnay. "Will the trestle bridge at Trubbach be finished in time?"

"The engineers promised to be ready no later than midday on the fifth."

"Good. Give Natalie my note and offer her my sincere regrets. How strong do you think the fort's northern defenses will be at St. Luzisteig?" he went on, his mistress dismissed from his mind, his gaze once again on the maps before him, his energies the past two months consumed with planning the offensive.

"The spies say it's impregnable."

The general studied the topographical drawings for a moment more, his brows drawn together in concentration, and then his head lifted and he smiled at his young subaltern. "Then I'll have to lead the attack myself."

"The fort is as good as ours then, sir," Henri Bonnay

replied, his smile flashing in the shadowed interior. The winter twilight was closing in on the room.

"It better be. We need that river crossing. Now, off with you. I don't want the countess descending on my household with Korsakov's wife there."

"Perhaps they're acquaintances."

"Let's hope not. One temperamental Russian countess is enough to handle."

"You *should* go and see the woman, sir."

"You handle it, Bonnay." Duras turned back to his maps.

"There's nowhere else to put her, sir."

"I'll sleep in your lodgings then. How would that be?"

"She seemed frightened, sir." His aide-de-camp's voice held the merest remonstrance.

"Well, console her then. She has her maids, doesn't she? I'm not playing nursemaid to Korsakov's wife, Bonnay, no matter how woebegone a look you cast my way."

"How could it hurt to offer her your assistance? Tell her she'll be returned once the offensive is past. Korsakov would do the same for your wife."

"My wife doesn't journey beyond Paris, my dear Henri. So, unless the Russians march into the city, Korsakov won't be required to play courtier to her. Not that she wouldn't be accommodating should he prove the victor in this contest," the general softly murmured, his marriage long ago bereft of all but chill politesse, his wife's indiscretions legion. But one did not divorce the niece of Talleyrand, foreign minister to the Bourbons and Napoleon alike, without jeopardizing a hard-won career. And his wife gloated over the position of consort to France's most victorious general.

"Five minutes, sir. I'll tell her you'll stop by."

Duras's mouth twitched into a half-smile. "Still trying to make me a gentleman, Henri?"

"You're more of a gentleman than the Bourbons, sir. The young lady seemed anxious, that's all."

"With good reason, I suppose. Very well, Henri, tell her I'll offer her my compliments."

"In five minutes."

Duras grinned, his handsome face taking on a boyish cast, the weight of his command disappearing for a moment. "*Ten* minutes, Henri, because I'm still in command here. But don't ask me to bow to the lady," he added, his dark eyes amused. "My corsair father would never approve."

"No, sir, very good, sir, I'll tell the lady, sir."

It took more than ten minutes, though. In fact, Colonel Bonnay had to remind Duras twice before he set his maps aside and left his makeshift office. Dark had descended by the time he crossed the frozen mud that passed for a street in the small border town on the upper Rhine. The night air was damp and chill, and his thoughts centered on his engineers working around the clock in the icy waters of the Rhine. He desperately needed that bridge to move his men and matériel across the river to attack General Korsakov's Russian corps, Austria's newest allies.

What exactly did one say to the wife of the man one hoped to destroy in three days? Not the truth, certainly.

There were guards at the front entrance of the burgomaster's house he was using as quarters. Bonnay was always thorough—a prime requisite in an A.D.C. Duras chatted with the men briefly, his easygoing rapport with his troops the reason they would follow him anywhere. And they had, in the five years since he'd earned his general's stars, and in the years before as well. His success was due in part to their devotion, although those who knew him well understood he had certain natural gifts of leadership separate from the loyalty of his troops—the power of quick decision, faultless judgment, boldness, dynamic tactical skill, and indefatigable determination.

All of which fueled jealousies not only in Napoleon but in the War Ministry, where political intrigues motivated promotions and assignments more often than ability. But they needed him here in Switzerland. He knew it and they knew it. He'd been given command of the single outflanking position between France and its enemies, the possession of Switzerland of vital strategic importance.

And in three days he began his offensive.

● ● ●

He knocked once on the parlor door before opening it and stepping into a blaze of candlelight. He didn't realize he had so many candles. And on second glance he saw he didn't; the scented tapers were all set in heavy silver Russian candelabra.

Two maids watched him from the fireside with wary, timorous eyes, their features Asiatic, their costumes Russian. There was no sign of the countess.

"Where's your mistress?"

"In here, General," a clear, direct voice replied in French. "Have you eaten? Do you play chess?"

And when he crossed the carpeted floor and stood in the open doorway to the small dining room, he saw Teo for the first time, seated before a small chess table, apparently playing both sides in the game.

Her dark brows arched delicately against her pale skin as she gazed at him. "Your engravings don't do you justice, General Duras. You're much younger."

"Good evening, Countess Korsakov. And you don't appear to be frightened. Bonnay gave me to believe my presence was required here to allay your fears." If she thought him young, she was younger still, he reflected, and exotic-looking. Certainly Korsakov could have his pick of women, with his prominent family well connected at the Russian court.

"The young colonel mistook my reticence for fear," the countess replied, a luscious small smile lighting up her brilliant green eyes.

"You're not afraid then."

She made a small moue of negation. "Surely, General, we both understand the rules. You'll exchange me for one of your officers now languishing in Austrian hands—when the opportunity arises. He'll be glad to come home and I"—her dark lashes lowered marginally—"will return to Korsakov's household. Do you play chess?"

"Yes."

Her mouth curved upward in amusement. "*Will* you play chess?"

"I'm sorry. Perhaps some other time."

"Have you eaten?"

He hesitated, debating the lie.

"You haven't, have you? You must eat sometime tonight, General. Why not now?"

He was a gentleman, despite his disclaimer to Bonnay, and it would have been rude to refuse when they both knew he'd have to have dinner at some point that evening. "Something quickly perhaps," he agreed.

Clapping her hands, she called for her maids, giving them directions for serving the general. "I'll join you at the table," she graciously said, rising from her chair in a shimmer of absinthe velvet.

She waved away his offer to help seat her across from him and sat instead to his left. "I recommend the ragout, and the wines of course are wonderful here. Korsakov is quite sure of his victory, you know. So sure, he ordered me here to keep him company," she went on, leaning casually on the tabletop, meeting his swift, searching glance with a smile. "I'm just making conversation. He doesn't confide in me, but my maids know everything."

Lifting a spoonful of ragout to his mouth, he asked, "How old are you?" She spoke with a girlish candor, and he couldn't decide if it was coquettish or artless.

"I'm twenty-eight."

"You look younger," he said, dipping his spoon back into the savory dish. Her porcelain skin and black hair, her wide, ingenuous gaze and lithe slenderness evoked a youthful delicacy.

"Korsakov likes that."

Was her tone jeunesse dorée, or just cynical? "Do you miss your husband?" he bluntly asked, tipping a tender piece of meat from his spoon into his mouth.

"Do you miss your wife?"

He gazed at her for a telling minute while he chewed and

then swallowed. "Will your husband want you back?" he softly inquired, ignoring her question.

"Yes, definitely." She sat back, a new coolness in her tone. "I'm too valuable to misplace. Korsakov has his own selfish reasons for—"

"Let's just leave it at that," Duras interjected. "I'm not interested in family controversy."

"Forgive me, General. I lack reserve, I've been told."

He ate for a few moments without replying, not inclined to discuss a relative stranger's reserve or lack of it, and when he spoke, his voice was blandly impersonal. "I can't exchange you now, with the state of the war, but we'll endeavor to make you comfortable."

"How long will I be here?"

"Two weeks to a month perhaps. We'll keep you safe." He put his spoon aside, the campaign once again intruding into his thoughts.

"Thank you. You didn't eat much."

He shrugged and pushed his chair away from the table. "I'll eat later. If you require anything, ask for Bonnay," he added, rising to his feet. "Good night, Countess. It was a pleasure meeting you." And with a nod of his head he turned and left. That should satisfy Bonnay, he thought, striding back to his office.

It was well after midnight. Only Duras and Bonnay were left at headquarters, when a guard rushed into the map room apologizing and stammering, obviously agitated, his broken phrases finally merging into a decipherable account.

The Countess Gonchanka, it seems, was in Duras's bedroom accosting General Korsakov's wife.

Swearing, Duras decided Natalie must be his penance for his multitudinous sins, and then, breaking into the guard's disordered recital, briskly said, "Thank you, Corporal. Bonnay and I will take care of it."

"Why me?" Bonnay instantly protested.

"Because I'm ordering you to," Duras said with mock severity, "and I can't handle two women at once."

"Rumor suggests otherwise," his subordinate murmured.

"Not, however, tonight," Duras crisply retorted. "Now, move."

The noise emanating from the burgomaster's second-floor rooms facing the street had drawn a crowd, and ribald comments greeted Duras and Bonnay as they approached at a run.

"The show's over," Duras said, sprinting through the parting throng.

"Or just beginning, General," a cheerful voice retorted.

"Everyone back to quarters," Bonnay shouted.

"He wants them all to himself," another voice called out, and the crowd roared with laughter.

"That's an order, men." Andre Duras spoke in a normal tone from the porch rail. "Back to quarters." At the sound of his voice, the laughter instantly died away and the troopers began dispersing.

"I hope the ladies obey as easily," Bonnay drolly said, motioning Duras before him into the house.

"Wishful thinking with Natalie," Duras replied.

Moments later, at the sound of the men entering the bedroom, Countess Gonchanka turned from her prey. "Damn you, Andre!" she screamed, hurling the bronze statuette intended for Korsakov's wife at him. "Damn your blackguard soul!"

Swiftly ducking, Duras avoided being impaled by the upraised arms of a Grecian Victory, and lunging for Natalie's hands before she could gather fresh ammunition, he caught her wrists in a steely grip. "Behave yourself, Natalie," he brusquely ordered.

"So you can't have dinner with me tonight," she shrieked, fighting his grasp. "And now I know why! You bastard, deceiving, libertine knave. You've someone new in your bed!"

"Christ, Natalie, calm down. She's a guest," he asserted, trying to retain his hold as she struggled in his hands.

"I know all about your guests," she hissed, twisting and turning, trying to knee him in the groin. "There's always a new one in your bed, isn't there?"

"That's enough, Natalie," he snapped, forcing her toward the door. "Bonnay will see you home." The Countess Gonchanka had overstepped even his lax sense of propriety tonight. He abhorred scenes.

"So you can sleep with Korsakov's wife undisturbed!" she screeched.

"No, so everyone can get a night's rest," he answered with great restraint, his temper barely in check. And transferring his charge to Bonnay's hands, he watched as the Russian countess who'd entertained him so pleasantly the last few months was escorted out of his life. He'd see that she was on the road back to Paris in the morning.

"Did she hurt you?" he inquired, turning back to Korsakov's wife, who'd found shelter behind a semainier.

"Does this happen often to you?" she asked pleasantly, emerging from her burled-walnut barricade.

"No, never," he retorted. "You're fine, I see," he added curtly, realizing immediately after he uttered the words that he shouldn't have verbalized his thoughts. But her slender form was too blatantly visible through the sheer batiste of her gown to ignore.

"Yes, I am." Her voice was amiable, not seductive, and the odd disparity between her sensuous appeal and her frank response suddenly intrigued him.

"What's your name?" he said when he shouldn't.

"Teo."

Her voice was genial and melodious, although the contrast with Natalie's termagant shrieks may have enhanced its sweetness. "What's your real name?"

"Theodora Ostyuk."

"Not Korsakov?"

"No, never." She smiled as she repeated the words he'd so recently spoken.

"Would you like a robe?" he abruptly said, because he unexpectedly found her smile fascinating.

"Do I need one?" And then she laughed—a refreshing, light sound. "Do you scowl like that often?"

"Natalie's too fresh a memory."

"I understand. Have you ever been just friends with a woman?"

It took him so long to answer that she teasingly said, "You must be ignoring me, General, although your reputation precedes you. But I'm not like Natalie," she went on lightly. "I'm actually faithful to my husband, so I'm not going to seduce you. Do you mind?"

"No, not at all."

"How ungracious," she mocked.

"I meant, no, not with Natalie's screams still echoing in my ears. Why are you faithful to your husband?" It was a novel attitude in the current flux and upheavals of society.

"Will you play a game of chess with me?"

"Now?"

Evasive but not a no, she decided, and she found she didn't want to be alone in the middle of the night with her husband's image freshly brought to mind, so she cajoled. "I could tell you about faithfulness while we play, and Natalie *has* rather disrupted my sleep," she reminded him.

"A short game then, while you define a faithful wife. A rarity in my world," he softly declared.

"And in mine as well. Men of course aren't required to be faithful."

"So I understand."

"A realistic appraisal. Should I put on a robe?"

"I think it might be wise."

He played chess the way he approached warfare, moving quickly, decisively, always on the attack. But she held her own, although less aggressive in style, and when he took her first knight after long contention for its position, he said, "If your husband's half as good as you, he'll be a formidable opponent."

"I'm not sure you fight the same way."

"You've seen him in battle?"

"On a small scale. Against my grandfather in Siberia."

"And yet you married him?"

"Not by choice. The Russians traditionally take hostages from their conquered tribes. I'm the Siberian version. My clan sends my husband tribute in gold each year. So you see why I'm valuable to him."

"Not for gold alone, I'm sure," he said, beginning to move his rook.

"How gallant, Andre," she playfully declared.

His gaze came up at the sound of his name, his rook poised over the board, and their glances met for a breath-held moment. The fire crackled noisily in the hearth, the ticking of the clock sounded loud in the stillness, the air suddenly took on a charged hush, and then the general smiled—a smooth, charming smile. "You're going to lose your bishop, Teo."

She couldn't answer as suavely because her breath was caught in her throat and it took her a second to overcome the strange, heated feeling inundating her senses.

His gaze slid down her blushing cheeks and throat to rest briefly on her taut nipples visible through the white cashmere of her robe, and he wondered what was happening to him that so demure a sight could have such a staggering effect on his libido. He dropped his rook precipitously into place, inhaled, and leaned back in his chair, as if putting distance between himself and such tremulous innocence would suffice to restore his reason. He gruffly said, "Your move."

"Maybe we shouldn't play anymore."

"Your move." It was his soft voice of command.

"I don't take orders."

"I'd appreciate it if you'd move."

"I'm not sure I know what I'm doing anymore." He lounged across from her, tall, lean, powerful, with predatory eyes, the softest of voices, and the capacity to make her tremble.

"It's only a game."

"This, you mean."

"Of course. What else would I mean?"

"I was married to Korsakov when I was fifteen, after two years of refinement at the Smolny Institute for Noble Girls," she suddenly said, wanting him to know.

"And you're very refined," he urbanely replied, wondering how much she knew of love after thirteen faithful years in a forced marriage. His eyes drifted downward again, his thoughts no longer of chess.

"My husband's not refined at all."

"Many Russians aren't." He could feel his erection begin to rise, the thought of showing her another side of passionate desire ruinous to his self-restraint.

"It's getting late," she murmured, her voice quavering slightly.

"I'll see you upstairs," he softly said, rising.

When he stood, his desire was obvious; the form-fitting regimentals molded his body like a second skin.

Gripping the chair arms, her voice no more than a whisper, she said, "No."

He moved around the small table and touched her then because he couldn't help himself, because she was quivering with desire like some virginal young girl and the intoxicating image of such tremulous need was more carnal than anything he'd ever experienced. His hand fell lightly on her shoulder, its heat tantalizing, tempting.

She looked up at him and, lifting her mouth to his, heard herself say, "Kiss me."

"Take my hand," he whispered. And when she did, he pulled her to her feet and drew her close so the scent of her was in his nostrils and the warmth of her body touched his.

"Give me a child," she whispered, some inner voice prompting the words she'd only dreamed for years.

"No," he calmly said, as if she hadn't asked the unthinkable from a stranger, and then his mouth covered hers and she sighed against his lips. And as their kiss deepened and heated their blood and drove away reason, they both felt an indefinable bliss—torrid and languorous, heartfelt, and most strangely hopeful in two people who had long ago become disenchanted with hope.

And then her maid's voice drifted down the stairway, the quiet intonation of her native tongue without inflection. "He'll kill you," she declared.

Duras's mouth lifted and his head turned to the sound. "What did she say?"

"She reminded me of the consequences."

"Which are?"

"My husband's wrath."

He was a hairbreadth from selfishly saying *Don't worry*, but her body had gone rigid in his arms at her maid's pointed admonition, and he knew better. He knew he wouldn't be there to protect her from her husband's anger and he knew too that she was much too innocent for a casual night of love.

"Tamyr is my voice of reason."

He released her and took a step away, as if he couldn't trust himself to so benignly relinquish such a powerful feeling. "We all need a voice of reason," he said neutrally. "Thank you for the game of chess."

"I'm sorry."

"No more sorry than I," Duras said with a brief smile.

"Will I see you again?" She couldn't keep herself from asking.

"Certainly." He took another step back, his need for her almost overwhelming. "And if you wish for anything during your stay with us, feel free to call on Bonnay."

"Can't I call on you?"

"My schedule's frenzied and, more precisely, your maid's voice may not be able to curtail me a second time."

"I see."

"Forgive my bluntness."

"Forgiven," she said gently.

"Good night, Madame Countess." He bowed with grace.

"Good night, Andre."

"Under other circumstances . . ." he began, and then shrugged away useless explanation.

"I know," she said softly. "Thank you."

He left precipitously, retreat uncommon for France's bravest general, but he wasn't sure he could trust himself to act the gentleman if he stayed.